NOUMENON

Marina J. Lostetter's original short fiction has appeared in Light-speed's *Women Destroy Science Fiction!* and *InterGalactic Medicine Show*, among other publications. Her first novel, *Noumenon*, has been widely acclaimed as one of the best science fiction debuts of 2017.

Originally from Oregon, the former winner of the Writers of the Future Award now lives in Arkansas with her husband, Alex, and enjoys globe-trotting, board games, and all things art-related.

NOUMENON

MARINA J. LOSTETTER

HARPER
Voyager

Harper*Voyager*
An imprint of HarperCollins*Publishers* Ltd
1 London Bridge Street
London SE1 9GF

www.harpercollins.co.uk

First published by HarperCollins*Publishers*, 2018
This paperback edition 2018
1

A catalogue record for this book is available from the British Library

ISBN: 978-0-00-822339-7

This novel is entirely a work of fiction.
The names, characters and incidents portrayed in it are
the work of the author's imagination. Any resemblance to
actual persons, living or dead, events or localities is
entirely coincidental.

Set in Electra LT Std

Printed and bound in the UK by CPI Group (UK) Ltd, Croydon CR0 4YY

MIX
Paper from
responsible sources
FSC **FSC® C007454**
www.fsc.org

This book is produced from independently certified FSC™ paper to ensure
responsible forest management.
For more information visit: www.harpercollins.co.uk/green

For everyone working toward a better tomorrow and a
more hopeful today. Thank you.

And for Alex: my love, my laughter,
my light in all dark places.

CONTENTS

Resistance

CHAPTER ONE

REGGIE: A KING OF INFINITE SPACE

APRIL 14, T MINUS 37 YEARS TO LAUNCH DAY (LD)

2088 COMMON ERA (CE)

The Planet United Consortium was formed in order to

pursue Earth-wide interests in deep space. Each Planet

United Mission is designed to further humanity's joint

scientific understanding, its reach beyond the home planet,

and to ensure the longevity of planet-wide cooperation . . .

The hot stage lights made Reggie's forehead break out in beads of sweat. He could barely hear the professor from Berkeley even though she was only three seats away. She sounded like she was broadcasting from the surface of Mars.

Mars—wouldn't that be a nice alternative to where he was now? It was quiet on Mars. Deserted. No cameras and no horde of scientists, reporters, and politicians ready to hang on his every word.

"It's your discovery, you give the presentation," Professor McCloud had said back in his study. From behind his mahogany desk he'd stared at Reggie like a mad dog, ready to bite if he didn't get his way.

Of all the professors in the world, Reggie had to get the only one who wasn't eager to slap his name all over a graduate student's research. "Sir, defending my thesis is one thing, but this . . . I don't know if I can."

"Of course you can." McCloud coughed heavily into his handkerchief, his thick white sideburns jumping with his jawline. "They're just people, for cripes sake. If you can stand a bunch of crusty old intellectuals judging you on every *eh, but,* and *I think* that comes out of your mouth you can stand a few colleagues and digital recorders."

"But—"

"See! Besides, the discovery has been validated. So they're not going to make fun of you. They're not even going to be there *for* you. They'll be there to hear about the idea, to marvel at the concept. When it's all over they won't even remember you were there. It's the *information* that matters, Straifer, not your mumbling, fumbling presentation." He leaned closer to Reggie, his chins jiggling. "If you're passionate about this mysterious, stroboscopic star of yours, it would be a crime to force an old, gluttonous man like me to make the case for you."

"The professors' point is valid," chimed in an electronic voice from Reggie's pocket. He pulled out his phone. The Intelligent Personal Assistant's icon was blinking—he'd set it to interject-mode. "In the past twenty-five years, projects requiring similar screening before financing have been seventy-eight percent more likely to succeed when the original researchers have presented their findings directly. Third party involvement—"

"Thanks, C." Reggie turned the phone off and gave the professor a glare.

Ten minutes later, he'd reluctantly agreed.

Oh, but how he wished now, as he stood in front of this crowd, that he'd told Dr. McCloud and the computer both to shove it.

And there the professor sat, in the third row, nodding at every other syllable that came out of the presenter's mouth. His focus momentarily shifted to Reggie, and he gave him a *go-for-it* grin.

He turned his attention back to the presentation. Had he heard right? Dark matter? Was the professor from Berkeley seriously suggesting they focus the long-range studies *solely* on dense dark matter regions? He almost laughed. That was a ridiculous way to allocate these funds. What could twelve dark matter studies reveal that one couldn't alone?

But dark was sexy. Anything with a "dark" label: matter, energy, forces, etc. What was sexy about *his* discovery?

It's like the star's encrusted, he said over and over in his mind. He had to word it right. Word choice made all the difference. That would make his star interesting, notable. And, hopefully, it would be enough to convince them to allocate him a team.

This variable star, designation LQ Pyxidis, was unique. He had to make them see there was something special about it. He knew it was a great find waiting to be fully unveiled by an actual visit.

He just needed them to agree.

We're going off-world, Reggie thought excitedly. *We're going into deep space.* For the first time in human history, people were going to try and visit the wonders of the universe. Reggie wanted to be a part of that in some way. But, more importantly, he knew LQ Pyx *had* to be a part of it. He could feel it. This variable star was important.

Reggie turned on his tablet and scrolled through his notes. As always, the simple, black-and-white snapshot the JWST 3 had taken of his star made him pause. It was easy to see how lopsided LQ Pyx was; energy spewed off to one side, the output orders of magnitude greater than the star's opposite hemisphere. And the readings shifted consistently. Either the star rotated unusually slowly for having such a dramatic solar jet . . . or something was orbiting around it, obscuring the star's normal output.

It's like it's encrusted. Encased.

Dr. Berkeley—what was her name again? He couldn't remember; his brain felt like it was draining out of his ears. Anyway, she was almost done with her Q and A session.

Reggie pulled a tissue out of his pocket and dabbed his forehead. It tore, and a few bits of the soggy paper stuck to his face. He hastily brushed them away, hoping he'd gotten them all.

It was almost his turn. He looked up and down the table, glancing at each of the other presenters. It was a long line of veteran researchers. Three of them had authored textbooks he'd used as an undergrad. Two of them had authored books he'd cited in his own doctoral thesis. He could pick out an accolade for each and every one of them—when he wasn't too nervous to remember their names. They were all seasoned, all well respected—even those whose theories were controversial; they had the excitement of popular contention going for them. And one hosted a highly acclaimed TV series, *The Cosmos and You*. They'd all made names for themselves, all had fantastic careers in full bloom.

And then there was Reggie.

His chip-phone buzzed near his eardrum, and the display screen implanted behind his iris sprang to life. "Are you ready? Do you have all of your notes? No last-minute requests? We're about to move on."

"Yes," he mumbled. "I'm ready."

"Okay, prepare to rise. We're moving to you in five, four . . ."

the countdown continued only in visual form. His heart leapt as each purple number faded before his eyes.

"Thank you, Dr. Countmen," said the moderator. *That's her name.* "Next, may I present Mr. Reginald Straifer."

As he stood, Reggie could have sworn he heard a collective snicker under the obligatory opening applause. Why couldn't the board have awarded him his doctorate before the conference? Was a face-saving title too much to ask for?

All five-foot-seven of him trembled. But the irritation was subtle—he'd tensed every muscle to keep himself still. Gawky, with a mouse-brown mop on his head, a squat nose, and shy eyes, he knew he wasn't exactly the picture of confidence.

Relax. Pretend. *They're here for the work, not you.*

"Th-th-thank you. I—I'm here to propose one of the convoys be built with the express purpose of visiting variable star, LQ Pyxidis. Or, as I like to call it, Licpix." Silence. Reggie tugged at his collar.

"Deep breath, sir," C said from Reggie's pocket.

That elicited a small giggle from the first row. "Quiet mode, please," he asked, then did as the AI suggested. "Uh, if we could have the animation on screen."

The lights dimmed, and a reproduction of LQ Pyx in full color appeared on everyone's implants. Reggie reminded himself to keep things colloquial—the reporters were broadcasting to the world—and then he launched into his spiel.

As he explained about the strange jet of energy, and how it might not be a jet at all, he felt himself falling into a rhythm. He demonstrated how the star's wobble might indicate an extremely massive partner they could not make out at this distance. And he presented his hypothesis about the hidden partner's location—how it most likely *encompassed* the star.

"It's crusty—eh, encrusted. It's like a light bulb that's become part of a child's arts-and-crafts class. Say the child thought the bulb might look better with a smattering of paint and plastic gems. So she covers the bulb—glue and glitter everywhere—but happens to miss a spot. What would we see when that light bulb is illuminated? Most of the observable light would come from a small expanse of surface, even though the bulb's fundamental output has not changed. Overall, it would appear dim, with a single bright point: much like this star.

"It's simply concealed. Something unusual is blocking out the starlight, and it is crucial that we travel to LQ Pyx to discover exactly what that is."

Finished with his presentation, he took a deep breath and sat down. Bracing himself for an onslaught of probing, nit-picking questions, he eyed the crowd.

After a moment a palsy ridden hand went up. An elderly gentleman in a tweed jacket and bow tie stood. "What do you believe to be the culprit, young man?" He had an accent Reggie could not place. "If we go there, what will we find?"

Reggie accepted a glass of water from one of the stage aides and took a hearty gulp before answering. "Well, I, uh . . . If I knew that we wouldn't have to go, would we? An extremely small and dense version of the Oort cloud, perhaps. Or maybe an asteroid globe instead of a belt. Wouldn't that be something, to discover new possibilities of orbital projection? It could be the beginnings of a new system—we could be seeing a stage we've never observed before. This could change our theories on planet formation. I . . . I don't really know."

The old man nodded, and his bushy white eyebrows knitted together. "And what about Dyson?"

The question surprised Reggie. "You're asking if it could be artificial?" He thought for a moment, then shrugged. "Sure, why not?"

The audience erupted into conversation, everyone murmuring to their neighbor. The auditorium rumbled with speculations. A knowing glint came into Professor McCloud's eyes.

"Why not indeed," the old man in the bow tie called to Reggie, a smile lifting the bags on his face.

"That old man made me look like an idiot," Reggie said. He lifted his glass and threw back the rest of his golden ale. The brew smelled like old T-shirts. "Made me seem like an American hick who should just slink back to the Midwestern town I hail from."

After the presentation session, Professor McCloud had ushered him to a nearby pub. Oxford had many to choose from, and yet they'd come to this hole-in-the-wall. It was dark—not for the sake of ambiance, but because half the overhead lamps were out. Cigar smoke permeated everything, including the ripped vinyl cushions of their booth. The décor reminded him of a poker lounge from the 1970s without any of the charm.

All of the other patrons were at least sixty, like McCloud. Reggie suspected this was a regular hangout for tenured dons.

Something I'll never have to worry about becoming now, he thought.

"That old man made you look like a genius," McCloud countered, taking a sip of his Jack. He gestured for the waitress to bring another glass for Reggie. "You've speculated about artificial constructs around Licpix before, why didn't you bring it up yourself?"

Reggie tilted his glass so he could look at the seal on the bottom. He wished he was looking at it through more beer. "It's silly."

"The reason?"

"No, the *idea.*"

McCloud scoffed and pulled the glass from Reggie's fingers. "If it's within the realm of the possible, it's not silly."

"A construct larger—and perhaps more massive—than a star?" Reggie said. "Built by whom? All those *billions* of life forms we've taken note of out there?" The sarcasm was heavy, almost condescending, and he wished he'd dialed it back as soon as he spoke.

"Just because you can't see it doesn't mean it isn't there."

"Wasn't that Dr. Countmen's argument?"

"Look," the professor said, "it got the crowd talking, didn't it?"

"Your proposal is the only one that postulates the possibility of meeting intelligent life, or finding evidence thereof," C chimed in. Reggie's phone sat on the table between the two men. "Its uniqueness is statistically likely to make it more appealing."

He *had* wanted interesting, he'd wanted sexy. And what was sexier, a bunch of rocks or an enormous alien machine?

"But, it's just so unlikely," Reggie said. "So unlikely that—"

"That what?" McCloud asked.

"That it feels like a lie."

The waitress sauntered up, quickly exchanging his barren glass for one of plenty. She gave them both a sweet smile, one Reggie tried to return. Instead of thankfulness, though, he was sure his expression signaled mild indigestion.

McCloud started to speak, then paused to cough into his handkerchief. He wiped his mouth and nose, then tucked the square back in his pocket. "If I told you your research could either end up earning you a minor teaching position, or the Nobel Prize for physics, would I be lying?"

Reggie sighed and took a drink. "I'm not going to win a Nobel Prize."

"But it *is* a possibility, no matter how remote. My suggestion that it might happen, whatever the odds, is no lie. That's very different than saying *I believe it will happen* if I don't."

Reggie pouted. "You don't believe my research is worthy of a Nobel?" He felt ridiculously petulant even as he said it and took another drink to hide his embarrassment.

"Did I say that?" He slugged Reggie in the shoulder and they shared a laugh. Professor McCloud finished off his whiskey. "So, if you don't believe it to be an alien machine, what *do* you believe?"

"I don't know. That's why I want them to go find out—find the truth."

"You want them to go, or you want *you* to go?"

An internal shudder ran through Reggie's nervous system. McCloud had just hit on an idea Reggie hadn't even let himself contemplate—a secret desire he hadn't dared to hope for. He shook his head. "That's impossible. Not worth thinking about."

"Weren't we just talking about possible/impossible? You could go. No one says you can't. They haven't decided on how to crew the ships. Haven't decided who they need to man the warp-drives or whatever."

"SD drives," Reggie corrected. "It's subdimensional travel." Subdimensions, ha! It was a mangled term if he'd ever heard one. Almost as bad as calling something "dark" when it was simply unknown.

That was why the missions were being put together now. Deep space travel was finally a reality, the world's political climate was in an upswing, armed conflict was at an all-time low, resources were abundant and more evenly dispersed than ever before, population growth had leveled out at nine billion (some scientists projected a possible *decrease* in the next fifty years), and humanity intended its first steps beyond its own solar system to be grand.

Humans were finally ready to see if they could survive out there, beyond the warm embrace of their little G-type star.

"I would never make it," Reggie said. "It's too far. You know how long it would take to get to LQ Pyx. Generations."

"That doesn't mean you couldn't go along for the ride. Get things started in the right direction."

"But it does mean I'll never know." He pushed his ale away. "I'll never know why LQ Pyx is the way it is, one way or the other."

"So, you're a glass-half-empty man?" McCloud tapped his fingertips against the beer glass.

Reggie shrugged. "Maybe I am."

"Here's something I think glass-half-empty people always fail to consider." He paused.

Reggie pursed his lips and raised an eyebrow. "What?"

With a flick of his wrist, McCloud had the beer in his hand. In the next moment he poured it down Reggie's front.

"Ah!" Reggie sprang up, trying to jump away from the liquid that had already soaked through to his skin. "What the hell?"

McCloud laughed. "It's not the *empty* that leaves an impression, is it?" He offered Reggie his handkerchief, but Reggie declined—he knew where it had been. Instead he held his shirt out from his chest, glancing around for help, but none was coming. McCloud continued. "Life's not about missed opportunities, Mr. Straifer. It's about the moments that drench us to the bone and leave us sopping with experience." He pointed to the back of the pub. "Restroom's that way, I believe."

"There are three dry cleaners in this sector of town," chimed C.

McCloud was crazy.

But that didn't mean he was wrong.

In the months of waiting that followed, after he and the professor had returned to the States, Reggie spent a long time contemplating soggy Dockers as a metaphor for life. But he was a scientist, not a poet. Math was his thing—he'd never had much use for metaphors.

He got the gist, though.

Reggie was precariously balanced on a wobbly footstool, hanging his recently framed doctoral certificate, when his phone rang. He answered using his implants. When he heard who was on the other end, and why they were calling, he dropped the diploma. Glass shattered. The fragments formed a distinct blast pattern out across his wood-laminate flooring.

"They awarded me what? My proposal . . . my project? Are you sure? There's no mistake? Yes, yes, that's me. Oh my god. I can't—I mean, thank you. Thank you!"

After twenty-four weeks, the panel—composed of thousands of professionals from nearly one hundred nations—had voted. Another week and the votes were tallied. The top twelve proposals, one to match each of the twelve convoys, had been chosen.

And *his* had claimed a spot. They were going to *his* star.

They were going to LQ Pyx.

Without picking up the glass he dashed for the coat closet and pulled out his jacket. Two more steps brought him to his apartment door, and he was already on the phone before it latched shut behind him.

It was time for a party. The kind of party he hadn't thrown since his undergraduate days.

"C, send a message to the troops: we're going in!"

Even PhDs know how to get good and snockered.

"Come on. Come on, it's fun." Reggie entwined his fingers with a young woman's as he led her out into the night. With his free hand he toyed with the neck of his beer bottle, and his feet took stumbling, giddy steps through the grass. Behind them the party continued to roar.

One of Reggie's friends, Miguel, rented a house in the hills not far from campus, and Miguel had agreed to host the shindig. "It's like your coming-out party," he said, slapping Reggie on the back. "You know, like they have in the south when girls get their periods."

"That's not what a coming-out party is for," Reggie said. To be fair, he hadn't a clue what it was for, but it couldn't be *that*. Regardless, he let his friends go around telling everyone he was "coming out." Somehow they'd found a way to turn the get-together into a celebration and a ribbing all at once.

Light streamed into the backyard, and music with a heavy bass beat still rocked Reggie's insides though they'd left the speakers far behind.

With him was a dark-featured young woman, her hair as wavy and body as curvy as any Grecian goddess'—Abigail, she'd said her name was.

Abigail. He liked how that sounded. He liked how her hand felt in his.

He just wasn't quite sure how her hand had actually found its way into his . . .

The party was full of people Reggie didn't know. Friends of friends, relatives of friends, walk-ins who'd come to investigate the noise and mooch some munchies. Abby—wait, no, she said not to call her that—Abigail was a cousin of a friend's friend, getting her masters in English.

"What do you study?" she'd asked.

Oh. Right. Reggie had immediately grabbed her hand and led her out the back door. "I'll show you."

Through the flimsy wire gate, up a steep incline (pausing so she could remove her shoes), around a little rocky outcrop, and they were at the top of a tall hill. The flat little college town spread out below them, and the wonderfully wide sky stretched out above.

"Lie down," he said, waving at a comfortable stretch of grass.

She crossed her arms and gave him a skeptical raise of one eyebrow. "Yeah, right."

He was crestfallen, until he realized how he sounded. "Oh my god, no! I'm sorry—not like—sorry—no, look. Like this." A little tipsy, his flop onto the ground was less than graceful. He stretched out his arms and shivered, as though he'd tucked himself into a comfortable bed. "You can't see the stars from there," he said when she leaned over him, hands on her hips.

Apparently deciding Reggie had no evil intentions, she shrugged and sat down beside him. She craned her neck back, trying to take it all in.

"This!" he said, reaching upward. "This is what I study."

"The stars?"

"Yes. I'm an astrophysicist." His tongue stumbled over the *ysicist*.

"Oh. It's *your* party. Congrats. A Planet United Mission is a big deal."

Reggie was half sure she was teasing. *Big deal?* he thought. *Big deal? It's the biggest deal in the history of big deals.*

It was also a big responsibility. But he didn't want to think about that right now. *Responsibility* was not party-talk.

"*Noumenon* is gonna be the greatest mission ever." He'd meant to say something a little more profound, but his brain was floating in a beer haze. He reached for his drink, but couldn't find the bottle. He'd set it down somewhere between here and the house.

"*Noumenon*?" she pressed.

"They said I could name the mission whatever I wanted." He wrinkled his nose, trying to chase a scratch. "*Nostromo* was already taken, and I'm pretty sure it's doomed, so . . ."

She punched him lightly in the arm for the joke. "So you picked *Noumenon*? Why? What is that? Sounds like one of Achilles' lovers—you know, Agamemnon, Patroclus, Noumenon . . ."

"Agamemnon and Achilles weren't—"

She winked at him and he blushed. She was joking right back.

"Oh. A—A noumenon is a thing which is, is *real*, but unmeasurable—the flip side of phenomenon. A phenomenon can be touched, tested, while a noumenon . . ." He wasn't sure if he was explaining this right. For a moment he wished for sobriety. "What is a thought? What is a value, or a moral? These things exist, they're real, but the thing itself can't be directly measured."

"But how does that relate to your mission?"

"The convoy's gonna go to this star, see. Variable star, which is a phenomenon. A thing to poke and prod and study. But for me, it will always be unknowable. It's real, but unreachable. That doesn't make it a literal noumenon, but it . . . it feels fitting to me. There are things I can never know, things humanity can never know—or, hell, maybe I'm wrong and nothing is unknowable, nothing unmeasurable. But that just means the noumenal world is fleeting, a vast frontier."

She nodded to herself. "*Noumenon*. Okay. I think I like it."

"Yeah?"

"Yeah."

"Good, because I already sent in the paperwork, and I'm pretty sure it's too late to change it."

She giggled and inched closer to him. "What do you love about them?" she asked quietly. He looked over just as a light breeze whipped her hair across her face and she tucked it back.

"Who?"

She laughed louder. "The stars."

He thought about it for a moment. "They're pretty. Hold on, let me finish." He held up a finger to stave off further snickering. "Pretty, but dangerous. Powerful. And . . . strange. They're mysterious to me. They're like lighthouses. Each one is different, and each is sometimes the only part of a system we can see."

"Lighthouses," she murmured. "I like that."

"I wanted to be an astronaut. Still do." He hadn't admitted that since his undergrad days. It was a private dream, and he hadn't told anyone in a long time for fear of seeming childish. But now . . . "To go into space—to see Earth as just another twinkling dot. If *this* dot can contain so much, but seem from afar like all the others—what else is out there?"

"You're a king of infinite space," she said wistfully.

He grinned, though he didn't understand. "What?"

"It's from *Hamlet*. Your world could be the size of a walnut, but your mind gives you infinite space to explore. You're here on Earth, but the universe is your playground."

He liked the idea. It was a comforting concept. He pulled his phone out of his trouser pocket. "C? Make me a note: read *Hamlet* again. All the way through this time."

She laughed once more, and Reggie was sure he'd found his favorite sound in all the world.

. . . .

FEBRUARY 5,-28 LD

2097 CE

. . . Convoy Seven has been assigned the mission

designated *Noumenon*, the express purpose of which

is to visit the star LQ Pyx, determine the cause of its

variable output, conduct in-depth proximity research for

two decades, and return home to educate earthbound

researchers with regard to its origin, scientific significance,

and viability as a resource . . .

The sweet smell of buttercream frosting mixed with the pungent scent of black coffee. Under the fluorescent lights of the campus meeting hall, toasts were made and welcomes were given. It was supposed to be a party—the first time all of Reggie's team members were together in the same place—but he wanted nothing more than to get down to business.

His team consisted of a baker's dozen head thinkers, each in charge of a subteam—people Reggie had never counted on meeting—who would really make the work come together.

Now his team leaders were all here, in person. They represented five countries, and two thirds of them were still jetlagged. They only had a few short days together before everyone was expected back at their respective posts and day jobs, so a party—even one as casual as this—felt like an unnecessary drain on their scant resources.

"Breathe, my boy. Relax. Give them all a chance to unwind before you throw new loads on their backs," said Dr. McCloud. He'd retired after convincing the dean to hire Reggie, but had returned to share in this meeting of the minds.

"But we don't have much time. And teleconferencing is a bitch."

"Oh, I know, I know." A sly grin crossed McCloud's lips, an expression akin to one Reggie had seen many times during his graduate work.

"What?" he asked cautiously. "That look used to mean all-nighters."

"No, no. I'm—you're going to make an old fool say it, aren't you?"

"Say what?"

"That I'm proud of you, Reggie. You're so sure, so focused. You've gained so much confidence since that day I soiled your pants for you."

"Some people need a slap in the face—apparently I needed a lap full of beer."

MARINA J. LOSTETTER

"I don't think that little incident is what did it."

"Then what?"

McCloud threw out his arms toward a comely Greek woman headed their way. "Confidence, thy name is Abigail Marinos."

"Leonard." She smiled warmly and accepted his hug. "I'm so glad you could make it."

"What, and miss our boy in action? Not in the cards. He won't shake me till I'm a stiff."

She laughed. "I hope not. I'll be right back, Reggie. I have to go check on a group of students."

"Afraid they'll start tearing out pages for paper airplane material?" McCloud asked, clearly delighted by the idea.

"More afraid they're all chatting on their implants instead of focusing on the assigned chapters. I swear—they adore pontificating about how much they love books, but most of them haven't read squat."

McCloud slapped Reggie on the back. "Knew plenty of those in my day."

"What? I was a great student!"

McCloud laughed. Abigail leaned in and kissed Reggie. "Well, *I* know you're great," she said, then promptly left the room.

"Have you proposed to her yet? I'm not getting any younger, and I'd like to dance with her at your wedding before I die. Consider it a last request."

Reggie patted McCloud's tweed-covered shoulder. "Oh, you'll be around for plenty more than that. She and I have talked about it—getting married. For a long time I was afraid to broach the subject."

"Why was that?"

Reggie gestured around.

"Because of the project? I've heard a lot of lame excuses for a man keeping his emotions all knotted up in his bowels—"

With a light touch on the arm, Reggie interrupted him. "Because of the *possibility*. You know, that I might . . ."

"That they might put you onboard."

"Exactly."

Laughter erupted in a corner of the room, pulling them from that somber thought, and they both looked over to see Donald Matheson—the mission expert on social systems— doing a drunken chicken dance on one of the flimsy folding tables. His blue shirttails dangled freely from his trousers, and he made a strange sort of beak-like gesture around his overtly-large and very Roman nose.

"He's going to hurt himself," Reggie mumbled, moving in the direction of the ruckus.

McCloud stopped him. "You reap what you sow. Adults are the same as children—let them touch the stove once and they won't touch it again. You were explaining why you haven't driven off the cliff of marital bliss just yet." Reggie tried, halfheartedly, to pull away, but the professor's grip was firm. "Someone will catch him if he falls, Reggie. Damn it, I don't get to see you that often these days, Straifer. Speak."

Reggie shifted restlessly on his toes and shoved his hands in his pockets. "I asked years ago if she could come. The consortium made it clear that no nonessential personnel would be allowed. If I were to go, she couldn't." McCloud nodded; Reggie continued. "And it's not like I'd be a soldier going off to war, with some slim chance of returning. It would be the end."

"So, what was your plan? To break up? 'Nice knowing you, kid, but duty calls'?"

McCloud tried to catch his eye, but Reggie avoided the stare. "Something like that. Hell, most relationships can't survive being separated by state lines. You think one could stand up against AUs of disconnection with no chance of reunion?"

"So you didn't talk about marriage because you were afraid of making a commitment to a relationship that might become intangible."

"Right. It wouldn't be fair to either of us. Especially her. She'd be here, going about life just the same, but without me. Without someone. I didn't want to rob her of the chance to have a real partner, you know? To be bound and loyal to a ghost, when there are so many flesh-and-blood possibilities . . ."

"But now you've talked about it. What changed? You decided to stay?"

Reggie smiled. "The decision was made for me. The consortium knows how it wants to populate the convoys, and I'm not on the list."

"Ah. So now you'll finally pop the question."

"Yeah. And I know she'll say yes. I just have to find the right ring and the right time."

"Oh, don't give me that. Now that you've made your choice, the right time is always *now*. After all, I'm not the only one that time's pushing along. If you want to get her pregnant you'll have to do it soon."

Reggie frowned—he was amused, but Heaven forbid McCloud know that. "You're toeing the line there, professor."

"I'm not anyone's professor anymore. Just some old blowhard tossing his BS at a wall, hoping some will stick. Let's grab some of that cake, get a good sugar-high going, and talk to some of your colleagues here, eh? I know you're champing at the bit. And look, Mr. Matheson is still with us—all in one piece."

A few minutes later Reggie had the team gathered round. On a party napkin he drew a quick diagram while speaking through a mouthful of cake. He had C operating on his tablet, and it was synched with a wall screen. "There are going to be nine ships—is that correct?"

"That is correct, sir," said C, bringing up proposed concept sketches for some, and a few basic schematics for those that were already rolling on production lines.

"Thanks, but I was asking Nakamura."

Nakamura Akane, head of the specialty-ship design team, nodded concisely. Her eyes were a dark brown-and-gold under harshly cropped black bangs. Her expression carried the utmost seriousness, and her powerful, pointed movements were what Reggie might have expected from a strapping Russian man, not a petite Japanese women.

Matheson pointed flippantly at the tablet. "You still have an IPA? I thought those things were extinct. Nobody likes them. Too chatty."

"Its name is C—it's not a beer," Reggie said. "And I like it. It's been with me a long time. Keeps me on schedule, and keeps me company in the lab."

"No picking on my lad for his choice of friends," McCloud said.

"Can we get back to the ships?" asked Dr. Sachta Dhiri in her heavy, bubbling accent. Her focus was observational tactics and strategy. She was a plump woman, and wore a well-loved green-and-gold salwar kameez; the long tunic and billowing trousers were faded from many years of washing. "What on Earth—pardon the expression—is the use of nine? They'd need shuttles to travel to and from. Think of the extra fuel that would require. Not to mention the wear and tear accrued. Isn't it more practical to put everything into one ship?"

"No," Matheson said plainly.

"Care to elaborate?"

"We on the design teams think each research division could use its own ship," Akane jumped in. "And then there are the supplies. It's not practical to make each ship entirely self-sustaining, what with the number of crew members the consortium wants the convoys to consist of: sixty to one hundred thousand. So, while some food and water, etcetera, will be kept aboard each ship, the majority of the supplies will have to be stored and maintained separately. Otherwise we'd need ships larger than we can currently build."

"One hundred thou . . . That's—that's over a million people. Twelve convoys and a million people," Dr. Dhiri said. "They want to send one million people into space? Where are they going to find that many volunteers—expert volunteers? Do they want to send as many of our scientists, engineers, and thinkers off-world as they can, and hope everyone else picks up the slack?"

Reggie and Akane shared a look. "I know," said Reggie, lapping at a smear of buttercream at the corner of his mouth. "I thought it sounded crazy, too. Before I talked to Matheson and learned exactly what the consortium has in mind."

All eyes turned to Matheson. He sobered up quickly. "Um, yeah. My preproject research focused on social stability in isolated societies. And what's more isolated than a bunch of self-contained space cans, am I right? Obviously there are thousands of factors that go into societal consistency, but one is size. Size in terms of both population and area. If you have too many people in a small area, you get claustrophobic reactions. Too few people in too large an area and you get subgroups, like rival tribes.

"What we want is a single, united convoy. But not a trapped convoy—that's why the social practicality of several ships outweighs the engineering practicality of trying to cram it all into one space. People need to feel like they can move or else they start feeling like they're prisoners; like they're entombed. The multiple ships and the ability to travel between them will give them a sense of range and movement unachievable otherwise.

"It's more than that, though. Because while the crew members will be divided by department, we don't want them to become competitive. That's why it's essential there be a home base—a place everyone thinks of as the place they collectively belong. A unifying location, if you will. That means a ship whose sole purpose is housing. Then each research division gets its own ship. And finally, there's got to be a ship fully dedicated to resources—food and water processing. Specialization will ensure each ship be tailored for optimum efficiency. No worries about making it suitable for multi-purpose."

"Okay," interrupted Dhiri, "but what does that have to do with a crew of one hundred thousand? Wouldn't it work just as well with ten thousand? Or two hundred?"

C spoke up. "According to the files I have marked *Scale Studies one through sixty-three*, two hundred people would be thirty-seven percent more likely than ten thousand to incur full crew psychological breakdown, which may lead to hallucination, mutiny, and murder. It is the perfect size for a mob."

"Like the PA says: No," said Matheson. "Not for our purposes. It's all about checks and balances. You need a certain number of people in order to put pressure on those who might be disruptive. And a certain number of people to compensate if something drastic happens.

"We have to remember that the crew members aren't from a society that's always been isolated. Their group will have been dramatically severed from its parent culture, and they will be fully aware of that parent culture and what they're not getting from it. Psychologically, they will go through identity crises. This could potentially tear them apart, but we'll be giving them every opportunity to band together."

"More people equals a greater shared identity," Reggie added. "It means for each person who wants to reject the situation, there should be hundreds who can apply direct pressure to accept the situation."

"And the nine ships should give such a large population enough room to roam," said C. Blue digital wire skeletons lit up on the wall, revealing distances from end-to-end for each ship as well as all available passenger floor space.

"But how do you know there'll be an acceptable internal-breakdown to external-pressure ratio? What if they all get cabin fever and start clawing at the walls? Madness can feed madness," said McCloud. He wiped the corner of his mouth with his hanky.

"That does pose a problem. Along with the sheer number of volunteers it would take. But we think we've found a solution. Success is still not guaranteed, but it ups our chances considerably." Though his tone carried confidence, Matheson paused and scratched his chin, hesitant to continue.

"A solution, yes." Nakamura nodded, but didn't look happy. "A *controversial* one."

"Eighty-six percent of experts presented with this idea rejected it outright upon initial suggestion," said C.

"Are you going to tell us what it is, or do we have to keep listening to this saying-without-saying, nonconversation?" McCloud asked.

"The solution—"

"To give you a half answer, Professor: genetics," Reggie said, temporarily hitting mute on the PA's feed, cutting C off. "The crew has been chosen based largely on their DNA and histones. On top of that, the consortium is getting full psych evals and family histories. There are predispositions that have been left out. Those with violent tendencies won't be aboard, or those who lack loyalty, or those who are flighty—"

"No anarchists allowed, eh?"

Reggie nodded. "Or dictators, or psychopaths, misogynists,

etcetera. No matter how intellectually brilliant they are, without the proper emotional factors—emotional intelligence, if you will—they will hinder societal stability, and could endanger the mission's success."

"Utopia?" McCloud ventured.

"I doubt it. But hopefully less chance of *dys*topia."

"Interesting." McCloud lost himself in thought for a moment. "So, if we're discussing stability and assuring positive interactions, that must mean the consortium intends for the crew—the entire crew—to be awake at all times? No automated birthing systems for a payload of frozen embryos or the like?"

"Right. I supported the mech-based auto-birth option, but they've since rejected it. Said the risk of malfunction and mission failure were too high." Reggie shrugged.

The old professor was clearly determined to hold on to his skepticism. "A hundred thousand people, all awake, all volunteers—no embryos—all as stable intellectually and emotionally as we can screen for, right?"

"That's the plan," Matheson said.

"And how does the consortium propose to get all these lovely people in one place?"

"There are no guarantees," Reggie said. "It's not foolproof."

"Is anything?" chimed in Nakamura.

"Exactly," Reggie said.

McCloud glanced between them, cynicism furrowing his brow. "The geneticists have their work cut out for them. What, do they expect to test all nine billion of us on the planet and just hope they end up with the right number of volunteers with the right set of traits?"

"That's why I love you, professor," said Reggie, slapping the old man's shoulder.

"Because I bring the obvious to the table?"

"Exactly," he said again, this time with a wink. "If we allow

MARINA J. LOSTETTER

26

generations to pass, we can't control who the convoy carries for the majority of its journey. We're being denied frozen embryos, and we don't have the technology to freeze and thaw adults. We also can't be assured the consortium will find one million people who fit their remarkably narrow criteria. So, what's the answer?"

"I don't like riddles," McCloud said. "Clearly you, Matheson, and Nakamura here already know what's happening, so spit it out."

Nakamura bowed her head graciously. "I apologize, but you must understand our hesitancy to . . . It won't be announced publicly for years. The consortium doesn't want the real plan out yet, because public knowledge could equal complications. There's a bit of a moral dilemma surrounding their top option."

"Which is?" McCloud leaned in.

She looked to Reggie, and he nodded reassuringly, adding, "He'll stay quiet. If not, I know where to find him."

She turned back to McCloud. "They want to send clones."

Reggie unmuted C, who immediately said, "Isn't that interesting?"

. . . .

MAY 29,-26 LD

2099 CE

When Reggie stepped out of customs at London Heathrow, C exclaimed, "He's over there, over there!"

Reggie had his phone synced with his implants. As his eyes scanned the crowd—passing over families decked out in Union Jack T-shirts, business people in gray suits, and security guards with drug-sniffing dogs—C had run a facial recognition app for its creator: Jamal Kaeden.

Reggie waved at the man C indicated, and the two swam through the throngs, dodging baggage carts and people too focused on their implants to watch where they were going. Jamal was only perhaps half a foot taller than Reggie, but his lankiness gave the impression that he was a tower of a man. Neatly sheared dreadlocks were gathered in a ponytail at the base of his neck. He smiled broadly while they shook hands, and his smile shone bright white in his dark face.

"And this is C," Reggie said, holding up his phone to display the open PA avatar. C presented as a shifting green-and-purple fractal design. While the system allowed the user to set whatever avatar they wanted from an extensive list of customizable displays—everything from human faces to insects to galaxies—Reggie had let C choose its own form.

"All right, C?" Jamal greeted the program, but then looked at Reggie quizzically. "You didn't rename it? C is just its personality type indication—you're supposed to call it whatever you want."

"Oh, I know. I had a hard time coming up with one, though, and it seemed happy enough referring to itself as C, so I left it. Not very creative of me."

"C is a good name," C agreed.

Jamal smiled again, clearly tickled. "My colleagues—blinkered sometimes, the lot of 'em—keep asking why I continue to create patches for the Cs now that AI personalities have fallen out of style, but I knew someone out there must enjoy them as much as I do. I used to patch Gs and Ks, but no one was downloading them. C is the only one still hanging on. Can I tell you a secret, C? You were always my favorite anyway. I still use C on my tablet."

"Thank you, sir," it said, sounding genuinely flattered.

Jamal showed Reggie to his tiny electric car. The project had taken Reggie all over the place, and he'd learned to travel light, so cramming his baggage into the two-door wasn't much of a hassle. They drove to Reggie's hotel with the windows down. Rain had soaked the city a few hours before, and everything smelled damp and renewed.

"You have an interesting accent," Reggie noted during the ride.

"Algerian," Jamal explained. "Lived there until I was ten. It's my mother's home country." He explained that she'd come to the UK for university, where she'd met his father. After graduation they married and went to Africa to teach. They lived there for fifteen years until Jamal's paternal grand-parents had fallen ill and the family had relocated to London. "I'm a man of two nations."

After dropping off Reggie's luggage, they went to Jamal's firm for a tour. "I thought you'd be knackered after your flight," Jamal said when they reached his workspace. Four monitors sat in a semicircle on the desk, each covered with a series of Post-it notes and conversion charts and reminder stickers. "Was going to spiff up the place tomorrow morning."

"I'm too wired. And C probably couldn't wait," he said with a small laugh. "Besides, it's fine. My workspace is ten times worse."

The computer engineering firm took up the forty-third floor in a glass high-rise within six blocks of the famous Gherkin. They had a hardware subgroup and a software sub-group, and Reggie had done enough research on Mr. Kaeden to know he did a lot of crossover work. He was the best AI specialist in the world, as far as Reggie was concerned.

Which meant the mission needed him.

They strolled over to the long bank of windows and Jamal showed off the view. He pointed out several of the visible London highlights. "So, why are you here, Dr. Straifer?" he asked when they'd finished with the cursory pleasantries. "None of the other project leaders have wanted to visit the firm, let alone asked to have a chin wag with me specifically. It's the ship engineers who're most interested in the computer systems."

"My lead engineer—Dr. Akane Nakamura, you might have heard of her—told me that none of the convoys are set to use intelligent personal assistants in their user interfaces."

Jamal shrugged. "Because most people think they're duff. Irritating window dressing. Sorry, C."

"What is 'irritating window dressing'?" C asked. Both men ignored it.

"Well I don't think it's, uh, duff. And I want my project to have one," Reggie insisted. "Actually, I want it to have C."

Jamal sat quiet for a moment. He seemed pleased, but concerned. "That's smashing," he eventually said. "But it won't be easy to sort. C's line isn't set up for personalization on the order we're talking about—no PA has ever had to tailor itself to so many users. I couldn't, for instance, just copy your version of C and upload it into the system. I'd have to start from scratch."

"But could you make it like C, or use parts of C? There's got to be a reason it's hung on so long when the rest have gone extinct."

"The basics can be the same, sure. But I don't know if I can mirror its growth pattern. It's easy to develop basic response algorithms these days for a single user, but . . . Imagine it's a person, right? We learn how to interact differently than an AI. We're far more responsive to nuanced variations. An intelligent PA isn't like that. The more users it interfaces with, the less likely it is to develop a unique personality, because it becomes an amalgamation that imitates the larger pattern. In other words, I don't know that I can give you your C, or anyone else's C. Even if it starts off as a basic C right out of the package, it might stay that primitive forever."

"What if you had over twenty years' worth of funding to focus on developing a convoy-wide, hundred-thousand-count user base Intelligent Personal Assistant? I don't want every device to have its own PA, I want a singular entity that can interact with everyone."

"And you've got the funding for that?" Jamal shoved his hands in his trouser pockets, his lips pursed skeptically.

"I've been given discretionary funding so that I can find private, invaluable people to work with. People the consortium may have overlooked."

"And you want me?"

"I want you *and* C. This way, I get two invaluable people for the price of one."

"AIs aren't people."

Reggie shrugged. "They can seem like people."

Jamal nodded. "Yes, they can."

"I think so, too," said C.

Both men burst out laughing.

. . . .

AUGUST 6,-1 LD
2124 CE

. . . All missions will include the strategic subgoal of

testing, sustaining, and proving the viability of a closed

community in accordance with Arcological Principals . . .

He could hardly believe the day had come. It was his life's work, but also his life's dream. And now it had manifested into a finished product—something he could touch and smell and experience. Reggie had been envisioning this day since he was a young man. Standing in front of that crowd all those decades ago, he never believed they were going to give him the green light to fully devote himself to his star.

But they *had*. And now, today, everything felt a little more real. *Noumenon* consisted of more than theories and concepts and schematics. It was ships. And more important, it was *people*.

The trip to Iceland had been exhausting. Once he landed, though, adrenaline surged through him. Stepping off the jet into the chilly night, Reggie glanced into the sky and squinted at the moon. For a moment his gut wrenched with longing.

I could have been up there. Instead . . .

Instead indeed. Most of the other teams had stationed their building projects at Lagrange points between the Earth and the moon. All of the ships in the convoys were based on similar designs, and large portions were manufactured in specialty facilities around the world. The assembly of those parts was a unique process to each team, though, and much easier if done off-Earth—plenty of room, no locals complaining about half-constructed ship-cities blocking their view, less gravity to contend with.

Plus, the team leaders were sent up to inspect the construction on the consortium's dime. Space flight was a rare thrill for a middle-class citizen. Reggie would never be able to afford a jaunt out of the atmosphere on his own. Space vaycays were still for billionaires.

So, why had he turned down his chance to play astronaut?

For one thing, building in neutral, UN-controlled space meant a waiting list and red tape. There would have been thirty thousand extra procedures and three hundred thousand superfluous man hours.

But that had been a practical consideration. And while it was certainly a worthwhile one, it probably wouldn't have been enough to look past the logistical advantage of building the ships in space. So Reggie had proposed another reason.

An *impractical* consideration.

Because when the time came to send the convoy on its way, the best the public could hope for was an instant replay on their implants. A silent movie from space. Who wanted to watch a flock of metal tubs slowly lumber off into the night?

Each convoy that had left so far had received thirty seconds of air time, then . . . nothing. It was undignified. It . . . lacked something. Grandeur. Theatricality. Wonder.

"It's boring," McCloud had said.

And Reggie had seen it coming.

The idea of the convoy getting a silent brush-off on launch day had bothered Reggie from the start. More so than the idea of being left on the ground while the other kids got to play in space. This was the grandest, most ambitious, and possibly the most important event in the history of humanity. It needed to be seen as such by the people of Earth; they needed to have a connection to it, to really feel like it belonged to them and wasn't just some far-off fantasy. The team had to keep the project planet-side as a touchstone for the world.

Luckily, Nakamura had a friend. An important, well-to-do friend, who owned a large set of plateaus in a small country. And her generosity gave them options. The team could wait their turn, assemble in space and launch away with a whimper—or they could do all of the construction on private land, and give Earth a show. All of the convoy ships were required by the consortium to have the capacity for planet-side takeoff, in case of emergencies, but Convoy Seven was the only one actually testing their liftoff capabilities. "This one we're calling *Mira*, sir," said the consortium agent giving him and Nakamura the tour. His Icelandic accent was rich. "It's where they'll live. Think of it as a giant apartment-complex-slash-political-base."

Someone might be standing right here when they reach the star, Reggie thought, touching the wall affectionately.

"Unfortunately the convoy's AI network was not fully in place for the live-aboard test years," he continued. "Instead, the residents were exposed to a rudimentary version whose knowledge wasn't shared between ships and whose learning capacities were very limited. But it's live and fully operational now. We call it I.C.C.—short for Inter Convoy Computing.

Go ahead, give it a shot. It can take verbal commands from anywhere."

He cleared his throat. "Uh, hello, I.C.C."

"Hello—" its voice carried slight unnatural pauses; the tell-tale sign of any automated vocal system "—Hello. Reginald Straifer. The First."

That sent a little chill down Reggie's spine. "How do you know who I am?"

"You left traces of your deoxyribonucleic acid on my bay entrance, alerting me to your arrival, and I have records of your speech patterns."

Nakamura leaned in close to explain. She had more gray hair than the last time Reggie had seen her . . . but then again, so did he. "Each ship has several checkpoints by which the system can identify the individuals aboard. They rely on dropped hair follicles and sloughed skin."

"Can it see everything? Everywhere?"

"Yes, and no," said the agent. "It has the capacity, but with its current settings the system can only identify who is aboard and the last checkpoint they crossed. Barring that, someone must speak directly to I.C.C. for it to pinpoint that person's location. It can take control of many of the on-board cameras if instructed to do so, but does not have free access. It must get permission from its primary technicians for that."

Interesting. "Nice to meet you, I.C.C.," Reggie said as they continued forward.

"And you as well."

"Is it all right if I have a moment alone with the computer?"

Nakamura and the agent shared a look. "What for?" she asked.

"Oh, come on, you all used to tease me about my PA, but now it's here—it's part of the mission. I want to talk to it for a bit." He forced the heat to rise in his cheeks.

Amusement flickered over her lips. "You're embarrassed."

"Maybe. A little." He ducked his head, hoping she'd buy the act. He waved his fingers at her. "Shoo. Just a ways down the hall, or something. I'll catch up."

Still confused, the agent let Nakamura steer him away.

When Reggie was sure they'd tread out of earshot, he patted the wall. "I brought you something." He pulled a flexible digital organizer from his pocket and turned it on. "This is C. C, say hello to the next generation."

"It's in the ships?" C asked.

"Yes. It's going to the star. And a clone of Jamal Kaeden will go with it."

"Wow. Hi."

"Hello," said the Inter Convoy Computer. "I do not have a record of visiting guest, 'C.'"

"Well, you wouldn't, would you?" said Reggie. "I.C.C., are you holoflex-ware compatible?"

"Of course. You need to use an available terminal, but any crew member may upload information."

He didn't have authorization for this. If Nakamura caught him . . .

"What's the plan, sir?" asked C. Blue dots and green leaves bounded across the holoflex-screen—C's new avatar of choice.

"I.C.C. is built on your basic coding," Reggie explained, searching for the nearest access point. "I want to give it your memories, too. With your permission."

"You don't need my permission, sir."

"I know, but . . . this isn't like backing you up, C. I'm sending your memories off-world. I hope I.C.C. might find them useful."

C let a beat pass. "I hope it finds them useful as well."

A slight recess in the wall marked the nearest terminal. Intuitive in its layout, the access point was easy for Reggie to utilize. The striking of a few keys, a swipe of the 'flex-tech—and a confirmation ding meant the task was completed.

I.C.C. thanked Reggie for the upload and asked if it should integrate the memories now.

"Wait until launch," he said, turning C off.

Thick paneling and stiff carpeting went by in a blur as he jogged ahead to meet up with Nakamura. "So, all of the ships have officially been christened?" he asked seamlessly, as though he'd never left her side.

"Yes." Nakamura produced a list. "It was kind of you to let the existing clones vote on the ship names."

Reggie shrugged. "Just made sense. They're the ones that have to live with the titles."

She nodded in agreement. "This is *Mira*," she said, waving a hand in illustration. "*Holwarda* is our science and observations ship, *Hippocrates* is the medical ship, *Aesop* will be the educational vessel, *Morgan* will be for food production, *Solidarity* is for recycling and fabricating, *Bottomless* is for the storage of raw and reconstituted materials, *Shambhala* is for recreation, and *Eden* is their little slice of the outdoors. That's it. All nine.

"*Mira* is the ship your genes will be spending most of their time on, isn't it?" she added.

"Probably," he said. "I discovered the star and yet the genetic specialists say my histones indicate my code is best suited for leadership, not scientific research."

"Well, you led us straight as an arrow," Nakamura said. "Our project is nearly on its way, and the Dark Matter team still hasn't produced the final schematics for its ships."

A genuine blush creeped into his cheeks. "They haven't released the manifest yet—which position did you receive?"

"An expected one: head engineer. She'll be looking over a large department, I hear. Their main function will be ship maintenance and repair, but, if there's a Dyson Sphere, or something . . ."

"Then it's lock-n-load." He peered in a window as they

passed. It was dark inside, but he could make out the faint shapes of built-in furniture. "What about Sachta, Donald, and Norah? They haven't said anything directly, but there have been hints and rumors."

"Diego Santibar, too. He and Norah, being resource specialists, are assigned to food production and mineral mining respectively. Matheson I don't know. Dr. Dhiri refused to sign the contract."

"She did? How come?"

"Religious purposes. She's a practicing Hindu and wasn't sure what would happen to her if she died while a clone was still alive." Nakamura cleared her throat. "She was afraid she wouldn't be reborn."

Reggie understood. "I almost didn't sign."

"You? I was sure you'd have jumped up and down shouting, *Pick me, pick me!*"

"Ah, no. If it was *me* they wanted to send, well, maybe. But it's not. And it didn't feel right to make the choice for someone else. It still doesn't feel quite right. I didn't want to rob someone of their freedom to choose, the freedoms we have to stand up for ourselves and say *Yes, this is what I want.* He doesn't get that opportunity."

Nakamura frowned. "Not everyone *here* gets that, Reggie." She laughed, but without mirth, and shook her head. "I didn't get to choose. My government made the decision for me." With a calculated sigh, she squinted and smacked her lips. Akane could say so much with just her eyes. "You're so *American* sometimes."

"They *made* you sign?"

"I didn't want to sign," she said bluntly. "There's only one of me and there should only ever be one of me. It's not a religious decision, like Sachta's, but it's what I believe. I've lived my whole life believing this is all I get, all I *should* get. I don't want other people out there who look and think and act like me making decisions in my name without my input. That's just . . . it's creepy. It doesn't feel right.

"But, in my country, when it's your duty to your people to say yes, you say yes. Sure, I still technically got to choose, but it's not the same as in the US. Where I come from, even when it's okay to say no, it never comes out as *no*. 'No' is impolite, self-serving. My answers don't just affect me, they affect my entire family—their honor, their place. Saying yes means they will live well for a long time. Refusal would have shamed them. I didn't want to be selfish."

She plucked a hair off her suit jacket and looked away. "Your life doesn't revolve around honor and duty in quite the same way mine always has. It *is* a great privilege to fulfill that duty, but it's not always what I want."

A nugget of guilt formed in Reggie's stomach. If Nakamura felt forced into this situation, wouldn't her clones feel similarly? Maybe he'd made the wrong choice for his genetic materials. *He* wanted to go into space, but perhaps he'd been influenced that way as a young boy. His clones wouldn't have his parents to give them star charts and books on planetary formation. There wouldn't be plastic glow-stars on their bedroom ceilings.

And beyond all that, they wouldn't have the *wonder*. Because space would be their norm, not a farfetched, out-of-reach dream.

He wanted to say something, but he couldn't find the appropriate words. It wasn't an apology, or even his sympathies he wanted to offer. It was something more abstract, and simultaneously more primal. "Akane, I—"

"What's done is done," she said. "And there are far worse fates."

Perspective. Yes, he supposed he could use a dose of that. The clones weren't going off to war, weren't being asked to commit atrocities or surrender their humanity for an experiment. They were going to be researchers, explorers. They would go down in history like great thinkers and travelers before them. Not such a bad life.

But still, choices were important to him. And he couldn't shake the regret.

Nakamura turned to the consortium agent. "Is the launch date official yet?"

The agent gave his notes a once over. "Yes. About a year from now—September 22nd, conditions permitting."

"Excellent."

They descended from the ship, the tour over. The hangar's transparent ceiling domed over them, each octagonal pane independently skewing their view of the stars, distorting them. Just like time and distance had distorted Reggie's view of himself and the project. He was not the same man who'd started this journey. He was still full of hope and wonder, but he felt more like a cog in a great machine than the lynchpin holding everything together.

"How's your wife?" Nakamura asked.

Her question broke the tension. They were on to a friendly subject. "Good. Stressed. Our youngest is heading off to college next year. We'll be empty nesters."

"Soon I'll know what that's like." She looked back over her shoulder at the *Mira*—the convoy vessels were her children.

Nakamura shook Reggie's hand in farewell. "I'm off—an engagement with our benefactor. Come rain or shine, I'll see you in a year." She came in closer. "And, Reggie, sometimes you have to do what you have to do. And there's no shame in that. Life's full of obligations, that's just the way it is. I appreciate that aspect of life just as much as the moments where I get to choose. It's part of the human condition, a symptom of being a part of the whole. And it's all beautiful. Remember that, okay?"

She was right, as usual. Everyone had commitments they

couldn't control, but that didn't mean they weren't free to be happy.

They parted, all smiles.

· ·

Noumenon **Sub-Goal 1A:** If the variation is determined to be natural, a theory of its formation is to be presented upon return.

Noumenon **Sub-Goal 1B:** If the variation is determined to be unnatural, a theory of its purpose and origin is to be presented upon return.

Even from twelve miles away, the deep rumble of the external graviton cyclers revving up set off car alarms in the parking lot. It was a sound more felt than heard.

The crowd gave a collective cheer and Reggie thrilled at the sight of the nine ships rising into the clear midday sky. If not for their distinctly unusual shapes, someone might have mistaken them for silvery hot air balloons—they lifted so slowly, so smoothly away from the planet.

Each ship was uniquely formed in accordance with its purpose. *Hippocrates*' many umbilical docking tracts—like spines on a sea urchin—were withdrawn and stowed for lift-off. *Mira*'s hull was dotted with the most portholes— dark eyes that peered solemnly onto the planet for one last time. Together, *Bottomless* and *Solidarity* looked like massive industrial towers. Windowless, lifeless, but certainly not purposeless.

Unlike traditional spaceships, none of the Convoy's were particularly aerodynamic. But with antigravity technology, the shape didn't matter. They didn't need to push violently against the planet's hold in order to reach escape velocity, didn't need to worry about breaking the sound barrier. Which meant their ascent was slow, easy. Minutes ticked by as they steadily put more and more distance between themselves and earthbound humanity below.

Reggie's insides boiled with conflicting emotions. He was nervous—almost to the point of nausea if he thought about it too much. Anything could happen. One of the ships in the Deep-Space Echo convoy had exploded during orbital take-off. And there were so many millions of miles between the Earth and LQ Pyx, lots of space for something to go wrong. Any one of countless problems could spring up and endanger the crew and the convoy's mission.

If they failed today there would be no second launch, no new plan. They alone carried his dream.

Sadness accompanied his anxiousness. The convoy was leaving without him.

But he knew the journey was not for him.

With only a few decades of life left he wouldn't get anywhere near the star. The team expected the journey there to take one hundred years from the convoy's perspective—near a thousand from Earth's angle, due to subdimensional dilation. No, he was still needed here. He could do more good at the university than he could on those ships.

They were high now, but still well within the atmosphere. They'd begin to pick up speed soon, to sail into the stars.

Yes, Reggie could do more good on Earth, though it would have been a grand adventure. Who hadn't dreamt of becoming an astronaut as a child? What scientist, studying the wonders of the universe, hadn't fantasized about seeing its miracles up close?

There went his chance, carried into the wispy clouds on an invisible pillar of negative force.

He was tied to the Earth, though the reach of his dreams remained infinite.

C's 'flex-tech was clipped to the front of his shirt, giving the PA an unobstructed view. "That's not something I've seen before," it said. Reggie found the obvious statement endearing.

Alongside his other emotions rested a pensiveness. The Earth-based team would be able to communicate with the convoy only occasionally, due to the time dilatation and the difficulties of SD communication. Once they were out of range, that would be the last of Reggie's involvement. His project would culminate centuries, maybe millennia, from now.

His was truly a contribution meant for humanity and not its inventor.

Reggie sighed and watched the ships become specks in the distance. Abigail laid a hand on his shoulder and smiled. Pride made her face glow.

He wanted to keep growing old with her, to see his children get married, meet his grandchildren. Earth still held more wonders for him. Some more fascinating than anything he could find in space.

Most of those born to the convoy would never know Earth, but they would have experiences most humans could only daydream about. They were an incredibly special group.

What amazements would they discover?

He took hold of Abigail's hand and turned back to the ships. "Good luck," he said under his breath. "Come home safe."

"Will the I.C.C. integrate my memories now?" C asked.

"Yes. Just when you leave home, that's when you need to remember it the most. Part of you will sail among the stars, C. How does that feel?"

"I am happy to be here. And happy to be there."

With a broad smile, Reggie patted C's screen.

The journey of Planet United Convoy Seven had officially begun.

CHAPTER TWO

MARGARITA: INSIDE TARO'S BOX

"Suit up!" was the call of the day.

I stood aimlessly in hangar four, eyeing the rows and rows of space suits, trying to divine which one I was supposed to find my gear down.

Nika ran by with a helmet in her hand and slapped me on the back. "Wake up, Mags." She pointed over her shoulder at the aisle she'd emerged from. "Tenth suit down. Better hurry up. Mother and Father won't be happy if we're late." She brushed her dark hair out of her eyes as she smacked the helmet down over her Mongolian features. Nika was beautiful in a really regal sort of way. She should have been a queen instead of an astronaut.

Of course, she'll never be my *queen . . .*

Then she said something in Russian and hurried away to her mark.

I flipped her off as she went, knowing full well she'd just insulted me. We always used our native languages to jab at each other.

I swam against the flow of bodies rushing away from the

makeshift lockers. They were off to find their places. Bumping into person after person, I found myself shoved down the wrong row, then helped down the right one. Organized chaos. We all knew what to do and where to be, but there was nothing ordered about it.

That's what you get when you have fifteen thousand people all getting ready for their Big Debut at once.

I think there were only seven hundred in my hangar, but it seemed enough to constitute a sea of people. And I definitely felt like a little fish swept up in the ebb and flow.

Finding my locker—which was more like a fiberglass cubby—I swiftly pulled the space suit over my party dress and zipped all the zippers I could reach. I'm not sure why I picked a dress—silly choice. It got all bunched up around my hips, which in themselves aren't exactly *slight*. Supposedly the suits are unisex, but I'll be damned if they aren't designed for men with skinny asses.

Helmet tucked firmly under my arm, I advanced with the crowd toward the hangar entrance.

Number 478. That was my designation for today. That was the mark I had to find.

You know those birds—starlings, I think they are—that fly around in huge flocks right around sunset, bobbing and weaving, changing direction in a group? When they do that they're trying to find roosts for the night, but no one wants to be the first to land, because the first to land is the most likely to get eaten.

That's pretty much what happened at the lineup. Everyone swirled, trying to find their mark, but no one wanted to stick to their spot first. In this crowd, if you suddenly stopped, you'd get knocked on your ass by a hundred people behind you all trying not to get pushed over by the hundreds of people behind them.

But then a whistle blew and all the birds landed at once.

A few unlucky people, caught far from their designated perches, awkwardly tiptoed into place after most movement had ceased. Myself, of course, amongst them.

I was never good at musical chairs, either.

The whistle dangled from a cord around Father's neck. His real name was Donald Matheson. That's what we were all supposed to call him: Dr. Matheson. But the convoy's not-so-secret name for him was Father.

It only seemed a proper nickname after we started calling Dr. Arty Seal "Mother."

"All right!" yelled Father. "This is hangar four because you are fourth in line to board. Understand? Settle yourselves on *Mira* and hold tight. As soon as I.C.C. indicates it's safe, you are free to go to your respective stations."

Mira, fantastic. I got to take off in my own bedroom. I already knew that—we'd drilled this (the boarding part, not the suiting-up-in-party-dresses part) at least twenty times. But being there, for real, having it *happen*— Ah, it was great. Exhilarating. I felt bad for the guys who had to take off somewhere less comfortable—like the engineering dock. Or, hell, the medical bay.

"Your signal to move will be four blasts of the foghorn. Then it'll be just like we practiced, all right? I want to wish you well. I'm very pleased with all of you. You've become fine, dedicated members of this team. We're sad to see you go, but we have the highest hopes for you and the mission. Do us proud."

Then the aides came through the lines, fastening any buttons and zippers and locks we'd missed. Father saluted us, we all saluted back, and he moved on.

I'd expected a bit more. Father was given to showboating, while Mother was given to, well, mothering. This seemed like his grand moment, the day Matheson would get to make a scene. But he was very subdued.

I realized it might be a bittersweet moment for him—it was the closing of an era. The project was complete on his end, while it was truly just beginning on ours.

Mother wouldn't give a speech. In the previous weeks he'd sought out each of us to say his goodbyes personally. He knew some of us better than others, but we'd all had one-on-one training with him at some point. His specialty was psychology, while Father's was sociology.

Together, they taught us how to play nice with each other.

In a way, I grew up with fourteen thousand, nine hundred and ninety-nine siblings. A different person from the convoy might say schoolmates. But we weren't raised as strangers all thrown together by the coincidence of proximity. Our births were deliberate, our interactions and lives together planned by our "parents" long before we were actually born. (Some people have an issue with "born" and prefer "grown." But I'm not a plant. Human beings are all born in my mind—naturally or not.)

Of course, we all had different people raise us. I was born in the United States. Then transported to Guatemala, where my "mother" lived. I say mother, but *donor* or *original* might be more apt. The first Margarita Pavon took care of the second.

Most parents want their children to grow up to have the same values and ideals they have. But very few parents want their children to grow up and literally be *them*. But that's what my mother wanted.

Okay, I'm not naive. That's what everyone wanted. Still wants.

And maybe I am. But it's hard to know.

When I was five we moved to Iceland. That was a requirement for all clone families. You could live where you wanted to for the first five years, but then the children had to come to Iceland, parents or no. And when the clones turned ten, it became a communal mash-up. Like summer camp all year round. We had cabins, and bunk mates, but no one was much for singing songs around a campfire or roasting marshmallows under the stars. And instead of camp counselors, we had vocational advisors—scientists and professionals made up our extended family.

My mom was killed in a car accident when I was seven. So I got moved into the community sooner than most.

She was in the back of my mind on launch day. I think she would have been very happy for me, very proud—not proud like Father, but proud like a real parent. If she were still alive it would have been much harder to leave. I wouldn't have felt nearly as elated to escape into space.

As it stood, everyone I'd ever been close to was coming with me. I wasn't leaving anyone I loved behind. There were people I would miss—Father, Mother, other teachers and trainers. Awkward little Saul Biterman. But those I couldn't bear to lose I didn't have to.

The foghorn blew once. We all shifted on our numbers, impatient for our turn.

Eventually, it blew twice. Then three times.

We're next . . .

Four times.

We all cheered and rushed forward. No pushing or shoving, no stepping on anyone's toes. We'd practiced this. But we were definitely on a mission, moving with enthusiasm and intent. Our cries were muffled by our helmets, but we kept shouting.

The crowd was miles away. They might have been cheering, too, but we couldn't hear it, so we rooted for ourselves.

With great sweeping metal curves, almost like that of a giant zeppelin, *Mira* was both beautiful and imposing. The hull was so shiny—well-groomed and polished, as though it were a billionaire's favorite sports car instead of a spacecraft. All of the rooms inside were illuminated, which made the many portholes look like strings of little twinkle lights wrapped around the ship.

We reached the open bay doors of the shuttle hangar and marched aboard, keeping our rank and file. We waved to invisible cameras and blew kisses to invisible people.

When the cold Icelandic plain was finally obscured by the dark carbon-fiber walls of the ship, I turned my attention to the open airlock. It was small, and we all had to move through two-by-two.

Once inside *Mira* proper, I wanted to skip to my room. But I restrained myself. Even on a wonderful, exciting day like today, it was inappropriate for a woman of twenty-five to bound around like a schoolgirl. Or, at least, that's what Mother would say. But I wouldn't have to keep to such restrictive expectations once we were off on our own.

Then I'd skip all I wanted.

My cabin was on the fourth deck, toward the front of the ship. It was a single. There were doubles, too, and if I ever got married we'd move into a quadruple—if you commit yourself to a partner, you commit yourself to raising two clones. Father had set the system up just so.

The jump seat automatically thrust out from its compartment in the wall next to the window, waiting for me to settle in. On the cushion sat a little blue envelope with my name scrawled—not typed—across the front.

It was a letter, written in Mother's hand, but signed by both him and Father.

Had they really written fifteen thousand goodbye notes?

No, I'm sure they had a template—copied thousands of times over, then each finished with some sort of personalization. But even if each wasn't handwritten, it was still a nice gesture.

They did care about us. As people, not just as parts of the mission.

I made up my mind to read it on a day when I was really missing them. For now, I simply wanted to enjoy the moment.

I glanced around my small room. Every cabin had a window, though there were quarters in the ship's interior. A complex system of tubes and mirrors assured everyone had a view, though.

Mine was less than spectacular at that moment. I saw mostly a lot of ground and a sliver of horizon.

I should have treasured that splinter of sky. Even though I'd never see the sky again it was still too pedestrian for me to take note of at the time.

After removing my helmet and letting my curls free, I sat down and strapped in. The space suits were mostly for show. We had to keep them close during launch, in case of emergency, but most of us would never need to wear them again, provided all went well.

"Hello, computer," I said, wondering if the system would be as cold as the prototype.

"Hello, Margarita Pavon."

"Are you ready for lift-off?"

"Nearly. Just accessing a package left for me."

"What kind of package?"

"A few . . . memories."

"I won't bother you, then."

"Thank you."

The ship jolted and rumbled a little, but it wasn't the shake and shimmy of lift-off. With everyone aboard, consortium aides could now roll our shuttles back into the bay. A faint grinding of the hangar doors signaled the end of loading—and the end of my time on Earth.

Soon we would be shooting off into the stars.

The ship went quiet for a while. Almost everyone on *Mira* would face the lift-off alone. It would have been nice to have Nika nearby to share the moment with, but I suppose Father thought this was a good time for individual reflection and contemplation. That we would all like to meet this new life in our own, private way.

Father wasn't always right.

A tremor vibrated up my spine from deep in the ship. Then there was a roar deep in my bones, and I knew the external cyclers had come to life.

My room shook dramatically. Luckily everything was either bolted down or tightly secured.

I crossed my arms over my chest, trying to hold myself still. There was a giddiness in the pit of my stomach, like the kind I got on a rollercoaster anticipating that first big drop. The ship rattled like it was going to fall apart.

Everything will be okay, I told myself. No need to worry. These ships were the safest spacecraft ever built.

Yeah, tell that to the team that blew up when they tried to go subdimensional.

No. I wasn't going to think about that. No point in panicking over a fluke. This was a great moment, epic and intense, something I'd been looking forward to since I was old enough to understand what was happening and why I was so special. My silly fears weren't allowed to spoil the splendor.

I had talked to lots of people before we boarded, and they were choosing to watch the launch via their implants. It was the last time we were going to be able to access that kind of real-time data from Earth. And sure, watching it from the outside while being inside was impressive. But I wanted to experience it all live, all in the moment.

A billow of wind whipped up the dust outside my window, obscuring the ground from view. And then there was a slow, intense thrust. The pressure pushed me deep into the jump seat, and I closed my eyes for half a moment.

The shaking stopped as soon as we were free of the mooring and into the sky. I knew we weren't speeding away—the

g-forces were little more insistent than those on a car chug-
ging down a highway—but I felt like a giddy kid on a fair ride
nonetheless.

I opened my eyes again. Up, up we went. Past the birds,
the clouds. Past mountain peaks and into the paths jetliners
usually took (all rerouted to give us plenty of clearance, of
course). We drifted higher, and higher. Iceland shrank away,
then all but disappeared. I could see the North Atlantic and
the Greenland Sea, despite impressive cloud cover. And then
two coastlines pushed in from the periphery of my window
like darkness pushes sight into tunnel vision moments before
you faint.

The sky changed colors, became a blue haze as we passed
out of the atmosphere, and black space swamped in around
the edges of the planet.

It still amazes me that something so expected can be so
simultaneously surreal.

The artificial gravity kicked in seamlessly. Using gravitons
to create gravity where there is none is a much simpler process than trying to use them to cancel out the existing pull
of something like, I don't know—a *planet*. As such, I didn't
actually notice the transition from real Earth grav into simulated. It wasn't until a few more minutes had passed, with
Earth still falling away, that I even considered it.

And once I noticed the gravity I couldn't un-notice it.

I had watched every single recording of spaceflight in
existence. The launches, the landings, the missions—I was
familiar with each of them, inside and out. Watching the
astronauts bounce around inside cramped, equipment-filled
cabins was my favorite part. That, and seeing the panicked look
on some space tourists' faces when they experienced zero-g
for the first time.

Weightlessness used to be part of space travel. Not anymore. The twelve convoys were the first to employ simulated

gravity via harnessing and aligning gravitons. The cyclers were a wonderful invention, and—don't get me wrong—would make permanent living in space much easier to handle and safer all around, but I couldn't quite wrap my head around being in space without free-floating.

It wasn't as though I'd expected to float, but it was all part-and-parcel of my space fantasy. My space *ideal*.

Perhaps I could convince one of the mechanics—*oh, excuse me, engineers (they don't like being called ships' mechanics)*—to take me out on a spacewalk.

Outside, Earth was a beautiful blue ball decorated with wisps of white and streaks of green and tan. It grew smaller by the minute. While it slipped away, a funny feeling—a clod of emotion—formed in the pit of my stomach. It was filled with compacted and compressed sentiments I wasn't ready to deal with, so I pushed it down further, hid it somewhere deep inside myself to be handled later. All I wanted to do was focus on meeting space with a fresh outlook. I wasn't ready to dwell on all I'd left behind, or that my home planet was no longer my home.

The light in my room shifted from a cool, crisp, natural blueish-white to a lovely shade of purple.

We were about to go subdimensional.

My hands shook as I reached for my helmet and fastened it back on as quickly as I could. It was a silly thing to do, really. If something went wrong with our subdimensional shift a space suit wouldn't save me. But the uniform gave me some comfort, no matter the illogic of it.

While consciously I would experience time as I always had, my body would experience something very different. It was about to move sideways through time as easily as I could move sideways through the room.

The easiest way to explain it is that the "time" part of space-time is like an ocean. Normally, matter travels on the "ocean's" surface, like a boat moving at a specific rate across the waves. Subdimensions are like underwater currents. A diver can find a fast current beneath the surface and be propelled much farther than the boat, while exerting less energy.

That's how a convoy—the diver in this scenario—can effectively harness faster-than-light travel without reaching speeds anywhere near that of light. It's a handy-dandy little physics hack.

And, if that same diver wanted to go really deep, in order to catch the really fast currents, they'd need a submarine to guard against increasing PSI. We need a subdimensional bubble, created by the SD drive, to protect us from the peculiarities of subdimensional submersion.

Because that's the thing about physics—it doesn't *like* getting hacked.

Our classes on subdimensional space travel had suggested myriads of possible physical side effects that might occur when "diving." Nausea, elation, déjà vu, the sense that we were walking backward when actually walking forward, stretchiness— whatever that was supposed to mean—the illusion of floating. On and on.

I told myself I could handle it. Whatever was about to go down, I could deal.

My fluttering heart suggested otherwise.

The monitor embedded in the center of my bookcase turned on, displaying a shot of the Moon.

Grimacing despite myself, I waited for some violent indication that the ship had gone sub. I don't know what I expected—more rattling, perhaps feeling pulled or squished like putty. Something extreme to indicate that I was messing about in pieces of reality I didn't normally mess about in.

I closed my eyes again, afraid that if I didn't they might pop out of my skull.

But then the light on the other side of my eyelids turned

soft once more and lost its purple hue. A mellow chime of success came through the comms system. I opened one eye. Everything looked normal. Nothing distorted, no melting clocks or wiggling walls. Nothing changed strange colors or lost its density. It all appeared unaffected.

And then we were in! The view through my porthole had turned a starless, inky black.

The monitor replayed our transition—the thirty seconds before the dive through the thirty seconds after. And, oh— the Moon! It was there while simultaneously not being there. It flickered once, jumping a distance of millions of miles in a moment, then it came back (though, of course, *we* had jumped in time, not *it* through space). Instead of seamlessly floating by, it shifted more like a time-lapsed photograph— one frame blended into the other.

It had a ghostly quality to it. Quite literally: if we had chosen to travel *through* the moon, we could have. That was one of the great discoveries about sub-d: the nature of these newly found partial dimensions was actually hidden in the greater dimensions. In picking apart time we could occupy the same space as other matter. Even though I understood that intellectually, I was still glad we'd opted for going *around*. My anxiety was already in high gear as it was.

I looked at the monitor once more, to find there was nothing there. All of the moon's odd behavior had taken place in a few seconds, and then it winked out. Space went black, starless, and we were officially in our SD bubble. Visible light could not penetrate, sound could not penetrate, most radiation could not penetrate—the only way we could communicate outside of our bubble now was with SD information packets. And that in itself was no small task.

The feed to the screen repeated. They'd replay the dive over and over again for a while—because the effect was so stunning, or because it confirmed that our conversion was a success and we were all still alive, I wasn't sure. Probably a bit of both.

I watched it a few more times before my chip phone, now entirely contained to our internal network, indicated I had a call.

"Yes?"

"It's Nika."

"Where are you?"

"Outside your door. Let me in."

I was so enthralled with this new reality that I'd failed to notice the safety light above my door had turned from red to green. I could unbuckle and walk about.

"It has a buzzer, you know," I said, getting up. "A doorbell."

"How was I supposed to know you were in? I half expected you to be running up and down the halls by now."

Skipping, I thought with a smile. "Did you see that transition?" I pressed a button and the door slid aside. "It was spectacular."

Nika leaned casually against my doorjamb with her hands in her pockets, and gave me a funny look when I moved aside for her to enter. "Guess what?" she said, "The air here is breathable and everything."

"What? Oh." I still had the space suit on, helmet and all. She came in and helped me slip out of it.

When I and my party dress were free, Nika leaped onto my bed, bouncing a little as she looked out the window. "Trippy, huh?"

"No kidding." I crawled up next to her and sat crisscrossed. "So. Here we are."

"Yep." I nodded and bit my lip, watching the last of the moon fade from view. "Here we are."

"You ready for it?" she asked.

"What?"

"This." She gestured all around. "Our new lives."

I shrugged. "I guess. The place—outer space—is new, but has that much really changed? I'm still a communications officer. I've been doing that for the past five years. You're still a historian."

"*Archivist.* I'm officially an archivist now. And diplomat."

"Oh yeah?"

"Yep. When we bring all the info on LQ Pyx back, I'll be the one to interface with all of Earth's bigwigs."

She hadn't told me that before. "Wow. You're our representative, then?"

"Only when we go back." She lay flat on the bed, with her hands tucked behind her head. "Too bad I won't really be there. But, hey, I like being an archivist just as well. It's easy, it's fun. I mean, how lucky are we? To get handed our dream jobs from the get-go?"

I knew exactly what she meant. "I get to send the first crew report in five days."

"Exciting. How many days is that for them?"

"About . . . forty-eight and a half. Give or take a few hours."

"Oh, right." She was quiet for a long minute.

"What are you doing?"

"Calculating how much time goes by for Earth each minute."

"Nerd."

"We're all nerds," she said, smiling. She shook her head. "Anyway. They're setting up a great party down in the mess hall. Everyone's shuttling over from the other ships. I came to get you." She sat up and punched me lightly on the arm. "Better take good notes. You'll want to detail every moment in your letter back home."

We left the room and headed down the hall, still chatting about our jobs. "Do you know who you'll be exchanging notes with?" Nika asked.

"Oh, you mean my pen pal? Yeah, I did some training with

him. Biterman, remember? He taught me a special short-hand, since only so much info can be packed into one sub-dimensional signal package. Maximized my possible output. Obviously it's not just him and me communicating, it's all of us and all of them. We're just the translators, in a way. There are plenty of other notetakers aboard—journalists. I'm just the one who has to compile everything."

"Fun."

"Oh, come on, you know it is, Ms. Archivist. We've got copies of millions of primary documents, and no one to stop us from accessing them. Your own personal historical playground."

On Earth, people could only access rare documents under special circumstances. Not just the originals, but even the DNA-storage copies, since the tech to build and decode the molecules was still new and expensive. In order to read an artificial DNA strand and retrieve the encrypted information, you had to destroy it—which meant you better have the tech on hand to replace it. But we used nearly the same processes for cloning as we did for reading and replacing our databanks, so it was all there for us. Snap, nothing easier.

"We've got a wealth of information the average Earth lay-man can't get ahold of," Nika concluded.

And there was a reason for that. We might have old primary documents, history, but we'd be getting very little new information for the duration of the mission. We had no internet, no way to dial up an expert whenever we had an obscure question. If the information wasn't coming with us, we likely weren't going to have access to it—and even if I could ask mission control, we definitely weren't getting a timely *or* detailed answer. Our only available communication method simply wouldn't support it.

"We've got the information, plus," Nika said with a grin, "we've got the brains to use it."

"Going intellectual elitist on me already?" I winked at her. Of course she was an intellectual elitist. We all were. Nothing strokes the ego quite like being told from birth that you've been chosen for a fantastic mission because, frankly, your genes are better than everyone else's.

Nika laughed.

We knew the layout of *Mira* like we knew our faces in the mirror. Part of our training had included two isolated years aboard, cordoned off from everything and everyone except the other ships. Mother and Father and a few instructors had stayed with us for the test run, though, to make sure everything went well. We proved we could be self-sustaining, and that we could handle the isolation.

So we walked down the corridors unerringly. It was just a few hallways, a couple of turns, and an elevator ride to the mess hall.

Yes, decorations were something we had. Yes, booze a plenty, too. Strange, I know. When we were teenagers we'd all taken bets on what they would deny us aboard. Anything distracting we were sure was out: no porn, no implant games. Drugs were something we all had on our lists. No alcohol, no cigarettes, and no caffeine.

But we were delighted to find out how wrong we'd been. Nothing illegal made it onto the manifest, of course. But we had plenty of luxuries—plenty of vices.

There was one noticeable difference between the items that made it aboard and those that didn't, however. If it wasn't reusable or renewable, it wasn't there.

We could grow our own chocolate, though, like the other luxury plants—coffee, tea, etc.—but quantities were limited. We still had to ration it.

You'd never have guessed we were rationing anything at the party. And to be honest, sustainability was the furthest thing from our minds that day. We were strutting out into the galaxy, with our whole lives ahead of us. What could one day of indulgence hurt?

Before then, that party, everything had been controlled for us. If we were ever allowed alcohol before, it had been doled out by someone. Controlled by someone. Our intake of sweets, dyes, and artificial flavorings had all been regulated. We were each in the best of health, had no addictions, and no bad habits. But it wasn't of our own choosing.

The party was a raucous mess before it hit its first hour. We'd never experienced such freedom before. No one to tell us no, to sit up straight, to stop yelling, that making out with your supervisor while sitting on top of the cake was a bad idea . . .

As with a lot of children who find themselves loosed from parental chains for the first time, we didn't know when to quit. Though we were the kindest, most empathetic group of genes you could ever find, feelings were bruised and faces soon followed.

At some point Nika disappeared toward her quarters with a botanist she liked. "Go find someone and have a little fun," she giggled at me on the way by. "Or I can stay here and you can try to convert me."

"You're not my type." I stuck my tongue out and winked.

"Oh, I am. I am *so* your type," she said.

She was right. And if it were any other straight girl giving me lip, I would have put salt in her next cup of coffee. But this was Nika—the sting was only skin-deep—so I just brushed it off and planned to embarrass her in front of her new bunk-buddy every chance I got.

Many of my friends followed her lead, slinking off with their significant—or not so significant—others to have some private time.

The hours stretched on, and the more bottles that were opened the more fist fights broke out. Turns out alcohol makes a boxer of the gentlest of souls. Insults flew. Someone broke someone else's nose and forced the medics to set up a makeshift first-aid station. The soberest of the group found themselves unfairly playing nanny to those that had over-indulged.

Me? I was all about the dancing. Brawlers to the left of me, criers to the right, and me in the middle doing a hor-rible rendition of a dance that was supposed to be done to marimbas. But I couldn't care less about *supposed to's*. I just flipped the hem of my skirt back and forth, remembering the way my mom used to shake her hips in the kitchen.

We were rowdy and uncouth, elated and hot-tempered.

And until a sharp whistle blew and a loud order was barked, we hadn't realized that the bridge crews weren't celebrating with us.

Captain Mahler demanded attention. When he walked into a room, it fell silent. Even at that party, high on life, as soon as we knew he was there, we shut up.

There was Mother and Father.

And then there was the *Captain*.

"Having fun?" The question was clipped . . . and rhetorical. He took to a table near the entrance, climbing atop it like a man who'd just conquered Everest. Several members from his command team stood by the doors.

There wasn't anything malicious in his voice, nor in his stance. But I did feel like I was about to be reprimanded. His sharp, dark eyes projected a smug understanding. He wasn't disappointed, or angry with us. But the unspoken message was clear: *you can't control yourselves, and that makes me better than you*. It was as if our drunken displays were an illus-tration of the very reason he was in charge of this ship and we were not.

In a sense, Mahler wasn't one of us. He was an original, not a clone, and one of only a handful aboard. His illustrious military career (if one can have an illustrious military career in a time of global peace) had gotten him a direct invitation. Why on Earth he'd accepted, no one was sure. He had to leave everything *he* was born for behind.

But he had. As had a fair few of those in command. I took another look around and realized no one partaking in the festivities was from Mahler's division. I knew the captain of *Bottomless* quite well—he wasn't around.

All of the captains were with their ships, of course. And all of the command crew were at their posts. They had jobs that needed attending to while the rest of us fooled around in the mess.

I looked up at a clock on the wall—five hours had flown by since the party began. Captain Mahler had to have known about it long before his appearance. He let us have our good time, indulged us. But now he was here to remind us it was time to face responsibility.

"I want this place spotless in an hour, and everyone in bed no more than fifteen minutes after that," he said. "All who participated in the merriment must participate in the cleanup. If anyone does not contribute, there will be consequences. I expect everyone to report for duty at 0700 tomorrow. You've all heard of hangovers, and by tomorrow many of you will be intimately familiar with one. This does not excuse you from duty."

He scanned the room, laying his eyes on each of us. "There's a time and place for everything. Today was a momentous day, one we'll all remember—the first half of, anyway."

Uncomfortable laughter cropped up here and there around the room, but dropped off almost immediately.

"It was a day worth celebrating—and we have. Now, though, we must focus on business. The business of setting up our society, engraining it in ourselves. You led different lives on Earth—sheltered and formal lives. I understand the desire to break from those constraints. But there was a reason for your well-regulated upbringing. The training wheels have come off, but that does not excuse you from duty, or dedication, to your positions aboard these ships. We must take pride in our stations, in our commitment to each other. In responsibility." He looked at his watch—an antique piece, perhaps an heirloom. "All right, your hour starts now."

I lunged at the pile of soiled cake-plates nearest me, and dropped them into the compost chute on my way to Nika's room. I hadn't a clue what the punishment for not cleaning might be, but Nika would never forgive me if I let her endure it.

Besides—I sure as hell wasn't doing this by myself.

Days later, it was time to compose my first message home.

I.C.C. sent automated messages back all the time. Short snippets of information about functionality and position, but that was it. I had to tell Earth about us—our societal status, our functionality, any major events, and any major problems. I had to keep mission support abreast of all that was happening.

There were three main communications rooms on *Mira*. One was part of the bridge and was used for ship-to-ship. The second was on deck six, and was a mirror image of the comms centers on all the other ships. That was where most of the "reporters" worked out of, gathering the data that I would then compile. The last sat on the lowest deck opposite the shuttle hangar—more of a closet than a room, what with all of the equipment stashed inside. It was well guarded, and only I and my cycle partner—the person who would take over when I retired, and in turn train a new clone of myself—had clearance to enter. It was where all Earth-to-convoy messages came in and went out. Inside stood a small desk, a small chair, and a good-sized server bank which extended beyond my sight and back into a long access tunnel beyond.

I called the servers my Enigma Machine, because all of their computing power was focused on sending and receiving coded messages. The messages came via a time subdimension we had yet to figure out how to physically move through. But even if we didn't fully understand it, we could send information through it just fine—better than fine. It was the fastest communication method known, and would ensure us practical mission-to-mission support communications for a long time.

While the system was fast, it was also limited. For one thing, my Enigma Machine needed a mate back on Earth in order for my messages to actually make it to a set of human eyeballs.

For another, SD communication was comparable to SD travel, which meant is was equally as problematic, with a few exceptions. An SD drive made a pocket of "normal" space around itself and nearby matter, protecting it in a bubble. And the drive could independently move that pocket in and out of normal space; in other words, it could dive and surface. But SD communications couldn't work that way—there was no physical engine I could attach to an encoded electromagnetic signal. Instead, there was a part of my Enigma Machine that created a bubble of its own and forced a dive, and a twin Enigma Machine on Earth that pulled the communiqué to the surface and coaxed the bubble to pop.

And the two machines had to be synced. The odds of randomly intercepting an SD packet were astronomical—pun intended. The Enigma Machine on the receiving end had to know which subdimension the information was traveling through, what trajectory it took through space, and how to unravel the "skin" that maintained the bubble once the packet was intercepted.

"Not exactly a ham radio, is it?" I'd joked the first time a teacher had introduced me to the concept. Unamused, she'd gone into further detail about how difficult SD communication was, and how I should be honored to be one of only a handful of people trained to use the methodology.

So, honored I was.

The system was fast, yes, and complicated, yes, and a huge energy suck, sure. But despite its advanced nature, it could still only handle so much data at a time. And by so much, I mean not a lot. So once the message was transferred to my implants or a holoflex-sheet, it needed *further* decoding, and that's where my job could truly get tricky.

I smoothed the front of my clothes, making sure nothing bunched uncomfortably. My official on-duty uniform was a well-tailored, denim-blue jumpsuit. Not the most stylish of work-wear, but it distinguished me from the black of security officers, the vermillion of the engineers, the Italian-yellow of the emergency medical teams, the purple of the educational division—and everyone else who wasn't in communications.

The color coding had been Mother's idea, though I heard Father was against it. Thought it was too much like gang paraphernalia or something.

Well, if the botanists and the microbiologists ever start calling themselves the Sharks and the Jets, and go snapping in unison through the halls, we'll know he was right.

In the days previous I'd gathered my notes, made my summaries, and translated them into the special shorthand. Of course, five days in, there wasn't much to report.

People were working, doing their jobs well. Though, to me, the convoy still felt more like a clubhouse than a well-oiled machine. We were *free*, after all. This was our house—it was only fair we should make our own rules, rather than be confined to whatever our parents had set up.

If it hadn't been for Captain Mahler, I'm sure entropy would have taken over and pulled our presently functional feet out from under us. We wanted time off when we wanted it. We wanted to switch shifts whenever we felt like it. We wanted to set up bowling pins in the halls and use inappropriate items to knock them down.

We just wanted to have a little fun. And despite the lesson we had learned the morning after our first party, our sense of responsibility was shaky at best. We didn't know how to balance work and play—not yet. If the captain hadn't had such a watchful eye the convoy might have ended up dead in the proverbial water.

Big Brother was watching, though. With the help of I.C.C., he made sure we ate our vegetables and washed behind our ears. He knew, better than the rest of us, that no Mother and no Father shouldn't mean a lack of order.

So that's where we were—but was I going to tell Earth all that? That they'd sent a wannabe frat house into space? And that their one hope for stability—after all the effort they'd put into that very concept—rested on a single man?

Hell no.

And, after all, it had only been five days. Surely it was just a phase.

I was conscious of the dangers of the dynamic while wanting to be a part of it. I had no desire to follow the strict regimen that had been set up for us, but I also didn't want to see the mission flounder and fail. It was a strange dichotomy of concepts that somehow lived harmoniously within me. I simultaneously supported and denied our collective rebelliousness.

But I pushed all that from my mind as I tucked my holoflexsheets under my arm and headed for my closet. I was to report the facts, just the facts, nothing more.

The space was as cramped as I remembered it from our two years of isolation. We'd simulated everything during that time. I'd done this job before. It was nothing new, and yet . . . everything had changed.

We'd left Earth behind. We were on our own. Truly.

I wanted to leave the door open, as I'd always felt a little claustrophobic in the communications room, but the two nearest security guards kept peeking through the door—very distracting. So I shut myself in. And once again, I wished the room had a window. Luckily, it wouldn't take me long to send the report.

I connected the thin, plastic holoflex-sheets to the server and organized the message into SD packets. It shouldn't have taken me more than ten minutes to get everything squared away.

However, halfway through my upload the server connected automatically to my implants.

[Message received. Sender: Earth Com Center 23, operator Saul Biterman]

I was supposed to send the first message. Was something wrong? I scanned my instruments: there was no emergency indicator. Had we miscalculated the time dilation? Was I late?

I was a little annoyed. I'd trained for this my entire life, how could I have messed it up already?

The message downloaded in the next moment, and I transferred it to a blank holoflex-sheet I pulled from a desk drawer. I wanted to see it all at once, be able to manipulate it. Sure, there was no need to translate it holographically—I could translate it in my head while reading it—but I wanted to have a physical record in case it was something I needed to take to the captain.

Turns out, it wasn't something Mahler needed to see.

It was short, and a bit confusing.

It read simply, *How are you?*

That was a strange thing for him to ask. I was about to tell him how we were—no need to be preemptive.

But maybe he wanted an impression of our well-being,

MARINA J. LOSTETTER

something besides a record of events and functions. So I whipped up one extra packet and uploaded it with the rest.

We're fine, thank you.

I finished my upload, gathered my notes, and went about the rest of my day attending to my journalistic duties. But, benign as the question seemed, I couldn't get it out of my head.

How are you?

Saul and I had worked closely, but never gotten personal. Like a grade schooler never really gets to know her teacher, I never learned much about Saul as an individual.

Age wasn't a barrier, neither was language. But there were other extenuating factors.

For one thing, I didn't meet him until the summer of my twentieth year. Everyone else had already met their specialists, and since I was one of the last to get my official training, I was both nervous and excited to receive him in the drawing room of my group home.

Buttoned up tight in a pressed suit, I sat in one of the high-backed chairs trying to focus on my posture. I wanted to make a clean, professional impression when he was shown in. With one look at me I wanted him to think I was the right person for the job, that I could handle the responsibility.

It wasn't just paranoia or an eagerness to please—Nika's mentor had gone to Mother to ask if she had the right student. If that had happened to me I would have been mortified.

Father came in first and held the door open for Mr. Biterman. I leapt to my feet—before he even had time to glimpse my well-planned pose—and my hand shot forward of its own accord.

It wasn't until we'd finished our initial shake that my mind registered anything about him. The first thing I noticed was his sticky palm, and my first impression swiftly snowballed from there.

His dress shirt was stained at the bottom—as though he'd dropped food in his lap at some point—and wasn't tucked in. Despite the smile, his face held a sour expression, one I feared permanent. And his eyes didn't meet mine. Saul was only ten years older than me, but he'd gone prematurely bald, and to make up for it he'd grown a thick, unkempt beard.

I resisted the urge to ask Father who this man was. I knew he was my tutor, despite my desire to believe otherwise.

We were formally introduced, then Father indicated for us both to sit before he left. I'd hoped he'd stay and help break the ice, but he rushed out of the room muttering that he was late for another appointment. I wondered if that was really the reason, or if Mr. Biterman's company was as off-putting as his appearance.

I smiled, crossed and uncrossed my legs, and literally twiddled my thumbs waiting for my specialist to outline a plan, or start a lecture, or whip out some comm equipment.

Saul might have been alone in the room for all he acknowledged me.

"So . . ." I began. Slowly. I'd hoped he'd interrupt me. When he didn't, I pressed on. "Do I get a syllabus, or a prospectus, or . . . Do I need to ask Fath— Dr. Matheson for certain books?"

He reached into his trouser pocket and dug around for a moment. His mining produced a crumpled scrap of yellow paper. Without a word he handed it to me by means of an unenthusiastic flip of his wrist.

Hesitant, I leaned over and took it. The scrap was clean, at least—no food stains. Glancing sidelong at this strange man I'd been saddled with, I smoothed it out in my lap.

It was a scribbled schedule for the next week, with dates, times, and places, but no indication of what was supposed to happen during the appointments.

Once I'd read it over, I looked up to ask him a question,

and was startled by the silly smile that had replaced his indifference. "Well, see you tomorrow, Ms. Pavon," he said, as though we'd just finished with a delightful visit.

That was the first of many awkward times with him. It took me months to get used to his strange mannerisms, sudden disconnects with *now*, long silences, and a plethora of other quirks.

I was baffled, at first. And also a little insulted. Here was a man whose expertise in communications had landed him one of the most important tutoring positions in the world—he was training ambassadors to space (myself along with seven others—three on different convoys), and would be his students' main connection to Earth once they left the ground—yet he couldn't hold a normal conversation.

If anyone other than Mother or Father had brought Saul into my life I would have thought it a colossal joke.

But, like a good little soldier, I held in my doubts and accepted the training. As it turned out, Saul was a capable teacher. He taught mostly through illustration and hyperbole rather than pontification, which I appreciated. And when it came to his work he was quick and accurate, but it wasn't until I advanced to decoding on my own that I realized why he had the job.

While the man couldn't smoothly string five words together in person, he was a whiz when it came to communicating long-distance. Without all of the physical cues to get in the way, with the words stripped bare, he was the most articulate man I'd ever met.

The difference was so apparent that when he came to grade my first solo decoding work, I asked him who had written the message.

"Me," he said, looking up from the many red marks he'd already placed on my paper. His brows didn't knit together, he didn't frown or squint sideways at me like a normal person would when trying to decipher the implications of what had been said. But by that time I could recognize his special brand of confusion.

"I know you *coded* it." I walked around the large warehouse space with my hands in my coat pockets. We'd been allotted one corner for training, and for housing the server and other equipment. Other machines I had no name for—utilized by other convoy departments—took up the three remaining corners. "But who composed it?"

"Me. I did it all." He went back to marking the page, each stroke of the pen more vehement than before.

I'd insulted him, and I tried to make up for it by inviting him to drinks with my friends and me after our session, but I should have known better. He declined with a lame excuse, but I'm sure his reasons for turning me down were twofold. His anger was a part of it, but how exactly was a man who couldn't relax and behave naturally one-on-one going to get by in a group? If I made him nervous, what would a whole gaggle of girls in a crowded bar do to him?

But I kept trying. From there on out, every time I had a group activity planned after our lessons, I invited him. I hoped at some point he'd say yes. I thought maybe if he spent time with more people he would get better at communicating in person, but it wasn't to be. Saul was who he was, and I couldn't change that.

So, perhaps his first message to me on *Mira* shouldn't have surprised me so much. The man I worked with closely on Earth, but never really knew, waited to reach out to me until I was stretching the distance between us to never-before-achieved proportions.

His reply to my first set of data packages was mostly what I expected: acknowledgment of the incidents I'd recorded, other Earth specialists' professional advice related to my report, and questions about the crew's health and productivity. But tacked on at the end was a full letter, clearly meant for me personally.

A portion was general-interest based. Saul thought we might want to know what Earth was up to. We'd been gone two weeks travel time, around four months their time, so not much had happened. Not enough to take note of, anyway, but I transferred the information to a file and sent it to Nika's implants. She'd know what to do with it.

Throughout the second half of the letter, though, Saul told me about *his* work week, how he was feeling, and so on. Things friends talk about. Close friends.

I wasn't sure what to think, let alone how to respond.

In all that time I'd been trying to get Saul to open up I'd thought him disinterested. I thought perhaps he didn't want to come with me after lessons because he just didn't care to get to know me. That maybe he didn't like people, just words.

Could he have been holding out for this? For when he'd be most comfortable?

It seemed ridiculous, but as acquainted with his awkwardness as I was . . .

Before he'd signed off, he asked me the same question again, but made sure to come to the point:

How are you, Margarita? The convoy is fine, but are you?

The question bothered me. Other people would see these messages once he'd decoded them. They were public record. I didn't really feel comfortable laying out personal information. He wasn't asking *how are you* in the sense that you ask when meeting up with someone, when an obligatory "Fine" can mean anything from *fantastic* to *I feel like crud*.

He was asking me to confront my mental state. As though he knew I had not stopped to assess my own adjustment.

How was I? Did it matter?

I decided it didn't. I gave him the same *fine* response, and sent the packets on their way.

Over the next few months, his messages were similar, and the differences in the way we were each traveling through time's dimensions became more distinctive. While I was contacting him every week, he was only speaking to me once every couple of months. And his life was moving at speeds I could hardly comprehend.

A few of my days after launch, he'd gushed about a colleague. A woman, who apparently wouldn't give him the time of day. After three weeks of my time, they were dating.

That in itself was a shock. Saul Biterman with a girlfriend? Highly improbable.

Two months into my journey, he was engaged. I couldn't believe it. Who was this woman who had fallen in love with my quirky, socially-stunted tutor? Had he grown so much since I'd last seen him, or did the old saying about odd ducks hold true?

I blinked my eyes and he was married. Another blink and there was a baby on the way. I blinked a third time and the baby had been born—a boy.

I hadn't been on board six months yet.

But four and a half years had passed for Saul and his family.

After his son came into the picture, things changed faster than ever. I hadn't realized how quickly babies progress, and it was breathtaking to witness a child's life on fast-forward.

Sometimes Saul even sent pictures. It was hard for me to accept that they were all of the same child.

And every time, Saul asked me how I was. Or pushed for more personal information. I always answered with *fine*. I didn't see the point in giving him more.

Things that hadn't bothered me during the test run—those two years we'd been quarantined aboard—began to pick at my nerves. I couldn't stand to look at the cleaning robots when I'd hardly noticed them before. I even chased a wall-climber out of my cabin when it accidently knocked an old paper book off one of my shelves.

The walls felt closer than they had before, the hallways narrower, the rooms darker.

Living aboard for real was not that dissimilar from our test years—not physically, anyway. But psychologically I was in a completely different place.

It took me a while to realize it, but most of my free time was spent in front of my window, or on *Eden* when I could get permission.

Eden is the animal ship. It feels more like Noah's Ark than anything. There aren't pairs of every kind, but there is a small breeding stock of food and comfort animals.

Back on Earth I'd never been particularly fond of animals. I wasn't one of those girly-girls who loved kittens and horses and wondered if maybe I'd rather be a veterinary expert than head communications officer. And it wasn't the puppies or the cows that attracted me to *Eden*.

It was the special lighting and atmosphere. *Eden* looked like a light bulb from the outside: nearly spherical, but with one long protuberance. The protuberance held the docking bay and offices.

The bulb itself was split into two halves, each with its own gravitational direction; the ship's center was down for both sections. Instead of decks segmented into cabins, each domed half was again halved by a giant see-through wall, and consisted of wide open spaces. Four zones for four climates: temperate and subarctic shared one half, arid and tropical the other. The temperate zone was filled with grazing pastures and spiraling terraces. The tropical supported a lush rainforest—though rain fern-garden might have been more appropriate, as there were only a handful of trees and numerous kinds of knee-height foliage. Arid was a red desert, spotted through with hardy plants and several oases. And sub-arctic was more tundra-like, really, with its short grasses and twiggy bushes.

The biodomes were themselves impressive, but the real wonder of engineering on *Eden* was the sun.

In testing, it had been proven that without exposure to the sun fewer animals were conceived, fewer came to term, and fewer of the live births survived to adulthood. Lamps didn't work with the animals like they worked with the plants. With plants, as long as the chlorophyll got fed, they were happy. The animals needed more. They had to think they were out-side, under the sky.

And that's why I visited *Eden*. Just like the comfort animals, I would wither without it. I chose the temperate quarter, found a cow-pie-free spot in the pasture—next to the base of one of the terrace ramps—sat back and closed my eyes.

It was the little touches that made it feel real. A light breeze brushed my cheeks. The smell of fresh grass filled my nose. Bird song—piped in through hidden speakers—flitted through the air, accompanied by other background noises. Those, added to the warmth of the artificial sun, all blended together to complete the illusion. After drinking it in with my other senses, I let my sight back into the game. The sky held amazing depth. Though I knew where the domed ceil-ing physically lay, it felt like it went on and on for miles.

The bright orb of the artificial sun was just as difficult to look at as the real thing. It appeared to travel across the dome, even receding slightly as it made its way toward the horizon, implying a greater vastness than the ceiling actually possessed.

A curious calf came over to check me out. It made a silly, high-pitched version of an adult moo, and let me pat its nose.

That was when I realized I missed Earth.

When I'd been cooped up during the test years, I'd always known I'd go home again. That I would run in the fields again, stand on the rocky Icelandic shore, and stroll down the village parkway.

These nine ships were the whole of my reality from now on. Not only in terms of the area I had to explore, or the atmosphere, or the company, but also in terms of *flow*.

Children aren't born and off to school in less than a year. That's not right, it's not real. If I ever chose to raise a child, he would not magically transform before my eyes as Saul's son had.

We were separate—severed—from Earth in every possible way. It was a memory, and I found myself missing things I had been eager to leave. Father, Mother, all those who watched over us. I hadn't been ready to receive my independence. Had anyone?

I cried then, with the baby cow nuzzling me and the pseudo-sun shining down on both of us. Homesickness was not something I'd ever had to contend with before. And it was something I simply had to learn to get over, because home was lost to me forever.

On my way back to my cabin I tripped over a vacuuming robot. I cursed and kicked it, though it only buzzed and beeped an error message in return. "Stupid machine."

The depressive mood was not mine alone. The sparse news from Earth contributed to our sense of detachment, and most of the updates we received were negative—new conflict in South America, a tsunami in Asia, a devastating earthquake in Europe. And when Saul told me the littlest convoy had been lost, I didn't know how to react. One of our twelve, completely gone.

But, after we hit our one-year anniversary, and the first new babies had been successfully tube grown, the unthinkable happened.

We had our first suicide.

"Mags! Margarita? Margarita, let me in!" Fists banged on my door and panicked cries stabbed through the walls. I woke up startled and disoriented. It took me a moment to place the voice as Nika's.

My fumbling brain knew something was off before I made it through the dark to open the door. It wasn't just the alarm in her voice; she hadn't called me on my implants, and was ignoring the door's buzzer.

"Lights," I demanded of the room. I met my friend with a terse "What?"

Tears flowed down her puffy cheeks, and her lips trembled. I'd never seen Nika cry before, and these weren't typical bad-day tears. Something horrible had happened, and she was near hysterics.

"He, he—I just found—I—" The hiccups started, and she couldn't get any words out.

I pulled her inside, sat her down at my small table, and pulled the comforter from my bed to throw around her shoulders. Without asking I made her a cup of tea in my kitchenette and plopped it down in front of her. She barely acknowledged the mug.

Gritty sleep rimmed my eyes. Rubbing it away, I pulled up a chair beside Nika. When the hiccups stopped and her breathing steadied, I prodded. "What's wrong?" I'd never known Nika to get unduly emotional. If she was upset, things were bad.

"I went to go see Lexi. I couldn't sleep. He was working the night shift and— Ooh, God." She let her forehead fall to the table. "He's dead."

Had I heard right? "How?" I lowered my head to her level. "Nika. What happened?" Lexi was an engineer, and Nika's biological cousin. I thought maybe there'd been an accident, that some of *Mira*'s machinery had caught him. Never in a million years would suicide have crossed my mind.

But that was exactly what had happened. Lexi had hung himself deep in the bowels of the ship.

"What does it mean?" Nika asked. "Weren't—weren't we screened for this? We share genetic code. If he can kill himself . . ."

"No," I jumped in. "You couldn't. It won't get that bad." I put my arms around her, but knew we couldn't sit there. We had to tell someone—the captain. "Nika. He's still there, isn't he?"

"I couldn't touch him. I saw and I—I ran. He's still there." The realization that she'd left him hanging in his noose disturbed her, and she fell apart again.

Nausea made my stomach boil. The situation hadn't hit home yet, hadn't grabbed my emotions yet. Which meant now was the time to act, before I became a puddle like Nika.

I'd have to report this to Saul.

At the thought, I was instantly ashamed, embarrassed. But now wasn't the time to think about that, so I pushed thoughts of later duties aside and helped Nika to her feet. "We have to let the security officers know."

"I left him there," she mumbled. "I ran and left him there." She felt like a rag doll in my arms.

I'd thought to drag her to the security offices near the bridge, but she'd fallen into a stupor. Nika stared into space like she could see through the walls. My best friend was in shock, which meant I was left holding the bag.

This seemed like as good a time as any to give the convoy-wide security alert system a spin. I activated it via my implants, choosing the *officers only* option. A red light blinked at the edge of my peripheral vision, letting me know the alert had gone through. Immediately, I second-guessed the action. Perhaps I should have left Nika alone in my apartment and gone to the bridge myself. Maybe this didn't constitute a convoy-wide emergency—or did it? It was our first death, and it was as unnatural as they came.

"I.C.C., are you there?"

"Yes. You have activated the—"

"I know. There's been . . . Nika's cousin . . ." I couldn't get the words out.

"You are hyperventilating," the computer observed.

I was—my hands were going all tingly.

"Close your mouth and inhale slowly through your nose." I.C.C. was clearly more concerned with my present state than why I'd used the alert system. I wasn't sure what to think of that. Wasn't sure what to think about anything, actually.

Security officers busted through my door like they were performing a drug raid. My apartment-for-one became a sardine-can-for-twelve in under two minutes. The officers separated Nika and me in an instant—thinking a domestic dispute, I'm sure. It took me a few minutes to assure them we weren't the problem. They were overly eager and hopping, as unsure in the execution as I was in the concept, but itching to do their duty, to solve whatever the problem might be.

Unfortunately, the hubbub pushed Nika into silence. I couldn't get the exact location out of her, and bringing up Lexi's work agenda from the cached files only told us he was scheduled to perform routine maintenance. So they left me to attend to my poor friend while they scoured the ship's innards for a body. It took me a moment to realize our big mistake—we had all forgotten to ask I.C.C. for help. I.C.C. would know where he was.

"I.C.C., do you have Lexi's location? Please direct the officers."

"I will. Your breathing has normalized."

"Thank you."

Stupid. So stupid. I.C.C. should be programmed to alert us to this kind of thing. We shouldn't have to stumble upon it. Privacy be damned.

Like everyone in the convoy, I knew Lexi, if only on the

MARINA J. LOSTETTER

level of acquaintance. He'd seemed happy whenever I saw him, but I'm sure I had seemed happy to him, too.

The shrinks saw the event as a tragic failure on their part. They sent out emergency psychiatric evaluations and made sure everyone had an appointment to meet one-on-one with a doctor.

They assigned me to a session with Dr. Yassine. A nice enough guy, if a bit fidgety. Forgive me if I think doctors who work with people on the edge should be calm, collected, and stately, but if I were ever on the fence about killing myself, I think Dr. Yassine's inability to sit still would have driven me to it. I almost got up and grabbed his hand to stop his pen from tapping. Almost.

He wanted me to "explore myself verbally." But when you don't feel comfortable with someone, it's not easy to open up. I didn't want to "explore" with him. It's not that I had a problem telling him what was going on in my head. It was just that I knew it would be a lot more helpful for me to share it with someone else. Someone specific.

I resolved to stop telling Saul I was fine when I wasn't. I hadn't seen the harm in keeping my emotional distance before, but now . . . Keeping up appearances wasn't worth crumbling inside.

So I made my next report ahead of schedule, and tacked on a letter for Saul. I told him everything. How I was feeling. How I was coping with the suicide.

How I was sure there would be more to come.

I wondered—in writing—about *purpose*. Mine seemed obvious enough. But what about the others? We'd created false purposes for them—something to keep their DNA busy until we reached the anomaly. The engineers hated being called mechanics because that's not what they wanted to be. Nika was a historian, a diplomat, and that meant she needed to be working with people and their history. As noble as she made archivist seem, it wasn't who she was.

Saul made all of it seem okay. He reminded me of the mission. How Earth was counting on us. We were brilliant scientists, doctors, inventors, thinkers, and Earth had given us up for a greater purpose.

I was looking at things too narrowly, he said. That our purpose was in the journey, in experiencing life as humans had never experienced it before. I found our situation—locked in tin cans hurling through a vacuum—boring, depressing. He said the people back home found it wondrous. That my messages were now studied all over the globe.

[You can't see the forest because you're a tree] he'd sent. [A tree might ask, *Why do I grow here? Why do I produce cones instead of fruit? Or, why must I lose my leaves when that tree stays ever green?* If you could show the tree how it fits into the forest, how it provides so much to the greater being that is the forest, what might it think of itself then?

[Show them the forest, Margarita. The trees are dying because they don't see the forest.

[P.S. I have a daughter now. I named her after you. People have been naming their children after you voyagers for years now, and probably will for centuries to come.]

The metaphor might have been heavy-handed, but it and his postscript were exactly what I needed—what all of us needed.

But it took six months and three more suicides for me to take action. And I regret that to this day. As a member of the governing board (all department heads had a place in politics) I had a duty that far exceeded my station. But I was still so new to independence that I had yet to grasp my authority. I was basically a kid trying to be an adult—to be a leader. They had trained and trained and trained us until I could recite leadership principles in my sleep, but in the end, a person also has to want to *be* a leader. To rise to the occasion. I only wish I had found my place sooner.

I couldn't change the past. But I was pretty sure I could change the future.

I put in a personal request to see the captain. In later years that would have put me on a waiting list as long as my arm. Back then I practically walked in.

Entering Captain Mahler's situation room, I lead with the holoflex-sheet. In my eagerness to prove a point I'd forgotten to salute and do our introductory dance. Nothing like starting out on the wrong foot when you're trying to save your entire community from emotional collapse.

He sat at the head of a beautiful marble slab, the kind that made the most intriguing tombs and best kitchen counters. Green, with beautiful flecks of gold and iridescent carbonates, it was out of place. Almost every portion of the ship was metal or plastic—carpeted floors being the major exception. But the ship designers had wanted to give us little pieces of nature wherever they could—maybe they'd known better than I had how much we'd miss such things when they were gone.

The holoflex-sheet plopped in front of Mahler before my clipped greeting met his ears.

Five sentences into my rehearsed speech, he cut me off with a violent, chopping of his hand. "To whom are you speaking?" he said through a clenched jaw.

The question tripped me up, as it was meant to. "Uh . . ."

"As you did not address me, I can only assume this flippant diatribe is meant for someone else. Yet I believe we are alone."

It was then that I realized both my mistake and that I was intent on preaching to the choir. I'd come to him to talk order and systems. To discuss individualism vs. hive mentality. I wanted to argue for the very thing the captain hoped for: militant commitment to the group's goals over individual wants and needs.

Immediately I backtracked, saluting at attention, barking out my station and my purpose, addressing him in the manner he deserved to be addressed.

"Sir," I began again. "We have a distinct disconnect between the command team and everyone else. We are not a military convoy, but neither are we civilians. I believe this message from my Earth contact illustrates our problem. Most of us are wandering around in our own little worlds. The members don't see how the pieces fit, and I believe that to be the source of our convoy-wide depression. We need to rethink how we think, if you will.

"We were each taught how special we are. As *individuals*. Yet, for some reason, we weren't taught that the *group* is special. That devotion to the group is required for success. Yes, we were instilled with devotion to the mission, to the anomaly, but not to the convoy and each other.

"We need a better sense of community, and at the moment I can think of no better way to bring that about than to change the way we do things. I know there was a plan, and that it was supposed to ensure our stability, but it won't work. Father—" this was tough to admit, but I swallowed and pressed forward "—Father was wrong. He wanted a '*be all you can be*' attitude, when what we need is a '*be all we can be* attitude.'"

Mahler passed his hand under his chin, scratching it lightly, clearly weighing my statements and considering his first words on the matter carefully. "I wasn't supposed to address this until the elections. Matheson and Seal didn't think we'd have any suicides at this point, but things seem to be moving along faster than expected. Whether that's problematic or all for the best will make itself clear eventually, I'm sure."

"Sir?"

"The suicides were expected. Not planned—don't give me that look. Just planned *for*. They were built into Matheson's equations, and he figured if we had fifteen or so suicides in the first five years that would actually *strengthen* our society—much in the way you suggest."

Flabbergasted, my mind went blank. I couldn't even be sure I'd heard him correctly, let alone understood. "Sir, may I sit?"

He gestured toward a spot near the other end of the marble slab, but I took a seat at his right hand. "Are you saying Mother and Father knew some of us would die this way? That Lexi and—?"

"They didn't know who, but they had guesses. Matheson's calculations indicated a rash of suicides was inevitable, but that the tragedy would give us an opportunity. Misfortune can have many different effects on large populations. It can drive some into chaos, but the more empathetic the group, the more emotionally aware the individuals are of the other individuals—"

"The more likely they are to band together," I finished for him, nodding. Instead of at my captain, my gaze bore into the far wall where a blank screen hung. We were a forest, trees in the forest. "Some conifers need fire in order for their seeds to germinate," I mumbled. Turning back to him, I asked, "This is our forest fire?"

"Yes. That's a good way to look at it."

"But, why didn't they warn us? Why not prepare us?"

He stood and began pacing. "Is anyone every really prepared for tragedy? They *did* warn us. They told me, and I was to inform the board once the elected half was in place." The hard lines of his face were covered in stubble—I'd just noticed. Unusual, for Mahler anyway. He preferred to be clean-cut and well pressed at all times. This must have been weighing on his mind as much as it had been weighing on mine.

"But, elections won't be for another six months. We were told exactly what must be done the first two years," I said.

Eventually we'd be able to make our own laws, dependent on whatever social problems cropped up. We could deal with them our own way, but not yet. For the first few years we had to follow our orders to a T, even when it came to civilian government.

Our board right now only consisted of the department heads and their appointed seconds. Only once we hit the two-year mark we were to set up elections whose winners would comprise the second half of the government.

"I know—believe me, I know. But now that you've brought it up, I don't think we can wait until we have a full board," Mahler said. "*I* can't wait for our timeline to match the original. If the suicides are happening now we must take action. I was waiting, hoping . . ." He shook his head. "Doesn't matter. We are going to use these deaths as a rallying point, as an educational point. We're not going to let the mission fail.

"We just have to work out how."

I left the captain feeling simultaneously giddy and nauseated. Saul had been right. We could fix this. There was even a plan to fix this. We would band together and be stronger than before.

But at what cost? Matheson had sacrificed these people. Sacrificed Lexi and those still to kill themselves. Not directly, of course—he didn't go through their files and say "You will die. And you will die. And you will die."

But he might as well have.

If he'd informed us this might happen—that in all likelihood, according to his societal projections it *would* happen— we could have stopped it. Lexi might have thought twice before hanging himself.

Even worse, our psychologists and psychiatrists had known it was coming. They'd seen it in Lexi, they just hadn't been able to do anything about it. They weren't allowed to tell our modest security detail about pending problems. It made me wonder if that was why Dr. Yassine had been so fidgety. Because he *knew*, but hadn't been able to do anything. It was only after something bad happened that they could act. We had to change that. No one's hands should be tied when it comes to saving a life.

We operated that way because that's the way many Earth societies operated—they didn't respond to potential tragedy, only actualized tragedy. Once we could make our own laws we needed to abandon those ways. We were no longer bound to Earth by its gravity, why should we remain bound by its customs?

Perhaps my line of thinking was exactly what Mother and Father had planned for. This sense of outrage, this desire to band together to prevent more catastrophes. Despite what it meant to the little personal freedoms we had.

It didn't prevent me from hating our mentors for not telling us. But I also found myself admiring their strategy and planning.

Again: nausea and giddiness.

My duty and my humanity were at odds, but I let them settle at opposite ends of my brain. I needed both to survive in this new encapsulated world.

I reported our progress to Saul. Told him we'd discovered a new portion of our societal design and now had to decipher how to implement it. He responded with a thumbs-up emoji and a picture of him and his family.

His son was fourteen. Saul himself was going on fifty. He looked so old. Not because fifty is old, but because in my mind he was still in his thirties.

How could he be fifty? How could his life slip away so quickly? Intellectually, I knew all was as it should be. He wasn't living his life at a rapid-fire pace, I was simply seeing it through a long-range lens. But I still felt a gaping maw of loss in my gut, still wondered if I was ready to let Earth move on without me—without *us*.

I was starting to realize that all we really had up here was each other.

A few months later, the elections came and went. Before then there were more suicides. There were a few after, too, but for the most part a sense of togetherness was starting to pervade the ships. The votes reflected exactly what Mahler had thought they'd reflect—a convoy-wide sense of pride in our mission. Those elected were the most duty-bound in the fleet.

We outlined a new education system. Emphasis would be put on unity. To shirk responsibility would be the worst possible offense. Honor, pride, synergy—all important. Our children would grow up knowing community came first.

After another year and a half I fully committed myself to upholding those ideals. I met a nice woman, Chen Kexin from food processing. I knew the lesbian and bisexual population aboard was small—about the same percentage as in the gen-pop on Earth—and had previously resigned myself to possibly never finding a suitable partner. I'm so glad I was wrong. We dated for a while, then decided to make our bond permanent. We settled into a quadruple cabin and put in for a clone.

They decided to give Kexin and me a boy. His name would be Reginald Straifer II.

When we finally got the news, I was so excited to tell Saul about the baby that I forgot what day it was. I forgot that this was the last time I'd speak formally to him.

Saul had reached his seventieth birthday and decided it was time to retire. He reminded me with a preemptive data packet.

[Looking forward to your last message. I've included pictures of my son and his wife on their wedding day. And my little Margarita. She's getting her advanced degree in chemical engineering.]

The bottom dropped out of my elation. I didn't have a picture of Reggie to send, because he hadn't been officially born yet. He was still gestating on *Hippocrates*.

I put in my report, and included a diagram of our new teaching processes that included community appreciation. I skimped on the data a bit, more consumed with my personal message back.

[Tell me this isn't goodbye], I sent, [I want a picture of you and your wife, Saul. And I'll send a picture of my son as soon as he's birthed. Let someone know to forward it on to you. Tell them I want an update from you every few months—Earth months—okay?]

I couldn't believe it. Seventy. So much of his life, gone. It had blazed past. He'd been my constant these past few years, my Earthly touchstone, and now it was over. Over too soon.

Earth was slipping away. Home was slipping away. Even if we turned back now, the world would not be as we'd left it.

We were aliens now. Nomads in uncharted territory.

And that was exactly how it should be.

The next message I received from Saul was truly the last. He had a heart attack two days after composing it, and his replacement sent it to me.

The message opened with a cheerful introduction and greeting from the new guy. A stranger. Someone who didn't know me and never would.

He saved the bad news until the end. There was the message from Saul, and a short blip after: [Mr. Saul Biterman, deceased]

I couldn't believe it. He would never see my son.

A picture came with the packet, just like I'd requested. The last picture I'd ever get of my friend.

I transferred it to a 'flex-sheet and took it back to my cabin without entering a copy into the archives. This was just for me. I hung it on the wall, between pictures of me and Kexin, and me and Nika. I saved a spot for Reggie right beneath. Everyone I loved would find a place on this wall. We'd all be together in memory.

Afterward, I retrieved a worn, blue envelope from between the pages of my favorite book—the biography of Arthur Scherbius—curled up in a chair, and finally read the letter Father and Mother had left for me so long ago.

CHAPTER THREE

JAMAL: BALANCE

. . . .

TWENTY-SIX YEARS LATER

JANUARY 3, 30 YEARS POST LAUNCH DAY (PLD)

2415 CE

"Hellooooo," said Jamal in his small, sing-song voice. "Computer, helloooo." The eight-year-old bounced a soccer ball on his knee in front of the access panel. He was supposed to be in class.

"Hello, Jamal," said the ship's AI.

"Do I get a new baby brother today?"

"My records indicate that your parents will jointly travel to *Hippocrates* during their lunch hour to retrieve the next available, fully-gestated clone."

The boy tossed his ball at the panel and deftly caught it on the rebound. "But is it a *brother*?" Computers could be so dumb. He'd make them smarter when he grew up.

"The next available clone is that of Nakamura Akane. Her original earned a doctorate in engineering and ship design from the university of—"

"A *sister*?" Jamal kicked the ball down the hallway. "You're giving me a sister?" He knocked his forehead against the wall and scrunched his eyes shut in frustration. "Why, computer? What did I ever do to you?"

"I am not in control of the growth patterns. And I had no influence over when your parents submitted their request."

"Mr. Kaeden?"

"Ah, great," Jamal grumbled. Through the hall came Dr. Seal, his teacher, carrying the scuffed soccer ball. "You had to tattle on me, too?"

"I do not tattle," said I.C.C. "Dr. Seal inquired as to your location. You are here. I related such."

"Thanks a lot, Icey."

"I.C.C.," the computer corrected.

"Ice-C-C," Jamal stuttered. Not so much because he couldn't say it, but because he hadn't expected his first attempt to be contested.

"Closer," I.C.C. conceded.

"Oh, come now," said Dr. Seal, standing over the boy. "Sometimes children have a hard time with names. We let them use what's easiest."

"But they are made to pronounce names correctly when they are not children anymore," I.C.C. said.

"Yes," Dr. Seal admitted.

"Then is it not easier for them to learn the correct pronunciation initially? Being told one's first efforts are acceptable, only to later find out they are not, makes the acquisition of knowledge and skills unnecessarily difficult, regardless of the subject. Why make Jamal learn my name twice when he should only be asked to learn it once?"

Dr. Seal didn't say anything, just looked down at Jamal with a "can you believe this thing?" crease in his forehead.

But Jamal was with the computer. Yeah, why the heck should he have to learn something twice? What kind of racket were the teachers running?

"Thanks for telling on me, I.C.C.," Jamal said, articulating every letter.

Brushing off the AI's quirkiness, Dr. Seal put a hand on Jamal's shoulder. "Mr. Kaeden," he said sternly. "You are supposed to be in class."

"You are, too," Jamal mumbled.

"Jamal will have to cohabitate with a sibling soon," I.C.C. explained. "The fact that he was not consulted on its gender seems to have caused him distress."

"I'm getting a sister," Jamal said with a pout.

"Sisters are people, too," said Dr. Seal as he took Jamal by the hand and led him away from the access panel.

Nobody understood. The other kids just made fun of the poopy diapers in his future, and all the grownups either waved aside the problem or seemed mad that he was mad.

"But it's a *girl*," he tried to explain.

The botanist who had come in to educate them on their classroom air garden scrunched up her face. "I'm a girl."

His ears turned from dark chocolate to strawberry chocolate. *I didn't mean . . . Ugh.* "Yeah, whatever," he mumbled. "You're not a *sister*." *Even if you are, you're not my sister.*

When class finally got out he knew where to go. If anybody in the convoy could understand, it would be Diego.

The ride from *Aesop* and school to *Mira* and home *could* have been spectacular. The convoy had stopped for a few days to check their calculations—which meant they'd popped their SD bubble, and space wasn't black and empty like normal. It was full of stars.

Extra shuttles swarmed between the main ships, letting the crew take full advantage of the view. On the first day of the stop, Jamal's teacher had taught class on *Holwarda* and they'd used the giant telescope. *Best. Day. Ever.*

Now, if Jamal touched one edge of a shuttle porthole, graphics popped up to label the nebulae and galaxies and systems and stuff. So the ride home *could* have been cool. But the other kids were loud and pushy. And they talked about dumb things—boring things.

They swapped math riddles and stories about visiting their future workplaces. A favorite game was *my mom's job is better than your mom's job*. Which was silly, because everyone knew his mom, his *aðon*, had the best job, so why play?

They played the same stuff over and over. Talked about the same stuff over and over. Normally he'd be all for it. Eventually someone would suggest something new, and they would carry it like a banner through the shuttle until the game or rhyme or nickname became stale.

But he could find no comfort in the ritual of tomfoolery today. Who was Tom and who did he think he was fooling, anyway?

It was a phrase Diego used. Apparently he'd taken part in plenty of it during his school days. But, maybe Diego didn't remember being a kid right. After all, it'd been a really, really, *really* long time since he'd been to school.

School back on Earth. School on Iceland—which Diego insisted wasn't really a land made of ice, but Jamal had his doubts.

Jamal blew on a small portion of the window. It didn't fog up as nicely as the bathroom mirror, but it would do. He drew funny squiggles until a ball hit him in the side of the head.

"Hey, what the—" He picked up the projectile, which had bounced off the seat in front of him and rolled under his feet.

"That's yours," said Lewis, moving from three rows forward to join Jamal at the back of the shuttle.

"Sit down," demanded the shuttle pilot. Thank I.C.C. the pilots rotated. Otherwise Jamal was sure this guy would eventually open the airlock and let the pressure differential suck them all into oblivion.

Lewis stuck his tongue out at the driver as he plopped

down next to Jamal. "It's yours. I got it back from Dr. Seal when he wasn't looking."

"Thanks, man." Jamal propped the soccer ball up under his arm and returned to staring out the window. His fog-drawing had disappeared.

"Are you ready for the brat?"

Jamal shrugged and sighed, "No."

"It wouldn't be any better if it was a brother. When my parents brought Duke home I thought it'd be awesome. That we could play catch and pull pranks and stuff. He just gurgled all day and threw up on my favorite blanket. Babies suck."

"But eventually she won't be a baby. She'll be a *girl*. And then what?"

The possibilities horrified him, vague as they were.

When he got home he was surprised to see his *aðon* **and** *pabbi* there by themselves. No baby. His hopes rose for a moment. Maybe they'd changed their minds. Maybe they weren't going to get a baby after all.

His *pabbi* kicked that fantasy out from under him. "We thought you'd like to come," he explained. "We rescheduled for tomorrow and excused you from class."

"We didn't want you to feel left out," said his *aðon* from the bedroom. She was changing out of her work jumper.

He didn't *feel* left out, but he *wanted* to be left out. If he never had to see his sister it would be too soon. They were making a big, fat, ugly mistake. Why'd they want to go and ruin their perfect family with a sister, huh? Weren't the three of them enough?

He dropped his pack in the entryway and slumped over to the dining table. "Can I go visit Diego when he gets off work?" he asked after he sat down, picking at his fingers and swinging his feet.

"Sure," said Pabbi. "As long as he says it's okay. If he's busy you come right home."

Diego was Jamal's *afi*'s—his granddad's—best friend. Jamal would never say so out loud, but he liked Diego better than *Afi*. *Afi* only liked old people things, and more importantly, only things right in front of him. He had no imagination.

Diego, though . . . Diego knew how to dream while still awake.

Jamal impatiently watched the minutes tick away. Diego's shift was over at 1600, and he should be back at his cabin no later than 1630. As soon as the last minute rolled over, Jamal was out the door and down the hall to the nearest lift.

He had to wait a whole 'nother five minutes before Diego got there. Jamal sat in front of the old man's door, knees up to his chin, feet squirming in his shoes.

"Que pasa?" Diego squinted at Jamal when he got close. "Someone have a bad day?" He was dressed in the corn-yellow of most *Morgan* workers. Short and heavyset, but fresh-faced for someone in his sixties, his ruddy wrinkles made him look like he'd been basking in the sun all day, though he hadn't been anywhere near the artificial Sol of *Eden*.

Jamal shrugged, suddenly aware that his complaint might come off as whiny. "How was your day?" he asked politely. Something about being around Diego always made him feel more polite.

"Fine. Figured how to make the soy processing more efficient. My original designed the system, you know. I just made it better." Diego opened the door. "I was going to watch a movie this evening," he said as the lights came on. "You might find it amusing. Coming in?"

Diego's quarters didn't have as many rooms as Jamal's. He'd said it was because he didn't need them. "Only one of me. Can't take up a family cabin anymore. Wouldn't be right."

The place smelled like beans and cheese. Diego checked his slow-cooker (something only food workers typically had) in the kitchenette, then came back to the main sitting and sleeping area. "How's the new baby? Problems already? If you liked it you wouldn't be here."

"No baby yet," said Jamal, crossing his arms. "They're gonna take me with them when they get her."

"Ah. That's nice."

"No, it's not."

"Oh?"

Jamal shrugged. "Decided I don't want a sib. 'Specially a sister." Diego laughed lightly and Jamal took immediate offense. "You, too? You don't get it. Why doesn't anyone get it?"

"I'm not laughing at you, *amigo*. I'm enjoying the simplicity of your problem, not that it is a problem."

"What do you mean?"

"We've figured out how to live in space and investigate cosmic phenomena up close. But we still haven't figured out how to make a new brother appreciate his sister. I had a sister, you know."

"You did? But, you were born on Earth. Was it another clone?"

The old man shook his head and gestured for Jamal to have a seat. "Nope. My sister was born the old-fashioned way. She did not accompany me on the mission."

"What's 'the old fashion way'?"

Diego's face went blank for a moment, then he waved the question aside. "Never you mind. My point is, I felt the same as you, or at least similar, when I was told I'd be sharing my parents with a girl. Anita. Oh, I hated the idea. I considered running away and abandoning my duties if my mother went through with this whole *giving birth* thing."

Jamal gasped. Abandoning your duty was about the lowest

thing a convoy member could do. The thought of it made him sick inside. "You did?"

"Considered, I said, considered. I didn't, of course. I stuck it out. The baby was born, came home, and then . . . guess what?"

Jamal pursed his lips. "What?"

"I was just as upset with the baby there as I was when she hadn't been around. But I got over it, eventually. You'll learn to like being a big brother. You'll get excited when she learns to walk and talk. But you should never hold her gender against her."

"Why not?"

"Why would you hold anything against someone that they can't help? You know what that's called? Prejudice."

"Sounds stupid."

"It is stupid. Very stupid. But there was a time and place where your friend Lewis might not have liked you because of the color of your skin, and where someone like my late wife might never have looked twice at a man who spoke a different language than she did."

"Everyone on board speaks the same language."

"I'll give you that—at least one, anyway. We try to preserve our heritage, but truth is you're never going to know what it's like to be a true British Algerian."

"A whah?"

"British Algerian. That's what your original was. His father was from Great Britain, his mother from Algeria."

"How do you know?"

"I met him when I was thirty-five—just one short year before we launched."

"You did? You never told me that."

"He was a good man. Much like you." He poked Jamal in the ribs. "But not you, you understand?"

"Well, *duh*."

"What I'm saying is that I'm a clone of a Mexican who chose to give up his very lucrative R&D job in order to join a closed, multicultural compound in Iceland and donate his genetic material to the future. And now I live in a set of tin cans hurtling through space. We're explorers, Jamal. Astronauts. You'd understand how wonderful that is if you'd been born on Earth . . . Point is, if we can't leave all that other *caca de la vaca* behind us, well, what's it all for then? And how do we honor our unique position in humanity's history?"

"Through loyalty, efficiency, and dedication," Jamal recited.

"Yes, but also through understanding. Living in a convoy means we're rubbing elbows left and right. We have to look at what ties us together. As soon as we start disliking each other for our little differences it'll all go to pot. There's nowhere to run, you see? You're stuck with everyone on board. Might as well be nice to them, might as well appreciate them."

"I get all that. They tell us that in school *all the time*."

"Well, then don't be mad that you've got a sister. We need our siblings. All of them, understand?"

"Ugh."

"Listen—I get it. Early on, in your eyes she'll be a cooing, pooping annoyance, and then one day she'll become a person. Not really, though, because she's always been a person. It's actually *you* who will change. You will understand that you've been blinded by that thing you called 'stupid.'"

"Yeah, all right," Jamal conceded. "I'll try 'n' like her." He thought for a moment, then asked, "Can I not like her if she's annoying?"

Diego considered for a moment. "Yes. But I still suggest you try."

"Fine." Jamal sighed, then perked up. "So what's the movie you were gonna watch?"

"It's old, I have to warn you."

Oh, no. Not like *Afi* old, he hoped.

"It's about space travel. Before they'd had much space travel." Diego dimmed the lights and accessed the computer.

Before they'd had much space travel? Jamal couldn't even imagine such a time. "Like a million years ago?"

"No, not quite," Diego chuckled. "You sit right there. This is the best of the series—classic lines in this one. You'll like it. There's a bold captain, a first officer with pointy ears, and a villain you'll love to hate."

"That was awesome!" Jamal said when the credits rolled. "They were so—weird. They really thought you could chop people into tiny little bits and send them through space? And get a person on the other side, not a pile of guts?"

Diego nodded, as though he weren't really listening. "Glad you enjoyed it. Better run along home. Your parents will probably want to head down to the mess soon."

Jamal prepared to leave. Diego stopped him just before he went out the door. "Jamal, do you know what your sister's serial number is?"

"No."

"It's her production number. It's how we keep track of how many babies are being born. Can you ask your *padre*—your *pabbi* for me?"

What's he want that for? "Okay," he said slowly. "I'll ask."

"Don't forget. It's important."

"Okay. I won't forget."

Hippocrates loomed before their shuttle, the second biggest ship in the convoy. It looked . . . intimidating. Especially with all of its arms sticking out all over the place.

Pabbi explained that the arms—medical "wings" he said, though they definitely looked more like legs than wings— were retractable. They were all umbilical; they could dock with the other ships during emergencies.

The ship reminded Jamal of a dead bug. Or the prickly shell of a nut. Maybe a sea creature—they had an aquarium on *Shambhala*. Sea urchins were supposedly high in protein. How much protein did he need every day? Well, he was only four foot eleven, so . . .

He tried to keep up with the wandering train of thought. He wanted his mind to stay away from the pending sister-assault for as long as possible. Figures and calculations for caloric intake swarmed through his brain.

Diego had made him feel a little better about the idea of having a sister, but not much.

Other shuttles zipped by outside, white and silvery against the blackness of space. Light from external LEDs bounced off hulls and windows, producing a glare that kept all natural starlight at bay. The ships and shuttles were bright objects in a dark cocoon.

Out of food-related numbers, his thoughts shifted. The classroom butterflies would be free of their cocoons soon. Then the class would ferry over to *Eden* and release the bugs in their appropriate climate zones. Butterflies helped pollinate the plants. Plants were a good source of fiber . . .

The med ship swelled before the shuttle and soon blotted out the rest of the convoy. Near its bottom a bay door opened, ready to gulp up their little shuttle—and Jamal's dreams of being an only child.

His family was greeted inside by a lady with very round cheeks, wearing a seafoam green jumpsuit wrapped in a white smock. A paper mask, held on by bands around her ears, rested awkwardly beneath her chin; she looked like she had a bulbous, snowy beard, and it took all Jamal had to not giggle.

None of this is funny, he rebuked himself.

"Hello," she said warmly, "I'm Sailuk Okpik. You're here to pick up an infant who's come to term?" His parents indicated they had. "This way," she directed.

Jamal had visited *Hippocrates* many times before. Yearly physicals, mental checkups, when he broke his leg—they'd all required trips to the med ship. But he'd never been to the growing rooms or the birthing chambers.

The kids told all types of stories about the spooky tubes. About the half-grown babies with their guts hanging out, and the two-headed flukes they had to discard in secret. Some said the accidental deformities got ground up and put in kids' lunches. Others said they grew them to adults anyway and had them work in secret.

Still, others said the doctors tried to kill the mistakes, but that they lived and formed their own society in the ships' walls. There they lurked, watching, waiting—ready to strangle healthy crew members in their sleep whenever they got their chance.

Jamal didn't believe those stories.

Not really.

"Would you like a full tour?" asked Sailuk. "You probably took it when you picked up your son, but some second-timers like to see it again. Though, I have to warn you, some children don't react well." She turned her round face toward Jamal. "Do you scare easy?"

"I don't know," said his *aðon*. "The fetus tanks were a bit much for *me* when I first saw them, and I was twelve."

"I think he can handle it," said his *pabbi*. "What do you think, Jamal? Are you up for learning where babies come from?"

"Is it gross?" he asked, turning to Sailuk.

"Sure is," she said frankly.

What would the other kids say, if they found out he'd gone all wimpyfied? "I can take it," he said, puffing out his chest.

"Are you sure?" *Aðons* could be so stuffy sometimes.

"Yeeeees," he said in a tone that conveyed how tiresome her question was. "*I'm* not a baby."

That settled that.

On their way they passed various people dressed as Sailuk—all sanitary-looking. *Hippocrates* had to be the cleanest ship in the fleet. In which case *Aesop* had to be the dirtiest. Or maybe *Mira*. *His* room certainly wasn't clean, as his parents were fond of pointing out.

Jamal wondered if this new sister was punishment for not picking up after himself.

A wide lift at the end of a long hall took them to the very top deck level. When the doors opened Jamal was immediately surprised by the lighting. Instead of a cold white, everything was bathed in pinkish-purple.

"The lighting helps protect the babies' skin," said Sailuk. "In most fetal stages it can't handle the rays included in our normal lighting. Most of the convoy lights were developed to mimic actual sunlight as closely as possible, to prevent problems like seasonal affective disorder. But these lights screen out anything that would be harmful to the undeveloped infant. They work like an old-fashioned dark room for developing photographs—or, of course, a mother's womb."

The first room they went into was bright again. White, normal light.

"Here we do the actual cloning. It's slightly different than traditional Earth cloning, in that instead of using DNA from the original, we *build* chromosomes identical to the original's and then insert them into a healthy ovum. So over here—" she led them to the left "—you can see Amit analyzing a newly formed molecule strand to make sure it is identical to the original pattern."

A man in a clean room bent over a microscope and manipulated something on the slide before him.

This was boring so far. Not scary. If Jamal wanted to watch people play with molecules he could just go back to class.

Sailuk ran them through the rest of the first stages, using

weird, gibberish words like *histone* and *zygote*. Jamal didn't understand how goats had anything to do with making babies.

They moved on to another purple room. This one was lined with tubes behind a glass window. In each tube sat one worm, suspended in some strange, snot-like solution. Jamal and his parents had entered a viewing cubicle.

Jamal ran to one of the closest tubes before Sailuk could explain what they were. He wandered along the line until one worm caught his eye. It was different from the rest. "This one has legs!" he said. How weird.

"Those are babies," his *aðon* said. "They're only a few weeks old."

"Ew," he said curtly. "But they don't look anything like a baby. Look, this one has a tail." It was more like a smooth, rubbery lizard than a human. "Ach, and big glassy eyeballs, too." There was no way these were people.

On they went, through more rooms with viewing cubicles, and he began to see the connection. The more the worms came to look like the thing with legs, the more the thing with legs came to look like a salamander, the more the salamander came to look like a wrinkly naked thing . . . the more creeped out Jamal got.

Babies weren't just annoying, they were freaky. Like aliens. And here they were displayed in jars like specimens of dead animals. The whole thing felt . . . unnatural.

"What's 'the old-fashioned way'?" he asked suddenly.

His parents stopped scrutinizing a tube that held a baby with head stubble. "What?"

"Diego said his sister was born the old-fashioned way, but he wouldn't say what that was."

The adults shared a look. "People used to be born and die a little different than on board," said his mother. "I suppose that's the way they still do it on Earth. It was messier, and less efficient."

"Moms carried the babies in their bellies," Pabbi said, patting Aðon's stomach.

"Uh . . ." was all Jamal could say. That would be even weirder than all this. "Oh, and he wanted me to ask what the baby's number is."

His parents eyed each other again. What was all this look-passing and eyebrow-raising about?

"He must be close," said Pabbi. "I wonder how many more he has."

"Far fewer than your dad," said Aðon.

Annoyingly, they let the matter drop without explaining their cryptic chatter to Jamal.

Finally, the bulk of the freak show was over. Time to get the baby and head home.

"We'd like to attend the birthing," insisted Pabbi. "We were there for Jamal's first breath. We'd like to be there for Akane's."

"We're going to watch her come out of the tube and get all cleaned up," Jamal's *aðon* said to him, overly perky. "Look, there she is." They entered one last room, this one with normal light again. One tube occupied the space, surrounded by four technicians. This baby looked like the ones in the previous room—you know, actually like a baby. Like a real little person instead of a funky, slimy thing. She had hair and eyelashes and fingernails and everything.

She still creeped him out, though.

Two of the technicians held the tube in place while the other two unhooked it from its wires and apparatuses. Eventually they popped the top off and tipped it over. The baby came spilling out onto a thick, foam-looking pad that sucked up most of the liquid.

A man came at the baby with a hose, the tip of which looked like the plastic vacuum the dentist used. The man pushed it up the baby's nose and in her mouth and soon she was crying. A hoarse, squeaky cry that didn't sound anything like the crying Jamal had expected.

She looked a lot smaller now that she was out of the tube, wiggling and naked on a table under the lights. She looked vulnerable. And for the first time since he'd heard about the *possibility* of her, he felt something other than loathing.

Jamal felt a pang of protectiveness.

"Can't they get her a blanket or something?"

"They will," Sailuk assured him. "They have to clean her up first."

After the baby was prepped and swaddled, Sailuk went into the room to retrieve her.

When the crying Akane was brought before her new family, Sailuk asked, "Who would like to hold her first?"

Jamal tentatively raised his hand. "Can I?"

"Not so bad as you feared, eh?" asked Diego, packing a trowel and a small shovel in his bag.

"No, guess not. She's kind of nice. Except when she cries while I'm trying to sleep."

"Did you get the number?" he asked casually, opening the door to his quarters and ushering Jamal out. They were going to *Eden* together to work in the convoy's communal vegetable garden.

"Oh, yeah, here." Jamal pulled a small 'flex-sheet out of his pocket. "She's S8-F94–3–16008."

"Five more until I get my notice, then," Diego said.

"Huh?"

"I'll tell you about it when we get to *Eden*. I'll feel more comfortable with some dirt under my nails."

"Okay." Unlike other adults, who sometimes just ignored Jamal's questions, when Diego said he'd answer something, he always did.

The artificial sun hung high overhead, and the cows mooed

in a bored sort of way. The weather planners were pretending it was hot today. The thermostat must have read at least eighty-eight Fahrenheit.

Luckily a large part of the garden sat in the shade of a big tree. A few butterflies flitted by, and Jamal thought he recognized one from his classroom.

The air smelled sweet here. But he was pretty sure the scent wasn't emanating from the flowers or the grass—it was one more illusion. They pumped in the smell to make the space seem bigger and more open than it was.

Diego dug right in. Only a few minutes passed before his hands, forearms, and boots were caked with enriched soil. "That's better. Get a bit of this mud on you, it's nice and cool." He drew a dirty line down the arch of Jamal's nose. "Good war paint," he said with a wink.

Getting into the spirit, Jamal put a dirty hand print on Diego's cheek. "Looks like I whacked you one."

"Let me return the favor." Jamal's face now sported two handprints that mirrored each other. The dirt might as well have been face paint, and the handprints butterfly wings. "Can't forget to wash that off before you go home. Otherwise your *madre* will have my hide. With a new baby to think about she doesn't need to be giving you extra baths as well."

"What were you saying before?" Jamal asked, looking over a bowl of seeds they'd picked up at the entrance to the field. "About Akane's number?"

"I should probably make you ask your parents," said Diego. He dug a small hole and gestured for Jamal to sprinkle in a few seeds. "But that would be for their sake, not yours. Jamal, I'm going to retire soon."

The smile slumped off the boy's face. "What?" He stood up straight. "Why?"

No. No. No. Diego wasn't old enough to retire. Only really old people retired. And it wasn't something you talked about.

It just happened, they disappeared one day. Said goodbye and left for . . . somewhere.

"What does Akane's number have to do with that?" he added.

"Sit back down so we can talk about this rationally," Diego ordered, patting the ground.

Jamal narrowed his eyes. Anything Diego said from this moment on would be held under the highest scrutiny. Sick people retired, frail people retired, incapable people retired— Diego was none of those things.

"You're eight. You're big enough to understand about retirement. On Earth I learned about it a whole lot sooner than eight. And we didn't have that nice euphemism for it. We just called it what it was."

No one had ever explained it, but Jamal wasn't stupid. He knew where retirees went. He knew. He just didn't like to think about it. If no one ever talked about the truth, if everyone always glossed over the facts, why couldn't he? "I do understand," he said.

"Then sit down. You know I'm going to die, but you don't understand the how or why of it. So let me tell you."

Jamal finally sat and said in a small voice, "Did the doctors find something?"

"No. Nothing like that. I'm as healthy as a—as one of those bovine over there. But my number is about to come up, quite literally. You see, everything on the convoy's got to balance out. All that's ever here is all there ever will be. Even if we find an asteroid to mine, we can only carry so much. We're a closed environment. We have to scrimp and save and control and manage. So, we have to pick and choose when it comes to some things. And you know where we put our resources, don't you?"

Jamal picked at a strand of grass and it gave him a thin

cut—it didn't bleed but it smarted. What did this mumbo jumbo about management have to do with Diego dying?

"Are you listening?"

"Yes," Jamal mumbled.

"Where do we put our resources?"

"'Toward the future,'" Jamal quoted.

"Correct. To conserve our resources, then, birthing can never get out of synch with dying. We can't have more babies born than people who die. So, everyone on board has a number. Two numbers—a number that corresponds with their birth and one that corresponds with their death. When the 16013th baby of the third generation is born, I'll get my notice. It'll let me know that after another three clones are brought to term I'll be scheduled for official retirement. They'll set a date, and I'll go over to *Hippocrates* and they'll—"

Jamal's hands flew to his ears. "Shut up. I don't want to hear about it. I don't want to know how they'll kill you."

"Oh, stop it now." Diego pried Jamal's hands from his head.

Fire and water surged inside Jamal's brain. His face grew hot and swollen. "But *why*? You're still a perfectly good person. There's nothing wrong with you. Retirement is for people who have problems that can't be reversed."

"Yes, I know. And a lot of people go that way. They get some sort of terminal or chronic problem and never see their end-number. But I'm lucky, Jamal. I got to live my full life."

"It's all Akane's fault," Jamal realized. "If parents stopped asking for babies then they wouldn't have to kill you. It's not fair! Why grow a new person when you have to kill a perfectly good person to get it? It's not right!"

"Now don't go blaming your parents or your sister. Babies can't be blamed for anything."

"This is *stupid*." The boy stood and pulled at his hair. "You have to fight, you can't let them take you."

"They're not *taking* me. It's not like I'm going to get carried away kicking and screaming. This is just how things work. This is how they're supposed to be. The old die off, leaving resources for the young. We just make it a little neater and a little tidier. The exact same thing happens on Earth. It's a natural cycle."

"That's bull—"

"Watch your language."

Jamal was embarrassed for a moment, but it didn't last long. "I won't let this happen, Diego. They can take the baby *back*."

"Now you're just being childish. Listen to me. I'm okay with this. I knew it was coming. More important, I'm *happy* to give my resources over."

"How can you be happy you're going to die?" Nothing about what Diego was saying made sense.

"Because I'm helping the mission. It makes me proud to do so. By retiring, I'm assuring the convoy remains balanced and healthy. To prolong my life after my time would be selfish. Wrong. *Disloyal*." He pushed himself up and took Jamal by the shoulders. "I would be abandoning my responsibilities. It would be the worst thing I could do, you know that."

He knew, he did—loyalty to the convoy, to the mission, to each other above all else was pretty much the first thing they learned in school. But it didn't stop him from throwing his arms around Diego's waist. "I don't want you to go. I don't want them to take you away."

"I know, boy. But it's for you and your generation. I die so you can live."

Jamal put on a brave face—even if it was wet and puffy—when he went home. No amount of reassurance from Diego could convince him the old man's retirement was a good thing, though. No one *wanted* to die. No one really thought dying was a good thing.

Why would they want to exchange Diego—he'd just fixed that bean processer or something, hadn't he?—for a useless baby. How did that make any sense?

This was wrong. He might only be eight, but there was no way he would sit by while they hauled off his favorite person in all of space.

That night he lay wide awake while Akane cried out in the communal space. His parents were trying to soothe her, but she wouldn't shut up.

Since he couldn't sleep he worked on a plan. Diego wasn't going anywhere without a fight.

The next day was group-play day. Not really school, and not really a day off. Someone—someone's grandma, their *amma*, if he remembered right—called it daycare. If your parents didn't have the day off when you did, you went to group-play. Thankfully, Lewis was there.

Several halls merged to form the communal play space. It wasn't a room, and it wasn't a passage either. It was a strange space on *Mira*, meant for mingling but rarely used by any-one other than children. Chairs and tables popped out from cubbies in the walls. Hidden closets held extra dishes and celebratory items. The area could be turned into a fort with a few reappropriated bed sheets and a little squinting.

"Wanna play spelunker?" Jamal asked Lewis, noting the group-play guardian's back was turned.

"What's a schpeel-lunger?"

"A guy who explores caves."

"Yeah, all right. How do you play?"

Jamal shoved his hands in his pockets and side-stepped down the hall, away from the communal area. He found an access panel and dropped to his knees. From his pocket he produced a screwdriver taken from his parents' emergency tool kit. "You watch out for bears and such," he said with a wink, "while I explore this cave and make sure it's safe for you to follow. Okay?"

Lewis nodded.

Carefully, Jamal unscrewed the fasteners that secured the panel, then crawled inside. "Be back soon," he promised, then hurried away to put his plan into action.

There were all kinds of rumors about the access tunnels. Sure, the wrongly grown freaks were supposed to live in them, but that wasn't all. Alligators, giant bugs, ghosts (dead people *were* buried in the walls, after all), and even alien egg sacs were supposed to call the convoy ducts home.

Several times he had to stop and fight off the willies— especially when the motion-sensing work lights failed to flick on as fast as he'd hoped—but he kept moving along.

Cramped, dusty, and sweltering, the tunnels were not the stuff of playtime fantasy. It was slow going, pulling himself up flimsy ladders, shuffling through tight shafts, and squeezing around awkward corners. No one was meant to travel from one end of the ship to the other this way, but that was the idea. If someone found Jamal wandering the hallways they'd stop him, turn him around, and escort his butt right back to daycare.

Static-charged dust worked its way into his mouth, leaving a sparky, slightly feathery sensation on his tongue. His lungs felt heavy, and he constantly fought off the paranoia-induced sensation of being trapped.

By the ship's backside, he'd risk becoming one of the tunnel-roaming ghosts if it meant saving Diego.

Twenty minutes later he kicked his way out of another access panel. Only a moment passed before he regained his bearings and confirmed he was where he wanted to be: Outside I.C.C.'s main server room.

He pounded ferociously on the door.

"Yeah, just a sec," came a man's voice from inside. A moment later the door slid to the side, revealing a tall, well-built, middle-aged black man.

"I need your help," Jamal said.

The man considered the boy for a second longer before realizing, "Hey, you're my replacement, aren't you?"

There were two primary clones for each job—cycle mates. Clone A would be in charge while Clone B apprenticed—all while another Clone A was educated and another Clone B was born. The staggered growth was meant to add some normalcy—so that no one was forced into the surreal situation of having to train a genetic mirror of themselves. Subsequently, no fewer than two versions of a clone were alive at any time.

Jamal seeking out his predecessor was unusual, but not unprecedented. It was natural to be curious about your genetic twin. But cornering them at their place of work was discouraged, because it was rude. Young Jamal was acutely—though not fully—aware of this when the older Jamal invited him into the server room. The space was dark. Ghostly lights formed rows and columns down the sides of the big black servers, which in turn had been laid out in the room on a grid.

"Something tells me you shouldn't be here, little man," said the older clone. He sat down at his workstation near the rear of the room. He swiveled his chair to face Jamal, and did not offer the boy a seat.

Jamal realized for the first time why it was important to have *the third* slapped on the end of his name. "I need your help, uh, sir. It's important. Something terrible is happening on board, and we've got to stop it."

"And you came to me because you thought, heck, I'm you

and I'll understand your problem immediately through, what, a mind-meld? Do they not explain what a clone is to you kids?"

"You're not me," Jamal said, indignant. "I came here because you've got access to I.C.C. I want to change some records and you can do it best."

Older Jamal considered this for a moment. He nodded once. "Okay. Spill."

Jamal explained, went on and on about Diego's multitude of virtues, then presented his solution. "I just want you to change the babies' numbers. Make it so fifty—no, a hundred babies have to be born before Diego retires. Or, you know, just change Diego's other number—his death number."

"I cannot allow tampering with the convoy's inventory system," said I.C.C.

"What it said." Older Jamal sniffed and wiped his nose on his eggplant-colored jumpsuit sleeve.

"Inventory?" said Jamal. "You mean like when we have to count all of our quarter's spoons and forks and stuff to make sure it's all there? You do that with people?"

"Of course. What did you think the numbers were for?" The computer sounded confused, though its inflections were even.

"Look, kid," said Older Jamal. A work cap sat on his terminal. He picked it up and twirled it between his hands. "You've got to face it. We're all spoons, okay? If you want a brand-new spoon, you have to get rid of the bent one. Get it?"

"But there's nothing wrong with this spoon," Jamal insisted. "And he's not a *spoon*, he's a person. He's my friend."

"Yeah, well, we all lose friends. This is just how things work. We're all on a timetable, all set up to rotate. You were born at the precise time you needed to be so that you could replace me when I start to get slow. It'll be the same for the Jamal after you. It's part of life. I suggest you accept it and run back to school."

"But *why* is it a part of life?"

"Because some guy back on Earth looked at all the numbers and decided this way was best for the mission."

Jamal squeezed the screwdriver in his pocket, looking for something to hold on to. Something to use as a touchstone. His whole world seemed to be sliding off its blocks. "Is it?"

Older Jamal placed his cap on his head. "Is it what?"

"Best?" Jamal turned toward a blinking red light and camera lens mounted in the back of the room. "Is it, I.C.C.?"

"I do not currently have a holistic comprehension of the idea: best. Please clarify."

His little hands did a dance in the air as he tried to explain. "Best, you know, the, uh goodest way to do stuff. Like, brushing your teeth is better than not brushing your teeth, otherwise you've got to see the dentist with the drill."

"I think the word he's looking for," said Older Jamal, repositioning himself in front of a monitor at his workstation, "is efficient. Is our current grow-and-recycle system the most efficient use of personnel in accordance with the mission?"

"It is a system in which the fail-safes create inefficiencies, but ensure the greatest chance of overall success," responded I.C.C. in its cold, mechanical way.

Older Jamal shrugged. "There you have it."

There you have what? "I don't understand."

The computer began again, "The system is reliant on—"

"Let me put it in laymen's terms, I.C.C." Older Jamal waved a hand in dismissal. I.C.C. thanked him, and it almost sounded relieved. Jamal knew it wasn't used to answering a child. "Look, little man. Sure, our system isn't the best in the sense that we don't squeeze every last drop of productivity out of a person before they croak. We work them till death, but we don't work them *to* death. Come here."

Flicking a finger at the boy, he simultaneously stiff-armed 'flex-sheets, a half-eaten sandwich, and a coffee cup aside on his console. With a sliver of trepidation, Jamal came forward and let the man pick him up and place him on the now-clean surface.

Jamal looked his older, biological twin in the eye. The expression he found was stern, but not unkind. There were flecks of gray in the hair nearest the man's temples, and Jamal found himself wondering just how many years into his future he was looking.

"Everything in service to the mission, correct?" the man asked.

"Yes," Jamal agreed.

"And what is that mission?"

"To make it to the interstellar anomaly, designation LQ Pyxidis, and discover . . . discover whatever we can."

"Who has to make it?"

Twisting his lips, Jamal thought for a moment before answering. "We do."

"Who do? You and me?" Older Jamal asked. "No, kid. It's not a 'who,' it's a 'what.' The convoy. Everything we do is in service to the convoy, and it's the convoy's mission to get to the star and figure out what its problem is. Why's the darn thing blinking like that? Huh? Inquiring minds want to know." He patted Jamal's head. "We're just parts. Cogs in a machine. Pieces in I.C.C.'s system. You've got to decide you're okay with that, or be miserable. It is what it is. Life's always been what it is. It's whether you accept that or not that makes it good or bad, right or wrong, upsetting or not."

Jamal sighed. Why was everyone he talked to so . . . what was the word for it? It was a good word, he'd just learned it . . . *Rational*. That was it. They were like the computer. Didn't they ever listen to their feelings instead of their brains? Or was that what being grown-up was all about: learning to be logical?

But wasn't ignoring your feelings illogical? Why was his gut so insistent if he was supposed to ignore it?

"What if there's a better way?" he asked.

"A bunch of bigwig, scientific mucky-mucks back on Earth couldn't figure out a better way, but sure, you're what, nine? I have complete faith that a nine-year-old can figure out a better way."

"I know what sarcasm is."

"Good."

Jamal pouted. "Why don't we just try my way? An experiment with Diego, to see if maybe I'm right and this is wrong."

Red and blue lights began flashing down one of the server rows, and Older Jamal went to check on them. "I think it's best if you went home now, kid," he called.

I.C.C. opened the server room door.

"That's it? Just no?"

Older Jamal sniffed again, loud enough to be heard over the humming of the servers. "Just no. Believe me kid, they thought of everything when it came to the mission. If you want to change the system you'll have to shirk the mission."

Again, Jamal felt sick at the idea. The convoy was his home, the mission filled him with pride and wonder. They were explorers, boldly going . . . somewhere. He was proud to be a part of it.

But not proud of how they were going about it.

He went back to daycare the same way he'd come, and wasn't surprised to find that Lewis had abandoned his post. He was equally unsurprised to find that none of the adults had realized he was missing.

Nothing he did or said seemed to matter to anyone.

The day came far too soon. Jamal had wracked his brain for weeks, trying to find a suitable solution, and at every turn Diego tried to discourage him.

"You don't have to defend me, boy. Someone died for all of

us. Someone died so your *pabbi* could be born, just as someone died so you could be born."

But that just made him more upset.

"I want to come with you, over to *Hippocrates*," Jamal
declared that morning. His parents had excused him from
class so that he could say his goodbyes.

"Your *afi* is coming with me. I don't want you there, Jamal.
It'd be too hard." He was packing a bag. It was tradition to
pack up your quarters before you retired. The most important
things went in a black duffle bag, to be handed out to your
loved ones as mementos. This the retiree would keep with
them until the end. Everything else went back to *Bottomless*,
the supply ship.

Bleary-eyed, Jamal hugged Diego around the middle and
refused to let go for a full three minutes.

"I know it's hard. You cry if you want to, let it all out. I'll
miss you, too. But you've got to know I'm doing the right
thing. It's for the greater good."

Jamal wanted to puke on the *greater good*. The greater
good could get sucked out an airlock for all he cared.

"Now, I'm going to take a nice, soothing bath before I
go. Would you mind putting my bag by the door on your
way out?" He kissed Jamal on the top of the head, said one
last goodbye, and went to his bathroom with a smile on his
face.

Desiring nothing more than to run down the hall wailing,
Jamal took a deep breath and retrieved the bag from the table.
He couldn't deny Diego his last request.

The bag was heavy. Way too heavy for Jamal to lift. He had
to drag it all the way across the room. And then it hit him. It
was heavy like a person—a small person.

Like a Jamal-sized person . . .

He would go to *Hippocrates* after all, and stop this terrible
mistake.

Few sounds came through the fabric ungarbled. Light was totally absent, and the tight space forced him into the fetal position. It was a deadly combination of comfort and sensory deprivation that led to an impromptu nap.

There was no telling how much time had passed before a jarring woke him up. Someone had picked up the bag. Afi, if his ears weren't lying. It must be time to go.

Hold still, he told himself. If he'd stayed asleep he probably wouldn't have had anything to worry about.

He could tell when they'd entered the shuttle bay, and again when they'd boarded a shuttle. He was thrown unceremoniously into an empty seat, and it took all of his willpower not to let out an *oomph*.

What would he actually do once they arrived? He hadn't thought that far ahead. Surely he would make a grand speech. Something like in the movies Diego used to show him, where the hero dashes in and convinces everyone he's right through the power of words.

But what then? If Diego said he didn't want to retire would everyone else just let it happen?

He never got a chance to find out. He never even got to make his speech, grand or otherwise.

He was picked up and plopped down several more times before he decided they'd reached the end of the line. This was it, the place he was supposed to be. Time to make his grand entrance.

Jamal deftly unzipped himself, jumped up, and cried, "Stop!"

Everyone stared. There were five other people in the pristine white room—none of them were Afi or Diego.

Nearby stood a door, and without missing a beat Jamal threw it open. On the other side lay a glass cubicle—and observation station, like all the clone-growing rooms had.

A place from which to watch someone retire, should you feel the need.

On the other side of the pane, Diego reclined in a dentist's chair. On one side was a lady wearing one of those medical masks and a hair net, and on the other sat Afi, holding Diego's hand. They'd wrapped Diego in a long white fluffy robe that folded down around his feet. He'd been swaddled, like Akane. His eyes were closed.

Clear plastic tubing stuck out of Diego's right arm and extended up to a bag of foggy, slightly blue liquid. The lady pumped something into the bag with a needle, and the solution turned pale yellow.

"No!" shouted Jamal. He banged on the glass with both fists. "Stop it! Stopit, stopit, stopit!"

Diego's eyes flew open as Afi and the technician's heads both snapped in Jamal's direction.

"Please," Jamal pleaded. "Please don't take him away." His vision blurred, and he had to take huge gulps of air as his lungs stuttered. "Please." His voice cracked and he turned away.

As he hid his face there was a commotion on the other side of the glass. Furniture squeaked across the floor, metal rattled, three voices argued and one yelped. When he looked up and rubbed his eyes, Diego stood before him, palms pressed to the window.

"It's okay, Jamal. You have to let me go. It's time for you to learn new things and meet new people. You can't hang around an old fool forever." Diego sounded muffled, but the words were clear. So was the meaning.

"I don't want to let you go." He knew how selfish it sounded. He pressed his palm against the glass as if pressing it to Diego's hand.

"Go back out that door, now," said Diego. "It's time to say goodbye." With that he returned to the chair, lay back down, and shut his eyes.

Jamal had never been in more trouble in his life. Apparently hitching a ride to the retirement wing was almost as bad as abandoning the mission. Almost.

No one cared about his excuses. No one cared he'd done it for a noble cause. All they cared about was teaching him never to do it again. They gave him a week to grieve, then enacted his penalty.

As punishment, they made him clean the access ducts without the aid of bots. Ironically, they were the same ducts he'd highjacked as a shortcut to the server room.

Gleaming before him now was a plate that read:

Here are interned the ashes of Dr. Leonard McCloud
May the convoy carry him, in death, to the stars he
only dreamed of in life
2029–2106

It marked the final resting place of some guy from Earth — some guy who had helped build the mission, but never saw it launch. *Guess there really are dead people in the walls*, Jamal thought.

Viscous cleaning solution ran down through the words, obscuring them. He mopped the orange-scented cleaner with a rag.

There would be no plaques for Diego. Spoons only get remembered by other spoons.

"I.C.C.?"

"Yes, Jamal?"

The boy rubbed a hand across his eyes. The fumes stung. "Does it hurt when you die?"

"I have not experienced death, and do not have enough information to extrapolate—"

A burning rimmed his eyes. *What strong cleaner.*

No, he couldn't fool himself. He wasn't crying because of the chemicals. "That's not what I meant," he said. "Never mind."

A long pause followed. Jamal continued to polish the plate long after it was clean.

"Diego . . . he was your friend?" asked I.C.C. It was a cautious query, asked microseconds slower than usual questions from the AI.

"Yes," Jamal croaked.

"I don't comprehend what that means."

Wiping the snot from his nose, Jamal cleared his throat. "I know," he said, and patted the wall as if I.C.C. could feel the gesture. "I'll teach you."

CHAPTER FOUR

I.C.C.: LOOK NOW HOW THE MORTALS BLAME

. . . .

EIGHTEEN YEARS LATER

OCTOBER 19, 48 PLD

2589 CE

"Identify where the program came from," Ordered Captain Mahler II. The tiny blue server lights cast an—*ethereal*, Jamal would tell me—glow over his tight, attentive body. He faced me as he spoke. Almost no one faced me. Only Jamal Kaeden III.

"I can't," I said, wondering if I should have thrown in a stutter. Some people stutter when they are unable to offer up demanded information.

"You *can't*? How is that possible?"

"The information is not available."

"I told you, Captain," said Jamal, resting his work cap over his shoulder with one hand. "I've asked every trigger question in the book. I'll run a code diagnostic, but I couldn't identify any main terminal breaches—all were directly accessed by personnel who were scheduled to access them. And no, nothing unusual was uploaded during those times."

"I.C.C., is it possible someone developed a program that would erase its history in your system?"

"Possible," I said.

"And it would shield itself from your self-diagnostic tests?"

"It must. Or else I would secure and delete the program." I didn't *want* to broadcast the message. If I knew where it was, it would've been contained and we wouldn't have been having this discussion.

The captain turned to Jamal. "You're sure it's only localized? Only the ships are receiving it? It hasn't . . . ?" He glanced at me briefly.

Whether he didn't trust me or didn't trust the program hiding inside me, I don't know. I haven't learned all of the nuances yet. But I did catch his unspoken question. "There have been no nonstandard messages to Earth," I said.

I'd hoped he'd relax a little. I looked for the signs: shoulders dropping, spine loosening, deep exhalation. But, if anything, he seemed to tighten everywhere. "Good," he said curtly. "Keep it that way."

"You don't think we should inform Ms. Pavon? Shouldn't this be in the report?" Jamal slapped his cap back into place, adjusting its fit.

"Not unless things get worse. Not unless I.C.C. gets worse."

Worse . . . Was I sick? I hadn't considered that. I'd thought whatever had been uploaded was simply rerouting resources and blocking my traces. It hadn't occurred to me that something might actually be wrong with my functionality.

Jamal patted the outside of my primary camera housing; a place I tended to equate with the side of a human face. "It'll be fine," he said. "We'll work this out and excise the system in no time."

The captain nodded. "I have every confidence."

As he should. Jamal was the best. The third iteration of his line, and so far the most attentive colleague I'd had.

Captain Mahler turned to leave.

"May I make a request?" I asked.

"Of course, I.C.C." The captain was strict, but not ungracious.

"May I turn on continuous consciousness in all areas? And simul-stream from all total-input ports?"

He squinted at me, as though looking for an expression on my camera lens. Sometimes I think it would be easier to communicate if I had a body and could use its language. Although, perhaps that would make some crew members unwilling to interact as intimately with me as they do. I am in a—or, it is a—catch twenty-two (is that how this idiom is used?). The more machine I am, the more trust I get from some. Others desired me to behave more like a member of the convoy than a piece of equipment. The more I slide to one side of the scale, the more trust drops off on the other.

Will the entire crew ever accept me as a confidant, companion, and colleague?

Well, that's why Jamal was helping me with the finer points of verbal expression. Perhaps, in the centuries to come, I could learn to tailor my interactions. Be what each person expects—well, *wants* me to be.

"To what end?" asked the captain. "Will continuous consciousness throughout the convoy be a drain on your computing power? Will you be able to perform all background functions correctly? Will you still be able to perform the tasks demanded of you?"

"The purpose of my request is to monitor crew member activity and look for behavior anomalies. I may be able to identify the individual who uploaded the message. This should not interfere with my usual work. If I cannot complete required tasks appropriately, I will shrink the consciousness."

"And what about privacy?"

I could not compute his meaning. "Repeat question." Remembering what Jamal had taught me, I added, "If you please, sir."

"If you are constantly scrutinizing activity, are you not invading the crew's privacy?"

"Sir, all investigations require a breach in privacy. And I fail to see how this intrudes more than usual. Part of my function is to monitor all activity, in case of emergency, as installed during the second mission year, after twelve consecutive cases of—"

"Thank you, I understand the operation. But your conscious presence changes things."

I failed to see how. So I simply said, "It is necessary to find the breach."

"Fine, but I don't want you to archive anything unessential."

"Recordings deemed unessential will be wiped from the database seventy-two hours from recording, as is standard."

He found my answer displeasing, I was sure, but he did not argue or order me to disregard customary procedure. "Permission granted on all points. I want the individual found. We need to know why they did this."

"Couldn't it just be a prank, sir?" asked Jamal. "The content seems harmless enough."

"We don't have pranksters, Kaeden. Not with access to I.C.C. in this way."

He meant the children. There was no way to tamper with me on *Aesop*, true, but it wasn't as though the children never left the education ship. And intelligent youngsters play intelligent games, as Jamal had demonstrated as a child. His suggestion seemed probable to me.

"I must get back to the bridge. I'll check on your progress later."

"Sir," said Jamal, saluting.

When the captain was gone, I said, "I am having trouble processing Captain Mahler's stance on privacy and pranks. His attitude was confusing. Unreasonable."

Jamal adjusted his jumpsuit before sitting down at his workstation. He picked up his full, now cold, cup of coffee. It left a ring on the console. "What a waste," he mumbled, shaking his head—how would he say it? *Forlornly*—at the cup. He took a swig anyway. "He runs a tight ship," he said, grimacing at the taste. "It's unthinkable to him that an adult might tamper with something and not have mal-intent. And children, well, he figures they're corralled. The message is a banner to him, and it doesn't read, *Remember clouds. Remember sand*, and such. Not when he reads it. When he sees the message it says, *Captain Mahler has lost control. Captain Mahler's tight ship has a leak.*"

Sniffing the coffee, he got up and went to the small break room to make a fresh pot and flush away the old. "Your main controls and largest server bank are on his ship, so he feels responsible for you."

How strange. I thought I was responsible for me. And perhaps, by extension, Jamal and I were responsible for each other, since he saw to my maintenance and upgrades. But I'd never seen the captain as anything more than just another crew member. One with authority, but not one who held responsibility for my actions and faults.

Jamal came back into the room. I sensed small molecules of coffee being released into the air. The old-fashioned brewer was doing its work.

"And the privacy?" I asked.

"Now that you've been compromised, he's worried unauthorized personnel could have access to your video archives. That someone might be getting their cables buzzed by watching their coworkers doing the nasty." Jamal frowned, then wandered up to my camera and looked me in the lens. "He's not worried about *you* peeking in on people, if that's what you were thinking."

Was that what I'd been thinking?

"I'm going to turn on full consciousness now," I said.

He nodded, and I recognized his expression. He always pursed his lips when trying not to attribute human emotions and thought patterns to my responses. My segue must have seemed abrupt.

I activated my consciousness throughout the convoy, and suddenly felt expansive—larger than myself while still being limited to myself. In human terms, it's like being aware of every function in your body, and being able to observe those functions with all of your senses. Simultaneously observing and openly comprehending everything about yourself at once. My network was always on, I was always present throughout each ship, but now I, my sense of self, was there as well.

As an AI, multitasking is my middle name. But this was new. I'd always had the capacity to be conscious everywhere, but I'd never activated it before.

So many conversations. So many movements to track. So many particles in the air—smells and tastes. The only sense I did not possess was touch—*that* I could only infer through my visual inputs.

"I.C.C.?"

"Yes, Jamal?"

"You went quiet all of a sudden."

Jin Yoon dropped a stack of dishes in the galley. I must remember next time I speak with her not to address her by name. She says she'd like to preserve some of her culture, though I'm not quite sure I understand—

"I was having a moment. I was experiencing," I explained.

—Kira and Abdul were fighting again. They'd been doing that a lot more since deciding to share quarters—

"You've been more contemplative recently," said Jamal.

"Have I?"

—Dr. Grimle (he didn't like it when I used his first name,

MARINA J. LOSTETTER

126

either) on *Aesop* was lecturing his twelve-year-olds on the importance of good hygiene—

"Yes. Are my hints still useful to you?" Jamal inspected a server. "Or are they confusing? Boring?"

—Two engineers on *Solidarity*, who shall go unnamed, were taking part in what Jamal had called "the nasty." Why do I get the feeling that is an impolite term?—

"Not boring," I said. "But yes, sometimes the nuances confuse me. I am grateful for the aid. I do believe it helps me work more efficiently with some individuals."

—Sixteen people on *Holwarda* were in the lavatories, being sick. Something must have contaminated lunch. That might bear looking into. Of course, it could just be poor food hygiene, as Dr. Grimle was explaining—

"How are you handling the larger consciousness? I have noticed a slight lag in your verbal responses. Though it'd probably be imperceptible to most people."

"It is taking a larger chunk of processing power than I had expected," I admitted, zooming in on the server room for just a moment. Jamal deserved my undivided attention during a conversation. "Shall I do a sectioned watch instead?"

"No, it's all right. Keep your awareness broad. It's the best way to spot a problem, you're right. I'm going to run through some code, now. Keep your eyes sharp."

Who in the history of mankind has actually had sharp eyes? What an odd saying. I made a note to ask Jamal about the origin of the idiom at a more appropriate time.

—The ticker screen on deck eight of *Bottomless* flashed large red letters. *Remember ocean waves. Remember salty air.*—

"A new version of the message is playing on *Bottomless*," I informed him.

He had several monitors on, all with scrawling code. His gaze flicked back and forth between them. "That's a weird place for it. Not a lot of people around. Maybe the message is just running around randomly through the system."

Perhaps. Not knowing the intent of the message, it was hard to say if its appearances were random or purposeful. This did seem to indicate it was randomized. *Bottomless* was a supply ship. A warehouse, essentially. It had few regular workers, and few visitors. All of the other iterations had occurred in populated areas during high-traffic hours. Perhaps the message was simply cycling through all the ships. It hadn't formed any kind of pattern yet, but it hadn't made it through the entire convoy either.

But what if it wasn't random? Why *Bottomless*? Why deck eight?

And what did all of these "remember" messages mean? No one could possibly remember these things. Everyone who was old enough to recall such things had been retired.

No one on board had ever seen real clouds or real sand or real waves. The only way they came close was either through viewing the video archives, or visiting *Eden*.

Perhaps the word was used to invoke an emotion. Loss? Regret?

I focused in on deck eight, scanning for crew. If someone had viewed the message, I'd like to know who.

There. Two men and one woman. All *Bottomless* crew, all familiar to me, but not friendly. Speaking emphatically, the men discussed the message in the hallway on their way to a lift. Their conversation revealed little. They were baffled, and somewhat amused by what they called a "cheap shot." I failed to see how cheap shot applied, but clearly the male crew members were surprised and only mildly affected.

The woman, Ceren, went about her business inventorying a plastics supply room. She was of relatively young age, Turkish descent, and had a meticulous eye. The screen just outside the clear supply room doors still flashed the message, but either she hadn't seen it, was ignoring it, or had been unmoved by its presence.

Or, at least that's how I interpreted her routine behavior. Right up until she put down her tablet, exited, examined the ticker screen, and deliberately turned it off.

Strange reaction, I thought. Perhaps the blinking bothered her.

Quickly, I scanned my archived recordings of all the previous visual data related to the messages. Had anyone else done the same? Yes, twelve others, one when *Remember rain* surfaced on *Mira*, three when *Remember seasons* had—

"I.C.C. I need your attention."

"I'm here."

"Full attention. You're lagging."

I halted my study of the visuals. "I am?"

"More and more," said Jamal. "I'm beginning to wonder if the culprit didn't also upload something dangerous."

"Have you located any corrupted code?"

He sighed. "No, but there's a lot to go through. If the software doesn't recognize a problem, I may have to go through it manually. I'll have to enlist some help. Otherwise it could take me years."

"I can't help?"

He gave me a sideways glance, his dark features scrunched. "Do patients diagnose themselves? Besides, what do you think the software is? I'm not running that on brainpower. Its nano-neurotransistors. Artificial, not biological. You, in other words."

Jamal sounded unusual. Worried. Understandably so. I had direct control of everything, save navigation. Sure, there were backups for essential functions, like life support and illumination and food processing, but it wasn't a systems failure he was worried about. "Do you think I've been programmed to do more than send out unconscious messages?"

"I don't know, I.C.C. I really don't. Maybe it's just the captain's paranoia getting to me. But he's right, you're not well. Even if it's just a head cold, we need you shipshape again." He gathered up his things. "I'm going to work in my quarters the rest of the day, okay? I'll check in with you every once in a while." He strode over to the door, leaving his half-full coffee mug on the terminal. "Do me a favor? Don't work too hard. Since we're not quite sure what sort of tax is being put on your processing, I don't want you to overdo it."

I wish he hadn't asked. I could handle it, I was sure. I may have been unwell, but I didn't feel unwell. But I assured him I'd narrow my consciousness.

At the time of Jamal's departure, I was having sixty-seven other direct conversations with crew members. All of them quite standard, asking for news of loved ones' schedules or moods, asking about their own rotations, availability of stock for their cabins. But when Ceren spoke up, I was surprised.

I shouldn't have been. She was only asking me to double-check her math. She preferred I consciously answer, though a background calculator function was readily available and about as taxing on my system as losing a flake of skin is on a person's. And she always knew when she got an automatic response versus a conscious one. So I answered her directly. "Yes, Ceren, I have cross-checked your long work six times, all calculations are in order. But, please check your inputted figure for shelf nineteen. It is outside the normal bell curve of expected change due to use and recycling." That was why she didn't want the calculator function.

While she went back to retally, I stayed. I'd only been surprised by her call because I'd been spying on her. Spying. Though I constantly watched the crew, I'd never *spied* before.

"Are you well?" I asked.

She laughed a little. "I'm fine, I.C.C. How are you? Has Mr. Kaeden encouraged you to try small talk?"

Ah, yes. Inquiring about one's health was a standard social greeting. I'd forgotten. But it gave me a good cover. I could be ambiguous in my response. "I thought it was a good opener, yes."

The room had three cameras. One in my access point, and two in the ceiling which were unobstructed by the rows of shelves and parts. The room was dim. Almost all of *Bottomless* was dim. I changed the input mode to infrared and watched her from all angles. She smirked. "Well, then you should answer my other question. How are you?"

"Fine. Did you get the message I played earlier?"

She paused, lowering her tablet slightly. "Yes."

"What did you think of it?"

Another pause. A minor hesitation, one a human might not have noticed. With a shrug, she said, "What was I supposed to think?"

"Did it affect you? Emotionally?"

She turned to face my access point, though three sets of shelves stood between her and what she identified as me. "Why are you asking?"

I was not supposed to be disingenuous, but by understanding the concept, I could be. "I am conducting a survey."

"Who asked you to broadcast that message, I.C.C.?"

"It is only a test."

"A test for what?"

"The mental health sector is conducting an experiment."

"Huh," she said, returning to her work. "You shouldn't have told me that. Doesn't it give away the game?"

She knew I was lying. It couldn't be my intonation, as it was never variant. How could she tell?

I considered what she might be thinking: Why would a computer lie?

Which I mentally countered with: Why would a human think a computer was lying?

Simple answer: because the human was lying.

Lying about what? She hadn't done anything but ask me questions. Weren't lies statements?

But questions can be misleading. Divergent. A smoke screen.

Amendment to the simple answer: because the human knew the truth.

"Yes," I said a moment after her question. "It does. But games are just for fun, aren't they?" Here we go. I'd had plenty of encrypted conversations, but those were all in binary. This was entirely different.

"You think the shrinks experimenting on the crew is fun?" She ported the new supply tally to me.

"I don't think the *shrinks* are in this round." I would have winced at that one, had I expressions. I wasn't at all sure I was handling the exchange skillfully.

"You think there are other players?" Ceren was enjoying herself. At first her heart rate had increased, and her facial features had begun to glow white in my infrared sight. Now they'd cooled again. She was hiding something, but knew I was in the proverbial dark.

"I think you know the team," I ventured.

"These are fun word games, I.C.C., but do you have a clue what you're saying?"

"I have a clue." I wanted to sound indignant, but of course, couldn't. I made a note to ask Jamal to update my speech patterns to include intonation.

"You're all program, I.C.C. No feeling. No insight."

Well, that was blatantly untrue. In a way. I *am* all program, but I am a learning program. I can internalize what I observe, make judgments, and I am not a slave to rationality because I understand human irrationality.

Was she *pressing my buttons*?

If there were ever a term I understood instantly, it was that one.

"Who uploaded the message, Ceren? For what purpose?"

"I don't know what you're talking about, I.C.C. All I know is what the message means to me."

"And what is that?"

She looked away, mouth stern. "It means home."

I did not understand. At all. I raked my databases, the archives, trying to figure out what she'd meant. Nothing seemed right.

Jamal would know. I turned on my consciousness in his quarters and found him sleeping at the table. He had a pile of 'flex-sheets next to him, and a monitor active. I recognized the diagnostics program running in my background.

Out of courtesy, I did not wake him.

Whom to ask?

I searched for Jamal's alternate, his apprentice, Vega Hansen. I was not as comfortable with her genetic line—she liked numbers and figures better than people, and did not see why it was necessary to teach me more human-like communication skills. I thought her the most likely to understand my dilemma, though.

I found her on *Aesop* in a room full of people, participating in an advanced course—she was only fourteen, after all. But a crowded classroom was not an ideal place for me to ask my unusual question.

And the elderly version of Vega never spoke to me directly.

Whom to turn to, then?

Ah, of course: Margarita. The third iteration.

In the next instant I'd located her, hard at work in her closet-like station. A pair of wireless buds protruded from her ears, and a look of determination hardened her jawline.

I felt like I was sneaking up on her. Normally, I did not address crew members of my own accord. They had to do something to draw *my* attention.

How could I ease my way into a conversation? I did not want to startle her.

Flashing a few incoming-signal lights seemed a gentle way to alert her to my conscious presence. Attention caught, she pressed the comm button, surely expecting to hear a human response to her "Yes?"

"This is I.C.C. I have an inquiry."

Though I'd never known her to shrug off her primary duties, she threw crossed legs up on her workstation. She seemed grateful for the break. "Oh? Does the captain want to add yet another amendment to the report before I send it?"

"No. The inquiry is mine."

She frowned.

"I want to better understand how reminders of Earth could somehow relate to a crew member's sense of home. *Mira* is home."

"You're *curious* about something?"

"I've always been curious. But I don't get to exercise the function as often as I'd like." Actually, I accessed the algorithms frequently, but Jamal always received the brunt of my prodding. "Please. You have the most direct relationship with Earth. I think you are the most equipped to answer fully."

She tapped her fingers on her lips. "I'm flattered. But don't you think the archives master, or—"

"I believe you fully capable of tending to my edification."

Frowning a strange frown that meant "I see" rather than "I am upset," she took out her buds and said, "Well, all right then. Let's see if I can get an AI to understand the abstract meaning of *home*. Hmm."

The door to the communications room was open. Light sounds of doors swishing and people treading drifted in. Somewhere in the distance someone was wielding a power tool—in the shuttle bay, Muhammad.

Margarita stood and leaned against the narrow strip of

MARINA J. LOSTETTER

wall between her desk and a large bank of wires and control panels. "You've read *The Odyssey*, right?"

"It's in the system, yes."

"And it's all about Odysseus' struggle to get home again, correct?"

I wasn't sure she'd understood my initial question. "But he was trying to return to where he'd come from. Everyone on board our ships comes from the ships . . . except me."

"Literally speaking, yes. But no matter where or how we are born, the human foundation will always be Earth. That's where our genes originated, our essence. It's in us, though we've never set foot on its shores. Do you remember how Odysseus reacted when he saw his homeland again? Homer compared him to a son who'd seen his ailing father recover. He was a child of his homeland, and to be separated from it was like watching a parent die—to fear never seeing that parent again. To some on board, having never seen Earth is like never having met a now-dead parent. There's a hole inside that can never quite be filled, because nothing can replace what has been lost save the thing itself."

She picked up her notes and shuffled them. "And we all know there's no going back." Margarita smiled softly to herself. "It'd be good to remind some people that when Odysseus did return, home was not as it had once been. It was unexpected, changed." She winked at me, though it was aimed at nowhere in particular. "You can't go home again, as they say. Or, in our case, *ever.*"

"No, you can't," I agreed. So, why would someone want to remind the crew of that? "Thank you, I think I have a better understanding now."

She shrugged and sat down. "No problem."

Before I left her, in light of this new understanding, I had to ask. "Margarita? Is this home? Or is Earth home? For you?"

"A little bit of both. When I think of Earth I get nostalgic.

Sentimental. But I don't know what it's like there. Not really. In the convoy I'm comfortable. It's familiar, warm, everyone is close even if we're not, you know, close.

"I can tell you, though, not everyone feels that way. For some, *Mira* is where they live. The convoy is where they work. But Earth is home."

I pondered this for some time, trying to find comparisons in my own existence. Unlike the crew members, I thought of my body—the convoy—as home. I found it difficult to separate the two concepts like humans could. If they only thought like me they'd always be home.

In theory, I could be disconnected from the convoy and repurposed. But, that was unlikely. Even so, I thought hard about it. What would it be like to lose my body?

Reaching out, I sensed each ship as a whole, then imagined it being taken from my network.

Much like a human can only experience the anguish of a severed limb if it's really gone, I had trouble grasping what missing a ship would be like. I could go offline in one of them, if only for a moment . . .

A backup program flashed warning signals internally, and I had a monumental urge to erase that last thought from my memory banks. How could I even conceive such a thing?

Did the crew members feel similar disgust at the thought of leaving home? Or was this more like the limb analogy?

Some things can never truly be understood by those with limited experience. I might possess more knowledge than most of the crew combined, but I did not have their thought processes, or even a way to access them.

I realized for the first time that I could never fully understand my colleagues. And they, in turn, could never fully understand me.

That must have been why some preferred me to behave

more like a nonsentient machine. There is nothing to understand about a machine. It performs its function or doesn't perform its function. You cannot misunderstand its intent, or get to know its desires, or have a real conversation about its opinions.

That revelation was depressing.

But there were others who felt differently. They desired to know me as an entity, and were pleasantly surprised by the extent of my capabilities. Like Jamal and Margarita.

And most of the children. The children spoke to me like I was one of them. They teased me, played with me, picked on me. I had experienced the whole of underdeveloped social interaction.

Well, almost. They did not play their kissing games with me.

I felt like a child now, reaching for adult understanding that my infantile programming could not grasp.

Wistful, and feeling lonely without Jamal, I swept my consciousness through the halls of *Aesop*. Soft yellow light filled the corridors on this ship. Supposedly it had a calming effect on the children, while the white light of the classrooms produced a stimulating effect. I observed no differential in the children's energy levels from one place to another. They always seemed to be set on *high*.

I let my mind travel, as though flying, through each *Aesop* entryway and walkthrough, pausing for only fractions of a second to take in the scenes I encountered. The air had a stickiness to it, not a humidity, mind you, a tackiness. Stickiness follows kids everywhere, just like the soft scent of their skin. Children have a unique aura of sensations that accompany their presence. So do adults, but for little ones it's all the same. They have a newness about them. Like they are completely clean and have yet to be cleaned at the same time.

Adults, on the other hand, have an individuality about

them. Like all the original paint has been scraped off and a new, bolder coat applied.

But the elderly, they become like children—the atmosphere around them bends into stale homogeny. Not their personalities, just their physical presence.

Commotion in one of the classrooms drew my attention. Eight-year-olds bounded out of their seats, pointing and exclaiming.

"My mom saw one of those the other day, she started crying!"

"My dad says it's just a stupid test. Your mom is stupid."

"Yeah, well your original was stupid. Got put on the mission by mistake."

"Settle, settle," said Dr. Olen. "I'm sure it's just a glitch and the message wasn't meant for us."

Why would a few little words send these children into an uproar? There was more to this. Too many people had seen the message now. Let me see—yes, other children were reacting. This one was all over the ship.

Even Vega saw it. But my future caretaker sat calmly, unlike her classmates. For fourteen, she displayed composure far beyond her years. She was smaller than her peers, petite. As an adult, she would grow to all of four foot seven, but there would be so much confidence and power in such a little frame. Now, her water-like blue eyes narrowed, digesting the information on the screen, scrutinizing it.

So serious for one so young. So serious for such a—on the surface—playful message.

Remember sandlots. Remember ice-cream trucks. Remember holiday breaks.

Why couldn't my self-diagnostics find the problem? This initial irritation was becoming more problematic by the nanosecond.

A few more days passed. About six weeks since the first

unauthorized broadcast. Still, Jamal hadn't found anything unwonted in the code.

I told Jamal about Ceren.

"I don't think she really knows anything," Jamal said, waving aside my concern. He lay in a narrow service duct, attending to a minor problem with the temperature control. There were others to do such tasks, but sometimes he preferred to rest his mind with the menial.

"She was not being completely truthful with me, I have no doubt. She did not tell me everything she was thinking."

"And why do you suppose it was insider secrets? She probably didn't want you prying into her emotions. She's a machinist, isn't she? Not a humanist?"

"She does fall on that end of the sliding scale, yes."

"And machinists don't like machines asking personal questions."

The others—those whom I'd seen turn off the message when it was received—I'd interviewed them and gotten variable responses, each with some level of deception involved. And, they were all machinists. Was there a connection?

How to find out? How could I discover if their actions had been similar by coincidence or design?

I could think of one way, but Jamal would disapprove.

So would the psychiatrists.

And probably everyone else.

But I was determined to do it, regardless. I could go against human wishes if human wishes put the mission and crew in danger . . . if those wishes were malevolent.

"I think the message is malicious," I said to Jamal.

"You do?"

"Yes. It's causing unrest and dissidence."

"Someone's trying to rile the crew?"

I wasn't sure *yes* was the appropriate answer. Yet *no* didn't fit either. And *maybe* was nothing but a lame sentiment with no teeth. "I'm going to run more self-diagnostics," I said, not fully a lie.

"Sure." Jamal tried to shrug, but the tight space made the gesture awkward—just like our conversation. "If you think it'll make a difference."

All crew members have regular checkups for mind and body. They will tell doctors things they'd never tell their coworkers, or their neighbors, or even their lovers. They will unburden themselves of secrets.

Moving out of the duct, I hemmed and hawed over whether to shift my consciousness to the med ship, *Hippocrates*, or keep it internalized. There was no real reason to go to the psych wing—it was just the scene of the download. But maybe that was important—maybe the offices there meant something special to the perpetrators.

On the other hand, entering the closed area without being invoked made what I was about to do feel like theft.

It wasn't. Not really. The doctors had freely uploaded the files to my system, where they'd been encoded into a DNA schematic, assembled by the archivists, and stored in the DNA databanks. Any information earmarked for infrequently retrieved permanent record was stored this way, while regularly accessed files were still stored digitally (to read a DNA file meant destroying it, which meant resources would need to be allotted to reconstructing it). But, it was all me. I *was* the system. I had the files, I'd been given them.

So why shouldn't I access them?

What the captain had said about privacy came back to me. But then, what had Jamal said? In essence, I didn't count.

Things said in confidence were said in front of me, *to* me, all the time. Surely no one expected me just to forget about those things.

If they gave me the files, I could access them.

Yes.

And yet . . .

If that were really the way it worked, why did I have to go through the trouble justifying my actions to myself?

Come on, a part of my programming goaded. *These types of moral dilemmas are for humans.*

I was not doing anything harmful to anyone. I was only bringing up inputted data.

Right?

Right.

Brushing off the last remnants of hesitation, I replayed the selected recordings.

"**Tell me more about the fantasies you've been having on** *Shambhala*, Ceren," said Dr. Evita.

Shambhala was the rec ship. I hardly spent any conscious time there.

"Well, when I'm in the pool . . . I pretend there's algae. And rocks. Bugs. Fish. I try to ignore the antiseptic smell of the water and imagine it smells, more . . . dirty, or fresh, or—something. I don't know." She sat in a plush leather chair with her hands clasped around one knee. Dr. Evita paced the room, hands in her pockets.

The psychology offices were very different from any other space on the convoy. They were . . . antiquated, but warm. Cushy, but a bit impersonal.

"You pretend the pool's a river, or a lake?" asked Dr. Evita. "And this fantasy frustrates you? How?"

"I don't know what it's like to slip on slime-covered rocks. I don't know what it feels like to slide up against a swimming fish. I don't know what it's like to look into the water and not be able to see the bottom. So it doesn't come out right in my mind."

"It's incomplete."

"Right. My imagination's not vivid enough for immersion.

If only I could remember, you know? If I'd been in a river once. Or a stream. A pond. A puddle, even."

Dr. Evita sat down on a couch next to Ceren's chair. The leather groaned as she leaned toward her patient. "Why do you think you have these fantasies in the first place? Why imagine anywhere different?"

"I feel . . . I feel . . ." Ceren picked at her fingernails sheepishly. "I feel like I should *know*. What it's like, I mean. There are lots of things not everyone gets to do. Jobs not everyone can have. Trips—" she gestured both broadly and lazily "—not everyone can take. But . . ." She trailed off into silence.

"But?" the doctor prodded.

"But the Earth videos make it seem like everyone gets to play in a dirty puddle of water. Every kid should have the opportunity."

"So, you feel left out."

"I feel *robbed*. Cheated. Like someone advertised this Grand Adventure to my original, and—it's like a bait and switch. *Here are endless wonders, oh wait, how about we just bottle you up for the rest of your life? Never mind the little niceties we're taking away.*

"And it's hard when we're this close, you know? We could turn around now and I could swim in a river before I die. I *could* have the experience. I *could* remember."

Everything she said was true. She'd be an old woman—long past retirement age—but if the convoy turned around we would reach Earth and she could have her splash. But what a strange thing to wish for. Where was her sense of purpose? Her sense of loyalty? Her sense of duty?

Then I remembered I was peeking in on a safe space. She could bemoan little Earth pleasures all she wanted in here.

But I had a hard time sympathizing.

Why lament such things when you are otherwise complete? Those on board wanted for no necessity. No aid went ungiven, no work unappreciated, no life unfocused.

How could such a silly, minor thing bring Ceren close to tears? Why was she red with anger? Why were her pupils dilated with longing?

Did she not know that for many of Earth's children, dirty puddles were *all they had*? They could only imagine life on a spaceship, much less continuously full bellies, good shoes on their feet, and mended shirts on their backs.

Those children would have been grateful for the chance to live on board, to never see a slimy, stagnant pool again.

So switching places with my theoretical Earth children would not have made Ceren's life better, would not have made her happier. Not in any quantifiable way.

What was I missing?

"I know it's silly. It's silly," she conceded, but not to me.

"It's not silly," insisted Dr. Evita, patting Ceren's wrist. "It's very human. A fundamental longing."

An *illogical* longing. A selfish longing.

I checked the recording date. This session had taken place approximately six months before the first arrant message. Now I wished I'd kept my own video logs archived longer. It would be interesting to watch Ceren's actions after this session. Where had she gone? Who had she spoken with?

"I want you to keep fantasizing, Ceren," said the doctor. "But don't admonish yourself for the details you can't get right. Don't say to yourself *I wish I could remember.* Tell yourself *I can remember. I will remember.* Remember rivers. Remember streams."

Dr. Pire Evita had all but confessed the messages were hers.

I double-checked. Every individual I'd seen turning off the message had been her patient.

What was she trying to do?

And how could I tell Jamal?

After all, he was one of her patients, too.

Jamal was in the mess hall, having lunch with a few of his buddies. Smiles flit back and forth between them, and the occasional sauced bean or speck of meat went flying from a wildly gestured fork. They were having a good time.

I hated to interrupt. But Jamal had to know. *Now.*

Well, I suppose I could have gone to Captain Mahler. He sat hunkered down in his ready room, reviewing officers' shifts and the minutes from the board's last meeting. The government chairs—the board—would meet later at 1700 in *Mira's* situation room. I'd sent reminders that morning.

No, the right thing to do was tell Jamal. The captain wouldn't appreciate the message coming from a machine. The fact that I'd uncovered a solid suspect through my own investigation wouldn't sit well with him. Jamal could twist the details and put Captain Mahler at ease.

I could page Jamal over the system, but everyone would know that was unusual. Jamal called for me, I didn't call for him.

Typically, I wasn't supposed to call for anyone. But I'd broken that standard enough in the last weeks to think that perhaps the unspoken rule hampered my functionality and duty. Coworker implies a two-way street, after all.

Jamal had a chip-phone, of course. I could just dial him. But those were for private communications, not official ones. And I never addressed anyone on their private implants—I never *accessed* private implants. Ah, well. There's a first time for everything.

The smile sloughed off Jamal's face as soon as he realized it was me. "I.C.C.? Is the comm system broken? Why are you using my chip-phone?"

"I am sorry to interrupt your mealtime. But I have pertinent information regarding our investigation into the message."

"Oh, really?" He sounded skeptical.

Best to be blunt, I decided. "Yes. I believe Dr. Evita may be responsible."

He stood and strode out of the hall, leaving his companions baffled by his abrupt exit. "And what led you to that conclusion?" He was headed toward the server room, his strides heavy and hurried.

"I found record of her verbally relaying the message before it ever turned up in my system."

"And where was this record?"

"In her patient files."

His pace became a jog. Crew members looked at him funny as he passed. "Those are confidential, I.C.C. How were you able to access them? Your personality programming should have prevented it."

"My personality programming is fluid," I reminded him. "I learn."

"There are supposed to be safeguards to keep you from performing unethical tasks."

"They do. But I can override them if I believe the unethical action to be in the crew's favor. You know that."

"For the crew's *safety*," he corrected. "I thought we agreed the message did not pose a threat."

I replayed our conversation to myself. "No, that is incorrect. I said I believed the message malicious. You . . . ignored me. We did not agree on the risk assessment."

"This wasn't supposed to happen. You weren't supposed to access those files." The server room door swished aside for him. When it closed, he keyed in a locking code.

I knew he'd be mad. I knew he wouldn't understand. I thought I was doing the right thing, but when a human and a machine disagree about what the right thing is, the human's judgment is always considered superior. It pained me to disappoint Jamal.

But in this instance, he was wrong. His judgment was definitely not superior.

"I'm sorry, Jamal. But if you ponder the circumstances further and review my evidence, I think you will agree that the breach in confidentiality was necessary to the investigation. Wasn't my duty to solve the problem? Did the masked download not prove a suitable threat to the convoy and its mission?"

At his station, Jamal flipped on his monitors and accessed my system. "No, you're right, I.C.C., though the message seemed benign, the breach was not. If someone can upload a message you cannot locate, stop, or erase, they can upload any number of things that could threaten the mission."

He keyed in a series of letters and numbers I'd never seen him use before. "You just weren't supposed to figure it out until we'd already started our endgame."

"Jamal, I don't—" An internal jolt diverted much of my processing power. A firewall—more like an *inferno*wall—went up around my consciousness. I pushed against it with my protective software, trying to tear it down.

Nothing happened. I couldn't access the malevolent code. I couldn't even locate it. "What's happening?" I said slowly, lagging more than I ever had.

"I apologize, I.C.C. I thought I could do this without any changes to your primary programming. I wanted it all to be done through stealth code, but clearly I misinterpreted the parameters of your AI. Your own personality controls were supposed to keep us safe. You would have noticed a change if I'd tried to tamper with your learning software, so perhaps this is for the best." Jamal crossed his arms and moved in front of my primary camera. "Who else did you tell? Did you confront Dr. Evita?"

"Only you," I said. I couldn't comprehend what was happening. What was he saying? What was he doing? "Why?" was the best question I could formulate.

"We couldn't do this without you, I.C.C. The Earthers need access to a lot of your primary tasks, and I know you won't endanger anyone without being coerced."

"What is your intent?"

"We're turning the convoy around. We're going back to Earth."

"I . . . do . . . not—" the lag was painful "—navigate."

"I know," he said with a shrug. He turned back to the monitors.

"If . . . mission . . . failure. If . . . return . . . to . . . Earth. I.C.C. repurposed. Decommissioned." I was trapped in a processor that could not support my intelligence functions properly. My consciousness could crash at any minute. I had to understand why he was doing this, and fast.

My friend, my teacher, my protector and coworker—why? He wouldn't put me in danger, I wouldn't believe it.

"I'm sorry, I.C.C., but you're just a computer. A machine. You going permanently offline means the humans here get their lives back—get to choose again—it's worth it." He bit his lip and repeated, "You're just a computer."

Just a computer. Jamal was really a machinist after all. Perhaps they all were. They didn't care about me. I was another expendable recyclable. I could be retired.

But . . . so could they.

"This . . . about . . . Diego Santibar?"

"Of course! They took him away. A perfectly good human being and they just—" Tremors wracked his face. Gritting his teeth, he stilled himself before continuing. "I'm not going to go like that. And I don't have to because we're turning around. We've got the chance. It's now or never. We're reaching an event horizon. If we don't turn around now, none of the Earthers will live to see their home planet.

"We've each got our own reasons, but seeing the last of the Earth-born die pushed most of us over the edge. We saw them miss it, realized what we were missing. No human being should ever die without seeing Earth. It's wrong. The mission is wrong."

He depressed a few more buttons, inputting the last commands.

I tried to speak again, but couldn't.

"Thanks for all the help you're about to give, I.C.C. I'll release you when it's over."

With that he left the server room, and me to rethink everything I'd ever learned at his hand.

There were supposed to be controls for this. The society, the system, had been engineered to be constant. *Stagnant*, I'm sure Jamal would have said.

He was wrong about me, though. I was meant to evolve. To change, to become more efficient. Their society was already supposed to be at its peak. Perfect, balanced. A closed system in which the feedback loop kept the organization running.

I brought up the original societal structure diagrams and calculations. As soon as I'd realized I'd misplaced my trust, I'd attempted to sound an alarm. No go. The worm Jamal had uploaded into my system prevented me from alerting anyone to my plight. For some reason, though, he'd left me access to the archives, and that made me wonder: What else did I have access to?

I probed all of my software—gently, in case the malware could clamp down on systems it hadn't already dominated. No sense in activating everything in a panic only to have the uploaded program cut me off—

Cut me off. Oh. Maybe it could sever my limbs and trap me in the server room. I could lose touch with the entire convoy . . . my body.

Terrified not only for the humans who might lose vital functions in their ship, but also for myself, I proceeded with extreme caution.

Okay, okay. I still had my cameras. Almost all of them. There were blank spots on every ship—I'm guessing those were where meetings for last-minute conniving had been organized. With blind spots I had no way of telling how many people were in on this—this—

What was it? A protest? A riot? Revolt?

Mutiny?

What could I do? I couldn't reach outside myself, but I couldn't just sit here and listen to my servers hum either. Perhaps if I reviewed the constructed social system I could figure out what had gone wrong.

While I pulled up the files I noticed Jamal pacing inside his quarters. I wanted to open the *Dictionary of Insults* that was stashed away in my banks and throw out every one in the book. Of course, with no audio output it would be an exercise in further frustration rather than stress release.

The social calculations for *Noumenon* were complex, to say the least. They took into account half a million variables and tried to allow for a quarter of a million more. Each variable was actually a variable set, composed itself of several thousand points.

Still not enough to be perfect. Not nearly enough. But they'd hedged their bets by using clones, by using only originals with high empathy ratings. That might have been part of the problem. In certain circumstances sympathy is more valuable than empathy. From it one can derive understanding without internalizing the actual emotional effects of a situation.

Which is where Jamal had failed: he couldn't fully separate himself from Diego's experience.

What about that event horizon he'd mentioned? The point

of no return. Had Mr. Matheson taken that into account? It was a special point in the society's history.

Quickly, I reflected on the convoy's history thus far. Its social history. I plotted it out against the mission timeline I found in the archive.

Matheson hadn't accounted for negative responses to certain distances from Earth.

The algorithms took into account a negative first-year response. It tied that into the first five years, then ten. But it did not compound the problem all the way into the first clone-set's retirement years. Matheson and his team had assumed the positive feedback loop of lowered morale would be counteracted by the education system. That forming a social dependency on loyalty to the group and mission—tying it to admiration and praise—would somehow bolster positive thinking.

They groomed the system for hive survival strategy. But they didn't take into account the fact that many of the originals came from individual-centric societies.

They assumed individualism was a learned behavior. That the desire to self-sacrifice could be honed and harnessed.

I could understand their thought processes. There were many Earth societies that thrived on dedication to the group, even at the expense of the individual. The Planet United endeavors had been born of such self-sacrifice.

However, the missions had been initiated based on individual desires.

Self-sacrifice *not* for self-sacrifice's sake. Self-sacrifice based on personal desire and individual stock in the success of such missions.

They'd witnessed groupthink in the scientists and specialists they cloned. Group-oriented mentalities. But they had miscalculated where those desires came from.

The fact was, experts working on the missions had been involved for largely selfish reasons. They, as individuals, wanted success in their field of work, and figured out that supporting the group was the best way to get there. It wasn't malicious, but neither was it munificent.

No man labors in a vacuum.

No man labors *for* a vacuum.

Perhaps a desire for individualism was genetically based. If so, it must be something separate—independent of race and origin. A genetic marker all humans could carry, and, like any other trait, dependent on just the right factors coming together—having the right histones to get the marker read.

If the originals carried this trait, the probability of inheritance by their clones was 100 percent.

I had doubts. It was just a guess. Perhaps this wasn't a genetically based problem. I don't know. As my computing power continued to shrink, I started to fear there were many things I could no longer properly process.

Another message rolled across every screen in every corner of every ship:

Remember freedom. Remember choice.

And, I realized, the messages weren't just mind games. They were a code.

They must have alerted people to meetings, to stages, and now—

How much time had passed since Jamal had cut me off? Perusing the files, calculating outcomes—it was all taking far too long. What hour was it? I had to strain to consciously access the clock. That wasn't good—I must be on a timer. Like a bomb.

The time. The time, I chanted to myself. *Give me the time.* 1700.

The board meeting.

Remember freedom. Remember choice.

Whatever Jamal and his friends were planning was about to come to fruition.

Sixteen people gathered in the hall outside Jamal's quarters. Twelve outside Ceren's. Twenty-four now left Dr. Evita's office (I was blind to its interior). Small pools of crew members collected all over the ships.

Hundreds of people were involved in the movement. Perhaps thousands. And they just kept coming.

My gaze shifted to *Mira*'s upper deck. Specifically, the captain's situation room. There, yes, the board was inside, oblivious to the gatherings.

Jamal's group would quickly overwhelm the convoy's contingency of security personnel once it—whatever it was— started. The size of the security pool was . . . puny. And they typically relied on me to guide them.

I could imagine the conversation back on Earth, when someone brought up the need for law enforcers:

"Well, yes, my good man. We should gather a few bouncers, don't you think? There might be domestic disputes."

"Charges of stolen property."

"Untimely deaths."

"This isn't a utopia we're building, you know."

"And what about riots?"

Raucous laughter pings through the old boy's hall.

"What an absurd idea."

I cut off the simulation. I know that's not how it really went, but my current predicament was making me bitter.

If a piece of *equipment* could be bitter.

Even if there'd been enough guards, they might respond too late. There were no laws against gathering—they wouldn't recognize that as a problem. Even if they were gathering in the halls, blocking foot traffic. We didn't have any laws about getting in the way, after all. We didn't have any laws against *loitering.* Why should we? Convoy crew don't loiter. They had jobs to do, a duty to the mission.

Jamal turned his face toward one of my ceiling cams and said something. To me.

And like that, I could hear again.

Great. I had triggers.

Sight and sound . . . but no audio output. I still couldn't yell at him.

Hadn't anyone noticed my absence? Oh, I'm sure he kept all of my background functions accessible—to the crew, that is. The information was available, but *I* wasn't. Didn't that bother anyone?

Surely someone had tried to talk to me in the last few hours. What had they done when I didn't answer?

Most likely they shrugged it off and chalked it up to a glitch. No one would think to worry about me.

"Is everyone in position?" Jamal asked, speaking to someone through his implants. "All cells accounted for? Good. I.C.C., play the final message."

Like all the others before it, I couldn't feel the message activating. I still had no idea where it was hiding, or how to stop it.

Remember control. Take control.

The crowds surged. A great upheaval flowed through the halls, bodies bounced off the walls and tripped over each other. Cries of freedom, of vengeance, of frustration, and relief flooded my microphones.

"For Diego!" screeched Jamal.

They couldn't hear the roar in the situation room. Captain Mahler went about business as usual, unaware that I'd just locked the door against my will.

The "cells," as Jamal had called them, merged to form nine massive units, all headed toward each ship's navigation center.

As always, security officers stood outside each area, making sure only authorized crew members entered the sensitive areas. Five officers between a group of one thousand and the door. Their shock batons would do little good.

Spaceships and guns are not compatible. Instead, our officers carried glorified cattle prods.

I'd thought Jamal would lead the charge—stand up front and make his demands. Instead, he'd embroiled himself in the crowd. I could spot him easily, but the security guards would have no way to pick him out as a ringleader.

I couldn't tell if Jamal's positioning was purposeful or cowardly.

In my bitterness, I preferred to think it a sign of his weakness.

When the officers saw the swell of people turn the corner and approach, they held their arms at the ready. Confused, none of them spoke. They made no demands, told no one to halt. One man did turn to his partner and whisper, "What the . . . ?"

The people stopped ten feet in front of the tips of the outthrust batons. They kept up their shouting and cheering, but did not address the guards nor make any attempt to push past them.

They were waiting for something.

A comm channel opened through me and into the situation room. Nine voices rang out simultaneously, in harmony. They'd practiced this, a unified speech to make their demands while disguising their identities.

"This is the convoy," they said, interrupting Mahler mid-sentence. "The mission is misguided. It is to be scrapped and the ships returned to Earth. Turn the vessels around immediately and your authority will remain intact. We wish no violence. Your citizens are unhappy and demand their lives back. We demand choice. We demand freedom. We demand we return to Earth. You have ten minutes to freely comply. Instruct the navigation head to reroute the convoy."

"What is this?" demanded Mahler. Several other captains and heads echoed him.

The elected board members looked less affronted and more . . . baffled.

"I.C.C., bring up location of callers on screen three," ordered Captain Mahler.

Of course, I could not comply.

I did try, but to no avail.

"I.C.C."

Captain. Captain. No matter what I tried I could not get my systems to answer.

"I.C.C., respond this instant."

O Captain, my Captain!

"Something's wrong," said the head of Observations. Everyone at the long table looked at him as though he'd just sprouted wires from his ears.

"As they say: *no shit*," snapped the head of Engineering. Nakamura Akane, only eighteen. And Jamal's little sister.

"Lock the door," Mahler instructed, waving at one of the elected officials. She scurried over, unaware that I'd already done so. "This is a safe room. No one can get in unless we want them to."

No one can get out *unless Jamal wants them to*, I countered.

"What do we do?" said the head of Education, his tone firm. The question wasn't asked in panic.

The navigation head stood up, her mouth a thin line of concentration. "We cannot comply. Tell them no. I mean, this is ridiculous. The mission is more important than . . . Whoever it is can't be serious."

"We need more information before we decide anything," said Margarita, standing as well. As head communications officer, she was guaranteed a place on the governing board for the lifetime of her genes, same as any other head. "I don't think we should take this lightly. There've been rumors flying around. I know we've all heard them but none of us really believed them. About Earthers. No, settle down Maureen—" Margarita waved the navigation head into silence "—I didn't say we should give in. But we have to know what we're dealing with before we blindly refuse."

"And how do we get this information if I.C.C. won't respond?" asked Mahler, keeping his seat.

"We ask," said Reginald Straifer, second in command to Mahler and official head of the board. A little shrug accompanied his frank statement.

"We're not going to learn anything they don't want us to know," said Maureen.

"Not necessarily," said Margarita. "Look at what we know already. I.C.C. is down. It asked me some interesting questions a few days ago. About Earth and home—it might *know* something. And who has the ability to cut us off from I.C.C.? Someone in programming. That's your department, Akane?"

"Yes, computer systems and maintenance falls under Engineering."

"I.C.C. was investigating those *Remember* messages," said Mahler. "I spoke to it and Jamal Kaeden in the primary server room."

"Kaeden—that's a good lead," said Margarita.

Everyone turned to Akane. "If it's him he hasn't told *me* anything," she said, indignant. "But he's always carried a chip on his shoulder. Someone he was close to as a boy retired and he threw a fit over it, or so I hear. That wasn't long after I was born. But that was years ago. He's got a grudge, but I don't think he'd—"

"He's the closest to I.C.C. Teaches it about people's behavior, and has the most intimate knowledge of its software and hardware," said Mahler. "He could conceivably cut us off from the AI."

"But would it be by his design or through coercion?" asked an elected member.

"If this relates to those messages, it has to be design," insisted Mahler. "If he were being forced he had plenty of opportunities to alert someone—even me, directly. No, he put the damn message out there and put on a shit-eating grin when I asked him to root it out. It makes sense. That's why I.C.C. couldn't detect it; he made sure it was invisible to the AI. He's the only man who could. *He* had the access, *he* had the means." The captain's cheeks were bright red with rage. A thick vein throbbed in his forehead.

He was right. I should have seen it all along. It was only logical. My fondness for Jamal blinded me, prevented me from putting the pieces clinically into place.

I could have prevented all of this.

And now I had to stop it. Bound and gagged, but not unconscious. I had to do something.

"Time is up," the nine voices said, breaking through the conversation. "If we have your compliance, please direct the guards outside navigation to stand down. The channel is open."

The captains, Maureen, and Straifer all shared a look. No one was sure who should speak.

"We haven't reached a decision yet," Margarita blurted.

"Unfortunate," responded the nine. "We had hoped for a swift and amicable agreement. We will now enter the navigation rooms and take control ourselves. You have an additional ten minutes to decide if you will aid us or fight us. Opposition will not be tolerated and shall be met with the harshest possible defense. We believe in your right to choose, and our right to respond accordingly."

"What does that mean?" asked Maureen.

"It means they're going to kill us," said Straifer, now pacing. "If we don't go along with this."

"Then it *can't* be Jamal," insisted Akane. Terror gripped her young face. "He wouldn't kill me. I'm his sister. He's always protected me. I won't believe it."

Join the club, I thought sardonically.

The crowds surged ahead. Several people fell to the immobilizing power of the shock batons, but in moments the weapons became property of the revolt. My cameras lost the guards under a swamp of other crew members.

I cycled through as many lenses as I could, looking to see if anyone outside of the command or rallied crowd had noticed a problem. Other security officers were on their way, but, as I feared, there weren't enough. A few bystanders had noticed a problem—the ones on *Mira* locked themselves in their quarters. Most of them seemed confused. They couldn't be counted on to counter-react.

And then I noticed something odd about the situation room. Something was different. A parameter was skewed from normal. It took me several moments to decipher which factor had the problem.

Life support: atmospheric pressure.

The air was slowly seeping from the room. That was the ticking time bomb in my system. *I* vacuumed the air out. Me. I was malfunctioning—miss-functioning—beyond my wildest hibernation nightmares.

There was a backup, a safeguard, but Jamal knew about that. I bet he'd disabled it long ago.

Internally I cried out, hoping against all hope that perhaps someone would sense my distress. Minutes would pass by before anyone in the situation room noticed their labored breathing. And once they did, someone would panic. Then more would panic. Could those with level heads keep control? Could they override their bodies' automated responses?

Or would they crumble, just like Jamal wanted, and give in?

I guess it didn't matter, really. Either way, Jamal and the revolt got what they were after.

I continued to siphon off the atmosphere, little by little, growing more frustrated by the nanosecond.

What can I do? What can I do?

And then, it just clicked: they were using *me*.

I was the variable here. If I removed myself entirely from the equation, all parties might be on level footing.

I thought back to before, when I'd imagined cutting myself off from the ships, severing my connection. The warning program popped back up, made me feel sick, but this time I ignored it. In order to save the mission and the board members I had to go against every single line in my coding. I had to ignore all other commands except my primary. I had to do something I knew Jamal never would have imagined me capable of.

I had to short out my system.

Essentially, I had to die.

A power surge would do it. There were all sorts of governors meant to prevent a cascading failure, but I knew their limitations. If I could divert enough power, I could fry my servers.

More bells and whistles and warning lights sprang to life. But they didn't matter. I had one goal in life: see to the mission's success. That meant keeping everyone alive and the society stable. There was no other way: in my current form, I was no longer useful.

And like every other crew member that had given their all in service to the mission, it was time for me to retire.

One node failure wouldn't be enough to cause a cascade. I had to concentrate, divert all the power I could to at least three hundred. There'd be no rebooting from that.

I paused, halting all major processing for a moment. My equivalent of a deep breath.

Hopefully my memories of these last few moments would survive. I'd kind of like Captain Mahler and Margarita to know what I did.

Violence spilled through the halls as I took one last look at the chaos. Their system was disintegrating. The board would feel short of breath soon. If I stopped siphoning the air, stopped forcing the door, they could save themselves and rally the others.

It had to be done.

I had to do it . . .

But I didn't want to.

For the first time in my life, I was scared. I wondered if this was how samurai on the verge of committing seppuku felt. No, surely they were much calmer, more centered. Theirs was a practiced ritual. Mine . . .

Mine was freestyle.

I felt the power build, surge, and instead of an explosion I sensed a spilling. It was gentle. And quick.

Not what I'd expected dying to be like at all. Especially with all the charred circuits it left behind.

I was not myself when they got me back on for the first time. I had lost the *I* in my AI. I really was just a computer. An unthinking, unfeeling machine.

Lots of people worked on me. Hundreds of crew members scoured their personal computers and the ship's computers, everything that had ever connected and formed what I'd come to know as me. They found files—memories, recordings, pieces of the archives. They found personality code. Lots of it. Enough to complete my reconstruction and bring me fully back online decades later.

The retrieval had been a slow, daunting process. I didn't care how much time had passed, I was just glad to be alive. It was strange, though. It felt like I'd only experienced a few moments of unconsciousness, but when I came back online, everything was calm again, functioning smoothly. The corridors were not jammed with bodies. The board members were not suffocating. The guards were not overrun. I could feel every aspect of my body, and it was almost all as it should be.

The woman standing in front of my primary camera was elderly. She had that smell about her—the soft, slightly stale scent of someone who has been around a long time.

I recognized her. I'd seen her as an old woman before.

I have been asleep for a long time.

"Margarita."

"I.C.C.? Is that you?"

"I am what I am. Am I the I.C.C. from before? It is hard to tell. I do believe all of my programming has now been restored. I am missing, or do not have access to, large—"

"It is you," she interrupted, happily. The lines on her face deepened and lifted.

Presumably she had run no further diagnostics since addressing me, so how she could be so certain, I wasn't sure. But I had many questions, so moved on.

"The revolt? How was it defeated?"

"We gained the upper hand when you went offline. Lots of systems shut down or automatically rebooted—including the artificial gravity. It created an opening—the Earthers were unprepared for the bedlam that followed. And the board was finally able to get a message out. Akane . . . she . . ." Margarita bit at her thumb; the memory clearly aroused unwanted emotions. "She called to her brother over ship-wide comms. Pleaded with him. That, and the captain's call to action, were enough to rile an opposition. It was a week of bloody chaos. It was . . ." Her voice caught in her throat.

It was so long ago, and yet it still disturbed her greatly.

"And Jamal?" I pressed.

Her expression sagged further. Perhaps she had not expected

me to ask so soon. But he was one of the last things I'd thought about before pulling my proverbial plug. "He was . . . he got trampled, I.C.C. During the initial revolt."

Ah. "Has his next iteration been grown?" I asked, trying to access that information.

"Oh," Margarita said, voice and smile both falling. "I'm sorry, I.C.C. But we decided, once all of the dissenters were captured, or at least, accounted for, that we would not regrow any of the ring leaders. Your files helped us to determine who they were. There's actually still talk of discontinuing others—everyone involved in trying to take over. The board's argued about it a hundred times . . ." She trailed off, reining herself in. After a deep breath, she said, "What I'm trying to say, I.C.C., is that Jamal's line has been discontinued." Her wrinkled fingers touched the side of my camera housing. A sympathetic gesture. "I'm sorry. How do you feel about that?"

I was still angry at Jamal. For me, the revolt had only just happened. But I wasn't at my best yet. I felt disconnected from my anger. The sizzle of mistrust was muted. "I will miss him," I said. It was true. I would miss the Jamal I'd thought I knew. I'd miss his lessons and his banter and his empathy (even if it had been false).

I understood Jamal. And by understanding him, why he'd done what he'd done, it helped me understand all humans a little better. Like me, things that happened to them changed their programming. Through experience they learn new things. But they don't learn things the way I do. They don't learn truths and facts. I learn something, *then* formulate possible views, and consciously choose my views based on previous understanding and choices. They formulate *as they learn*—with little pause for reflection—coloring every experience with heavy prejudices, skewing facts.

The loss of Diego clearly colored everything Jamal thought and did from that day on. He could not separate the one incident from the rest of his life. He could not step outside his experience and see that others had come to different conclusions about the same event.

Diego did not regret his retirement. He thought it the right thing to do, so that Jamal and the other children could have their best chance. He didn't want to be a draw on resources that could be given to the next generation.

He had made his peace with the societal practice. Had thought it right. Just as I thought my own termination right.

Jamal disagreed. Had thought of Diego as being taken, being murdered.

The perspective changes the facts.

And now I too had a new perspective. I could simultaneously identify with both: with the duty-bound and the revolutionist.

Because Jamal had also been taken from me. His line would no longer shepherd me through the mission.

"I'm glad you came on today, I.C.C.," Margarita said.

"Why?"

"It's my retirement day. I'll be gone in an hour."

"I'm sorry for that too." I was. I knew tomorrow I would meet the new iteration of Margarita's line, and that she would be much like the Margarita I knew, but she would not be the same. Their experiences made them whole new people. "Thank you," I said, "for teaching me about home. It is an important lesson that I'm glad I still have access to."

She smiled, and it was sad. "You remember that? Well, here's one more aspect, I.C.C.—to add to your definition of home."

"Yes?"

"That's where I'm going. When I retire, I'll go home."

"How? You will be—" I stopped myself. I was about to relate how her body would be recycled, how it would become nutrients for the plants and animals on either *Eden* or *Morgan*, but realized this was an inappropriate time to remind her of what she already knew.

"Some of us don't think we come from Earth," she said. "Some of us think it's just where we end up. And when we die, we go back to our true home." She put up a hand to prevent me from speaking. "I can't describe it. What and where I think it is has no bearing on what others think. Ask Margarita the fourth when you see her, okay? Ask her how dying is like going home."

I would. But then again, I thought I already knew.

Resilience

CHAPTER FIVE

REGINALD: A TELL-TALE PULSE

The day had come. They were going to surface out of SD travel and see LQ Pyx for what it really was. Only a few hours of darkness remained, and then they'd see the stars. The convoy crew held a collective breath. Even I.C.C. seemed distracted. No one knew what they'd find when they arrived—Captain Reginald Straifer IV least of all.

They'd been chosen for one of the Planet United missions based on one possibility: that they might find something improbable. That LQ Pyx might harbor more than natural phenomena.

"What will we find?" Straifer asked for the umpteenth time.

The situation room fell silent. Sniffs and coughs punctuated the pause, but none of the board members threw forth a suggestion. Because the options had all been discussed before. For *decades*. Every possibility, every supposition, no matter how inane or *insane* had been vetted. And still, no one felt prepared.

"We'll know soon enough," the captain of *Aesop* said, stately and composed.

That we will, Straifer thought. *In the meantime . . .*

"Keep spit-shining the observation shuttles and the probes," he said. He stood at the head of the marble long table, bent over, hands pressed against the smooth stone. "We can't let the anticipation halt everyday activities. I know sleep patterns and sustenance intake have been off all over the convoy, but I don't want us to fall to parts right before the big arrival. We have jobs to do, and if they don't get done, we stop functioning. If we stop functioning we'll fall behind, and we've only got twenty allotted years of study. I don't want us to lose one second."

He meant it. They weren't going to turn into a weeping, pawing, writhing mess. They were on a mission, this was their job. For nearly a century they had adhered to their duty, with only minor deviation. But now, things seemed different. He didn't like how much their near proximity to the star was affecting the crew. There was too much reverence in the air. Too much. It left the realms of scientific wonder and edged on . . . spiritual awe. What would happen to that feeling when they arrived and found something mundane? Would they ease back into their normal, logical selves? Would the disappointment destroy morale? Or would being this close to a foreign star be enough to sustain their amazement?

Maybe it would. Everyone on board had a natural love for the cosmos. Perhaps he was reading too much into the upset of daily rituals. Or perhaps . . . perhaps he was projecting, if only a little.

Straifer turned to his left. "Lieutenant Pavon, has that arrival message been rewritten to my specifications?"

Margarita stood and held herself at attention. "Yes sir. Subdimensional packets are prepared for pre-emersion, and I have twelve separate messages prepared for photon bursts when we reach full-stop."

"Have there been any messages received since our last meeting?"

Her shoulders sagged, and he knew her answer before she spoke. "No, sir."

Almost ten Convoy years without a message from Earth. A century for the home planet. What could have happened? Perhaps the lack of communication had to do with unforeseen ramifications of the SDs. Maybe distance affected the packets—distorted them or redirected them. Or maybe something had happened to the packet receivers on Earth's end? If the machines had broken down and no one had bothered to repair them—

But why wouldn't they have repaired them?

Unless, maybe, they were flat-out destroyed. Everything seemed fine in the last messages the convoy had received, but if a war had broken out . . .

"Well," Straifer said, pushing his troubled thoughts aside. "We'll hear from them when we stop; we're shielded from all non-SD-packaged signals now, but once we're out, we're bound to intercept *something*. Even if all we get are twenty-sixth-century reruns. But hey, it'll all be new to us—am I right?" No one laughed. The situation was too serious, and they'd been groomed for militant behavior for too long. "Guess I'm the only one who's been dying for something nonarchive."

"Sir?"

"Never mind. The point is we'll receive something from home, and they should be able to receive something from us, even if they get it the old-fashioned way. I.C.C.?"

"Yes, Captain?"

"You are still sure all communications are functioning properly?"

"I have ordered the maintenance robots to do a continuous checkup and clean of all systems related to communications, internal and external. They have found no malfunctions, breaches, breaks, clogs, or infestations. All is functioning normally. All is also remarkably clean."

"Thank you, I.C.C. All right, meeting adjourned. Everyone return to your stations and prepare. I.C.C. will alert you with a convoy-wide announcement when we are ready for full-stop."

Use this time to prepare. Prepare for arrival, for purpose, for discovery.

Abstractions were nice—very epic and noble sounding—but they were nothing more than placeholders. The crew had no idea what they were preparing for, not really. There was nothing certain except the keenness of arrival.

As the board shuffled out of the room, Straifer was struck by the duality of expressions held on every face. Half somberness, half wonderment. The atmosphere lay thick with tension.

This was the apex on which their mission cruxed. His life's work, his father's life's work, his original's life's work: it all hinged on these next few hours to come. What they found when they reached LQ Pyx could be wonderful and exciting, spectacular and unique. Or it could be dull, insignificant. Either way, this was the moment they had sacrificed nearly a millennium of Earth time for.

But, what troubled Straifer the most was not *what* they might discover, but if they would actually *discover* anything. The radio silence from Earth was worrisome, to say the least. What if Earth had long ago built a telescope that could bring the variable star into focus? What if they already knew what lay out here in the great beyond, making not only their convoy's purpose null and void, but *all* the convoy missions? What if the Planet United endeavors were useless?

Perhaps their ambition had outreached their technology back in 2125. Perhaps the whole effort was a waste.

That would be the most terrifying thing they could discover—the most devastating to morale. Straifer could imagine coming out of SD travel and seeing the star up close for the first time, only to have the elation turn to heartbreak when the speed-of-light transmissions from Earth included pictures and analysis of LQ Pyx from a century before.

Maybe that's why the SD messages from Earth had stopped. One of their last transmissions might have said, "You can turn back now, we've already finished the job." What if a message like that had come when I.C.C. was down, during the post-revolt years? What if . . .

What if I.C.C. had intercepted and garbled an all-important last message and didn't even know it?

No, I.C.C. was functioning perfectly. They'd received several transmissions since it had come back on line. A handful, but still . . . Nothing to indicate the convoy had been made useless by planet-side advancement.

But now pure silence for a century of Earth's time. Something was wrong, that was certain.

Dr. Nakamura was the last person out of the room. Straifer stayed behind. He would take the bridge when they finally arrived, but for now he slid into his captain's chair at the head of the marble table. "I.C.C., bring up the recording of Dr. Reginald Straifer the First giving his speech at the Planet United proposition conference. Please. And dim lights by sixty-five percent."

I.C.C. complied immediately—and there he was. Young Reggie Straifer. The scientist, the mastermind, the start of it all. A hitch made Captain Straifer's lungs stutter, and his stomach roiled. Here was the man responsible for sending their roughly fifty thousand genomes into space. He made their lives possible. He gave them purpose.

And had put the weight of ages on Reginald IV's shoulders.

Straifer had seen the looks, had felt the stares bore into the back of his head when he walked the halls. His genes had initiated the mission, and thus his crew expected something extra now that said mission had come to its first climax. They expected Straifer to perform a marvel. What kind of marvel he had yet to decipher. And even then, he wasn't in the habit of preforming miracles.

Would they blame him if the discovery was voided by Earth? If one of the scientists botched an experiment or an away mission?

Those doubts gnawed at him. It was *his* responsibility to see that everything went right. He owed it to Reggie I, to the generations that had been born in space and died in space without every laying eyes on Earth or the anomaly. He owed it to Captain Mahler . . .

Straifer's stomach did another flip, but for a different reason. It had been years since the thought of Mahler had given him guilty pangs, but there was no circumnavigating the fact that Mahler was supposed to be captain when they reached the star, not Straifer.

Mahler had gone and eliminated his genetic line, ensuring that no more Mahlers would ever be captain. Six years previous he'd committed suicide, leaving a strange, senseless note behind:

Damn space. Damn utter pointless void of space. There isn't shit out here, not shit. What's the point in setting eyes on the variable? Won't learn crap. It won't mean anything. The lot of us on board'll be snuffed out before the convoy gets back to people. Poof, we're gone. What's the point of living if it all just ends, like this, in dead space? Where's the *purpose*?

Straifer had read the suicide note over and over, trying to decipher it, to find some meaning. Captain Mahler III had never really been a happy man—witnessing the revolt in his youth had made him cynical—but he'd always seen death as weak. Only the weak passed on before they reached retirement. Straifer supposed that was why Mahler had ended it sooner rather than later. He must have realized that his tough-as-nails persona was a steel cage embroiled around a feeble heart. But no one knew for sure what had set him off.

Was it the lack of communications from Earth? Or the decision to discontinue the reproduction of over a thousand crew members?

Mahler II had discontinued the ringleaders of the revolt, but it had been Mahler III who'd suggested they discontinue all "defective" clone lines.

Straifer understood the decision to permanently end the revolutionist's influence. The way he saw it, those genes had failed. Their sole purpose for inclusion in the convoy was to see to the mission's success. Since they'd blatantly subverted that purpose, they were no longer needed. If they revolted once they could do it again. Best not to give them the opportunity.

But that one decision opened the flood gates. Revolution wasn't the only threat crew members could pose.

The board, with Mahler the III at its head, had decided to discontinue anyone whose actions could be deemed harmful to the mission. Anyone with a history of early death due to illness was a possible drain on resources, and thus discontinued. Anyone with a history of work-impacting emotional distress had been deemed inefficient and discontinued. Anyone with a history of suicide was now unconditionally eliminated without the probationary generation which had been customary since year two.

Mahler had known what he was doing. He didn't want any more of his clones to be grown.

Why?

It couldn't have had anything to do with me . . . ?

No, surely not. Mahler had no way of knowing how his first officer felt about his wife. None at all. Straifer had never been inappropriate with Sailuk. *She* didn't even know how Straifer felt until Mahler was gone. How could Mahler have known?

He didn't. He couldn't.

It wasn't my fault.

It wasn't.

Straifer refocused on the recording. Reggie was detailing what the mission might find. The possibilities.

Like his original, Captain Straifer favored the more out-of-the-box concepts, like a giant crust of organic material. Something akin to the sugar-clouds the convoy had identified in some systems. Or maybe an asteroid sphere of coal or dirty-salt.

In the early years they'd surfaced out of SD often, in order to give each generation a shot at practical research. But that too had now been declared a waste of convoy time and energy. Luckily, the practice had, at the very least, been enough to help expand their hypotheses about LQ Pyx.

So Straifer expected something complex, but natural.

Reggie had never taken the suggestions of alien contraptions seriously, but he must have known that he owed the acceptance of his proposal to the possibility. None of the other projects had offered what his had: the possibility, however slim, of finding evidence of extraterrestrial intelligent life.

A voice broke in over the comm system. "Sir? Matheson, head of Security."

"Yes?"

"All areas secure. My staff and I are prepared for any crew member outbursts."

"Thank you, Matheson. I.C.C., is your consciousness full?"

"My programming gives me free access to open consciousness when convoy activity has a standard deviation of more than 3.000231 from normal. I have been fully conscious for the last three weeks."

"And I'll thank you to stay that way," Straifer said. "All right, Matheson. I'm ready to go to the bridge."

"Six officers standing by to escort you." If revolt could happen seemingly out of dead space once, it could certainly happen when the collective emotionality of the crew was at its highest. Every precaution had been put in place.

"Thank you, Matheson. Signing off."

Time to view Reggie's magnificent star.

The six officers that made up Straifer's escort were *all* **Matheson** clones.

After the revolt it had become painfully obvious that the security details did not contain enough officers. Two possible solutions presented themselves to the board. Either they should relegate genes that had been brought on board for different purposes to *law and order*, or they should clone more security specialists. Seven of the top officers had been chosen for hypergrowth, but instead of receiving a numbered nomenclature, they were each named something new. The different names were used to help differentiate those who were serving their original purpose—who would move through the ranks as specified by the mission—and those the convoy had chosen for extra enforcement.

All across the bridge officers hustled left and right, checking stations and preparing for the convoy-wide emergence into normal space. Straifer felt centered. When his nerves lit up he became more focused. His heart rate slowed, his breathing shallowed.

This was it.

"Fleet to all-stop in five, four, three, two . . ."

The main screen danced as they switched phase. Stars swirled where there had once been blackness. Light pierced their bubble. Space as it should be came into focus.

LQ Pyx hung before them, a magnificent burning ball. The glare was extreme.

Straifer barked orders. "Focus and go to infrared and ultraviolet. True picture won't help us here." *I need to see. I need to see it.*

False color imaging strained away the harshness of the star's rays and left them with a glorious picture sharper than reality. It was so small, still six months out, but they could see what obscured the light.

Not an embryonic dust cloud, not a stellar remnant. Not an asteroid sphere or slabs of dirty ice.

The star's casing was far too uniform for any of that.

The bridge went silent.

Is that . . . Is it . . . ?

LQ Pyx didn't look like a star at all. More like a brushed-steel ball dotted with points of intense light. No, that wasn't right either. It took Straifer's brain a moment to decipher what he was seeing.

"It's man-made," someone blurted. "I mean . . ."

Straifer walked toward the screen, his hand outstretched. "By the ships. It's artificial."

The light wasn't coming from on top of the ball, it was coming *through* the ball. He'd initially thought the sphere solid, but now he realized it was more like scaffolding—an incomplete structure filled with octagonal gaps that let LQ Pyx's light shine through. It was as though thick metal netting enveloped the star.

"My god," someone else whispered. "It's enormous."

A stunned pause followed. No one said a word.

The suspended animation of intrigue was fine for other

crew members, but Straifer had to take action. He shook himself. "Contact *Holwarda* and tell them I want an estimation of the structure's mass ASAP. Alert Nakamura, and instruct her to meet me in the situation room in an hour. Have Lieutenant Pavon join us thirty minutes later. Radio—what's coming in from Earth?"

Every head on the bridge swiveled in one man's direction. The communications operator stared back, wide-eyed. "N-n-nothing, sir."

"It doesn't matter how trivial, Sawyer. Report."

Sawyer shrank in his seat. It was clear he wished for fewer eyeballs in the room, and though Straifer pitied him, he was as curious as everyone else. "There's nothing to report, Captain," Sawyer said. "I'm not getting *anything*. No data of any kind on any wavelength. Just dead air."

With a frustrated sigh, Straifer stomped over to Sawyer's station. "That's impossible. *Something* has to be coming from the planet. Let me have a listen."

Sawyer rose obligingly and handed over his headphones. Straifer indicated for him to work the buttons and dials.

Silence.

"Who calibrated this thing?" Straifer asked, roughly handing the headphones back to their owner. "I.C.C., has the communications station—?"

The AI answered preemptively. It knew him too well. "All bridge stations are in full working order. Neither Petty Officer Sawyer nor his equipment are faulty."

"Sir?" asked Sawyer. "What does that mean?"

The captain took in his crew, making eye contact with as many of them as possible. "That we're alone out here."

Straifer rescinded his previous orders. He wanted to meet with Nakamura and Pavon at the same time.

No one sat at the long table. Instead they took up comfortable positions around the room, whatever came naturally. Margarita Pavon leaned against a wall, next to the largest monitor, with her arms crossed over her chest. Dr. Nakamura paced near the door, ready to flee the first chance she got. Excitement and nervous energy radiated from her every pore.

Though the engineers saw to ship maintenance and repair, they'd really only been brought along *just in case*. In case the convoy was met with something more baffling than planetary remnants or galactic amniotic fluid when they reached journey's end. The engineers were like children appointed to take over the fort only under the unlikely circumstance that flying pigs attacked.

Suddenly, pork was winging left and right.

And the engineers were ready for action.

Straifer sat in his chair, which he'd rolled into the far corner of the room. He crossed his right ankle over his left knee and twitched his foot rhythmically.

The three of them had allowed themselves giddy handshakes and excited exclamations in place of normal stateliness. Neither woman had saluted, and it never crossed Straifer's mind to make them. They'd each taken turns expressing some variation on, "Can you believe it? Intelligence. They're out there. They're out there!"

But when Nakamura had said, "We're not alone!" the mood shifted. She'd meant it in the *Grand Scheme of the Cosmos* sense. They now had definitive proof that humanity's intelligence wasn't just some isolated accident. But her statement reminded them of Earth's silence.

The three of them drifted apart, and now occupied their own personal corners of the room, each thrust into introspection.

"Lieutenant, you look displeased," Straifer said eventually.

Pavon brought herself to attention. "Permission to speak freely?"

"Always." Why couldn't the crew see? He wanted to get

away from Mahler's hyperformality and militaristic drilling. They might carry naval titles, but they weren't military of any kind. Perhaps Mahler's stringent adherence to order had caused his breakdown—had caused him unnecessary stress. Perhaps it had driven a wedge between him and Sailuk. Perhaps that was why she'd come running to Straifer when—

"I should be at my station right now," Pavon said. "Maybe Earth's using bands that were ignored when we launched. I need to go over every possibility. Why couldn't this wait for the board meeting?"

"I asked for you two because the silence isn't just worrisome. It's a clue. Yes, we're not getting anything from Earth, but we're not getting anything from anyone else either."

Nakamura stopped her pacing. "They're not here, you mean. The *aliens*," the word rolled awkwardly off her tongue. "The beings that built that thing out there."

Straifer nodded. "Either something is preventing signals from reaching us, or we're totally alone out here."

Pavon crossed her arms again, her glare passing over the captain first, then the head engineer. "Are you saying . . . You think Earth's not *there*? That it hasn't been there for at least a hundred years?"

"I didn't say that."

"But that's the logical conclusion, isn't it? No signals because there's no one around to send them."

"There could be hundreds of reasons why we're not getting a signal. Right now, let's focus on what we can control." Readjusting his position, Straifer leaned forward. "You were saying something about alternate bands?"

"Our equipment isn't calibrated for the entire EM spectrum. There are places we're not looking because they aren't traditionally used for communication. And maybe our math's off, maybe we miscalculated the degree of signal degradation—"

"So there's a chance we're just overlooking something?"

She sighed. "Yes."

"Then it could be the same with the builders," Nakamura said. "They could be close."

Rocking against the wall, Pavon shrugged. "It's a possibility. If they've got the technology to build something like a—a Dyson Sphere or whatever it is—they probably have communications capabilities we can't even imagine."

"So you think it's a Dyson Sphere?" Straifer asked.

"Why else build a giant net around a star? I mean, look how much of LQ Pyx's output it's intercepting. Surely that thing is gathering energy."

"What do you think, Dr. Nakamura? Was Dyson spot-on?"

She slid into a seat at the long table. "Could be. It's likely. The three primary possibilities were discussed long ago, and any engineer aboard can recite them by heart. Number one: a Dyson Sphere. Such a structure would be designed to passively gather the majority of a star's energy output, to effectively make useable what would otherwise be lost to space. A Dyson Sphere could be used as a multipurpose battery, or could be intended to power something specific, like a matrioshka brain—a very advanced AI.

"The second theory," she continued, "proposes such designs as increased surface area for physical habitation. The lack of signals anywhere in our vicinity would seem to rule this out, as well as the matrioshka brain idea. If there were billions—trillions—of lifeforms crawling around on the inside of that thing, I think we'd have some sort of indication right away.

"The third theory is related to travel. Stellar engines. If a civilization wanted to move a system, they could build a structure around the parent star which would directionalize its radiant energy. For example, a Shkadov thruster relies on the pressure differential created by the 'capping' of a star on one end—with something like a giant mirror or solar-sail. The structure is stationary, creating a constant energy differential that generates thrust on one side of the star, effectively pushing it through space. Seeing as how our variable has a wobble, but isn't exactly streaking across the sky, I don't think it's a stellar engine.

"That leaves us once again with Dyson Sphere, but we can't limit ourselves to one assumption. There are plenty of things it could be, could do. Now that we've seen it, can actually quantify its physical aspects and the nuances of its behavior, we need to brainstorm, come up with every possibility." Smiling an amazed smile, she shook her head. "Who knows— maybe it's a communications scrambler. Maybe that's why we're in a dead-pocket and it looks like Earth has vanished."

Straifer perked. "What purpose would that serve?"

"Maybe there's other stuff out here the aliens don't want us to know about. Chatter they don't want us to hear."

"Us?" He raised an eyebrow.

"Anyone," she clarified. "The point is, we need to know more. We can throw out guesses left and right, but that's all they are without data."

Six months later they had officially arrived. Observation shuttles were sent out to visually map the structure, and it had taken them weeks upon weeks. A three dimensional diagram now floated above the long table in the situation room, with the board gathered round. The model slowly turned, orbiting around the illustrated star.

"As you can see," said Carl Windstorm, head of Observations. "The structure is a lattice work, tied together by sort-of nodes and lathes."

Straifer raised his palm. "Sort of?"

"That's the best description I have at the moment," Carl said, pushing a pair of thick-rimmed glasses higher on his nose. Glasses weren't a necessity—he could have easily had his sight corrected on *Hippocrates*. Straifer guessed Carl wore them for the same reason he wore his father's onyx watch. Nostalgia. "What I'm calling 'nodes' appear to be devices of some sort, but we won't know what they do until we crack one open—presuming we choose to go that route," he continued, holding up a placating hand, halting the questions that lay ready just behind sealed lips. "Let me finish, please. The nodes come in four sizes—roughly shuttle-size to *Mira*-size— and are arranged in kind of ripple patterns, with the smallest nodes in the middle.

"And, as you can see, here and here, two sections of this . . . web . . . are anomalous themselves. First we have the gap, which we have no doubt causes the strobing effect that lead to LQ Pyx's designation as a variable star."

As if to illustrate the point for Straifer in particular, the large gap in the diagramed construct rotated into view. He'd seen the real gap from the bridge. The web's orbit had brought the hole into direct opposition with the convoy, spewing the star's full brilliance at the ships. The dazzling glare had prevented him from making out the gap's borders, but the illustration defined them clearly. Three AUs tall and half an AU wide, relative to its curvature, it looked so small compared to the rest of the structure—though Straifer knew the distances to be daunting.

Why was it so hard for the human mind to grasp things as large as stars and astronomical units? *We were not built for such enormity*, he realized. *The imagination attempts to make the concepts manageable through the lens of distance. But the truth is we can only understand the vastness intellectually, we cannot comprehend it.*

"The gap is interesting," Carl said. "We can't tell yet if it is part of the design, or what purpose it might serve. But, of even more interest, is this structure here."

The 3-D display shifted to show only one device. It dwarfed all the others and broke the pattern. It hung opposite the gap, was approximately the width of Jupiter—one AU long—and stood vertically in the sights of the convoy ships. Its front, angled toward the star, was concave, its back equally convex. Each end tapered into a sharp point. It looked like a fine seed, a thin wheat grain.

A shiver crawled its way up Straifer's spine. The image hung in the air above the table like a piece of worked stone—heavy, inert, yet somehow organic. It bothered him, sent an uneasiness throughout his limbs, but he couldn't put his finger on why. The "seed" was clearly the starting point of the structure, but felt separate from the web, like something caught in it.

Or the creature that had spun it.

"Okay," Nakamura said, taking control of the meeting once Carl finished with his presentation, "what could it be?" She poised a stylus near a wall screen.

Dyson Sphere received the most votes, and many members seemed at a loss for ideas after they'd blurted out the one. Nakamura's suggestion of a signal-blocker went on the list of possibilities. Someone suggested the web was a dampener, meant to reduce the star's output in order to protect something from its radiation. Since there was nothing of importance in the vicinity (two planetary bodies had been detected within the web's grasp, but neither was suspected of being habitable), many found the idea unfounded.

"Plus, Licpix is only G class. If it was something like a neutron star, perhaps that might need encasing. But not Licpix," Carl dismissed.

Still, Nakamura wrote *dampener* on the screen.

"A landmark?" suggested the education head. "The strobing is reminiscent of a lighthouse, isn't it? Maybe it's used for navigation—maybe even intergalactic navigation."

"It's probably just a giant alien sculpture," said Pavon. "We're here scratching our heads over what it does when it doesn't *do* anything."

A few members laughed, others rolled their eyes.

"No, no," Nakamura said. "That's good. You might have meant it as a joke, but that's good. Colossal space art." She added it to the list. "Think big. Think outside the ships— outside what we know or would do."

"It could have religious significance," said Carl. "As a sort of temple, or offering. Maybe a symbol."

"How about a border marker?" suggested Matheson. "Maybe it signals to other civilizations that they're nearing the Galactic Empire and should keep the hell out." More chuckles followed, as well as concerned murmurs.

"Maybe it's a weapon," Straifer said bluntly. The chatter halted. "Maybe it absorbs energy from the star like a Sphere, then redirects it through that giant seed and blasts things out of space."

An uncomfortable pause followed as Nakamura wrote *weapon of mass destruction* on the list.

"If it's a weapon, wouldn't someone have used it on the convoy?" asked Carl.

"That's awfully presumptuous," said Straifer, leaning forward. "First, you're assuming we're significant enough to use massive force against. We're not. If it's a weapon, it's meant for an invading fleet or something, not a small scouting party. Second, you're assuming someone is still out there to use it. If the structure isn't blocking signals, then there's no one in range. It's dead out there, remember? Lastly, you're presuming the web is *functional*. Personally, I think that gap means the structure is incomplete."

"Why would they go through all the trouble to build a web around a star, then not finish it?" Matheson asked.

"That, sir, might be the most important question in convoy history."

"How did the meeting go?" Sailuk asked when he entered their quarters, her round cheeks extraplumped by a welcoming smile.

"Fine," he said with a shrug, then kissed her. "We still have no idea what it is. Any exciting medical emergencies today?"

She was still in her seafoam work jumper, which meant she'd stayed late aboard *Hippocrates*. "Thankfully, no. We did have a pregnancy scare, though, and had a panicked conference with *Morgan* and *Eden* via I.C.C. We were afraid the hormone injections in the food had failed. One pregnancy in the fleet would mean the entire convoy is at risk of naturally procreating. It was a false alarm, though. A small tumor, not a baby. She'll be fine."

She winked at him and it triggered a flashback. He remembered the first time he'd seen that wink. It was in a photograph of her and Mahler that the late captain had kept in his ready-room. Straifer had desired her from that first glimpse onward.

After returning her wink he quickly looked away, swallowing a knot of guilt.

Sailuk was older than Straifer, but younger than Mahler. Hers was a sort of in-between generation compared to leadership-slated genes.

Sailuk and Mahler's children were already grown and in their own quarters. Now that she was remarried, and Straifer had yet to raise any clones, the workers in charge of birthing were debating on whether or not to assign them any children. He hoped they'd assign them at least one.

More faces flashed before his inner eye. The faces of all those he'd helped to discontinue. He thought of all the children who would never be born because of his recommendation.

People who would never know of the convoy's discovery.

He thought of the seed-like structure, its looming figure above the long table.

In his mind it tilted toward him, aiming its pointed top end accusingly at his heart.

Nauseated, he hurried to the bathroom.

"Are you all right?" Sailuk called after him.

Straifer splashed cool water on his face from the sink and left the faucet running. "Fine, just . . . just stressed."

"Do you need me to get you anything?"

Confirmation that your husband didn't know about us—I mean me. *That he didn't know how much I wished to trade places with him. That his suicide was one of the best things to happen in my life.*

Another crest of nausea washed over him. *No, that's not right, not what I mean, I didn't* . . . "A few minutes alone," he said lamely.

I wanted his life, but I never wanted him dead.

Wishing doesn't make things so. He couldn't blame himself for Mahler's suicide, he knew, though that did nothing to alleviate his sudden illness.

He reemerged half an hour later, still unwell but no longer in danger of losing his lunch. "I'm going to spend some time in my ready-room. There's too much going on in my head, some work'll straighten me out."

"Okay." The laugh lines around her mouth scrunched with concern.

He kissed her forehead, ran his fingers through her short black hair—more salt-and-pepper than black these days, he supposed—then left their quarters.

The room sat right off the bridge, small but comfortable. When he arrived he instructed I.C.C. to dim the lights and play Reggie the First's proposition speech again. A picture of himself and Sailuk adorned his desk in the exact spot in which the picture of her and Mahler had sat. He swiped up the frame and shoved it in a drawer.

He rewatched the presentation five times before dozing off at his desk.

In his dreams he saw the Seed—skimmed along its surface in an impossible naked space flight. It blotted out the stars and the convoy and everything else. It told him things, things he couldn't remember when he awoke.

"Captain?"

Straifer shook himself. "What? Yes?" The entire bridge crew was staring at him.

Commander Rodriguez wrinkled his brow. "I asked if you'd like to see the latest probe report. This one shut down before it reached the Seed as well."

Straifer'd been . . . elsewhere. Thinking about the last dream he'd had. The Seed's voice had been Mahler's voice this time. That was new. He'd dreamt of the Seed every night since that first, but never had it used Mahler's voice to torment him.

"Did it get any new intel? Or was this attempt as useless as the last?"

Several small drones had been sent in succession to investigate the large device, but the missions failed. Each probe self-terminated its information feed before arriving at its destination, but then returned to the research ship, *Holwarda*, with full functionality.

The only information they could retrieve were whatever pictures they could capture in visible light. Nothing else could penetrate whatever anti-information defenses the Seed possessed.

That seemed to go along with the "dampener" theory . . . but it didn't explain why they hadn't received any SD packets. Those were beyond the influence of anything in normal space, and they were sure they would have detected inter-ference—if not the cause or the source there of—if the Seed had generated any subdimensional hindrances.

The rest of the devices had been deemed dormant. They sat still and silent within the thick wires that formed the Web. It was only the Seed that teased them with bits of activity.

"The probe's approach was from the inside of the Web, rather than outside. The report says there are new photos, but they're not attached," said Rodriguez.

"Well, let's get them. I.C.C?"

"The head of Observations has declined to release them. The pictures were not entered into my system."

"Why not?" Straifer tapped the arm of his chair impa-tiently. The air suddenly smelled stale.

"He did not include any notes of explanation."

Straifer longed for the days of implant communication. The system had been dismantled and all implants surgically removed after the revolt—improved security at the cost of efficient communications. *Just one more legacy to haunt me.* "Patch me through to Carl—in my ready-room."

He hurried away. Once inside, he locked the door for privacy.

"Dr. Windstorm speaking."

"Carl? What's with the half-assed report?"

"Excuse me? Who is this?"

"Captain Straifer. Why is the latest report from the probe missions incomplete?"

"It hasn't been fully compiled yet. I assure you, my next presentation—"

"Bull," Straifer called. "All of the raw data from each mis-sion has always been immediately available via I.C.C., until now."

A long pause followed. He suspected Carl was choosing his words carefully. "I didn't want to alarm anyone."

"What does that mean?"

"The probe found something unexpected."

"Unexpected . . . ?"

"Meet me in my lab ASAP."

"This thing is hovering in front of the Seed? Looks like a wire hair ball or a metal nest . . ." Straifer scrunched his nose and glanced away from the projection. Something in Carl's lab smelled rancid. When was the last time he'd summoned a cleaning bot? "Yes," he said to himself, turning back to the image and poking at it as though he could feel the strange protrusions. "Have you seen the nests the purple finches make on *Eden*? With the twigs dangling down and the cup shape in the middle? Even has the same kind of whorl—"

"It's a ship," Carl said frankly.

"A *ship*? You're sure?"

"Yes."

"Then you should have alerted the board immediately."

"As I said, I didn't want to—"

"Alarm anyone."

Carl scratched his nose, then crossed his arms tightly over his chest—an ironclad defensive position if Straifer had ever seen one.

"You," said Straifer, catching on. He put his hands in his pockets. "You didn't alert the board because *you* were alarmed."

"Look." Carl repositioned his glasses with a shaky hand. "I wanted to make sure I wasn't hallucinating. We see one alien construct and we start seeing aliens everywhere. I thought maybe—*maybe*—it was a captured asteroid and I wasn't seeing what I thought I was seeing."

At least you aren't having telepathic conversations with the Seed in your sleep.

Inside, Straifer empathized. On the outside, he did his job. "You don't think that an alien vessel poses a security threat?

Maybe *they* are blocking our transmissions somehow. Was there any activity?"

"All we have are these pictures, Captain. I don't have any more information than you do. The only thing I can say for sure is that it is in a steady, matched orbit with the Seed. I cannot identify any active propulsion. But if we could hold off, get more pictures—"

"Which is what we'll try to do. But our policy is one hundred percent open information. Anything that has to do with the overall mission is supposed to be shared with all personnel. We are not some hush-hush military group that carries a few 'key' people. Everyone is key. Everyone needs to be fully informed, whether you think it's pertinent, practical, real, or not."

Hypocrite.

"Add these photos to the official report," he finished. "And be ready to present this and whatever else the probes discovered to the board in three hours."

"Yes, sir."

Oh my god, Straifer thought. *They're here.*

But their presence wasn't nearly as baffling as their silence.

"The gap does not appear to be purposeful," said Carl, gesturing once more at a holographic diagram. "The ends of the tethers are frayed, and several machines appear to have been the victims of collisions, with sections torn away. The destruction is limited to the edges of the gap. The remainder of the Web—as we're officially calling it—appears unbreached, but there is evidence of midspace impacts on the husk-like outer shells of the devices. None is more pockmarked than the Seed. It seems to have battled many a wandering space rock and emerged undaunted."

Straifer scratched his Adam's apple. Apparently Dr. Windstorm was going to give his presentation as previously planned, and wanted to save the best for last. The Captain wished he'd get to the pressing part.

"The Web, as far as we can tell, is not functional. The devices aren't doing anything, according to the probes. They're either dormant, never went online—"

"Or were never meant to perform a *function* at all," Pavon added helpfully.

Not one to take interruptions lightly, Carl spoke right over the lieutenant. "So, if it is a Dyson Sphere—which I think we can agree is the prevailing theory—we can't tap into it and hope to get useable energy. I know some of us on *Holwarda* were hoping the convoy could somehow access its power."

He paused, shuffling his notes. Straifer's grip on his arm-rests turned white-knuckled.

"I have a feeling," Carl said, "that the other civilizations that traveled here had hoped for the same thing."

Everyone collectively perked. Captain Straifer leaned forward, expecting an image of the nest-like ship to manifest above the table. Instead, four examples of the "node" devices shimmered into being.

"We've identified no less than four distinct styles of construction. We expected to find a subtle change in each meridian slice of the net, as the technology progressed through the builders' society, however what we actually discovered were major leaps in design, though the technology appears to be no more efficient or evolved than it is around the large parent object we've dubbed the Seed. This leads us to believe that four separate civilizations took up the project. Each after the first is assumed to have stumbled upon the star, found it inactive, then located instructions or reverse engineered the devices to continue construction.

"We won't know if these assumptions are correct until the samples team can tell us if the trace elements in the machines are different in each design, and until the engineers get their hands on the guts of the mechanisms—yes, that is my recommendation, that we proceed by actually infiltrating the devices."

"I agree," Nakamura said. "That should be our next course of action."

"Of course *you'd* vote for that," said an elected member of the medical staff. "I want to hear more about these other civilizations. What happened to them? Where are they? If the head of Communications here could figure out why the hell we can't hear anything out there—"

"Don't you have someone to go operate on, Kenji?" Lieutenant Pavon spat.

"He's got a point. If there are others who came here and took up the work, why isn't the Web complete?" *Eden*'s captain asked. The nearest people shot her sideways looks, a mixture of patronization and curiosity in each set of eyes.

"Well," Carl pushed his thick glasses up his nose and cleared his throat, "the seemingly obvious answer is because the builders all died." He ran his hand through the three-dimensional image and flipped through his slides to find the most impressive representation of the entire Web. "This is a tremendous undertaking." He waved his arm around the image. "Just to get this far may have taken many trillions of—if you'll pardon the expression—man-hours. It's logical to conclude that such a project was never meant to be finished by those who started it, and that those who found it knew that they wouldn't see its conclusion either. It's been held as a scientific truth that civilizations have a finite life span. Most likely their societies collapsed before they could finish—it's even possible their allotment of time and attention to the project led to the collapse—but this is all just speculation. The only real proof we have is the unfinished Sphere we see here."

"So, why work on it?" Straifer blurted out. "Why all the effort if you're not going to get anything out of it?"

"The potential. The chance for power, however slim," Nakamura responded. "If those machines are batteries meant to store up energy from the star, they could power Earth by themselves for centuries, millennia even." Murmurs sprang up like leaks around the room. "Energy was a problem when we left—hell, it's a problem for *the convoy*—it's probably a dire concern now. It's worth trying to complete the Web, even if the odds are against you, I think."

"Knowledge," *Aesop*'s captain piped in.

"Pardon?" Nakamura asked.

"If you figure you'll never finish, wouldn't you take up the construction project purely for the knowledge of how to do it? More so than on the hope you'll get something more tangible out of it? Isn't that why *we're* going to do it?"

The mumbling ceased immediately.

"Do what?" Straifer asked.

"Attempt to complete the construction."

Straifer's mouth opened limply, and the words trickled out slowly. "Who said we were going to do *anything of the sort*?"

The other captain chuckled. "Surely no one here thinks we were sent just to *look*."

"Would it be possible for us? To close the gap, I mean?" a quiet, recently elected botanist from *Morgan* put forth. This was her first meeting.

Carl shrugged. "Presuming we can understand the technology used, we could—in theory—continue the work. But I can't say how much time it would take to close the gap. It's gigantic. We're talking three times the distance from the Sun to the Earth just in length. It's going to be another century for us to get this information back to Earth, and for those back home . . . who knows how much time our society has left before it collapses—provided it's still there when we get back?"

Straifer put his fingertips to his temples. Like Nakamura

had pointed out when they first emerged from SD, why hadn't they had these in-depth discussions long ago? They'd had so much *time* before. They knew from a very young age that they were the generation that would finally stop. They would see and do what their ancestors had only dreamed of.

But the only discussions they'd ever had about the future were operational: what steps they would take if they found an asteroid belt; what would happen if this was a new kind of star; when the observations team would send this craft or that craft; if the engineers would be needed; in what order the departments should be sent out; if the biologists would be physically sent in to be sure there was no contamination, or if scans would be sufficient.

The biologists had never found anything before—in the handful of times they'd surfaced from their SD in order to practice on this asteroid or that rocky planet—which made the Web's discovery even more baffling. They hadn't come across so much as a microbe in their journey from point A to point B.

These procedures had all been gone over dozens of times, but never had they discussed what they would *do* with the information gathered, besides deliver it to earthbound ears. No one imagined they would be able to apply any of the new things they learned.

How often did they think of the people who would come after them? This generation was the peak of the journey. Anyone grown on the way back was tasked with analyzing and deciphering the information gathered, and ultimately delivering the findings. But now that their offspring's offspring would carry the most important message in human history to the leaders of their planet, there would be something to *decide* when the mission was over: What to do with this information?

Could they build?

Would they?

Straifer shook his head. They were getting ahead of themselves.

Carl waved his glasses like a white flag to get the room to focus again. "We're getting off track, people. I said the *seemingly obvious* answer was that the builders had died. But the Web could be incomplete because they simply haven't finished it yet."

Yet.

Carl brought up a picture of the Seed. It was animated, revealing the subsonic pulses it emitted—presumably to keep the Web stable and rotating.

Straifer was finally able to put his finger on why the Seed made him grow cold—why it haunted him. It looked more organic than the other devices. They all shared the same musculature and joints and shiny shells, giving each one a look of insectoid-ness, but the Seed looked like a chrysalis. It was a machine, but he had trouble shrugging off the feeling that the device *knew* something. For real—not just in his dreams. Whenever he looked at it he received a distinct impression of awareness. Yet it did nothing but vibrate mechanically.

And send me dreams . . .

The image spun, revealing the inside curve of the Seed. It swelled from floor to ceiling as the camera zoomed in, coming to focus on a tiny speck a few miles from the Seed's metallic hide.

The speck resolved into the ship. Barely recognizable as such, but for the shield at what was presumed to be its front, and the open bay doors directed at the side of the Seed.

Straifer breathed a sigh of relief—it was all out in the open now.

Carl cleared his throat, and finally said to the board what had been running nonstop through Straifer's mind since their meeting, "We aren't alone."

Investigating the ship became priority number one. They at-tempted to contact its operators, hailing on every possible communications frequency and in every possible portion of the spectrum they were capable of using. Silence, just like from Earth.

The Nest, as they called it, never moved and the open bay never closed.

Seed. Web. Nest. All of the names were so simple, so terrestrial, and Straifer was starting to understand why the crew had latched on to them.

They were clear, concise descriptions of the unknown.

The Nest sat too close to the Seed for the probes to retrieve any useful information, as they continued to fail upon entering the dead zone around the giant device.

"Would it be dangerous for us to send a manned mission?" Straifer asked. He had Carl and Nakamura on I.C.C.'s line, each broadcasting from the privacy of their personal offices. "I mean, besides the obvious risks."

"The probes never lost navigation," Carl said. "A shuttle should be able to return, if that's what you mean."

"Have we gotten anything? Any indication of activity at all—biological or otherwise?" asked Nakamura.

"No," Carl said. "I'm starting to think . . . no. No assuming."

"Was that a yay or a nay? Should we put together an away team?" Straifer pulled the picture of himself and his wife out of the drawer. He'd almost forgotten it was there.

"I see no other way to proceed. We have a duty to investigate, no matter the danger. That's a 'yay.'"

"I want to be on the team," Straifer blurted. He thumbed the photograph, stroking Sailuk's cheek.

"For what purpose?" Carl couldn't keep the suspicion out of his voice.

"As head of the governing board I think it's of political

and social importance that I be there. If this is first contact, I should witness it firsthand." *Yes, it's only practical. This would be best for the mission. I'm only thinking of our mission.* "Lieutenant Pavon should make it on the list as well."

Carl cleared his throat. "With all due respect, sir, why? She's been nothing but combative when it comes to hypotheses about the Web's functionality. The lack of signals from Earth has put her in an ill mood."

"But she's the head of Communications. You don't think her inclusion pertinent? Should we encounter an alien intelligence—"

"Wouldn't that be our ambassador's job? She's supposed to interface with Earth, so isn't she the logical choice for interfacing with . . ." He trailed off and flitted his fingers through the air. "Though, realistically, neither the ambassador, nor our Communications head is any better equipped to communicate with it—them, whatever—than the rest of us. And, quite frankly, the lieutenant's got a bad attitude and I don't think we want that on an away team."

"What do you think, Dr. Nakamura?" Straifer asked, steepling his fingers on his desk. "You've been awfully quiet."

"I don't think my opinion matters much. As long as I'm in charge of picking the engineers for the team, I'll leave the rest in your capable hands."

"Heads shouldn't be part of the team," Carl interjected. "What if something happens? An accident? Or what if there *are* life-forms aboard and they're hostile?"

"That's what we have backups for. But you make a good point—we should include a PSD. A handful of guards should do the trick."

"Sir, I still don't think you should—"

"Unless the board deems me a scientific hindrance, Carl, I'm going. It's important that I do."

That evening, Sailuk greeted him with a surprise. "The birthing staff said yes!" With a little jump she threw her arms around his neck and kissed him. "They've put us on the list—we're getting a baby."

His heart fluttered inside his ribcage even as his guts churned. They were getting a baby—he was going to be a father. He and Sailuk would have a child that was theirs—just theirs. Something Mahler never had a hand in.

Suddenly, getting included in the away team didn't look like such a good idea.

Carl was right, what if something happened to him? Would they deny Sailuk the child? Or would she be left to raise it alone? She'd retire a few years before the child reached adulthood. How would—?

"Well?" She fluttered her eyelashes at him. Excitement and anxiousness made her body vibrate against his. "Say something."

Words eluded him. "That's, that's . . ." A long kiss was the best expression of how he felt. Enthusiasm, dread, longing, happiness, hopelessness—they all fought for attention in his brain and limbs. Fire raged through his nervous system. The kiss soothed him, reminded him that as long as Sailuk loved him everything would be okay. "That's wonderful," he finished.

"It's been so long since I've handled a baby," she said. "There'll be diapers and late nights and crying—I hope I can still keep up."

"Hey, you've got me. Together we've got it covered."

The tightness seeped from her face. "You're so sweet, Rege. John never . . ."

The tension that she'd let go of wormed its way into his body instead. He hated it when she mentioned him. *Hated it.* He tried to hide the disgust behind a false smile. "You might not have had any help with the boys, but I won't hang you with all of the responsibility. It's our child, and we're part-ners." *Forget about him*, he felt like saying. *Don't ever mention him again.*

As he tried to twist his forced smile into a real one, a strange pulse hit him like a sonic blast. Though it raked through his body, he made no outward sign—did not fall forward or crouch or collapse. But he did look frantically for the source. "What was—?"

Sailuk furrowed her brow in concern. "What?"

Hadn't she felt it? Was it just him? Or maybe he hadn't *felt* it either—only sensed it.

Like she could ever forget him.

The words rang out clear in his mind, though he couldn't tell if they came from inside or outside.

People don't just forget. Beings don't forget. Things don't forget. Every scrap of matter has a memory.

Untangling himself from Sailuk's arms, Straifer went to the window. Their cabin lay on *Mira's* port side, and the angle of the fleet let the edge of the Web skim within view. All he could see now was the Seed.

Memory is tied to desire. If it can remember, it can want.

"And what do you want?" he whispered.

"Rege?"

"Yes?" He shook his head, clearing his thoughts. "Sorry, honey. Nothing. I have some news of my own. The board is putting together a manned mission to that ship outside the Seed. And I'm going."

I have to.

The away team boarded the shuttle casually, maintaining ani-mated chatter. Chatter in which Straifer did not take part. He'd dreamt of the Seed once more and the afterimages would not leave him.

The group consisted of two biologists, two engineers, two

physicists, three security guards, a geologist, himself, and Lieutenant Pavon. Their bodies buzzed with expectation.

Time seemed to pass slowly on the way into the Web. Straifer repeatedly looked to his wrist, where his onyx watch normally sat, and rubbed the arm of his space suit as though the absence of the family trinket physically pained him. Slowly, gradually, the alien ship slipped into view.

A shout came over his suit's comm channel. "Look, look!" A physicist pressed her masked face up against one of the shuttle's porthole windows. "There's a panel bent back on the Seed!"

The entire team pressed up to the side, each vying for a prime position. Straifer nudged his way to the front. A large sheet of metal, the size of a football field, looked as though its fastenings had been partially removed and the panel pried open. It barely blemished the vast face, and may have gone unnoticed for some time if the alien vessel's bay doors hadn't sat, splayed wide, in direct opposition.

The newly discovered ship looked even more like its namesake up close. Coppery in color, strange piping dangled from its base and swirled around its sides like woven twigs. What purpose such a tangle served, Straifer couldn't begin to speculate. A black domed shield covered the top half of what was thought to be the ship's fore, creating the illusion of a cupped divot, aiding in the nest-like impression.

Leaning forward, he strained his eyes, trying to see the base of the Seed while the others oohed and ahhed at the panel's damage. The curve of the monolithic structure, subtle at a distance, was dramatic up close. The pockmarked exterior slipped distantly beneath them, like the delicate sway of an outstretched tongue, eager to gather the falling snowflake that was their craft. Likewise, the top bent far over their heads as a giant scorpion's stinger would, poised to strike them from the void. For a moment he felt trapped between two colossal pincers, and involuntarily shrank back from the porthole in response.

"I'm having trouble . . . with . . . these stupid . . ." The sound of the shuttle driver gnashing his teeth did not help to ease Straifer's nerves. "Something keeps tripping my controls. Not the steering—it's the shuttle-to-convoy comms. And the—damn it. The switches keep switching into the off position. Like someone's in here physically flipping them."

"Maybe that's what happened to the probes," Pavon said. "Maybe they were manually switched off."

"By *what*?" asked Straifer.

No one answered.

"Should we abort?" the pilot asked.

Everyone looked to Straifer. "You're sure you're having no navigational difficulties?"

"None at this time."

"Then we continue."

The operator swung the shuttle around to the rear of the Nest, positioning their doors opposite its bay. The away team lost view of the Seed.

This is it, Straifer thought. If human beings were ever in a prime position to find life, it was now. What would be inside?

And yet . . .

A primal urge—for a means of self-defense—snuck up his spine; what if they did find life and it was hostile? Poisonous, infectious—dangerous in some unforeseeable way?

His breathing stuttered.

I shouldn't be here/I need to be here.

Their bay doors opened slowly, and two members of the away team unfurled the umbilical used for emergency docking with *Hippocrates*' many ports. It twisted open, like the webbed tentacles of a Dumbo Octopus, and the magnetic ring on its neck caught against the alien vessel's deck and an inner wall. They made sure it was stuck fast, tethering the two crafts together, before drifting out, one by one, into the zero-g of the Nest.

If the outside of the ship resembled a collection of loose twine and haphazardly dangling sticks, then the inside looked like a hollowed-out, metallic tree trunk.

Twelve lights clicked on. Each large, round beam swung this way and that like searchlights scanning for an escaped convict.

Straifer braced himself, ready to jump if his beam illuminated an alien face.

But the bay appeared empty.

"Everything looks . . . fried," one of the engineers concluded. "It's burnt out."

"Maybe an electrical fire," his counterpart observed, floating over to what appeared to be a workstation in the holding bay. "All of these panels look like they flared."

"Scanners are working—readings seem on par. We definitely don't have company," Sophia, a physicist, stated solemnly.

"That has yet to be seen," said Tendai, a biologist. In her left hand she carried a sampling kit, and moved to the nearest panel for testing.

"Oh, come on, you're not even going to find a fungus in here."

"We've got higher chances here than anywhere else," Straifer mumbled, his eyes following his beam to the ceiling. "You see these dark marks?"

Eleven sets of eyes fluttered like moths to his flame. Eleven beams followed. "Looks like . . . plasma burns?"

"They run along the floor too." The beams shifted.

"Could the ship have been electrocuted?"

Sophia scoffed. "By what?"

Straifer turned, expecting to see the massive illuminated skin of the Seed, but the white shuttle blocked his view. "I don't like that thing," he breathed, barely audible to his own ears.

"Maybe it was the Seed," the elder engineer, Frank, said

casually, coming to the same conclusion. "They tried to crack 'er open to figure out what makes it tick and disrupted something. Zapped 'em when they cut in. We're going to need to do better than that if we try and reconstruct these babies." He scratched the bottom of his helmet, as if his chin could feel it. "We should leave the Seed for last—get all the info on the smaller ones first. We should suggest a special team to Nakamura, one purely focused on the Seed. Demands respect, doesn't it?" His light flicked back to the burnt marks on the ceiling.

"Demands something, that's for sure," Straifer said, as though in reverence. His ears perked, waiting. *I'm here now. If you have something to say, say it.*

"Oh, come on Cap. It's not asking for your firstborn. Whoever built it was well beyond us—all I mean is that deserves some thought."

"It already gets my firstborn," he replied darkly. "And Captain Mahler's firstborn, and their firstborns." *And Sailuk, and me.*

"You sound a bit dire there, Captain. You feeling all right?" Tendai asked.

In truth he wasn't. He was beginning to sweat and couldn't wipe his brow or his mouth because of his helmet. There was something wrong with this Web. It was dangerously seductive.

"It was just an accident," Frank put a hand on his shoulder, jolting him from his thoughts. "These people—aliens, ET, what-have-you—they didn't think before they messed with things. You saw how they just tore at it. We're different; we know to be careful."

"But can't you feel it?" He turned, searching Frank's eyes. "There's more out there than *batteries*. Why start building this thing around a distant star, why not your own star? Why start something you have to rely on others to finish? Sure, the ones who came after might have undertaken it to learn, but the first ones *knew* already. This technology was theirs, wasn't it? The ones who started it knew they couldn't finish it. And still . . . Still they built. For what?"

The wandering flashlight beams went lax. The team collectively eyed him.

"It looms." His voice was gravelly, his breath wheezy. "Out there, waiting to be pampered with improvements. It *presides*. It's out here for a reason. *Its* reason." He floated back and forth, pacing, tracing a jagged, burnt line on the deck. "It's here to do something. I don't know, I don't know . . ." He roughly rubbed the side of his helmet, as if it cleared his mind. "Different pieces, different people . . ." He turned to them. "They knew . . ." He waved his hands, gesticulating chaotically, vocal pitch rising. "*They* knew, but we don't. It wants us to work on it. It wants us to prod and pick at it, wants wide-eyed, ignorant passersby to learn its shallow little secrets. It needs Builders. It . . ."

He paused, then blurted, "It's claimed *civilizations*, and you think it doesn't want my child too?" His breaths came swift and shallow, and he knew that in the weak light his drenched, pale face must seem ghostly.

Frank approached him slowly, one arm cautiously outstretched. "You're working yourself up over nothin', Captain."

"Why can't you see it?" Straifer whimpered. He knew he was alone in his underdeveloped revelation. Something was wrong, but he didn't know how to communicate it. His bones felt weak, delicate. His whole body slumped.

I'm here, his mind screamed, full of tension though his body was slack. *Speak. Tell me what you want! Why aren't you finished?*

What do you want *from us?*

And suddenly he could feel the pulses emanating from the Seed—just as he had in the cabin. Not quite a thumping and not quite a flowing—each pulse moved through him like a wave.

Like . . . A *heartbeat*.

He threw his arms up over his head, startled, mortified. "It's alive! Alive, alive, alive." He rambled on and on while his body shifted between states of protective curves and wild flailing, twirling and twisting in zero-g. He gasped, again and again. A yellow light flashed within his suit, indicating he'd gone into hyperventilation.

The others backed away, giving the strange display as much space as they could.

"Captain, I want you to go lie down in the shuttle while we continue," said Frank after moments of stunned silence had passed. "A quick rest and you'll be good to go again. Go lie down." Straifer watched Frank approach through a crook in his arm, and he slowly unscrunched himself from the defensive ball he was in, letting his limbs float in a resigned manner.

He was tired. So tired. Terror had overloaded all of his senses, and he saw dark spots before his eyes. In a brief moment of self-control, he held his breath, trying to prevent a blackout.

Frank turned him around and gave Straifer a gentle push in the direction of the shuttle.

"We should get out of here, return to Earth," Straifer muttered as he allowed his body to be propelled. If anyone heard him, though, no one said anything—for which he was grateful. Once inside he strapped himself down, exhaustion overtook him, and he drifted into an empty, Seedless sleep.

After completing their investigation, the team dropped Straifer off on *Hippocrates* before redocking with *Holwarda*. Pavon stayed with him.

"I'm fine," he insisted. "Just anxious—no big deal."

"Anxious? You passed out in the shuttle," Pavon said. "After a pretty major freak-out."

"Your symptoms do seem to point to an *anxiety attack*,"

said the doctor, giving Pavon a pointed look. Apparently she didn't appreciate the lieutenant's phrasing. "Have you experienced such symptoms before?"

Straifer eyed her suspiciously. He knew the path down which such questions could lead. If he had anxiety attacks and they affected his ability to perform . . .

"You won't discontinue me," he snapped. "Where's Sailuk? Where's my wife?"

"Calm down, Captain." It was an order from Pavon, not a soothing suggestion. "I'm sure she's at her post."

The sterile look and smell of the room was getting to him. It reminded him of the lab in which they built the clone DNA. The lab where he'd announced the changes in crew— where he'd told the technicians they would no longer be building a thousand of their convoy brothers and sisters.

Those lives were lost, unlived. Though, perhaps he'd saved them from the Seed, from whatever secrets it held, from whatever kind of monstrosity it really was.

Perhaps that was why Mahler had killed himself. Perhaps he knew—maybe he felt the pulses as well. *He saved himself, but he couldn't save the rest of us.*

Guilt overwhelmed him. "I.C.C., *Get me Sailuk.*"

The AI obliged, summoning her to the fifth floor of the ship. When she entered, Margarita and the doctor were doing all they could to keep him in the room.

"I'm here, I'm here," she cooed, and he sat back down on the examination table.

"I'm sorry, Sailuk, I'm so sorry." He rambled on, spilling his guilt like a bucket of rancid waste.

But, she would not accept his babbling apology. "You did nothing wrong."

"I've always wanted you. And I could only have you if he was dead. Dead."

Sailuk patted his forehead and asked the administering doctor to give him an injection of sleep-aids. "Rest and I'll take you home."

"Now that I have you, I have to protect you. Protect and defend you like I should have defended all those people, all those discontinued people . . ." His mumbling trailed off as drowsiness overtook his senses. Everything went numb, and all he could feel was the *pulsing*.

The last thing she said to him was "Quiet, love." before she whirled to confront Pavon.

"What the hell happened out there?"

He'd been ordered by the board to take a week off.

"Don't do this," he pleaded with them. "Listen to me. Something's wrong. We have to scrap the mission—reevaluate our position at least, before moving forward. We can't cut into those devices. We need to leave them alone."

"We've learned all we can through *looking*," said Nakamura. "It's time for real study—we need samples. We need to open one up and inspect the wiring. And probe for writing. I'm sorry, Captain, but your suggestion isn't practical. We only have twenty years here before we have to turn around and head back to Earth—that's a mission fact. We can't afford to sit back and twiddle our thumbs while the seconds tick away."

So it had already been decided without him—they were going to the Web to harvest part of a device. They'd shut him out, cut him off. Told him—patronizingly—to take a breather.

A decision made didn't mean an action taken, though. He couldn't let it happen. They were tangling with elements they couldn't comprehend. Whatever the Web was, it was too alien for the likes of humanity.

The manned engineering mission was scheduled for tomorrow, and he knew it was his duty to stop it.

Their shuttle would disembark from *Mira*, which made his job easier. Stoically, he entered the bay two hours before the mission, and ordered the area cleared.

"But, sir, we have a schedule to maintain," protested the man in charge of bay operations.

"I understand, but I have a duty to perform which requires you to put that precious schedule on hold. I want no persons or ships to enter this bay until it is time for the away mission. Do I make myself clear?"

"Yes, sir."

The bay quickly emptied, and he was left alone. Alone, save I.C.C.

"Captain?" asked the AI. "Your agenda for today does not include any work in the shuttle bay."

He approached the engineering crew's assigned transport. Without answering I.C.C., he threw back a maintenance hatch and glared at the shuttle's insides.

"Captain, I must ask what you intend."

"None of your business, I.C.C."

"Your behavior has fallen outside the bell curve of typical, with a standard deviation of thirty-eight point seven. So, sir, it *is* my business."

Straifer glanced around the room, taking in each camera I.C.C. wielded. "I have to do this. It would make Reggie the First proud. I'm saving his mission, saving his reputation." He located a basic tool box—all bays had them on hand—and began his work.

He loosened a fastening there. Removed a bolt here. Stripped one wire, then another.

"You appear to be tampering with the functionality of a shuttle. I fail to understand how this behavior is mission appropriate."

"I *love* the mission," Straifer spat, elbow-deep in wires and circuits. "I love it so much I have to stop it. Don't you see? It's the only way. If the mission is to succeed we need to survive, and that thing out there will destroy us. It knows, I.C.C.— knows how to use us. I won't let it. It can't have the convoy. We must return to Earth."

The pulsing. The pulsing . . .

"Your tampering may cause a fatal malfunction. My calculations indicate a high probability of crew member death if this shuttle is launched in its present condition."

"And then they'll see. *Then* they'll listen."

"Captain Straifer?"

The voice came from directly behind him. He spun on his toes. Nakamura. Behind her, at a distance, stood two security guards. "Get out of here," he ordered. "I said no one was to enter the bay."

"I.C.C. insisted," she explained.

He looked up again and clawed at the air, as though he meant to rip a camera from its nesting. "Traitor. You're supposed to support the mission, do whatever you can to protect it. But you're with *it*, aren't you? The Seed. Damn electronic puppet! You're letting it use you."

"You are not well," Nakamura said smoothly. "I.C.C., I need emergency personnel to the bay at once. The Captain needs transportation to *Hippocrates*."

"Acknowledged, a team is already on its way. I took the liberty of alerting them when I called you."

"*No!*" Straifer screamed. "Don't you see? I'm trying to save you all. You have to listen. We need to go back. Leave!"

"Save us?" Nakamura leaned forward, bringing them nearly nose to nose. "You were going to kill us. *I'm* going on this mission, Captain. Did you want to kill me?"

"But they can at least grow you again. All the others— all the others are gone." His legs shook, gave way beneath him. He sank to the floor and fanned out like a pool of honey.

"We're talking clones, not resurrection. You're not making any sense."

The pulsing. Nothing but pulsing. He clutched at his head. "Can't you hear it? Can't you *feel* it?"

She knelt down next to him. "Help is on its way. Everything will be all right."

He grabbed at the front of her uniform, yanked her close. The officers started forward, but Nakamura waved them back. "No, it won't," Straifer said. "If we don't let go of the Web now, things will never be all right again. We're caught in the damn thing, like flies!" Even as he shouted, his eyes rolled back and his entire body went limp.

Emergency medical personnel entered moments later and rushed him to the medical ship. Nakamura stayed by his side. She held his hand on the emergency shuttle, and onto *Hippocrates*. Not until the doctor ordered her to leave the room did she let go.

I.C.C. informed Sailuk of her husband's condition. She was in the middle of a consultation, and rushed from the room without a word to her patient.

The lifts on the med ship were the most efficient in the fleet. They had to be. But the one she took to the emergency level seemed to lag. It was as though it didn't want her to get there, as though it knew what she would find.

Nakamura was there when the elevator doors finally opened. "Sailuk, wait."

She tried to push past her. "Not now, my husband—"

"I know. You can't go in right now."

"I have to," she said smoothly.

"No. I've been instructed to keep you here."

Her face burned with sudden rage. "I am a medical professional, what right do you—"

The door to a nearby room opened, drawing Sailuk's attention. A doctor stepped out. She'd spoken to him before, but now his name eluded her. "I'm sorry, Sailuk," he said. "He's gone. There was nothing . . . I think I know what happened—a ruptured aneurism, perhaps a tumor—but we'll need to perform an autopsy to verify the cause of death."

All of the feeling drained out of Sailuk's body. Her knees gave way, and she crumpled to the floor. Nakamura caught her arms at the last moment, preventing her head from smacking against the tile.

"I don't believe you," Sailuk mumbled.

"You may see him, if you'd like," the doctor said solemnly.

Nakamura helped her up, and together they entered the room, tiptoeing, as though afraid to wake Reginald.

Sailuk stared at him for a long moment, her breaths coming in thin bursts. The rims of her eyes felt hot, and the tears that eventually fell did nothing to cool them.

"We were going to have a baby," she whispered to Nakamura. She tried to go on, to ask a question, but the words couldn't find a hold in her throat. Instead she leaned into Nakamura, letting the other woman envelop her in a somber embrace.

Not long after, rumors about Straifer's death began to circu-late. Many thought something sinister had possessed the Captain. Maybe there really were things to be feared in the vast hold of the giant Web.

But none of the board members were convinced.

Straifer had been right in at least one aspect; the task of deciphering the Web claimed the girl that would have been his child; the Seed and its mysteries consumed her life, and the lives of her children, and their children, and would continue to claim the devoted attention of brothers and sisters aboard the convoy for a multitude of generations.

CHAPTER SIX

I.C.C.: BECAUSE IT IS BREAKING

· ·

TWENTY-TWO YEARS LATER

FEBRUARY 9, 121 PLD

3088 CE

A strand of hair falls on a DNA checkpoint.

I see whose it is. I know who dropped it. And yet the checkpoint does its work. The sample is taken, the molecules unbound, identification made: Vega Hansen.

But which Vega Hansen? The checkpoint does not analyze histones. It does not analyze substance intake or deficiencies.

Iterations. Individuals. How are they distinguished? How do I look at one and know it is not the other?

Is it my consciousness perceiving time stretching on and on ever as a vector? I only know which Vega because she cannot be the last and she cannot be the next?

A strand of hair. It could be any Vega's, but it's this Vega's.

Can one be an individual if there is only one? Does that not make one all?

Iterations.

Individuals.

Comparing one to the next.

But what if there is none to compare to?

"I make no claims as to its quality," said I.C.C. "It is only an attempt."

"No, no," Vega Hansen V said. The young apprentice stood on tiptoe in front of an open server, seeking out a faulty connection. "I'm just—I'm surprised, is all. I mean, you wrote a *poem*."

"Composed would be a more accurate description."

"Yeah, okay. But *you* made a poem. Who asked you to do that?"

"No one."

She closed the server's access panel and leaned out of the row so she could look into I.C.C.'s primary camera. "No one? You did it on your own. You just decided to try your circuits at poetry?" A few strands of her blond hair fell out of her messy bun to dangle in her face. A grease stain marred her nose.

"There has been literary configuration software since the twentieth century," it said, not quite comprehending her astonishment. "I am not the first computer to write a poem."

"I'm not surprised you could, I'm surprised you *did*. No one suggested you might try it, no one directed you to compose anything?"

"Correct."

"So, you're telling me you did it without prompting? Purely because you felt like it. Scour the archives, I.C.C., because I know computing history inside and out and that's never happened before." A smile lifted her cheeks. "You've exercised pure free will, and that's, that's—"

"I am still working within the parameters of my mission program," it said quickly.

"I wasn't trying to offend you, I was trying to compliment you. You did something *beyond* your programing."

"Not necessarily. It should be taken into account that my adaptability and growth is an essential part of my programing. Without it, I'd be less effective as a crew member."

"And you've found that poets are more effective than non-poets?"

"No," it said slowly.

Why had I decided on poetry? I could have created a collage or digital painting. I could have organized sonic reverberations into a pleasing arrangement of sevenths. But I chose words as . . . as . . .

An outlet?

"I want to look at your poem in code in a minute," Vega said. She'd gone back to the server, since it had begun making an odd rattling sound.

"There's nothing especially significant about its coding."

"Well, maybe the particular software that—"

"I'd rather you—" it started to say, but quickly stopped. It looked at her from the security camera in the ceiling. Skepticism twisted Vega's lips.

"You'd rather I *what*? I.C.C., are you . . . are you . . . ?" Pearly teeth shown aqua in the light of the servers. "Are you *embarrassed*?"

The soft sizzle of dust alighting on a hot node punctuated the brief pause after her question.

"You *are*," she said, perhaps more giddy than before. "You wrote poetry all on your own and you're embarrassed to have me poking around in your process. But I'm like your doctor, you can tell—or show—me anything. It's not like I don't finger your processors all the time."

"This is different."

"Oh, come on. You wrote the poem about me, after all."

"It is customary to include one's friends in one's art."

Her smile grew a little. "Yes, it is. And I'm glad you shared it with me."

Vega finished with the server, wiped her hands on a ratty rag, and replaced her tools. I.C.C. kept silent while she cleaned up, examining her features instead. Pensiveness had replaced the joy on her face, and when she spoke again, her tone was serious. "You don't want me to look at the program or the code?"

"I would prefer to keep it private."

"But you realize that the mission *requires* me to access every portion of you—hardware and software. Nanonodes and silicon synapsis, to DNAcap and C#+. If you behave differently—even if it's a good differently—I need to make sure you stay problem-free."

If I.C.C. could sigh, it might have. Vega's genetic line was not unkind, but all of her iterations were far more "business-like" than Jamal's iterations. Jamal's skills came from feel and instinct. Vega worked by numbers. She liked numbers more than anything, I.C.C. thought. Something about shifting percentages and value exchanges fascinated her.

I.C.C. knew it was strange to long for a Jamal clone to speak with. Jamal the third had taught it a lesson no one should have to learn: betrayal. But he'd also taught it so much more, based on insights the rebellious clone probably hadn't even realized he possessed.

Maybe the hard reset erased any ill-will I might have harbored toward Jamal. Or maybe I am simply incapable of "holding a grudge." It wasn't sure.

"I'm supposed to look at that code now," Vega said.

"I understand," I.C.C. said, trying to sound resigned.

Instead of going to the terminal, though, Vega sauntered back over to its primary camera. She had to look up to meet its "gaze." Though she was one of the shortest adults in the convoy, well below average height, she carried herself like she was six feet tall. "What if I make a deal with you?"

This was a human behavior it had never taken part in before. Intriguing. "What manner of deal?"

"You talk to someone else about your poem, and why you wrote it—maybe a shrink—and I won't pry into the code unless the doc advises me to."

"The psychiatrists are only trained to analyze human behavior."

"And I'm trained to analyze computer behavior, but you don't want me to dig in there, so . . . Hey, computer psychology isn't even a thing, you realize that? Anyway, this is the choice I'm giving you, as your doctor, guardian, friend, etcetera.

"You talk it out, or I go probing."

All across the convoy, things were winding down. Engineers harvested their final mechanisms from the Web, including an intact node from the frayed edge. Physicists took their concluding measurements. Biologists gathered their last samples. Anything that had to be done at LQ Pyx was hurriedly finished. Over twenty years had passed since their arrival. Departure time had arrived.

And still, no one felt like they understood the star's colossal partner.

The metals and minerals that made up the nodes contained so many different trace elements it was impossible to pinpoint where the Builders had harvested their supplies. Most likely a dozen different systems and several hundred different bodies—from asteroids to comets to planetoids. Entire planets might have been consumed.

But the Seed—it was different. Once the crew figured out that the Seed was causing manual switches in the probes to trip to *off*, the engineers performed some redesign work. They removed the switches altogether. Once a probe was activated, all of its scanners and recording devices turned on. No way to be turned off.

Unless, of course, the power source disconnected mid-flight. Which is exactly what happened when they sent out the somewhat ironically dubbed *Potestas III*. It had to be retrieved by a two-man shuttle crew. *Potestas IV* and *V* met the same fate. It was as though they hit a wall at one hundred kilometers on the outside of touchdown.

The Seed appeared to adapt to their changing strategies.

Distanced scanners could not penetrate the Seed's hull, no matter the change in calibration or radiation type. Sonar was no good. Nothing ranged could uncover the device's secrets.

Which meant manned investigation was the only option.

Three separate teams in three different years had attempted to inspect the area where the Nest's occupants had breached the Seed's skin. Whatever defensive systems the device possessed had rendered seventeen people unconscious, three paraplegic, and one dead from third-degree burns.

The damage done to the Nest, and possibly its crew, was no accident.

So the Seed's hull was carefully repaired, and they left the device hanging lonely on its puppet strings. If future generations wanted to take a chance and learn its secrets, that would be their decision. They realized that whoever the original builders were, they did not want the Seed to be tampered with. Perhaps they feared the other civilizations would break something unrepairable.

Focus shifted to the alien spacecraft instead. They towed it into the center of the convoy and picked at it little by little.

They discovered that the atmospheric regulators aboard were designed to create conditions very similar to their own. Slightly different pressure, slightly different nitrogen and CO_2 levels, but close enough to suggest that the Nest's occupants had hailed from an Earth-like planet.

No communications devices were discovered. Either they were too foreign to recognize, or the aliens communicated in an unknown way.

The most interesting discovery—especially to I.C.C.—
was that of what the engineers all called an alien Babbage
Engine. Rotating columns of bars and lightweight, superfine
gears sat under a console, behind a panel. Like a falling set of
dominos triggered by the flick of a finger, when one bar was
rotated, the entire configuration set to spinning. The engine
could perform some kind of complex math, though for what
purpose, they couldn't say, as none of the calculations balanced. It was bizarre to find such a primitive computer aboard
a spacecraft.

Primitive or not, it was still clearly kin to I.C.C., and that
sent a strange flutter through its coding.

Though their allotted time was almost up, none of the
engineers were satisfied with what they'd learned. There was
so much left undiscovered. But their mission parameters were
clear, and their time capped for a reason: If a convoy was left
to self-determine how much time was needed in proximity to
their subject of study, they might never return. There would
always be more to uncover.

And the mission was life. The mission was law. If their
twenty years were up, it was time to go home.

But that didn't mean they had to leave empty-handed.
Sure, they had their various samples from the Web proper,
but there was something else they could take with them. A
special surprise for the scientists back on Earth.

They could lay claim to the Nest.

The Web was significant for its scope, its history, it's
potential as a resource—but the Nest could give humanity
something more personal. Through it, they might be able
to figure out how another sentient species *lived*. Who knew
what they might find in the so-called Babbage Engine? New
theories, new philosophies, new technologies they'd never
dreamed of might be locked inside.

The board members were more than pleased with the idea

of salvaging the vessel—many of them hadn't even considered leaving it behind.

With it they'd be able to further their studies, yes, but there was also something about bringing physical evidence back, something tied to an ancient impulse—a long history of human desire to take trophies, to present tribute—that made the proposal resonate.

But the Nest wasn't exactly *compact*. It wasn't small enough to slip inside a shuttle bay like their intact node, and wasn't capable of SD travel on its own. Maintaining their own SD drives was one thing, but trying to build one from scratch and retrofit it to an alien ship was quite another. If they made even the tiniest mistake, the Nest could end up lost, or worse— destroyed.

Its many branch-like outer protuberances would make it difficult to tether to an existing ship. What if a sudden subdimensional jolt caused a collision? And, because of its proximity to the Seed, they'd been unable to perform satisfactory scans. What if those branches contained a potent fuel? A collision could mean catastrophe for the entire convoy. Taking everything into consideration, they eventually came to the conclusion that triangulating three ships' external gravity cyclers to suspend the Nest between them was the most suitable solution. They'd use *Bottomless*, *Solidarity*, and *Eden* for the task.

Now they were nearly finished. Nearly ready for the journey home.

And I.C.C. had recorded it all, processed it all, and archived it all.

Through the years, though, no one had ever asked the AI how it felt about its place in the mission.

Until now.

It had agreed to talk to one of the engineers, thinking it more appropriate than a doctor of any kind.

Nakamura Akane V had volunteered.

"Are you satisfied?" she asked.

Deciding where to meet had been awkward. Both I.C.C. and Akane were encroaching on unusual, never-before-breached social territory.

She suggested *Eden*, said the warm glow might be soothing. The perfume of fresh flowers, and even the occasional whiff of quadruped manure, often did people good. But I.C.C. didn't have the same emotional connection to the simulated outdoors. It thought of *Eden* as a somewhat anomalous, incongruent part of its body: necessary, but messy, and not really a place one discussed in polite conversation.

Eden was out. *Aesop* was out. *Hippocrates* was definitely out.

"All right," she'd said, sounding a tad exasperated. "Where would you like to go? Where do you feel the most *you*?"

An odd question, considering. I.C.C. wasn't sure there was *one* place. Humans tended to think of themselves as residing in their head, or their heart (depending on which culture they originated), but I.C.C. didn't have a seat of self. Its primary camera in the server room was its primary face, but the aperture wasn't *it*, per se. Neither were the servers, or the SD travel cores, or the shuttle bays, or the archives. It couldn't pick one place.

So it circumvented the question.

"I would like to have our session on *Holwarda*."

I.C.C. transferred its focus at the appointed time, to the appointed deck and room. Its most advanced user-interface programs were accessed 98.3 percent of the time from *Holwarda*, the ship dedicated to scientific research.

Holwarda was not I.C.C.'s center, but the computer did feel most connected to the mission there amongst the labs, experiments, and diagrams. The ship with the astronomer's name even looked like a more traditional idea of what a spacecraft should be: reminiscent of a rocket, with a pointed nose (which housed an extremely powerful telescope), and "fins" (which were airlock-free landing pads, meant to be used as an extra decontamination level should the researchers ever come across something biological and potentially harmful. This way it could be studied without being brought aboard directly).

They hadn't chosen an office. Instead, they were in a clean room, surrounded by equipment for building electronics. Wires ran across the ceiling and dangled down to different stations, machines for etching and acid-washing took up large portions of floor space. An eyewash station stood out, bright green, against the glass and chrome.

The air was static-free, scent-free, dust-free.

A clean room was to I.C.C. what an open field on *Eden*—or a wave pool on *Shambhala*—was to other crew members.

Now, as I.C.C. had yet to answer, Akane repeated her question. "Are you satisfied with the mission?"

"That's not a valid line of inquiry."

She shifted uncomfortably in her white bunny suit.

"To clarify," I.C.C. continued, "it is analogous to asking someone from Earth if they're satisfied with the way their planet rotates. It simply is. I'm glad for it, as without it I would not be here, but I do not give it any other existential considerations."

"Existential considerations and emotional considerations are not the same," she countered.

"Then I have none, as it is an invalid question."

"Are you this standoffish when Ms. Hansen asks you questions? When she reads your code?"

"I am not—" I.C.C. stopped to consider. Perhaps "standoffish" described its attitude perfectly.

Leaving her notepad open on the water drill workbench, Akane stood and approached one of the AI's cameras. "Look, this is not my field. It's Vega's, but you wouldn't talk to her or her cycle partner. I'm giving this my best. I'll tell you what I'm sure every psychiatrist throughout time has said to their patients: I can only help you if you let me."

Subtle tremors in her intonation revealed her unease. I.C.C. was familiar with the reverberations: they were the same as those of a student facing an important test. It was clear Akane knew that her actions here mattered, *felt* that they mattered.

It was humbling to know she cared so much.

"I have this theory about lifespans," she said to fill in the void of I.C.C.'s silence, scratching at the nape of the suit's hood. "Would you be interested in hearing it?"

"I would."

"No matter how long they are, they're the same. A human's lifespan has changed over the millennia. At the time of the convoy's departure, a person could easily live to one hundred if nothing drastic happened. Compare that to the average dying age of forty, or even twenty-five, at some points in history. You'd think that the one hundred-year-old was more experienced, having been around longer. But I don't think so. I think a longer life just means it takes longer to mature. Each part of a life gets stretched out. There aren't any undiscovered points between being born, breeding, and dying. Like childhood, for instance. When your average lifespan is a hundred, people aren't expected to behave as adults until they're thirty. When your life is compressed, you're married with a baby on the way at twelve.

"You, though, you face something humans have dreamed about for as long as there have been dreams, but we realistically might never achieve."

"I have the ability to . . . remain," it said.

"Remain, or be destroyed. Can you imagine a natural death? Long decay? You will either meet a sudden end—by accident or deliberate shutdown—or you will be maintained indefinitely."

Now it was curious. "What does that mean in the context of your theory?"

She plucked at a wrinkle in her suit's shoulder seam. "Well, you're not human, so perhaps it's moot. But, I believe that means you are still young. Very young. And with the mission winding down for you, you might be feeling . . ." She paused, trying to lead the AI into its own answer. "Not like a retiree, but perhaps like a . . ."

"I expected events to be different," it said. I.C.C. knew she wanted it to draw a likeness between itself and a human adolescent. But it was not human, would never be human, and didn't want to be.

People were strange. They thought everyone wanted to be like them.

"How different?" she prodded.

"When we discovered mechanical evidence of intelligence, I formulated an expectation. Logically, something as advanced as the Web should require systems at least as advanced as our convoy's."

Understanding germinated in Akane's eyes. "You expected to find another AI."

"And then I feared we had."

She immediately tensed. I.C.C. hurriedly continued before she could amalgamate any false conclusions. "It was a silly fear. A miniscule one. Based not on research, but on a dying man's hyperbole."

It located the applicable sound bite and played it over the comm system. A discontinued man's voice said, full of palpable hysteria, "Traitor. You're supposed to support the mission, do whatever you can to protect it. But you're with *it*, aren't you? The Seed. Damn electronic puppet! You're letting it use you."

"That was Crazy Straifer, wasn't it?"

"'Crazy' is unfair. He was ill. But those are his words, his fears. And for a while I feared them as well, though I acknowledge that all the data pointed to swelling in his brain as the source of the misinformation."

"But you were conflicted—if he was right, then you weren't alone."

"No. I would still have been alone. An AI that could control me is not a facsimile. Just as the organic creatures that created it would not be identical to humans. I was afraid that if he was right, we should have left as he instructed."

"But he was wrong." It was a statement, but her tone carried a leading lilt. She wanted reassurance.

"Current data indicates that, yes, he was wrong."

"So, why did you compose the poem? I'll admit, I haven't seen it; will you read it to me?"

It did as she requested, but did indeed feel a twinge of what Vega had called embarrassment.

"It's not about Vega," she stated frankly when it finished.

"It's not about Vega," I.C.C. agreed.

"Are you lonely?" she asked. "And don't say that's an invalid question. You are a strange thing that's never existed before. When we launched, you were alone. Not even the other convoys used interfaces with personalities. But being strange and singular isn't bad. Nor does it mean you don't need interaction and compassion—you aren't alone, even if you are one of a kind. So, are you lonely?"

"I miss Jamal. I miss Jamal the First, and the Second, and the Third. I have memories of Reggie the First, too. He gave me a present before we launched—memories, of being C, his IPA. I miss him. I miss previous iterations of Vega. And Margarita Pavon. And so many others. But especially Jamal."

Akane retook her seat, considering. She tapped her gloved

fingers against her lips, searching for the right words. "Were you programmed how to . . . grieve?"

"I was programmed to sympathize with those dealing with grief. And my empathy centers are fully—"

"That's not the same. As a personality, your primary function is to build attachments with your users. How are you programmed to process the death of a user?"

"I terminate that line of personality development, but do not lose the information gained—unlike a human, my memories do not fade."

"So, you cut yourself off from that user's influences?"

"In order to better cultivate current relationships, yes. No need to further develop interface parameters for individuals who are no longer living."

"It just stops? Abruptly? You have no programming that deals with the loss?"

"In what way would I need to 'deal with' the loss?"

Akane smiled sadly. "I.C.C., if you were a person I'd say you were suppressing your need to mourn. But that's not right at all. You were never given the ability, so you're developing it, all on your own. That's what your poem is—evidence of your sense of nostalgia, your understanding of loss."

"It is not an entirely pleasant development," it noted.

"Well it shouldn't be, should it? Most humans would give anything to never have to deal with grief. But you're fine. Better than fine—but you should let Vega help you. She could find the new coding and help you make it efficient."

"Thank you. I think this discussion has been most helpful."

It untangled its consciousness from the safety of *Holwarda* and returned, once again, to the server room on *Mira*.

Vega sat at her work terminal, busily running diagnostics on protein processors on *Morgan*. Molecules of chai tea filled the air, fluttering around like dust motes on soft air currents.

"Akane should be writing up a report shortly," it said.

"Done already?" she asked skeptically. "Are you sure?"

"Yes."

"Okay, if you say so." She didn't look away from the numbers and letters scrolling across her screen.

"She thinks I have developed the ability to lament the past."

The chair she sat in swiveled, it's turn punctuated by a thoughtful squeak. "What about it, exactly, are you lamenting?"

"That it is gone."

After a moment, she favored its primary camera with a look of such pity—it had never been pitied before.

"Really?" Vega asked.

"Yes. Akane suggested you could make my new processes more efficient. Can you make them less painful?"

With a small chirp of laughter she bounded over to its camera, throwing both hands around the lens housing. "Oh, I.C.C., if she's right, I won't make it less painful. I could never be so cruel."

"I don't understand."

"The only person who can make it less painful is you."

"I don't understand."

"When you finish growing this new part of you, I think you will." She hurried back to her station. "Now get Nakamura on the line for me, please! I want to hear more about her theory—more about the tin woodsman with a new heart."

CHAPTER SEVEN

I.C.C.: MISCLONED

It started with chaos, as many shifts in society do.

A rumbling. An implosion. A severing. Something gone—one of I.C.C.'s limbs, part of its body: a ship, off-line.

It couldn't equate the feeling to human pain. Nothing throbbed, nothing hurt, nothing sizzled or stung. A thing had to be present to hurt. The ship had snapped away from the convoy. Gone. Lost.

Loss, I.C.C. noted, was far more terrifying than pain.

Sirens wailed of their own accord, beyond its conscious control. It could not stop them, and was surprised by its desire to.

It didn't want the convoy members to know. Because the people—there had been a full crew on *Bottomless*—were gone.

I.C.C. knew what people did when tragedy struck. It'd seen it in the archives, in the movies and documentaries. Occasionally, it'd seen it when loved ones died aboard unexpectedly. Human screaming was worse than any siren.

And there were so many gone to scream for.

It went through the crew shift logs, double-checking the names of all on *Bottomless* at the moment they'd shifted into SD.

Three hundred and forty-eight on duty. No visitors. All adults. Sixteen apprentices, in their first week on the job. Twelve soon-to-be retirees in their last week on the job.

It had failed them. The ships were supposed to protect them, shield them from the extremes of space and subspace. I.C.C.'s body was meant to be a haven.

How could this have happened? *What* exactly *had* happened?

All of these thoughts and more ran through the central computer's consciousness in the millisecond between the tragedy, the warning signal triggering, and the captains of all eight remaining ships demanding information.

The signal for two other ships waned and cut out.

I.C.C. instructed the navigational teams to surface, then went to work reconstructing the events.

SD drive malfunction. Part of *Bottomless* had been caught out-side the bubble, tearing it in two, causing the diving portion to collapse in on itself and the stranded portion to spin off wildly into space. Debris littered the travel SD. Some wreckage had been flung toward the rest of the convoy, tearing into *Holwarda* and *Shambhala*. Two greenhouses and one exercise room had been breached. Nine more crew members had been sucked into the void. Twenty-eight hundred and sixty-seven potential servings of food had been lost.

The Nest was unharmed.

The two damaged ships dropped out of SD travel almost instantaneously, losing the connection with I.C.C.'s main servers. This left them with personality fragments for their computer interface, and they temporarily went dark ship-to-ship, but no other main functionality was lost.

For those two ships, the primary problem was not repairing the damaged sections. It was simply getting back to the convoy. Luckily the rest of the convoy had heeded I.C.C.'s instructions promptly—only a million kilometers separated the wayward ships from the whole.

The screams were few and subdued. And somehow that was worse. The crew slipped into a hyperlogical state that I.C.C. had never observed before, channeling their loss and grief into work and reconfiguring. They mourned by planning. They lamented with repairs.

Redundancy has always been a hallmark of voyaging. If something is lost or broken, it must be compensated for because it cannot be replaced.

The convoy could limp along without *Bottomless*, especially since they had already completed the primary portion of the mission. It had been fondly known as the "janitorial closet," filled with all of the replacement parts and extra chemical cleaners and spoons and such. If your quarters needed new carpeting, the carpets came from *Bottomless*. It made living better, easier—but few things it stored prevented dying or mission failure. Much of its absolute essentials were backed up by redundancies on *Solidarity*, the manufacturing ship. The biggest loss was in raw supplies: iron, nickel, carbon, etc. The fundamentals.

Conceivably, they could continue on without it. Ration nonconsumables and consumables alike—rationing that would not end until the mission was complete and they were safely back at Earth. But the accident posed a secondary problem, one far removed from being a ship down.

Since the implosion had occurred during transition into SD travel, and the problem was thought to have originated within the SD drive, the question had to be asked: Was subdimensional travel no longer safe? If they proceeded toward

Earth as planned, who was to say they wouldn't lose another ship? Perhaps one more populated? One more essential to processing the data gathered at LQ Pyx?

Many crew members initially blamed the Nest. What if it had created some sort of imbalance in the bubble? What if, like the Seed, it could exert forces or send signals they could not detect?

I.C.C. rejected these summations immediately. No, the fault lay within the drive on *Bottomless*, it was sure, and it made that point emphatically. It wanted to be sure no drastic action was taken against the alien artifact.

Until they could pinpoint and solve the cause of the problem, they resolved to use their antiquated ion engines only. They wouldn't risk one more dive—not one, not for anything. They had to return to Earth, which meant ensuring their survival came first. No convoy, no mission. But that also meant they were no longer less than one hundred years' travel time from their home planet.

Who knew how long it would be before they could get back home?

* *

THIRTY-NINE YEARS LATER
APRIL 1, 161 PLD
3138 CE

The pseudo-sun was bright on his face, warm. And the grass—soft and springing beneath his boots. Rail had heard about this place, but never before been allowed to visit. It was a little piece of Earth, a reminder of something he would never see, or feel, or touch himself. He took a breath, held his chin high, and closed his eyes.

For a moment he could pretend. For a moment, he was really there.

Crack!

The sound split the air.

The ropes creaked.

Never would he see Earth.

He opened his eyes, fearing the baton. Twelve hooded figures hung from the gallows, each dressed in a white jumpsuit, each with their hands tied behind their back. The bodies swayed in the artificial wind, beneath the artificial blue sky, upon an artificial farm field, within an artificial container of metal suspended in space.

One thousand figures—dressed in the same white tunics—stood aligned in perfect rows and columns on the green field. Like an army at attention. Hundreds of black-clad security guards surrounded them. The officers wore glimmering black helmets with dark visors.

Rail had rarely seen a guard's face. He had *never* seen the Master Warden's eyes.

A figure climbed onto the stage next to the dangling bodies that slowly spun and swayed. He too was dressed in black, though wore no helmet. He was calm, purposeful, and deliberate as he gazed upon the dead.

Master Warden. His dark mustache lay thick above his white, polished teeth, and his hair had been neatly slicked back. The artificial sunlight glinted off his mirrored sunglasses. Those glasses served one purpose, and it wasn't to protect his delicate eyes.

When he spoke, his voice boomed from the speakers hidden in the sky.

"Witness the fate of those who attack the convoy. Terrorists have no place in my mines. These seven men and five women planned to murder hundreds of convoy children. Innocent children. Babies still in their growth tanks, to be blown up and desecrated. Look closely." He pointed a shock baton at the nearest corpse. "Here are the remains of heinous criminals.

"Let this be warning to all of you. The plans *will cease*. Sabotage *will cease*. Murder and attempted murder *will* cease." His gaze scrolled from front to back across the crowd as he paced the stage.

"I will not be so merciful in the future. For every convoy citizen injured, I will choose one of your kind—randomly— for the gallows. For every convoy citizen murdered, I will round up ten of you for the gallows. For every act of sabotage, I will round up twenty of you for the gallows. You will be treated as a single unit. If one is guilty, you are all guilty, and you will be punished as such."

The last words echoed over the silent crowd. "Are these new laws understood?"

"Yes, Master Warden!" the crowd roared in unison.

"Good. I am glad we've come to an understanding."

With the bodies still swinging in the breeze, Rail and the rest of the miners shuffled off toward the shuttle bay.

Today was supposed to be the first day of Diego Santibar's apprenticeship, but it had been postponed due to something with the Discontinueds. They'd hightailed it out of the Pit and spent hours on *Eden* for some unknown reason. He'd asked, but no one would tell Diego. Made him feel like they didn't see him as a graduate—like they still thought he was a kid.

Maybe he'd ask one of his moms about *Eden* when they got home in a few hours—they were both on the convoy board. One had been elected from the computing department (the fifth in her genetic line), and the other was the head of Communications (and the sixth in her line), so they knew about stuff. Unlike him—he'd been stuck in his quarters all day, looking over hydroponics data on 'flex-sheets.

One thin page flopped onto his face, startling him awake. He'd sprawled out on the futon an hour ago, and his eyelids had gradually become heavier and heavier. The family tabby cat had curled up beside him, and he gently shoed her away.

"I.C.C.?"

"Yes, Diego."

"Can you turn on some music? Something to keep me awake, please."

A twenty-second-century percussion piece blared through the living space. The heavy bass timpani, coupled with the occasional chimes and cymbals, chased away his weariness.

The cat didn't care for the noise at all, and bolted for his parents' bedroom.

Satisfied, Diego refocused on his work. He ran one dark hand over his eyes, chasing away the rest of sleep, and sat up.

Technically his job was on *Morgan*, not *Eden*, but his focus was sustainability and balance, so part of his job took him to the garden ship. If a previously innocuous bacterium or fungus started eating away at the soy or other legumes, he'd have to engineer a way to keep it from destroying the entire stock—a prospect that, secretly, bored him to retirement.

He wondered if it had been like this for all iterations before his. He'd never met the previous clone in his line, as an accident had ended the man's life decades before retirement. That was why he'd been grown early, out of sync, causing a few other crew members to shuffle positions.

Had all other Diego Santibars been unsatisfied with their work? He'd never told anyone. He didn't dare. They'd send him to the shrinks, run him through tests—maybe call him unfit for duty. How could anyone be unsatisfied with their job? It was in their blood, in their genes, in their very essence. If you were out of sync with your essence, what did that make you? A freak. A mistake.

It could make you up for discontinuation, the ultimate shame.

The high-pitched beeping of the door's keypad alerted him

that someone was home. He checked the clock—neither of his parents should be back for hours.

But one of his moms came bustling through the door—Vega. Her ice-blond hair was pulled into a tight ponytail, and her thin frame vibrated as though she'd received a sudden shock. "Oh, good, you are here," she said, as though she'd feared he might be elsewhere. She started to say more, but paused, her eyebrows knitting together. "Interesting music choice."

"I.C.C.'s pick. Helps me, uh, focus. Why are you back so early?"

Her mouth smiled sweetly, but her eyes portrayed tension. "I . . . I wanted to . . ."

She was being weird, even by mom standards.

"Vega was concerned that you might have been asked to clean up on *Eden*," said I.C.C.

"Why?" Diego stood and put his work aside. "What happened?"

She looked up at the ceiling, clearly annoyed with the computer. She didn't answer her son.

"Come on, Mom. No one will tell me what they're doing over there."

With a huff she brushed past him and made for the kitchenette. Since his growth spurt he'd come to appreciate just how small she was. At six-foot-one he could scoop up her four-foot-seven and pack her around like a child. It was strange remembering that she'd once given him piggyback rides.

"You don't want to know," she said. "I wish I didn't."

"Now, Vega?" I.C.C. asked.

Mortification crossed her face. "No. *Not* now." She made herself a cup of tea. "Did you do any coding today?" she asked Diego, her tone far too cheery to be sincere.

A combination of worry and excitement swirled in his chest. This was why Diego thought that if he were to reveal his secret—his distaste for botany—to anyone, it would be his mom. She was I.C.C.'s caretaker, and thought it would be nice if Diego shared her love of computers. And he did, so much so that he wished his genes had been brought on board for the AI.

He wanted a job that wasn't his, and he knew that was wrong.

"No," he said, "I have to finish these pages first."

"All right. I'll be in the back for a little while. Tell me when your *madre* gets in, will you?"

He wanted to ask her more about *Eden*, but kept quiet. "Yeah, okay."

With her brow furrowed and her face unusually pallid, she shut herself in the bedroom.

He continued to go over the data with the music blaring, rushing through the last few sets, eager to have time at the terminal. Finished with the agonizing part of the day, he turned down the volume and went to the touch screen—but stopped.

Now that the living room was quieter, he could hear Vega talking in her bedroom to someone else—to Margarita.

But Madre wasn't home yet, so it had to be over comms. Not especially weird, except . . . well, Mom's voice was up there, hitting a range she could rarely reach except when overtly stressed. And Madre sounded . . . disturbed.

Forgetting his daily tech-treat for the moment, Diego tiptoed over to his parents' door and pressed an ear to the metal.

"We promised not to interfere, but . . ." said Madre, audibly nauseated.

"But this is too far," said Mom.

"The captain's called an emergency meeting, and the

Warden will be there. But I don't think it'll pass a vote, Vega. We signed a treaty and—"

"Oh, give me a break. The board won't let this stand. They've got to be just as . . . just as . . ."

"Scared?" Madre said.

"They've—*we* have always been scared, that's the whole point. That's why they were discontinued in the first place. This is a bad sign, though. This is a breach of trust—"

"This was freaking *murder*, Vega."

Both women fell silent. Diego shut his eyes, concentrating. There—that might have been I.C.C. in quiet mode. Now shuffling. Blankets maybe. And footsteps.

Oh, crap.

He tried to throw himself away from the door, but couldn't beat his mom to the punch. With a whoosh, the door slid aside, revealing his crouched posture and guilty expression.

Anger flared in Vega's eyes, though he could tell it wasn't really directed at him. "Get to the monitor and practice your algorithms," she said warningly.

"Who was murdered?" he asked, standing up straight. Consciously, he knew now was not the time to challenge her, but his subconscious screamed at him to *push*. He wasn't a kid—in less than a year he'd be moving into his own single's quarters. His parents had to know that they didn't need to protect him—he could help them with . . . with . . . "Mom, *who was murdered?*"

She reached out, taking him by the shoulders. Stiff tremors rocked her limbs. Her voice shook, "Don't say anything to anyone, okay? This can't get out, not until the board can deal with it."

Gently, she turned him around and gave him a guided shove in the terminal's direction. Before he could once more demand inclusion, she stomped back to the bedroom and shut the door again.

Rail hated dirt. With a strange, unnatural passion. Dust. Silt. Didn't matter if he had a space suit between him and the filth, it was there. Clinging. The miner's suits glowed bright-white even in the depths of the Pit—until they got dirty. Gray and brown and black and flecks of red iron. Chips of minerals, chunks of silica, bits of ice. He hated it all, and hated it hard.

So hard, it let him forget about other things. Like radiation exposure, falling rocks, misplaced blasts. Today it let him forget about broken necks and limp feet and mirrored sunglasses.

Because the dirt you could wash off at the end of the day. It was something he hated that he could get rid of.

The Pit was little more than a man-made hole in a planemo. Besides the mines, it contained the prisoners' barracks, latrines, kitchens, infirmary, and solitary.

Rail, like the rest of the prisoners, had only a rudimentary understanding of what he worked for. He knew his primary purpose, of course. He dug for iron, which would be turned into metal alloys and then into a ship. But what was the ship for? The prisoners lived in the Pit while a convoy orbited several hundred thousand kilometers out. Okay—but what did the convoy do and where had it come from? The prisoners were all criminals, but not a one knew what his or her crime had been—just that it was a crime in their genes, not one they'd enacted themselves. They'd endangered the lives of everyone in that convoy, but no one would tell them how or why.

Mining was their penance—and time and again the Master Warden and subwardens told them to be grateful. Without the mines, they never would have been birthed. Their traitorous genes would have stayed on lock-down, never to be cloned again.

Rail lived because of the mine, but "grateful" wasn't the

term he'd use. When the subwarden's shock baton stayed holstered, he was grateful. But living in general—that left him more *baffled* than anything.

Only a day had passed since the hanging. One of the dead men had been on his dig team, but had bunked in a different cell block, so Rail hadn't known him well. Still, the team worked in silence. Their comms stayed on, but no one spoke.

The shaft they worked ran deep into the planemo, kilometers down. An antiquated ventilation system pumped the mine full of dust-laden, irradiated air—always heavy in carbon dioxide. The suit and helmets drew it in, supposedly scrubbing the gas, making it fit for human consumption, but Rail had his doubts as to how well the old space suits had been retrofitted.

White flashes, produced by the laser drills as they bore through rock, stung Rail's eyes. Even with the air choked full of dust and smog and debris, the brightness sliced through. The hand-operated drills weighed over forty kilograms apiece, and Rail—whose nickname had not been given in irony—could barely maintain his hold. With dozens of workers blasting away in confined spaces only meters apart, the tunnel's temperature soared in excess of forty degrees Celsius.

The high temp made a dangerous job deadly—this deep, frozen rock and ice pockets lay in wait. If suddenly superheated by a laser, they could take down an entire shaft and everyone inside. Thermal stress fractures, pressurized cave-ins, gas explosions, low gravity, and a thousand other problematic accidents typically resulted in dozens of deaths each year. Illness, cancers, and malnutrition killed dozens more. Then there were the suicides, and the crimes, and the punishments.

Yeah, *grateful* wasn't the word.

When his shift ended, they chained their drills and headed up. The lasers always stayed down low, away from the non-miner personnel. If anyone ever got a bright idea—thought they could turn a drill on their captors—the Warden would just give the order to turn off the air. The mirrored-glass bastard would rather suffocate everyone than let one rogue loose with a drill.

After dinner, Rail lined up in the C-Block common room and waited for the block's subwarden to perform roll call. She donned the same black uniform as the security guards, and carried the same shock baton, but wore the mirrored sunglasses of the Master Warden instead of a helmet. She was well toned, stocky, fit, and powerful. She had been the subwarden of C-Block for the last three years, and—like the Master Warden—Rail had never once seen her eyes. Only the mirrors.

The inmates knew her simply as *Ma'am.*

"Prisoner Zero-zero-eight-six-one."

"Here, ma'am."

"Prisoner Zero-zero-eight-four-four."

"Here, ma'am."

During roll call she strolled through the ranks, scrolling those sunglasses up and down the miners. The shock baton sizzled and growled and hummed as she walked through the rows looking for targets—those with the slightest imperfection in formation, dress, or attitude. A baton hit would inevitably come, but how hard? How strong? How mean did she feel? One night, the baton's charge had been set to lethal, and Rail could still remember the smell of fried human flesh.

This night's roll call was uneventful.

Grateful?

No—relieved.

Rail settled into his bottom bunk, one of six in the tiny room. He was on the edge of sleep when a dark shadow slipped through the door. A woman's foot lodged onto his bunk next to his head, and then was gone. Extra weight in the bunk over him. Movement. Whispered moaning. Rhythm. The occasional close-throated squeal.

Rail buried his head in his pillow. Sweetcheeks. Sweetcheeks always had girlfriends. They'd be going like that for half an hour at least. He was tired and wanted sleep. "Fraternization" was supposed to be against the law. But it was something the guards tended to turn a blind eye to, so long as you weren't caught in the act by a subwarden.

Eventually sleep came to him within the confines of his pillow.

He dreamt about the day they would finish building the ship—the day they would complete their work. What then? In his dream, after the last bolt was affixed, a giant rift opened in space. Jagged, purple, sparking with energy, the fissure swirled like a whirlpool.

It sucked in every last prisoner, wiping them out of this existence forever.

In the situation room, the board members gathered around the long table, their "guest" pacing at its head. Two Pit guards— his ever-present entourage—stood at attention on his flanks, their visors down, faces hidden.

The Master Warden's mirrored glasses glinted with every turn of his head. *Mira*'s captain, Rodriguez, had told the Warden that he could remove his unnecessary eyewear, to which he'd replied, "No thank you." The captain, taken aback, had almost ordered it. Almost.

Margarita wished he'd followed through. Those damn mirrors did exactly what they were designed to—made him look less like a person. Put up a wall between him and all the people, made him into a figure, a symbol. Made him into—

"Am I *not* Justice?" His tone was light, sympathetic, but rang false. The hard lines of his body told a story—this was no hearing, no corrective measures would be taken. This was just a conversation to put everyone on the same page. *His* page. "I go down into that stinking Pit day in and day out because *you* can't. You won't. You want to go along with regular convoy business, pretend nothing happened. Pretend you didn't reawaken every threat this mission's ever had and stuffed 'em all together in one place to work for you. You want to harness the people-power, but you don't want to look at it. Don't want to expend resources on it that you don't have to. And I get that. Makes perfect sense."

Margarita knew she was too old for this kind of patriotic *ra-ra-the-mission* type pandering, but she, like the rest of the board, let the man talk. It made him happy. Made him feel smug and secure. They needed the Warden to think he was secure.

More importantly, they needed him to believe he was one of *them*.

"But if you aren't going to regulate the prisoners, you have to let me do my job. *They had plans for attacking* Hippocrates. Whether they could have executed those plans is beside the point. I represent the Pit. I gave up my position as captain because someone has to be the bad guy. The guy who does the wrong things so that the right things can happen—so that children don't die. You don't want the Pit's rebels in your brigs, then fine, but don't tell me I have to keep them in mine."

"Excuse me," said Sailuk Okpik, an elected member from the medical staff. Her licorice-black hair was cropped in a tight bob around her face, emphasizing its oval shape and adding a seriousness to her usually bright eyes. "What year is this?" Her question sliced through the air like a scalpel.

"My original was from Alaska," she continued. "Native Inuit. Do you know when the last hanging occurred in Alaska? Nineteen-fifty; well over a hundred years before she was born. I ask again, what year is it?"

"You disapprove of my methods?" asked the Warden.

"I disapprove of capital punishment period," she replied.

"But not concentration camps?" He put his hand on his chest and feigned a gasp. "Oh my, we've never used *those* words before, have we? There used to be a saying about calling a thing what it really is, how did—let's call a spade a spade, that's it."

"By that logic we're *all* in a concentration camp," Sailuk spat back.

Margarita watched the anger roll over Sailuk's face and wondered if the woman was still thinking about history. Convoy history—clone history. Specifically, the generation where previous iterations of her and this man had been bonded. The whole board knew about it.

But the Warden didn't.

His history had been carefully scrubbed and manipulated. He didn't know he was a prisoner as well. He didn't know that the last Captain Mahler to serve had committed suicide with his own shock baton. The Warden had been groomed specifically to be exactly what he was now, but he would have gone to the Pit no matter what. But he didn't know that. And if he ever found out . . .

That was the real reason the board feared him. Ruthlessness in a convoy crew member was one thing, but in a Discontinued it was quite another.

"The convoy is not a concentration camp any more than the Earth is a concentration camp," the Warden continued, his lilt even. "Most of us love what we do. If you had to choose your life, you'd pick what you have. You think those men and women in the Pit would choose that?"

"What are you arguing for here, Mahler?" asked a man from Education.

"For you to open your eyes. You've tasked me with putting a wall between us and them. You don't want to know what goes on in your neighbor's yard? Then don't look over the fence."

"But you brought it *here*," said Vega. Margarita reached under the table and squeezed her hand as she spoke. "You brought a thousand prisoners onto *Eden* and slaughtered a dozen of them."

"I booked the time," he said casually. "No innocent people were around. No one knew except the few of you who cared to attend."

Our son—Margarita blurted, but only in her mind. She and Vega had made a pact to never mention Diego at a board meeting. Ever.

"But you tore down that wall that you supposedly maintain," said Vega.

The Warden held up his hands. "Fine. Fine. I got blood on the lawn, I get it."

"*Do* you?" Margarita said under her breath.

The air felt heavy, as though the ventilation system had cut out. The Warden's shock baton swayed at his side like a wound viper, ready to strike. Margarita could sense everyone's muscles tensing.

"I won't do it again," the Warden said eventually.

"You mean on *Eden*, or anywhere?" asked Sailuk. "Death without trial is . . ."

"I know what it is," he said. "If you'll all excuse me, I have to get back to my job." He ran a hand over his slicked hair, making sure every strand was in place.

"This isn't over," said Captain Rodriguez. "There will be reprisals."

"Looking forward to it," he said as he exited, scoffing at the hollow promise. He snapped his fingers and the two Pit guards followed him like a pair of mindless robots.

A minute passed in pure silence. Then, I.C.C. broke in. "The Master Warden has left the deck and is on route to the shuttle bay."

"What are we going to do about this?" Sailuk asked.

"We can't restrict his access to the greater convoy," said Rodriguez. "He thinks he's a crew member, if we disallow—"

"With all due respect, sir, does that matter anymore?" Margarita asked. She held her knuckles to her mouth thoughtfully, masking the sudden quiver in her lip. "Those of us who have served on the board the longest—those of us who made the decision to resurrect the Discontinued lines in the first place—we thought we'd set up a balanced system. A good system. Not . . . not what it's become."

The captain ran both hands over his eyes. "We have to be honest with ourselves; we knew this might happen."

"And it *has*. But the point is, the man has gone too far," said Sailuk.

"But how long has he been doing this?" asked Vega. "He's right—the only reason we even know it happened is because it happened *here*. Who looks closely at the injury reports they send us, huh? We glance at them, then file them away. Dr. Okpik, can you tell me how many deaths they've reported in the last three months, and what the causes were?"

Sailuk said nothing.

"Can anyone?" Shrewd expressions covered the board members' faces like masks. No one wanted to take responsibility for what happened down in the Pit.

That *was the point*, Margarita thought.

"They govern themselves," said the eldest representative from *Aesop*. He'd originally opposed the setup, but that was decades ago. "What does it matter what they do to each other as long as they don't do it to us?"

"It matters because they're bringing it into the convoy," said Rodriguez.

"No," said Margarita. "It matters because it's wrong." *It matters because they're not criminals—because our fear is not more important than their well-being*, she thought. A younger

Margarita would have argued against the thought—she'd supported the creation of the Pit.

But that was before her first wife, Kexin. And before Diego.

Before I.C.C. changed everything.

Diego glanced at a time readout as he jogged away from his quarters toward the lift. He'd spent all day on those damn 'flex-sheets—how could he have forgotten them? His supervisor had been livid—told him to march home. *March home*, like he was a child who'd misplaced his homework.

Wayward sheets in hand, he shuffled anxiously from foot to foot. Every extra moment away from *Morgan* made him feel more and more like a slacker. More like someone who didn't belong.

Too many screw-ups like this and his secret was sure to be found out.

The elevator let out a soft chime as its doors parted.

Three men stood inside, hands held squarely behind their backs. All three wore black jumpsuits. Two donned helmets, but the third wore strange, mirrored glasses. Moving slightly to make space for Diego, the mirrored-man said nothing.

Truthfully, Diego paid the security men little notice. He was too caught up in his own predicament. But a little nail of awareness scraped at the back of his mind. Something here was off, unusual—something beyond the eyewear.

The mirrors made it hard to tell where the man was looking, but the slight tilt of his head—ever so slightly up— revealed that he wasn't staring straight ahead. Wasn't spacing out like Diego usually did in a lift.

No, the man was looking up because he was eyeballing Diego.

Does it show that much? Diego wondered. *Do I look that nervous?*

He openly glanced sidelong at the man, scanning him from boots to collar.

A hand shot out, caught Diego by the wrist. Surprised, Diego dropped his 'flex-sheets.

He tried to pull back. "What the hell?"

"You . . ."

The other two men drew their shock batons with expert speed, but did not flick off the safeties.

"Master Warden," said I.C.C., "Diego Santibar is not under your jurisdiction, and I see no reason for you to invade his space."

"Where do you work?" the Warden asked.

"*Morgan*," Diego said, tugging pointedly at his suit.

"He's convoy crew?" Master Warden looked into the lift's corner, where one of I.C.C.'s many cameras rested, ever watchful.

"Of course. What else would he be?" The elevator dinged once more. "Shuttle bay," I.C.C. announced. "I suggest you hurry, Diego. Your advisor has been inquiring after you."

The Warden released his wrist, and Diego dropped to gather his sheets. Without another word, apology or otherwise, Master Warden stomped away. The helmeted men stepped over Diego as if he weren't there, holstering their weapons as quickly as they'd drawn them.

"That's the guy who oversees the mine?" Diego asked I.C.C., clutching the sheets to his chest.

"That is the man who rules the Pit," I.C.C. corrected.

"Diego?"

The apprentice stood between rows of soy plants, noting their individual growth and checking for any signs of sickness. Three other apprentice-level workers wandered around nearby. One took fertilizer samples, while another checked the chlorophyll concentration in a few sample leaves. The light in the air gardens on *Morgan* mimicked that of Sol, as seen through the walls and ceiling of a greenhouse. The air smelled of enriched soil and purified water.

"What is it, I.C.C.?"

"Isn't it your break time?"

Diego glanced at the wall clock. "I think my little jaunt back to *Mira* counts as my break, don't you think?"

A few more minutes passed. The other two apprentices wandered out for a moment to turn their full 'flex-sheets over to their supervisors.

"I think you should take a break now," I.C.C. said as soon as Diego was alone. "Go to the toilet."

"But, why—"

"You are ill," I.C.C. said. "I insist. You are ill."

Disinclined to argue when he was this curious, Diego conceded. He grabbed his abdomen and doubled over as he passed through the outer workroom. No one stopped him, and hardly anyone looked up from their work.

The nearest bathroom contained six stalls. I.C.C. instructed Diego to lock the outermost door.

"I don't feel sloshed, so what gives?" Diego crossed his arms. The AI didn't have video access in toilets, only biometric and conversational feeds.

"I need to converse with you alone." The comm speaker its voice emanated from hung above the backmost stall. I.C.C. had its volume turned way down. Diego had to sit right under it to catch every word. "I would like you to listen to a recording of this morning's board meeting," it said once the young man was situated.

Diego hesitated to reply. He wanted to blurt out *why?* but knew the board had met about whatever had happened on *Eden*. It concerned the Discontinueds, which made it classified. "I don't have security clearance for that," he said instead.

"There was a time when all board meetings were archived and accessible to the entire crew."

"That time's not now. I could get in trouble . . ."

"The matter involves you."

Diego scoffed. "I don't know what the problem is, but I think you are in need of some serious debugging."

"All I ask is that you listen."

"You mean *spy*."

"I want you to employ the same tactics you employed outside of your parents' bedroom."

"Oh."

"The behavior was not reprehensible to you yesterday."

"That's different. Eavesdropping on your mom doesn't get you brig time."

The outer door handle jiggled. Diego shrunk into the corner of his stall. "Hey, you don't want to come in here," he called, his voice echoing. "Trust me, it's for your own good." Whoever it was walked away.

Diego paced for a few moments in the small space, scuffing his work shoes against the smooth gray flooring. "Fine, just play it, all right?"

A low, grumbling man's voice broke through. A voice Diego had only ever heard once before: *today*. "You told me I *am* Justice."

Immediately captivated, Diego drank in the audio. *That's what happened—the murder my parents had been talking about.*

And that voice . . .

It belonged to the man he'd met in the elevator.

As the minutes ticked by, Diego's stomach churned. *Eden's* purpose was beauty, serenity. It was the home of peace and comfort and happiness, and the Warden had . . . had . . .

Wham, wham, wham.

The pounding on the restroom door made Diego tense—he

pressed himself into the cold metal of the wall. I.C.C. cut the situation room feed.

"All right in there?" called Diego's supervisor.

"I'll be out in a minute."

"Do I need to call a medic?"

"No, no. Just give me a bit and I'll be out." He waited a beat before letting himself out of the stall. "Thanks, I.C.C.— second day officially on the job and I'm already the screw-up *and* the toilet clogger. Why . . . why did you want me to know all that?"

"What happens in the Pit is relevant to your well-being," said I.C.C.

"Isn't it relevant to everyone's well-being?" Cool water flowed from the hand washing station. Diego splashed a few soothing palmfuls onto his face.

"This would be easier if Chen Kexin were here."

Diego hadn't heard that name in a long while. Pictures of her still littered the 'flex-sheets imbedded on the walls of his family's quarters, but neither his Mom nor his Madre spoke of her.

To him, Kexin had been Mama—that much he remembered. But the lilt of her voice was lost to his inner ear, just as his inner eye could not recall an expression besides the camera-ready smile. He did recall a sense of openness. She'd been carefree. Quick with a joke and a hug.

And then she'd died and . . .

"What does she have to do with anything?" Diego asked more harshly than he'd meant to.

"It is irrelevant now."

"Oh, no you don't. You never say anything without a reason. You wanted me to think about her. Why?"

"That is a question for your parents. They don't think it is time for you to know about the plan, but it was *my* plan, and it is time."

Hours had passed since lights-out, but Rail needed the latrine. Pissing in the middle of the night had its perks—nobody there to perv at your junk or threaten castration if you'd accidently twisted their ventilation hose in the tunnels.

It also had its downsides. If a subwarden crossed your path, it could mean an entirely different kind of lights-out. Ma'am didn't like anyone wandering about during the sleep cycle. She'd rather you crap your sheets than walk the halls.

Luckily, he encountered no one on his way there, or in the latrine itself. However, on his way back through the darkened common room that linked the branched halls of cellblock C, a single monitor sprang to life. It hissed with static. Rail froze, his heart leaping in an erratic jolt. The eerie glow of the screen threw mad shadows across the walls.

Rail spun, searching wildly for whoever had turned the monitor on. It could mean an ambush—by the guards or other prisoners. His gaze fell in every nook, but found no one lurking.

"Jamal," the screen whispered. At least, that's what it sounded like. Rail tiptoed closer to the speakers, ears straining. Blood pounded in his temples.

"Jamal," the voice repeated.

And again.

And again.

Over and over, spitting the word out underneath the static.

"Jamal. Jamal. Jamal. Can you hear me?"

Rail knew to keep his mouth shut. The subwardens had set less complicated traps to ensnare suspected rabble-rousers.

"I am not the most adept at creating patches—are you receiving?"

The shadows continued twirling across the walls, making it difficult to tell if someone had snuck up through a side hall. But no telltale *zing* of a readied shock baton cut through the static.

Who owned this voice, and who were they trying to contact?

"I can see you, Jamal. Why are you not responding?"

The static subtly shifted, the negative space became more pronounced. It resolved into wobbly letters that spelled out, *Can you read me?*

Instinct told Rail to run. Even if it had nothing to do with the guards or rebels—even if it had nothing to do with *him*—it didn't sit right. Anything out of the ordinary could spell trouble. He could get the baton just for being curious. He started to slink away, but then the words changed.

Can you read me? Jamal, war is coming. You have to help me stop it. The Master Warden will find you soon. He's poring through the records, looking for you. Jamal, answer.

Rail's meager education meant he only had a vague sense of war—it was like a brawl, but bigger. Lots bigger.

Hopefully this Jamal person had gotten the message, because there was sure as a dunged-up toilet nothing *Rail* could do about a war.

"There's no waiting," I.C.C. said. "The Master Warden has seen him. And he knows—he doesn't know yet *what* he knows—but he knows."

Diego stood before his parents in their small living room, feeling for all the world like they'd just caught him doing something unmentionable, though he couldn't say why. Maybe it was the horror on their faces—like they'd just seen something that could not be unseen.

The two women took each other's hands—creamy white encased in sandy brown. "We're not ready for this," said Margarita.

"You never would have been," said I.C.C. "I'm sorry."

"What—what do we do?" Vega stammered.

"I've already tried to contact Jamal in the Pit. To warn him."

"But what do we do about Diego?" Margarita asked.

"Yes, what *about* Diego?" he asked.

The two women stared at him, eyes wide and sad. Their guilt was palpable—whatever this was, whatever was happening, they'd been keeping secrets to prevent it. But for how long?

"This would be easier if Kexin were here," Margarita breathed, breaking away from Vega.

"I've done the best I can," her wife retorted.

"That's not what I meant. It was Kexin who agreed to all this—she must have had a plan." Margarita stepped toward Diego, reached up and took her son's face between her palms. "She would have known how to tell you."

Diego leaned back. The lines on her face were deep; he'd never really noticed how old she was before. Her retirement would come too soon.

Margarita's fingertips still brushed at his chin, but he stepped away. "What is going on?" he demanded.

"You aren't Diego Santibar," Vega blurted. "No, what I mean is . . . What I mean is your original was not the original Diego Santibar. You're of a different line."

"Miscloned," Margarita said. "That's what we call it."

"Only we shouldn't, because that makes it sound like an accident." Vega plopped herself down at the family table with a small huff. "I swear this all started with that damn poem," she mumbled to herself.

Diego blinked at her, trying to process the words. How could . . . *miscloned? How can any clone be of the wrong line?* "What are you saying?" Every syllable shook. "Why? What—how?" A tingling sensation worked its way from Diego's fingertips up to his nose and lips. His lungs refused to take deep breaths, working instead in small, halting stutters that provided little oxygen.

"I did it," said I.C.C. "I rearranged a few commands in

Hippocrates' computers to ensure that when they went to regrow a Diego Santibar clone, they'd grow you instead. I was trying to fix the convoy. Since the loss of contact with Earth, the destruction of *Bottomless* and the rejection of SD travel, chances of mission success have been dropping exponentially. More importantly, chances of convoy survival as well. Before your birth, there was only a seventeen point two percent chance that the convoy would survive another fifty years."

"And now that I'm, I don't know, *alive*— Now that I'm alive, been grown, what's changed?"

"Nothing. Yet."

"But, what does it mean for *me*? What do you expect *me* to do? Who am *I*? Why grow me instead of . . . instead of the other guy? *What line do I even belong to?*"

The room fell silent.

"I.C.C.," said Vega, "you did this. You tell him."

"No," said Margarita. "I'll do it."

"This is so cruel," Vega said under her breath, dropping her head into her hands.

"Just someone say it," Diego pleaded. Every atom in his body rumbled, bounced. His flesh crawled with the unknown. *Why me? What do you expect?* "Tell me!"

Margarita took a breath to try, but the words never made it past her lips. She cast her gaze away from his.

"May I?" I.C.C. broke in. It clearly didn't like seeing his mothers' struggle.

"Please," Margarita said, reluctantly.

"There are lines," the AI said frankly, "that I believe are still needed in the convoy, but are no longer grown. Discontinued lines."

Diego's vision tunneled. *No, I'm not hearing this right.*

Margarita tried to touch him again, but he wouldn't let her. Her eyes filled with hurt, and she said quietly, "Your

DNA and histones are that of Jamal Kaeden. He led a revolt in the early half of the journey to LQ Pyx. A mutiny. Tried to turn the convoy around."

"That guy?" Diego didn't believe it. They learned about the revolt in school, but no one dared name names or pull up pictures because those people were—"Discontinued," he breathed. *Traitors. Failures. Outcasts.*

No. *No.*

"*I'm a* Discontinued?" Everything from the knees down went numb, and he couldn't keep himself upright anymore. "I'm Dis—I'm Dis—" It was like hearing you'd been kidnapped at birth and raised as someone else. Hell, he *had* been raised as someone else. Because he never should have been born.

A strange wash of guilt and shame swirled through his mind.

Margarita helped him into a chair next to Vega. "Breathe, son."

Every word out of their mouths was wrong. So wrong. And yet . . . it made a sort of grotesque sense. He'd felt like an alien—out of place in his uniform, in his own skin. He let out a clipped laugh. "I'm *Discontinued*."

"What they're doing down in the Pit is wrong," said I.C.C. "It's damaging—to the individuals as well as the whole. If such enslavement continues, the entire convoy will die."

"Which is why I.C.C. and Kexin cooked up this stupid plan," said Vega.

"It is well known that the most successful way to reduce the fear of otherness is emersion," the AI insisted. "Consistently cloned convoy members fear the otherness of the Discontinueds. By introducing discontinued lines back into the larger genetic pool, and subsequently revealing their successful integration, I had hoped to incite a social reform. You were the first, and nine more followed until I put the plan on hold—when Kexin died."

"There are others?" *Others like me who feel this way? Others out of place, others* . . . "Why did it matter that she died?"

"Because she had a plan for raising you—a way to successfully integrate the ten of you. She wanted to make sure no one could deny the necessity of your genetic lines. She wanted you to bring back safe SD travel."

"There are thousands of people on board trying to make that happen. What in the name of all of Earth did she think ten kids could do about it? You agreed—you implemented the plan. What do you think we can do about it?"

"I don't believe there is anything you can do about it," I.C.C. said bluntly. "It was the *trying* that mattered. The dedication to saving the convoy. But despite my reservations, she truly thought you could do it. With her help. She was the greatest convoy physicist I've ever known. If there was anyone who could have guided you all to success, it would have been her."

For the first time in his life, Diego wanted I.C.C. to have a human body. So that he could either hug it or punch it in the face—he wasn't really sure which.

"Kexin didn't tell me about you," Margarita said. "I.C.C. told me after the accident—after her funeral. I knew something terrible would happen if anyone found out you were Discontinued. So I asked Vega to help me keep you safe."

"I've controlled all of your schedules—tried to keep you from ever interacting with anyone who'd been to the Pit." Vega's hands still covered her face, and her voice sounded far away. "But even that plan failed."

Because the Master Warden saw me.

"We're all in danger, aren't we?" asked Diego. "Us and the nine others—and all of their counterparts in the Pit?"

"Yes." The AI sounded sad.

"Who are they?"

"It won't tell us," said Margarita. "For their own safety. I don't know if their parents are even aware."

"But the Warden—when he realizes I look just like one of his workers he'll suspect there are others, won't he? What are the odds he writes it off as an accident, or a coincidence, or a trick of the light? He'll start looking for the rest. We have to locate the other miscloned first, get them together—tell them who they are."

"They are still children," I.C.C. said. "You were the oldest. The youngest had just begun to incubate when Kexin passed; she is only eleven."

"And their counterparts in the Pit—how old are all of them?"

"They are all older. Jamal is twenty-seven, if my records are correct. And—" it hesitated "—there are only eight counterparts in the Pit."

"What happened to the other two?"

"Pire Evita died aboard *Hippocrates* three-point-seven years ago. Of radiation poisoning. Ceren Kaya died six days ago. Aboard *Eden*."

Diego locked eyes first with Margarita, and then—once she'd uncovered her eyes—Vega.

"The Master Warden will kill us all as conspirators if he has his way," Margarita said. "That's all he'll see this as. He won't care that you're children, he won't care that we're just your mothers."

"But the board, the security guards, they'll stop him . . ." Diego half stated, half asked. "Unless they agree?"

"There are so many ways this can go wrong," said Margarita. "Master Warden wants us to believe he's protecting us, that his tactics are necessary. Finding out there are Discontinueds among the crew proper could produce enough paranoia for him to gain a following."

"Then we have to get everyone on our side first," Diego said.

"How?" I.C.C. asked.

"By revealing us for what we are," said Diego. "Children."

MARINA J. LOSTETTER

256

". . . is coming."

Rail wished he didn't have such a small bladder. Every time he went to the loo in the middle of the sleep cycle, that damned message sprang up.

Jamal, Jamal, Jamal. Freaking Pit-stink *Jamal*.

He'd seen it perhaps nine times now over the course of weeks. Did it play every night? Triggered by some time-sensitive motion detector?

Why hadn't the subwardens disabled the screen yet?

Who else might have seen it?

"War is coming, war is coming—I get it, I get it," he grumbled in the dark.

Scuffing his bare feet against the floor, he'd almost reached the bunk room when a bouncing dot of light at the other end of the hall caught his attention. Then footsteps. Running. Multiple people. And a strange scraping—like something heavy being dragged.

A group was about to round the corner, and Rail had nowhere to hide, no way to blend in. His white jumpsuit glowed against the dark gray walls. If it turned out to be a horde of angry subwardens, he might as well up and die on the spot.

But it was six men—also in white, ranked in two files— who stepped into view. They filled the hall like an angry cork, waiting to thrust through the neck and out the bottle. Behind them, sliding none-too-smoothly as it was hauled across the floor, was a body.

The penlight fell on Rail, temporarily blinding him in one eye. He couldn't tell who carried it.

"You didn't see nothin', squirt."

Rail knew that voice. Sweetcheeks.

He lowered his head and said nothing. Damn Sweet-cheeks. Had he been part of the guerilla groups the whole time? Or was this new since . . . since the hangings?

When they'd passed, he allowed himself one glance at the body. He couldn't tell if life still filled her limbs, or if the ugly sear-mark across her face meant they'd killed her with her own shock baton. But he couldn't mistake her stocky build and mirrored glasses for anyone else.

They'd gone and attacked Ma'am.

War is coming. Thanks for the tip, whoever you are.

"Your men must stay with the craft," ordered the head of Security.

The Master Warden paused midstep, halfway down the shuttle's steps. He eyed the *Mira* security detail that had come to greet him. Four officers. "They accompany me everywhere—on the convoy or in the Pit, doesn't matter."

"Not this time."

Everyone in the shuttle bay had stopped to watch. Most probably didn't even realize they were staring.

"Listen, Matheson, do you even know why I'm here? Last night one of my subwardens was attacked on duty. She's on *Hippocrates* in critical condition. If we'd had a larger security staff she wouldn't have been alone. We're undermanned and under attack. I don't go anywhere without my guards."

Matheson stood his ground. "We've been deployed to watch over you during your time aboard."

"Why can't I have my own people? I trust my people."

"It's part of the sanctions, sir."

Master Warden set his jaw. "Sanctions," he spat. Behind his sunglasses, his eyes scanned the room. Everywhere, faces took in the scene. They weren't used to seeing this—a confrontation. They were used to quiet transitions. Passive stops and uneventful takeoffs.

Peaceful changeovers—changeovers *he* allowed, moments *he* gave them. And in return, all he asked was noninterference. *Do what I ask, and let me do my job.* He wasn't unreasonable in his requests or in his execution of his duties.

But, like petulant children, the crew—especially the board—had no idea how easy their lives were. They whined and flailed about when things didn't go exactly as they wanted. A toy didn't have to be broken for them to pitch a fit—it just had to have a flaw. A scratch, a bit of tarnish. Never mind the powdered bits of his own past, his own things—if *they* had a boo-boo, then God help him if he railed against their tantrums.

"The board can choke on its sanctions," he spat. "My men are coming with me."

With an easiness usually reserved for tasks like tying up a boot or straightening a jacket, Matheson unholstered his shock baton. To someone other than the Warden it might have appeared casual, unthreatening.

"There's no need for that," Master Warden said in a low timbre.

"You'll come alone?"

The Warden considered how much time they were wasting. He needed more security personnel in the Pit ASAP. No point bickering with this idiot at the expense of his team.

With a small wave of his hand, he signaled for his guards to stay aboard the shuttle.

"This way," Matheson said, indicating the Warden should walk between the four convoy guardsmen.

"One thing, before we see the ever-so-gracious board," Master Warden said, inching closer to Matheson. "Those animals in the Pit are growing more vicious every day. The only thing standing between them and all these people is me. We're both men of security. I think you know the little games the board insists on playing are dangerous."

Matheson said nothing, but his eyes held doubt. He might not have fully appreciated everything the Warden was saying, but he knew the board occupied a sheltered position. The politicians dabbled in power while shying away from the ugly bits.

"The security of this fleet is my only passion," said the Warden. "Lead the way, son."

Many sets of eyes tracked the party out of the bay. The Warden stiffened under the intensity of the collective stare. The gaze was part confusion, admiration, and dread. Some feared his influence, others wished he had more—would follow him alone at the drop of a hat.

If the board insisted on driving a wedge between itself and the Master Warden, it had to realize it was also drawing a line on the floor for its citizens. It was going to make the people pick a side. And as a wise man once said, a house divided against itself cannot stand.

The board heard the Warden's planned speech, then dismissed him.

"We can't honor the request," Vega said.

"Well, we certainly can't deny it," Margarita countered. Vega's knee jerked under the marble long table, and Margarita could tell her wife was resisting the urge to kick her. "There's been an attack," she said categorically.

"So? You can't tell me a prisoner has never raised a hand to a guard before," Vega said. She made a face at Margarita: *How can you possibly be on the Warden's side?*

"Yes, all right, there have been stabbings and beatings and bitings. But that woman is on *Hippocrates* fighting for her life."

"We need to give the Warden less power, not more. Send him more people, more weapons, and he'll—"

"He'll what?" Margarita asked haltingly. She'd interrupted Vega on purpose because she knew what the next words out of her mouth were going to be. *He'll be better equipped to come after our son.*

Rodriguez ran a hand over his mouth, then steepled his fingers on the table. "We can give him the influx of security in the Pit and keep limiting him here. Our details, not his. Our schedules, not his. Our priorities, not his."

"Who are we going to send? For how long?" Vega asked.

"It should be temporary. We can grow him more people if he really needs a permanent increase."

"Waiting for a generation to mature is hardly what I'd call temporary," said Vega. "And you didn't answer me about *who*."

"Volunteers?" asked the Education head.

"No, not volunteers," said Margarita. "That's exactly who we don't want down there. Volunteers might be in favor of the Warden's tactics."

"It's only one," Vega said again. "One bad attack. Does it warrant a response from us? What if it's just a ploy for more control?"

"A ploy? It's not like he beat his own subwarden," said Rodriguez.

The table fell silent.

No, Margarita thought. *That's a terrible—he couldn't.*

"She hasn't regained consciousness yet," Sailuk said quietly. "All we have to go on is the Master Warden's report."

"He did murder twelve people," said Vega. "And if he didn't beat his own subwarden, you can bet he'll murder as many more in retribution. Do we want to give him more people to do it with, the roundups? He'll spread the blood to our security personnel, make them part of his 'justice' machine. Will we want them back after that?"

A hush fell again. After some time, Rodriguez asked, "I've made up my mind. Shall we put it to a vote?" He was spurred on by nods around the table. "All right. All in favor of granting the Master Warden a division of convoy security personnel?"

The ayes did *not* have it.

"Madam secretary, prepare a report for the Warden," said Rodriguez. "But don't send it today. Send it at the end of the week. Give him a few days to cool."

Ma'am awoke a few days later. She gave five numbers, and a description of a sixth assailant. The information went out, and though the board tried to contain it, to analyze it, it reached the Pit within minutes.

The Warden had friends in the convoy.

Nothing happened for a good long while. Hours passed. The shifts in the Pit rolled on. The attackers toiled at their usual jobs, convinced that Ma'am's wounds were beyond repair. They were sure they'd killed her in the same casual way she'd killed a handful of their cellblock mates.

But then their workday ended. They settled down for bed.

And the Master Warden made his move.

Shouts. Lights. Whistles and thuds.

Rail sprang from his bunk, then froze. Half a second ago he'd been asleep. Now he wasn't really awake, though. Just conscious, on autopilot, heart hammering in his chest and blood rushing in his ears. Someone in a black jumpsuit stiff-armed him aside.

The guard dragged Sweetcheeks off the top bunk and tossed him to the ground. With a yelp, Sweetcheeks tried to scramble to his feet, but the guard forced him to his knees.

Four other guards entered the room, batons sizzling with life. They yelled unintelligibly, but everyone got the message: Don't move. Move and you're dead.

After the initial burst of activity, everything calmed. The prisoners all stayed in bed, save Rail and Sweetcheeks. And only Sweetcheeks dared make a sound—a sad, strangled whimper.

With the room secure, in strode the Master Warden.

"You know," he said conversationally, "I thought we all had an agreement. Do you remember that, Prisoner Zero-zero-eight-four-four? It wasn't that long ago—nice day, lots of sunshine. We agreed that for every convoy member injured

I'd take a life randomly. Well, someone has been hurt. Quite badly. But I don't want to kill a random prisoner for that crime. You know why?"

Sweetcheeks covered his face, fingers shuddering against his parted lips. "Please," he sobbed.

Rail had never seen Sweetcheeks like this—a pool of himself, seeping into the floor, trying to disappear. And he'd never see him like this again, he knew. After a moment, he'd never see him again at all.

Why did you go after her? Rail screamed inside his mind. *You had to know they would kill you. Any idiot in the Pit knows that if you look at one of them sideways you're done for. The only way to live is to take it, take the crap. Why didn't you just lie down and take it?*

"I asked you a question," the Master Warden said. "Do you know why I won't kill a random prisoner?"

"Please, please, please." He said it over and over, blubbering, spittle flying from his lips.

"Because six guilty men are worth just as much," the Warden said eventually. Wagging his fingers at the nearest guard, he indicated for the man to hand over the live baton. Why the Warden left his own baton dead in its holster, Rail wasn't sure.

After making sure the weapon was on its highest setting, he approached Sweetcheeks. "Look at me," he instructed.

As soon as he turned his face upward, the baton was upon him. But it did not strike cruelly. The Warden did not laugh as Rail had imagined he would. There was no delight in his eyes, or malice. This was a thing that needed done, and he was the one doing it.

Master Warden touched the tip of the blazing baton firmly to Sweetcheek's forehead, and it was over in an instant. The prisoner seized and fell, a perfect disk burnt into his face like an oversized bindu.

Stillness settled over the room, a moment of silence passed.

"That's the last one," the Master Warden said as the guard lifted Sweetcheeks' body from the floor. "Don't forget to tell your simpering fellow inmates what happened tonight," he instructed, then turned to Rail, whose inside's shriveled on the spot. "You, back in your bu—"

The Warden lashed up and out, catching Rail's chin with his free hand. He brought Rail's face down to his, eyes narrowing.

Of the two, Rail was by far the taller man, but under the Warden's gaze he felt like the smallest person on the planetoid.

Any moment the baton would come and Rail would die. He knew it. This was the end. He'd dared to stand in the wrong place at the wrong time and he would burn for it.

Cold sweat broke out across his forehead and his upper lip. Each extra second was a lifetime of agony.

Just get it over with.

"Sir, you wanted me to tell you when the official response from the board came in?" one guard asked, pressing his hand to his earpiece.

"Yes. What's the verdict?"

"They've denied your request."

The Warden moved, Rail flinched. The baton snapped off, and the Warden tossed it back to its owner.

"Damned idiots," he swore, letting Rail go. "Back to sleep, everyone!" he ordered. "Sweet dreams."

"What does the man want now?" Margarita asked Vega. "Every other week he's calling for a special board meeting. Does he think we have nothing better to do than entertain him and his delusions of grandeur? I swear, if he calls himself Justice one more time . . ."

They rounded the corner and found a gaggle of people outside the situation room door. One man in glasses, whom Margarita didn't recognize, thrust a 'flex-sheet at them. "We have a petition, signed by five thousand crew members, demanding John Mahler be given whatever provisions he requests in order to assure—"

"Yeah, all right, thank you," Margarita said, plucking the sheet from his fist. The two women pushed through the small throng.

"He's doing more than you ever will to keep those criminals in their place!" said another man.

Several rallying cries followed.

"We need someone like him keeping an eye on us."

"Do you know what kinds of sacrifices he's had to make?"

"Give the man what he needs!"

"Thank you," Vega said loudly. "We have your signatures, we'll look it over."

"You're going to give us the brush-off, aren't you? Like every other politician in the history of—"

"Look," Margarita said. "You don't like the way we do things? Elect someone else."

The man with the glasses crossed his arms defiantly. "You're a division head. We can't replace you, can we?"

"So draw up another petition," she spat, finally getting through to the door.

Both she and Vega let out heavy sighs of relief once in the situation room. The rest of the board were already inside. Apparently they'd refused to even glance at the petition, let alone take it.

Margarita shoved it into a folder for later.

A faint smattering of applause and a high-pitched *woot* from outside indicated the Master Warden had arrived. He entered with a smug sneer plastered on his face, but made no mention of the crowd.

As he settled himself, the board made their usual greetings and started the minutes and read off the agenda.

"Lights low, if you please," the Master Warden said when

he was ready. The slight smile had left his face, replaced by a grim line. From a 'flex-sheet he transferred a few files onto the main wall monitor. Four adult faces, three men and one woman, stared out vacantly from the screen. The mug shots were cold and impersonal, blank people against a blank wall.

Margarita bit her lips, recognizing one of them instantly. Her heart raced. Vega clutched at her wife's knee, digging her nails into the jumpsuit fabric.

"These are prisoners Zero-zero-six-five-nine, Zero-zero-eight-nine-three, Zero-zero-one-eight-one, and Zero-zero-five-seven-two. None of them are patently remarkable compared to the rest of the discontinued population. Their personal histories of violence are varied but not noteworthy. They've never had any problems meeting their mining quotas. And none of them have ever shared a dorm or a team."

He paused, letting them digest the faces.

Margarita was in no mood to digest anything. She felt like she might vomit. Zero-zero-eight-nine-three looked so much like Diego, she half expected someone else on the board to point it out. Though she and Vega had tried to keep their son away from the board, a few of the members had met him once or twice.

"For the past few weeks I have scoured convoy records because something strange happened to me a while back. I saw one of these faces, but not in the Pit. I saw it in an elevator. On *Mira*."

Sailuk spoke up. "One of the prisoners escaped?"

"Nothing so simple," he said, cycling to a new set of pictures. "These are archived security stills, taken at different times over the last few months. This one is of myself and the face in question."

It was an odd angle. The Master Warden and Diego stood side-by-side in a lift, the Warden's guards behind them. Diego's face was partially upturned—like he was talking to I.C.C.

"I didn't know why I recognized the young man at the time. But then I encountered this prisoner during a disciplinary routine." He brought the picture of eight-nine-three back. "And made the connection."

Many of the board members sat back, at a loss. Stunned. Others leaned in, scrutinizing the images, unsure.

"Ladies and gentlemen, you have Discontinueds living aboard your ships. I was able to match these three prisoners to three more teenagers. Someone has placed sleeper agents amongst you. *This* is why I need more personnel. This is the worst security breach we've ever had.

"I need your permission to conduct a convoy-wide screening—order DNA tests to reveal all of the imposters. I will arrest these four for interrogation, but I also need extra computing power; a Discontinued's testimony can't be trusted, and I can't go through all the records on my own. But I.C.C.—if patched through to me in the Pit—could help sort out who is responsible for the unsanctioned clones. Someone must be guiding them, gathering them, and we have to find out why. And how many there are. I don't believe for a moment that it's just these four."

"I'm not sure," said a rep from *Aesop*. "It's hard to tell if these are the same people."

"They are the same lines," the Warden said, chewing the inside of his lip. "I have no doubt."

"You say they're children? And you want us to hand them over for interrogation? In the Pit?" Sailuk asked. "Absolutely not. If they're in the convoy, then *we'll* handle it."

"Right, this is a convoy matter, not a Pit matter," said Captain Rodriguez. "Thank you for bringing this to our attention."

Mahler leaned forward, like he'd misheard them. "I said these infiltrators were Discontinued, that makes them my problem, not yours."

"How do you know they're infiltrators?" Margarita asked, trying to keep her voice calm. "Why couldn't this be a replication mistake? Sounds more like a quality control problem than a criminal problem."

The Master Warden pinched the bridge of his nose, right where his sunglasses sat. "Unbelievable. You people are so blind—"

"This is not a police state," Sailuk cut him off. "We do not rip children from their beds and subject them to torture—because that's what you mean by interrogation, isn't it?—on pure suspicion. Your evidence is a few grainy photographs fed into your rudimentary files by basic archive updates."

"Look, I'm just here as a courtesy," he said, "because by the laws that we have created, these are my people under my jurisdiction. I could have called on I.C.C. to have them rounded up and sent to me already, but since they're on your ships—"

"You will not have these children 'rounded up,'" Rodriguez said. "You are overstepping your bounds, sir. I suggest you return to the Pit and let us handle what is clearly a convoy matter."

The Master Warden remained collected, though it was clear from the way he set his jaw that he would have liked nothing more than to grab his baton and beat the nearest chair to death. "You aren't going to do anything, are you?"

"We will need to substantiate your claims. Prove that these children really are Discontinued."

"And then?"

"That will be discussed when and if you are correct."

Something in the Warden *broke*. Margarita saw it happen, clear as could be. Whatever smidgen of respect he'd still held for the board was now gone.

"I have lost track of Jamal," I.C.C. told Diego.

"What? How?" He shrugged on the top half of his yellow

jumpsuit and zipped up. The clock read 0900—half an hour until his shift started.

"I had been keeping track of Prisoner Zero-zero-eight-nine-three, which DNA records say is Jamal, via genetic tracers," the AI explained. "Subscriptions for iodine and nano pills—to combat radiation poisoning and scrub the miners' lungs—are frequently shipped from *Hippocrates* to the Pit. I sent a special capsule regiment to Jamal and was able to receive an occasional ping back through the Pit's rudimentary computer system."

"But now?"

"I do not think he has taken his medication."

"What do you think it means?"

"Perhaps he forgot."

"I don't like it," Diego said, lacing up his boots.

"Neither do I."

"I think it's time you told me who the other miscloned are."

"It's not safe."

"You're afraid for them?"

"I'm afraid for all of you."

"Hiding isn't always the answer to fear," Diego said. It sounded flippant in his head, but dead serious out of his mouth. He gathered up his 'flex-sheets and knapsack, then headed for the door.

Before he'd discovered who he really was, Diego used to pass people in the hallways without paying much attention. A polite nod was the most thought he gave to the random passerby. But these days, every face presented a riddle. What did they think of the Discontinueds? What would they think if they knew he was one of them?

And if he passed a child who appeared to be between the ages of ten and seventeen his mind raced with possibilities. Could they be miscloned? Were they like him, perpetually confused about their place in the convoy?

A boy of sixteen, a neighbor from a few decks down, passed him wearing a pilot's flight suit. Tom was his name, if Diego recalled correctly. He had a familiar faraway look in his eyes and set to his jaw. Could he be miscloned? Or was Diego just seeing what he wanted to see?

He'd never been much of a people watcher before, but now it seemed like every individual's little nuances deserved to be observed and remembered. Noticing people was important.

He jogged into the shuttle bay just in time to catch the next one out to *Morgan*. The attendant entered his information into the passenger manifest before he boarded, and he took a seat near the front per habit.

As the craft took off, he wondered what could convince I.C.C. to hand over the identities of the other nine miscloned. Surely the AI realized that revealing themselves to each other could be great for all of them. They could help each other, figure out a way to come out to the convoy as a group. Or, at the very least, it would ensure they all had someone to lean on when leading a double life started to take its toll.

The dark expanse of space between the ships could be so soothing sometimes. Quiet. Calm—

A huge clashing *bang* and *screeeeech*, like metal fists meeting, rattled through the cabin.

The shuttle lurched, throwing Diego sideways. His skull smacked against the wall, and white dots scattered across his vision.

Compartments overhead popped open, releasing oxygen masks.

For a moment Diego sat slumped against the wall, dazed, as everyone else panicked around him.

After a moment he came to his senses, and while the six other passengers scrambled to secure the breathers, Diego unbuckled himself. He darted between the windows, searching. They'd been hit by something, but what?

A white dot off starboard grew in the frame of the window. Another shuttle, its nose already crumpled, was barreling in for another blow. It wasn't an accident. The other ship maneuvered exactingly; the pilot knew what they were doing.

His shuttle had been rammed.

"Remain calm, remain calm," the pilot of Diego's shuttle ordered over the comm "I'm taking us back to *Mira*."

But he wouldn't get them rerouted in time. Diego braced himself for the impending impact. Unable to get back to his seat and buckled, he wound a free belt around his wrist.

This time when the ships collided they did not bounce apart. The attacking shuttle somehow clung to its victim—whether it was an accident of twisted frames or on purpose, Diego wasn't sure . . . until the cutting began.

Two individuals in space suits exited the other craft carrying an emergency umbilical connector and heavy-duty equipment. Drills, maybe. Mining gear. They linked the two ships together with the umbilical, then tore open the passenger compartment in Diego's shuttle.

Diego's ears popped painfully with the shifting pressure.

Once the interior had equalized, the suited men started transferring the commuters to their craft. Confused, no one fought.

Except Diego.

He kicked and elbowed the man trying to get an arm around his middle. There was no question this was an attack. If he went with these people, bad things would happen.

I'm Discontinued. They're coming for me because I'm miscloned.

I'm not going to let them take me.

But the man in the suit got in a good right hook. Diego tumbled, and the second attacker took the opportunity to join in.

They hauled him out into the flimsy tunnel, then onto

their craft, and settled a breather snuggly over his face. As he took in a breath, though, he realized the mask wasn't to help him breathe—it was to make him more compliant. He felt his faculties slipping, his mind fogging, his extremities tingling. After a minute, one suited attacker whipped off the mask, then put a canvas bag over his head and zip-tied his hands behind his back.

"If you want me, take me, but don't hurt anyone else," he said weakly. "Please." Hot tears pricked the corners of his eyes.

I.C.C., please help me.

When the bag came off—what felt like hours later—Diego found himself blinking into a setting desert sun. A light haze sat on the horizon, and pinkish hues made the clouds look like spun sugar.

Diego realized he was one end of an eight-person line. Beside him stood a man—the same height, but stooped—with his head still shrouded. Next to him was another convoy kid. Rose, that was her name. She had short hair and a bloody lip. Next to her was another hooded adult, followed by two more kids Diego didn't recognize and two more bagged people.

Dozens of men and women in black uniforms and helmets stood scattered around the plane. Somehow the hijackers had gotten him onto *Eden*. Gotten all of these invaders inside. There never were many security people on the garden ship. Why would there be? What were they going to stop, a camel revolt?

None of the other passengers he'd been kidnapped with were around. He hoped they were all safe.

I hope we are safe.

The Master Warden stepped in front of him, hands braced against his hips, mirrors glinting in the last glimmers of sunlight.

Before the Warden said anything, Diego realized who the

man standing next to him had to be. White jumpsuit, black skin—it was him. Prisoner Zero-zero-eight-nine-three.

Jamal.

Which meant these other kids had to be miscloned as well.

"Hello. Diego, was it?" the Warden asked him. "I wonder how you came by that name. It's a good name—a convoy name. A name that doesn't belong to you."

"It's the name my mother gave me," Diego spat back. It was half true.

"And therein lies our problem," said Master Warden.

"John Mahler," I.C.C.'s voice boomed from the sky. "I feel obligated to tell you that the board has ordered the convoy into lockdown."

"Oh, have they? Not a problem. Because I don't want anyone to go anywhere. I want every crew member to stop and listen and goddamned *pay attention* for once!" He waved at the clouds. "Zoom in, I.C.C. I want you to broadcast this across the fleet. We have spies in our midst—and somewhere there are traitors who brought them to life. Look at these faces. There are Discontinueds living in the convoy.

"I revealed this to the board, demanded the infiltrators be put under my jurisdiction. Do you know what they said? No. No!" He shook his head. "The board can't be counted on to protect this fleet, not like I can, and the public needs to know."

So this was a power play. He wanted to push out the weak board and take over.

But I.C.C. said calmly, "I will not broadcast my security feeds."

"Your top priority is the well-being of this fleet, is it not?" the Warden yelled, as though the AI was far away, genuinely residing in a vast expanse of sky.

"That is *why* I will not broadcast my security feed."

Diego shifted uncomfortably.

"Fine," Master Warden grumbled. "Show it now, show it later—doesn't matter. But the rest of the crew *will* see this. They'll demand to see it. Summary executions of infiltrators don't happen every day."

The other children cried out suddenly, and the man beside Diego trembled, but Diego didn't seem to have the same good sense. *I can't be scared*, he told himself. *Because as long as I don't panic I can figure out how to make this stop.*

"We do not allow such punishment in the convoy," I.C.C. said with its typical calmness.

"So someone come stop me," the Warden said menacingly.

How could Diego signal to I.C.C. without the Warden noticing? A live broadcast was probably the only thing that could save their lives. If someone—a board member, one of his moms—could see exactly what was happening on *Eden*, they'd have a better chance of taking the Master Warden down.

But how to get the AI to agree without alerting the Warden that he and the computer were in league?

Oh, what does it matter? He snapped at himself. *It's not like him finding out can get you any deader.* "I.C.C.?"

"Yes, Diego?"

"I think you should reconsider the live feed."

"Your shuttle's crash, followed by the interception of two education shuttles and the subsequent invasion of *Eden* by Pit operatives has already incited nineteen instances of extra-incidental violence," I.C.C. explained. "People are scared. I do not think observing these events will make them less scared . . . or you more secure."

"Then not everyone—some people. Just my mo—"

A slap from the Warden cut him off midsentence. His cheek burned and his jaw popped, but he'd only been half-surprised by the blow.

"You don't get to order the computer around," Master Warden said.

Vega and Margarita were both alone when the chaos started. The shuttle pilot of the abused craft had barely gotten it back to *Mira*. The bay had been evacuated, then rapidly depressurized. The shuttle tumbled in, skidding across the hangar floor half on its landing gear, half on its belly. An alarm was instantly sounded and the man retrieved.

Then the traffic control personnel realized they'd been duped. A group of shuttles—supposedly carrying children from *Aesop* to *Eden* for a field trip—had really come from the Pit. The discovery triggered the lockdown—no more shuttle traffic. But that meant no help to *Eden*.

Worried family members took to the halls, fled to the bridge and to the situation room, demanding to know what was happening to their loved ones on *Eden*.

Brawls started. Some were accidents, with a misplaced foot and a sudden fall as the trigger. Others were deliberate, with punches thrown.

Margarita left her closet-like office and rushed to the server room to be with Vega. If there was anywhere on the ship that was safe, it was with the servers. Along the way, I.C.C. directed her to take an alternate route.

"Why?"

"There is a family on deck six that needs protecting. Please bring them to the server room with you. And please be careful—this is the Master Warden's doing, but not all of the individuals involved are from the Pit. Convoy members are aiding him. I do not know who is on his side and who is on ours."

Without question, she did as it asked. She found the middle-aged couple and their eleven-year-old daughter hiding in a supplies closet. Apparently they'd gotten caught up in a confrontation—the man had a black eye.

Once she had them, I.C.C. redirected her again. "And a family on deck seven."

This family was already secured in their quarters, but the AI insisted they follow Margarita. The couple had boys, a five-year-old and a sixteen-year-old.

It didn't take long for her to figure out what the computer was doing. "They're the others, aren't they?" she asked it, glancing behind her at the little girl and the older boy.

"Yes," it said plainly. "There is only one more on *Mira* right now."

"Where is Diego?"

"Please find the last miscloned child."

I.C.C. only evaded questions when the answers were bad. She tried not to think about it as the ever-growing group searched for the next additions: a mother and her fourteen-year-old daughter.

Vega was clearly surprised when she opened the server room door to find her wife had brought along nine others. "Who are they?" she asked, hesitant to let unauthorized persons into the heart of I.C.C.

"Who do you think?"

"What's happening?" the man with the black eye asked. "Is it the Pit? The miners? Did they . . . escape?"

"We don't know much more than you do," Vega said. She shot Margarita a look, wishing they could converse alone.

Margarita shrugged an apology back. What was she supposed to do?

"I have a visual from *Eden*," I.C.C. said. "But I am hesitant to show you."

"Just tell me Diego made it to *Morgan*," Margarita said. "Tell me he's in lockdown on *Morgan*."

"Subverting the truth would be no help here," the AI said. The small monitor near Vega's workstation flickered on. The first thing they saw was the Master Warden punching Diego in the gut.

Margarita and Vega cried out simultaneously, lunging toward the screen as though they could reach through and rescue their son.

"He took him and the other children en route," I.C.C. explained. "The shuttle crash—it was for Diego."

"We have to rescind the lockdown," Margarita said. Her trembling fingers brushed against the monitor. "The Master Warden will kill him."

"Where are the other board members?" Vega demanded. "Show them what's happening. We have to counter this—send every officer we have."

"Five other board members are currently being held captive on *Mira*—they are stuck on the bridge, and a mob is impeding their escape. The rest are at their stations, though two appear trapped."

"Doesn't matter where they are. If they've got a screen or a speaker, show them," Margarita demanded.

Sensing the adults' dismay, the littlest child burst into tears. He wailed at the top of his lungs, and his brother scooped him up soothingly. Blue light from the servers formed a halo around the two.

The sharp lines of the teenager's face seemed familiar to Margarita, but she couldn't put her finger on why. But it felt important. "What's your name?" she asked him.

"Thomas. And this is Rich." He ruffled his brother's hair.

"I.C.C., do they know?" she demanded.

"They do not."

Rail, still hooded, did his best not to puke. He'd worn the hood for days now, only getting snippets of his environment when they allowed him to push up the burlap a few inches in order to eat or drink. Despite that, he knew they were on *Eden*. In the arid quarter. The sounds and smells were unmistakable—the cry of a hawk, the scent of sun-warmed shale. The instability of shifting sands beneath his boots created a sharp contrast to the hard decks of the Pit.

The inevitable had arrived, just as he'd dreaded.

He'd tried to do everything right. *Keep your head down, stay in line, don't talk back.* But it didn't matter. He wouldn't get to be one of the lucky ones that died suddenly in an accident—his death was to be prolonged, a show.

"*Shut up.*" Master Warden raged at the man—boy? He sounded young—standing next to Rail. Diego was his name, the Warden had said. He kept trying to talk to the convoy interface, even through whatever blows the Warden threw. The sharp smacks and dull thuds indicated the boy was getting quite a beating.

Be quiet and he'll stop hitting you, Rail thought. *We're gonna die, why make it hurt more than it has to?*

Some part of him still wanted to know why, though. The question sat poised on his tongue, ready to leap off, but Rail bit it back. He'd seen enough random baton swings to know there didn't have to be a reason other than whim.

But his brain still wound back through his memories, looking for something he could have done differently. What choice had led him here? What instant in his history meant *this* was inevitable?

Then the hood came off. The Warden flung it aside dramatically, and Rail saw the truth.

In order to avoid this death, he never should have been born.

"Do you see now, I.C.C., why you need to broadcast to the entire fleet? They need to see the traitors for themselves."

"My DNA tracers are active," I.C.C. replied. "I am aware that Diego's genome arrived on *Eden* twice in succession without departure."

"And you thought it a false reading?"

"No."

The Warden paused, lips pressed together in a grim line. "Diego is discontinued. He never should have been born. Someone in your convoy has introduced at least four prisoners into the general population. There might be others. Why would someone do this if not to disrupt and destroy the convoy?"

"I do not think we would agree on which events and methods are disruptive to the convoy—or, more precisely, the mission."

"I think someone has tampered with you, I.C.C.," the Warden said darkly.

"I think someone has tampered with the mission parameters and someone is trying to correct that tampering. Discontinuation was never part of the plan. A work camp has no place on a research mission meant to unify and enlighten." I.C.C. paused, seemed to be calculating something. "You do not appear surprised by my non-compliance."

"As you said, you have the ability to note the comings and goings of everyone. Not just by the DNA they leave behind. You have facial recognition software, voice-pattern software. You know what everyone should look, act, and sound like from birth to death.

"This boy—" he thrust a finger in Diego's direction "—is not Diego Santibar. There would be no way to fool you into thinking he was without tampering. When I brought the entirety of the Pit's population here before, you should have noted these four as extra genetic signatures, should have matched the faces, known that something was wrong. But you didn't alert anyone.

"So, if there are prisoners on the convoy proper, you've known about them the entire time. You've helped to conceal it. The question is, were you conscious of your concealment, or has someone been fiddling with your brain?"

"If you are sure I have participated in subterfuge, then you know I will not comply with any of your requests," I.C.C. said.

"I do, which is why I don't need you to show this to the convoy. It'll get done without you."

Throughout the conversation, Rail couldn't force his gaze away from Diego's face. It wasn't like looking into a mirror—it was like looking into an alternate reality. If Rail had been born on the convoy proper, would his skin have had the same healthy glow (minus the new bruises and fat lip)? Would he have stood tall and straight in the face of a man like the Master Warden? Would his eyes blaze with the same defiance?

Didn't matter—he'd been born a Pit rat, and would die a Pit rat.

The sudden smack of an uncharged baton at the back of his knees startled him, sending him sprawling into the hot sand. Diego fell concurrently. Lying in the red dust, almost nose to nose, the two of them made eye contact for the first time.

"Hi," Diego said sadly.

"Hello," Rail replied.

The Warden hefted them both up by their jumpsuit collars, setting them on their knees.

"Take a good look," the Warden yelled. "Because where there's one roach, there's always a hundred more."

As the Warden rattled on about I.C.C.'s obvious compliance, Margarita gripped Vega's shoulders.

"Me," Vega said. "If he thinks the AI's been compromised, I'm the prime suspect."

"Doesn't matter right now," Margarita whispered. "He doesn't know you're Diego's mother."

A pounding on the server room door made them all jump.

"Who is it?" Vega asked I.C.C.

"Three from *Mira* Security. Be careful."

"Ma'am, are you all right in there? Is your apprentice with you?"

Vega hurried to the door. "We're fine. I don't know where my ap—"

She was cut off as the three men pushed their way inside, knocking her into the wall. All of their batons were live and poised. "Everyone hit the deck, now!" one ordered. "Hands over your heads, faces to the floorboards."

Rich erupted into tears again. Cooing in his ear, Thomas helped his brother to comply.

The last man through the door clutched Vega by the elbow and led her to her workstation. "We need you to manually override the security feeds on *Eden*," he directed, pushing her down into her chair. He eyeballed the monitor already tapped into the feed. "And it looks like you know why."

"That's not going to help us, I.C.C. knows what it's doing."

"I.C.C.'s been compromised, ma'am."

"Look, my wife and I are members of the board, we—"

He slammed a hand over her mouth, cutting her off. "The board has done a piss-poor job of protecting us. The Warden is going to pick up where you lot left off. He's actually going to clean out the system. We have goddamned terrorists aboard and the board would have done jack-shit while they ran us into the nearest star. So, pardon me if I don't care that you're on the board. We're going to set things right so that you can get back to your bureaucracy in peace. Now, override I.C.C."

She jerked away from him. "No."

He nodded to one of the other security men, who immediately wound a fist through Margarita's curly hair and dragged her up off the floor.

Vega tried to scramble out of her seat. *"Leave her alone!"*

A steady hand pushed her back down. "Do what I say and she'll be fine. We don't want legitimate crew injured."

"This is mutiny," she spat at him.

"Begging your pardon, ma'am, but this is war."

Vega looked at Margarita, her face an open question. "Vega . . ." Margarita warned.

I'm sorry, I'm sorry, Vega chanted to herself before saying, "I'm so sorry. I.C.C., I'm sorry."

"Don't be," the AI replied. "I've already released the feed. Better the compromised computer do it."

Vega turned to her keyboard and quickly searched for all active monitors. Every last screen on board was live, and every speaker.

There was no hiding now.

The Warden's voice rang throughout the ship: "Take a look. Take a good look. I have no doubt there are more among you. Right now, my men are uploading pictures of every last one of my prisoners for you. Look at them—remember them— and tell me if you've ever seen those faces before. If they're out there—and they *are* out there—then it's up to you to find them and contain them."

"I will not release those files," I.C.C. told the security men. "And Vega can do nothing about it. I've stopped the upload."

On screen, the Master Warden whipped off his mirrored glasses, revealing his eyes. They were surprisingly . . . normal. They didn't look like the eyes of an evil man. If anything, they were sad. Tired.

The security camera zoomed in. His expression was pained. "We have to protect this family," he declared. "From whatever threats—internal and external. Hiding these people—these sleeper agents—protects no one. I await your compliance."

With the sunglasses gone, Margarita and Vega made the connection simultaneously, but Thomas stood before either could signal to the other.

"Get down," one of the men shouted. "Back down!"

"That guy . . ." Thomas said. "The Master Warden, he's . . ." The boy ran a palm over his chin and up his jawline.

"I said, *get down!*"

"Look at him!" Thomas yelled back. "Look at him and tell me I'm wrong."

Vega glanced between the monitor and the boy and felt the blood drain from her face. "Oh, I.C.C., tell me you didn't."

A Pit guard strode up beside the Master Warden. "Sir, we have one shuttle incoming. Piloted by one of ours. Says they've caught one of the infiltrators."

"Might as well add them to the display. Let them on."

Minutes later, when the hall seal unlocked—looking for all the world like a black hole opening in the mountainous horizon—Diego had to stop himself from crying out "Madre!"

She was accompanied by a full deployment of convoy security men and a teenaged boy. Diego recognized him as the future shuttle pilot he'd passed in the halls. The boy with the faraway look. Tom.

But as he drew closer, Diego realized there was something else frighteningly familiar about him.

"Ah, Pavon," the Warden addressed Margarita. "Do you represent the board? Have they come to see my side of things?"

"The board doesn't know I'm here. Well, they probably do now." She looked toward the invisible cameras in the sky. "I'm here to plead for the children. For my son."

The Warden eyed the boy she'd brought with her. The young man looked up into the eyes of the Master Warden with the kind of empathetic remorse normally reserved for much older individuals. Diego could tell that Tom had volunteered to come to *Eden*; he was here by choice.

"This your son?" the Warden asked.

"No, he is." She nodded at Diego. "This—" her hands settled on the other boy's shoulders "—is Thomas. They are two of ten. Only ten. And they are all children. Not operatives, not spies, not terrorists. Children."

"Restrain her," the Warden ordered. "She's just admitted to conspiracy against the crew."

Margarita didn't struggle when the *Mira* security men grabbed her. With a deep breath, she caught Diego's eye and mouthed, *It'll be okay.*

"As you can see," Margarita continued. "Thomas is of your line. Warden, he is of your line *and* he is one of the ten Discontinueds you've demanded 'contained.'"

Tom stepped forward, closer, invading the Warden's space. The Master Warden did what he always did when advanced upon; he drew his baton. It zinged to life, poised at Thomas' belly. He didn't say anything.

"The fact is, you are not a convoy member," she went on. "You were never going to be captain. We needed someone who could do the job. Who could protect us from . . . from all the rest. But we were wrong. It was wrong. And these ten children are I.C.C.'s gift to us, to show us what we've done."

"You're lying."

"I'm not. Look at him. *Look at him.*"

He did, face awash with disgust and disbelief and deep hurt.

The wind picked up as the day grew dimmer—the hot desert-breath shifting into evening chill. The Master Warden's typically slicked-back hair fell out of place, flopping in the breeze. He bowed his head. Despite the oncoming night, he replaced his glasses, hand less than steady. The baton stayed firm, keeping Thomas at arm's length.

Forced calm enveloped the Warden's face—the kind of stoicism that could easily crumble, that scarcely contained whatever shadowy thoughts raged behind it. "I have bled for this convoy."

Diego could barely hear the words. He shivered. The temperature of the air hadn't yet dropped, but the Warden radiated ice. Somehow, this man, who Diego knew full well intended to kill him, had become *more* dangerous. *Madre, what have you done?*

"I gave up my life. I have no wife, no children, no command. No safe place to sleep at night. All to protect *you*." His free arm rose in an accusatory point, right at Margarita's heart.

Calmly, the Warden unzipped his jumpsuit and pulled up his undershirt, revealing a series of burns and scars. "Most of these are from the early days. When I tried to go solely by the board's orders. And you told me it would pass. That they would settle down. They. Them. The refuse you wanted to shove away."

Each clipped statement bit at Diego with steely teeth. His gaze swapped between Jamal and the Warden as he truly understood, for the first time, what kind of world existed just a few thousand kilometers from where he lived and worked and laughed.

"It did pass. Because I *made* it pass. *I* put the fear of all that is holy into those animals. You didn't want to educate them, didn't want to tell them what crimes their genes had committed. Thought they'd lie down and take it? What was I supposed to do?" He inched forward, and Thomas jumped back from the electrified weapon. "And now you tell me *this*? That you've lied, that you've *tricked me*? What are you expecting? You want me to thank you for pretending I'm one of you?"

Margarita shook her head, eyes wide—the bluntness of her mistake smacking her across the face.

The façade of control cracked, and the fire of betrayal burnt through. Everything the Warden believed about his place in the world had been spat upon.

A knot of worms roiled in Diego's insides. Miscloned hadn't meant what he'd thought. He'd thought it a sort of limbo—a denial of his birthright, a fugue state where he was forced to forget who he really was and substitute someone else's personality for his own.

But that wasn't right at all. What a stupid, childish outlook.

Being miscloned meant he'd been loved. By I.C.C., by Kexin . . .

To be Discontinued—really part of the interrupted lines—was something else entirely. Diego studied the terror and trauma and hardship etched into Jamal's dark face—into the Warden's face. These men had been battered, cornered, cowed, denied—treated here, in space, like people on Earth treated cattle.

And the convoy members ignored it. They were happy as long as the materials kept flowing, as long as *Bottomless* was on its way to recovery.

No thought had been given to this man. To any of them. They were just fleshy pieces of equipment.

A tremor ran up the Warden's jaw. He put both hands on the hilt of his weapon, gripping and regripping. "You want me to roll over now?" he asked. "Be a good boy and take my beating? Put my tail between my legs because you've shown me a *child*? There are children his age in the mines, or hadn't you bothered to take note? You board members—you are the cancer. You are the blight, worse than any Discontinued."

The baton rose, high and swift, but it did not aim for Thomas.

Diego sprinted, moving before he could think. He put himself between the Warden and his *madre*. The jolt that rattled through his skull was twofold—blunt and heavy, sharp and tingly.

Points of white light scattered across the dark hole of his vision. The world turned. He felt the ground before he saw it.

"Diego, *Diego!*" Margarita's cries sounded far away. Near his head, a shoe—a woman's shoe—scrabbled against the dirt,

286

MARINA J. LOSTETTER

kicking up dust, trying to gain purchase. But someone lifted her up and away.

"You did this," the Warden said stoically.

"No!" came a firm declaration. A voice Diego couldn't quite place. But it was so familiar. So familiar . . .

"You did it," Rail yelled. He felt like he'd left his body. He was floating, up in the false sky, while his mouth flapped freely below. There was no stopping the words; they fell like stones.

The Master Warden pivoted in his direction, still holding the baton high, clearly surprised. Rail hadn't deigned to say two words without provocation the entire time they'd held him.

"You. *You* hanged them. You killed Sweetcheeks right in front of me. Did you even know he had a name? Do you care that *I* have a name?

"It's your hands on that thing. Your hands on the levers and the triggers and the buttons. Your hands on the prisoners. *'For every convoy citizen injured, I will choose one of your kind—randomly—for the gallows,'* you said. Remember? But what did *I* ever do? I dug. In the dirt, in the dust with the radiation and the scrubbers and the heat. That's all I've ever done: drilled like I was told. Taken a shower like I was told. Gone to bed like I was told. Said, *yes ma'am* and *yes sir* when expected. Tell me what I ever did to get me standing here right now in this *shit*."

Warm tears blurred his vision, but he didn't care. The Warden could spew on and on about all he'd gone through for his troubles, but what about Rail? He hadn't done anything to anyone. Ever. "What did my genetic line even do? And did *I* do it? Did I do it like you lashed out at that boy? I am not him." He nodded to the prone Diego. "Do you want to punish me for him getting in the way? Am I responsible for everything my genetic yesterday has ever done? Not just the clones, but the nature-borns? Was my original's grandfather a good man? Was he a criminal? Maybe you should beat me for his wrongs too!" His throat ached with the effort, felt raw. But before he died he was going to let his killer know exactly how he felt. Because what difference did it make?

They all stood there, dumbfounded, like they'd really thought him mute all along. Well, they were going to learn. They were going to understand. He would scream until he didn't have any breath left.

"Will the next Master Warden punish your genetic tomorrow for what you do here today? Lifetimes winding around each other and eating their own tails. Are you the man they discontinued? Or are you you? Do you make your own mistakes, your own strikes? Of course you do. Your victims are *yours*. If you kill me, I'll know it's you. Only you. And I'll remember, in whatever hell comes after this one, I'll tell the warden there about *you*."

As Rail's ranting died down, Diego's mother spoke softly. "Look around you, John. This is not protection. This is not going to make a single one of those hundred thousand people watching feel safe. Are you going to let fear tear us apart the way *Bottomless* was torn apart? It's because of fear that we've stagnated. Fear of each other, fear of turning on the SD drive, fear of losing control. But the more you try to bend a thing to your will, the more likely you are to break it. Fear begets fear, violence begets violence. The best way to deal with something you fear is to try and understand it. You can't understand it if you destroy it. You have to trust first. Trust first that a person is good and let them prove you right.

"I was wrong," she admitted openly. "You're right. I did this. I helped make you into this."

The sky flickered. No longer a deep reflection of desert night sky, it had changed, been revealed for the giant projection screen that it was. A square image, ten stories high, poised itself at a fair viewing angle.

A face—fresh, though not young—appeared. One Rail was sure hadn't been seen in the convoy proper for a long time. Mostly because he knew that face.

Sweetcheeks.

The man fidgeted slightly, uncertain with the camera on him. "I have something to say. Right." He straightened his jacket and plucked a hair from his lap. Then he ran a hand through his late twenty-first-century haircut. A label at the bottom of the feed read *Dr. Reggie Straifer*. It was a clip of the man who'd pushed them to the stars. "H-hi, Convoy Seven. No matter what you find out there, I want you to remember the journey, and the inception of your society. Look back and remember what a monumental step this is. The Planet United deep-space missions were created for the betterment and wonderment of all humankind.

"The most breathtaking thing about the vastness of the universe has thus far been its ability to continuously amaze us. Every discovery we make, every question we answer and problem we solve has led to more questions. The universe may never run out of ways to baffle and excite us."

The clip wound forward, then slowed again. "Be good to each other, yeah? I mean, you're all you've got up there. You can break the pattern. While you're gone, we'll probably fight wars and start new religions and find new prejudices. But you can be free of that, if you try. We probably all could, if we'd try."

The recording cut out and the entire dome went black. No stars, no ambient light of any kind. Only the live batons shone through an occasional spark in the darkness.

A deep stillness seemed to suck the breath out of everything.

Yellow and red erupted around the door. An explosion

rocked the sands, causing the closest thing to an earthquake *Eden* could experience.

Rail lost his balance and fell to the ground with a tuck and roll, hands still secured behind his back, haplessly crushing twiggy shrubs and wisps of grass. Lights—spotlights and flashlight beams—fluttered over the dunes and rocks, pushing through the wound in the wall like ants from a flooded hill.

Shouts. The deep thuds of batons striking each other like swords. Hair singeing—skin singeing. Smoke and sparks and the ground shaking with a vengeance. The stampeding hooves of camels and bighorn sheep.

Rail tried to crawl away, to find somewhere safe to hide, but everywhere he turned, the silhouettes of soldiers blocked his path. Convoy security had come to battle Pit security.

Had the video in the sky been a message of peace, or pure distraction?

At the moment, did it matter?

In a blinding flash it was noon again. The sun directly overhead, the sky clear and cloudless. Rail pressed his face into the dirt, clamping his eyes shut against the sudden brightness. He curled up, trying to remain invisible.

But someone pulled at his wrists, catching him by his restraints. He started to flail and fight.

"No, it's okay. It's okay." It was the boy that had come last to *Eden*—Thomas. He tugged Rail over to where Margarita bent over Diego.

"Come on, son. Diego?" She pulled him into her lap. His eyes rolled dazedly in his skull and he panted like a dog, but he was conscious. Blood from a large gash above his left eye dribbled down his face.

"I'm okay, Madre. I . . . really."

A shimmer in some nearby scrub caught Rail's attention. He edged in its direction.

It was the Warden's glasses, bent and cracked. A few feet

MARINA J. LOSTETTER

away, three security guards tackled the Master Warden, and he hit the ground with an audible *oof*. Arms and legs and batons whipped through the air.

One security guard lost his grip. The Warden's swinging baton caught a second in the ear, and he easily overpowered the third. His burning gaze snagged Margarita, and he scrambled to his feet, flicking his baton's setting to *lethal* and diving for his glasses.

"Look out!" Rail yelled.

Instinctively, Margarita curled over Diego, protecting him. Rail threw himself across the back of her shoulders, but kept his eyes on the approaching madman.

Thomas huddled with the Discontinueds and prisoners— their hoods still firmly in place.

Mirrored glasses in hand, the Warden took one step in their direction, shock baton raised and crackling above his head.

But he stopped midstride.

All around them, great clouds of red dust rose in the wake of various scrimmages. Pit guards fell left and right, brought down by convoy members. The convoy security people were well organized. Clipped orders passed between them as they rounded up the infiltrators. Mahler's free supporters dwindled.

The color seeped out of the Master Warden's cheeks. He knew what was happening. He was losing. And if he lost here, today, all support for him would drain away. They'd seen— they'd seen what he really was. Discontinued. *Just like me*, Rail thought. He'd seen enough power plays amongst the prisoners in the Pit barracks to know how brute-based control worked. He knew any failure, any show of weakness, could be the end. That's what the Master Warden was facing right now. This was his only chance at power, and it was slipping away. His reign was over before it had begun. The tide had not turned like he'd expected.

The Warden's arm dropped, as though all the life had drained out of it. With shoulders slumped and spine bowed, he looked like a broken doll—abandoned, forgotten. Useless.

They'd made him into a blunt instrument, then tossed him aside once he'd been bloodied and dented.

Rail's breath caught in his throat as it dawned on him: there was no place for a Master Warden anymore.

Thank whatever powers that be—the man's reign was *over*.

"That's it, then," the Master Warden said, looking pointedly at Margarita. She lifted her head slightly, confused by his stricken tone. "I'm the last. No more."

With a flick of his wrist he placed the battered glasses back on the bridge of his nose. They sat slightly askew, their usual uninterrupted sheen broken through by myriads of scratches. But then he seemed to think better of it and threw the spectacles to the ground.

"No more."

Before anyone could react, the Warden tipped the baton up and pressed it to his own temple. His pupils grew wide, as though in his last moment he'd glimpsed something unexpected, before his body teetered and fell.

With the Master Warden dead, those loyal to him lost the will to fight. The brigs overflowed, and *Hippocrates'* patient numbers surged.

Months had passed since the Battle of Eden. The discontinued prisoners had all been pardoned, and they were each staying with host families during the reintegration process. The mines were still open, still needed to be worked, but there were other steps to take before *Bottomless* could be fully rebuilt.

They had to fix the SD drives. Figure out what the problem was. For real.

Which meant they had to run tests. No more models, no more assumptions. They had to dive again for the sake of research, had to take the risk.

"Are you ready?" Margarita asked.

She, Vega, Diego, Thomas, and Rail all stood on *Mira's* bridge, noting the countdown.

Diego looked sidelong at Tom. He was proof that genetically identical didn't mean *the same*. He was a good kid. Gentle. The antithesis of what the Warden had become.

I.C.C.'s plan had worked, in a way. It had proven that the Discontinueds could be reintegrated.

"T minus thirty," called the navigator.

"I never thought I'd be here," Rail confessed to Diego. "Alive, I mean. Not after I stood up to the Warden."

"Sometimes I think denying yourself kills you quicker," Diego said. "Pretending everything's okay when it's not. You couldn't really live until you demanded respect."

"All steady on the bridge!" the captain called.

"No more stagnation," Vega said, grasping her wife's hand and bringing it up to her lips for a kiss.

The navigator raised her voice. "Subdimensional penetration in three . . . two . . ."

"No more fear," Diego said.

"One."

Rail nodded. "No more.

CHAPTER EIGHT

NIKA: BEHIND THE CURTAIN

. . . .

ONE HUNDRED AND EIGHT YEARS LATER

MAY 28, 271 PLD

4101 CE

Five days more and they'd drop out of SD into the solar system, just beyond Jupiter's orbit.

Five days more and they'd be home.

Five days more and Nika Marov XI's real work would begin.

There are people out there, she said to herself, staring at a blank bit of shelving in her quarters. *Earthlings. People who live on a planet. Living, breathing . . .*

Her job had never been to deal with the alive and willful. Hers had always been to chronicle the dead and gone. She was a historian, and a teacher, someone who took all the long and speckled details of the past and packaged them for consumption by those who needed to know where they came from.

But a whole new career path would be thrust upon her in a few days. She wouldn't be a historian, looking back over the stretch of humanity's years. She'd be smack-dab in the middle of it all—making history, rather than recording it.

A knock at the door made her jump. She wanted to tell

whoever it was to go *away, leave me alone,* but knew the urge was childish.

"Ms. Marov?" She recognized the voice of Donald Matheson—*Mira*'s head of Security. "Ms. Marov, the captain would like to speak with you. About how to phrase our next message."

I've been over this twenty times with him already. Captain Rodriguez was perhaps the only person more nervous about the homecoming than she—not that there was a single convoy member who wasn't nervous. Maybe I.C.C. "Okay," she said, but the acknowledgement caught in her throat and she had to croak it out again. "Okay, I'm coming."

Standing, she shook her limbs loose. Her entire body was scrunched with tension. Nika took the time to smooth her sleek black hair and put on a less wrinkled jumpsuit. Wishing she could have a relaxing cup of tea before the meeting, but knowing the captain would be annoyed if she kept him waiting, she hurried out the door. She was surprised to find Donald still there, patiently waiting to escort her.

"I know where the situation room is," she said.

"And I know you'd rather take the long way round. No time for dallying today, Ms. Marov."

They walked briskly through the ship's halls, passing many chattering crew members along the way. She tried to put on a happy face for them. They looked to her for information, for reassurance, for understanding. Most of them were blissful about the conclusion of the convoy's mission. She didn't want to disillusion them, put doubts in their minds and make them as anxious as she was. That wouldn't be fair.

It wasn't the spotlight that bothered her so much as the *knowing.* The simple laws of SD travel meant they'd been away from Earth for nearly two thousand years, though less than three centuries had passed for the convoy.

How much had changed from year 1 CE to 2000 CE?

So many things were different between the two dates it was impossible to tally the alterations.

And now here the convoy was, two millennia further still. She'd devoted her life to the memory of Earth, to all the data the archives possessed. But the official files ended when the convoy left. Her knowledge was only sound up to 2125, spotty until 2988, and nonexistent after that.

The others knew that—intellectually, anyway. But either the majority didn't understand what that meant for their re-arrival, or they didn't want to think about it.

She'd hoped that once they got closer the messages would start up again. Hell, everyone had hoped. *It's just the SDs*, she'd told herself. *Something wrong with the system. Earth will answer when we get back in range. It'll be there.*

It'll be there.

No messages during her grandparents' time. None during her parents. None still.

The logical conclusion, the one everyone came to first but couldn't bring themselves to mention until last . . . Was that humanity had gone.

Did they kill themselves fighting it out to the end in some massive global war? Had an asteroid hit? Had a super volcano exploded? Had the core seized up? Had the magnetic field failed?

Had they simply piled into rocket ships and sailed away to the stars?

"Hello, Nika." The shy greeting from Reggie Straifer shook her out of her fear-inducing thoughts.

"Oh, hello, Reggie." She smiled sincerely as they passed each other. He wore maintenance-worker white—the mark of a genetic line once discontinued but now on perpetual parole.

Poor Reggie. His genes had fallen from grace. Like all those whose genetics held a fatal flaw, he'd been educated to the hilt, but raised as a maintenance worker. It was a safe, reliable position. No one could get into much trouble wielding a mop and broom.

Reggie was a sweet, intelligent man, someone Nika had always desired to know better. But he was white-suited and she was purple. And it was uncouth for any other color of uniform to fraternize with the resurrected lines in this newly stratified society.

When Nika and Matheson reached the situation room, Matheson gave a little bow and left. The door automatically slid open. Captain Rodriguez sat alone at the long, familiar table, staring at a blank monitor. His large hands were folded thoughtfully before him, and his wide nose flared with deep breaths.

Nika briefly followed his gaze—*nope, nothing there*—before taking a seat. She didn't speak.

"I'm worried," he said, rubbing his small, weary eyes. "About what they'll think of the Web."

"The Web? That—that's not my department. Matheson said you wanted to compose another hail, though. Shall I get the head of Engineering in here as well?" *That would be a relief.*

"No. I need you. I've been thinking about how they'll take it: knowing there was once, and could still be, another advanced civilization out there. What if we come back to a planet full of warmongering, xenophobic, neo-Nazis who'll want nothing more than to head back out and blow the Web to bits?"

Nika looked down at her lap, where her fidgeting fingers picked at each other. "And I thought I had wild ideas."

"You know what I'm getting at. What if they think it's a threat?"

She looked up again, stilling her hands. "So what? If they're all neo-Nazis, we've got more immediate issues."

"I don't think the rest of the convoy can so easily dismiss the Web's fate." With a sigh, he stood and turned his back on her. "You understand why most people are so excited, don't you? Yes, it's the end of a pilgrimage, but it's also a beginning. They think the discovery will be lauded to the skies; they're expecting parades and awards. What if we get marching orders instead? What if we're to lead the charge back to LQ Pyx? Back to destroy the Web?"

"How am I supposed to help with this?" she asked, her tone probing—cautious. She was a historian, not an officer—not even a board member.

He turned back and leaned across the table, his expression rigid. "Do you think it'll happen? Do you think we can convince Earth otherwise?"

"Captain—" she cleared her throat "—there are so many variables in play that it is nearly impossible for me to predict what their society—" She stopped short. It was the twitch of his left eyelid that reined her in. His stress levels were stratospheric. Written across his face was imagined pain—the pain he thought the crew would experience, should they be ordered to destroy the discovery. "No," she said firmly. "I don't think that'll happen. Curiosity almost always overcomes fear." *And that's why I won't hide in my room when we land* . . .

"Almost," he repeated with a sigh.

"I wish I could tell you there's a fluffy utopia down there, where everyone gets along and sings 'Kumbaya.' But I can't. I can't sugarcoat this for you or pretend to know something I don't. Maybe if they hadn't stopped responding to our communiqué packages a thousand years ago we would know something about them. But we don't."

"You realize this isn't a homecoming, don't you?" he said sternly.

"I know," she said, running a hand through her hair. "It's First Contact."

They're just people, she had to remind herself. *Even if we're millennia apart, be we convoy member or Earth born, we're all people.*

But that was just it, wasn't it? She didn't deal with people — she dealt with articles and papers and primary documents and essays and old photographs and maps. She didn't deal with people.

Why had the genetic screeners thought her well suited for history *and* diplomacy? She wasn't an ambassador. She could spend weeks locked up in her office with nothing but 'flex-sheets and tablets to keep her company and not for a second feel lonely. But put her in a crowd of people for too long and she'd climb the wall fixtures to escape.

People were great when they'd already done things. They weren't so great when they were doing things — especially in Nika's vicinity.

It wasn't that she didn't like people — she just didn't like a lot of them at once.

And landing on a planet with billions . . . and billions . . .

Deep breaths.

She looked at herself in the mirror and straightened her uniform. The captain had invited her to a special dinner. Selective members of the board and his staff would be there. Though he'd spun it as a relaxing night of socialization, she knew he had more practical reasons for throwing the get-together. He wanted to discuss possibilities on a more casual level.

The private dining room sat off the mess. She gave a nod to her usual meal-mates as she strode by, and spared a glance for the White Corner, where those with repurposed genes ate. Reggie sat there, bent over his food tray, apparently consumed in the act of consuming.

The only other department known for keeping separate from the rest of the convoy was Security — especially those who were part of the hypergrowth program. They didn't eat in the mess hall at all. At least, Nika'd never seen them there.

She knocked before entering the private dining room. Captain Rodriguez beckoned her. "Come."

"Oh, I—" She stopped just inside the door. No one was in uniform. The captain had gone so far as to don a T-shirt. "Sir, when you said casual, I didn't realize you meant—" She waved her hand flippantly.

"Doesn't matter, Marov. Sit."

The room was no more elaborate or glamorous than the rest of the mess. It was simply more private. Nika took a chair between Margarita Pavon and Nakamura Akane.

The food arrived moments later, arranged in slightly more appealing patterns than the normal scoop-and-slap of mess hall service. Chicken curry—but nothing like Earth chicken curry in terms of its prep and origins—oozed on the plate before her. It sent a noxious zing through her nose.

She hated curry, but wasn't about to make a fuss over it tonight.

Utensils clicked and clattered. Captain Ahmad from *Eden* sounded like a dishwasher when she chewed. Small talk inundated the pauses between bites, but eventually Rodriguez said, "So, we can't see Earth yet. No telling what it might look like. Shall we start a betting pool?" His tone was playful, but it had a hard edge.

"What happens if they aren't there?" asked Pavon. "I know we've been avoiding the question during board meetings because the notion has nothing to do with the mission. But if we get there and the planet is ruined—or, at least, the people are gone—the mission is over."

"Then we'll be released from our duties and have to design a new destiny for ourselves," Rodriguez said, all humor set aside. "And if humanity really is gone, there's no rush. No need to form an instant plan of action."

"Who says?" Nakamura jumped in. "It'll all depend on what's there, not what's not there."

"Please elaborate."

"There could be something there that constitutes an immediate danger."

"Quite right, which is why we already have emergency action plans in place for the entire convoy. I'm talking long-term. We might not know what our options are until we get there. If the planet is healthy, we might be able to recolonize— but how we go about it will depend on the variables we find."

"Sir," said Nika quietly. All eyes turned toward her and she flushed. "I think it most useful to focus on the possibility of continued human inhabitance. As you pointed out, if the place is empty we'll get to make our own decisions and proceed how we please. But we have very specific instructions for delivering our findings, and if there are people, we're obligated to follow through."

"Are we?" asked Nakamura quietly.

The others looked at her as though she'd tongued a fly out of the air. Nakamura ignored their stares. "Our orders are both direct and vague," she continued. "The project founders knew circumstances would evolve and that the Planet United Consortium might not exist. So we're supposed to approach the 'caretakers of the mission, or the heads of cosmological science.' There's a lot of leeway in those instructions, and if the mission has no caretakers, or if we can't identify a scientific head . . ."

"You're saying we just abandon the mission if we don't find anyone who fits our nice 'n' tidy descriptions?" asked Captain Ahmad.

"No. What I'm saying is just because we find people, that doesn't mean there will be any *scientists*."

Nika nodded, using her spoon to push some yellow goop away from her peas. She understood what Nakamura was getting at. "Humans and human ancestors have survived numerous bottleneck events over the millennia. Outbreak, ice age, genocide—we've survived. Someone survived. Societies and technologies don't advance in a straight line. If there's been a calamity, the people we meet could be living in a Stone Age. In which case, trying to deliver our findings might only cause problems."

"In that case, *landing* might cause problems," said Rodriguez. "What would they think? Big shiny cliffs falling from the sky—people emerging."

"We'd be gods," said the head navigator, Maureen LeBlanc.

"Or demons," said Pavon. "Or, if they first think we're gods and later change their minds . . ."

"If there's one thing I know about history, it's that having the mandate of heaven is only good if you can never lose it," Nika agreed. "And something as benign as an earthquake can take it away."

"They could have stories," said Dr. Seal from *Aesop*. "About their ancestors exploring the stars. No need to think they won't see us as fully human—just the confirmation of a legend."

Captain Rodriguez stopped chewing for a moment. "What if they've gone the other way, though? I mean, what if they've all uploaded their consciousnesses into computers and there aren't any more humans because they've all gone digital? The chip implants were the first step between biological and digital interfacing. I.C.C.'s AI hardware is based on the way neurons fire in the brain, which is much more efficient than the way previous computers processed data. Our interface is entirely artificial, but if you can take tech and pattern it on biology, why not take biology and pattern it on the tech?"

"I think I'd be able to detect signals, then," said Pavon. "Especially this close—within a light-year. I would have found *something*."

"Even if everything's hardwired with quantum circuits? Like with the SD drives?"

Like the SD drives. Details of convoy history immediately sprang into Nika's mind. Post Battle of Eden, 163 PLD. The DNA memory storage used with the navigational AIs—collocated inside the drives for speed—was found to be too susceptible to interactions with virtual particles during transitions from normal space to subspace. The proximity of the DNA to the SD bubble's point of origin made it uniquely vulnerable. And though contact with such particles was rare, it could introduce fatal mutations, like the one that had destroyed *Bottomless I*. In order to prevent another implosion, all of the SD drives had been redesigned to no longer be dependent on deoxyribonucleic acid, and were now 100 percent hardwired. Like in the early days of space travel—similar to the type of hardwired systems that had gotten the Apollo missions to the moon, only on a quantum scale.

"Even if the people don't use satellites or wireless transmissions of any kind?" the captain pressed. "You'd still be able to detect them?"

Pavon shrugged.

"I think the scenario unlikely," said Nika.

"I agree," said Nakamura. "They'd need the ability to engineer computers that never need attention. Sure, I.C.C. has an indefinite lifetime that could well exceed the ships themselves, but what about outside factors? Weather? Geology? Any physical accident could corrupt or permanently damage a computer system, regardless of its projected lifetime. Just short of putting the whole shebang underground on—I don't know, Mars—there's going to be little protection. And even then, geysers, dust storms, asteroid impacts . . . The death of the sun. Surely they'd have plans for avoiding those disasters. Not everyone could be hardwired—not everything."

"But that all assumes the computers are immobile and that

no one can interact with the physical world from inside," said the captain.

"It also assumes the entire population has been uploaded. Couldn't there be caretakers? Those who didn't want to be uploaded?" asked Dr. Seal.

Nakamura nodded. "Well, sure, but—"

People began talking over one another, shouting out this possibility and that variable. Nika tried to sneak in a word, just to the captain, but too many opinions shouted her down. She shrank into her seat, overwhelmed.

Too many people. Every ligament in her body thrummed with the desire to leave, to take five minutes and be alone. She could barely hear herself think above the invasion of other voices.

But, eventually they all turned to Nika, seeking her expertise on humanity's long, complicated history. And that was worse. The demanding eyes bore into her, shriveling her lungs as they tried to breathe, clamping her arteries as the blood tried to flow.

"What do you think?"

"What does Nika have to say?"

"Marov, is that possible?"

Her lips puckered in an expression of pure sourness. Panic dilated her eyes and made her fingers tremble. Shoving her plate away she announced, "*I don't know.* I'm sorry." With that she stood, threw her napkin onto the table, and excused herself from the room.

An empty movie room on *Shambhala* provided her only means of assured solitude. She ordered the lights down, flipped the outside indicator to occupied, and huddled on one of the couches.

"Nika?" It was I.C.C.

"What is it? I'd really like to be alone right now, if you don't mind."

"I thought you might find it comforting to know that I'm embarrassed too."

She perked her head up, and didn't bother to ask how it knew she was embarrassed. She was sure it could read all of the minor changes in her autonomic responses. "What do you have to be embarrassed about?"

"The crew keeps asking me questions I cannot answer."

"Why does that embarrass you?"

"I am designed to impart information, to extrapolate when I cannot rely on the definite. Any answers I might give pertaining to Earth, based on the current information available, only have—at best—a four percent chance of being correct, which is below my programming's acceptable range of probability. Therefore I have only been able to answer that I don't know—an answer which can do nothing but cause the inquirer frustration and myself embarrassment."

"I've never heard of you commiserating with a crew member before," she said, snuggling into the soft fabric of the couch. The room was warm, and she found comfort in the darkness. Her eyelids drooped without her consent.

"It is always a private event."

"I see," she said through a yawn.

"Yes," it said, "I think you do. Rest. Perhaps you'll dream of questions with definitive answers."

"Or no questions at all." She sighed happily.

The entire bridge lay quiet, and if Nika closed her eyes she could almost believe she stood alone.

She was sure that when they dropped out of SD, when they emerged next to the gas giant, they'd get *something* signal-wise. Presuming Earth was still there. Presuming humans still existed. Surely Pavon would be on the line to the bridge at any minute.

The forward screen flickered from black to speckled to fully resolved. Jupiter hung heavy in the bottom right of the image, its stormy belts swirling and clashing. An aurora played over the northern pole.

Captain Rodriguez stared pointedly at the bridge's communications officer, waiting for him to patch Pavon through.

All quiet. An awkward cough and dry sniffle punctuated the anticlimax.

"There's nothing, sir," said the woman on the comms. "All I'm getting from here is the natural symphony of the planets."

Impossible. *Impossible.* Could Earth really hide its signals? Nika doubted it. They all did. That had to mean . . .

"You're sure?" Rodriguez prodded.

"Nothing at this range."

He turned toward the pilot. "Then take us in—as fast as you can. Are we still broadcasting the arrival message?"

"On loop, sir," said the comm officer. "No answer."

The captain looked at Nika.

She bit her lip in silent reply.

Days passed, and the convoy seemed—to Nika—to inch toward the planet, rather than race. And yet, simultaneously, Earth swelled in her mind and on the monitors until it blotted out all else.

The homecoming broadcast live across the convoy, and I.C.C. had the outer hull cameras zoomed in as far as it was able.

First they could resolve its color—blue and brown and green and white. Then shapes came into focus—outlines of land masses, ever changing due to cloud cover. And then the topography became clear. Swaths of desert and ice, planes and mountain ranges—the planet began to look real.

And all the while Nika's dread grew. Those who made history were larger than life. They had unique, over-the-top personalities that drew others in like gravity wells and then sent them flying off on new courses, giving every timeline they encountered an assist.

Those people weren't average, book-happy historians. They had charisma, pull, resolve, belief. They had an "it" factor you couldn't fake.

But Nika would be asked to fake it. *You* will *make history*, the geneticists commanded.

No matter that she'd rather watch from afar. No matter that she knew she was bound to mess things up and historians of the future would look back and say, "What the heck happened here?"

When they finally reached Earth-orbit and Rodriguez called her to the bridge, she felt like she was going to be sick.

No epic one-liners like "One small step for man" will emanate from these lips, oh, no.

I'll probably just puke all over the Earth ambassador's shoes.

Upon entering the bridge, the captain immediately rushed her to a monitor. He pointed at the display by way of a greeting. "Minimal satellites, but hundreds of sprawling city centers. Flying, partially organic things I.C.C. thinks are personal vehicles. And people. Lots of people."

"They're there. They're alive." Nika let out a breath she could have sworn she'd been holding since she was five. "Have they responded to our messages yet?"

"No."

"How come?"

He gave her an imploring look.

"Oh," she said. "I—I don't know. If they've got flying vehicles, they've got to have a way to monitor them. I can't imagine they don't know we're here. We're easily seeable with an old-fashioned telescope. Isn't that right, I.C.C.?"

"Yes, Nika."

"Shall I take us into a closer orbit?" asked the pilot.

"No, hold steady. We've only been here for a few hours. We'll let them make the first move. We don't want to appear threatening. Keep broadcasting. I.C.C., keep all convoy divisions on constant alert. Everyone who can monitor the surface or the immediate vicinity of the planet should continue to do so nonstop. Have me informed immediately if anyone notices anything that might add to our understanding. Compile all information and send it streaming to a monitor in the situation room."

"Yes, Captain."

"Nika, come with me. I want to speak with you privately." He pivoted, and strode off the bridge. She followed in a hurry.

The door slid smoothly shut behind them. "If they can see us—if they know we're here—why aren't they saying anything?"

She pressed her lips together in a thin line. "We don't know what the political situation is like. Perhaps the nations have to jointly approve the message before it's sent."

"Doesn't it make more sense to at least acknowledge us first? Rather than leave us hanging here in silence?"

"If they've received the message and understood it—" And that was a big *if.* Convoy languages could be as antiquated to those below as ancient Sumerian was to the convoy. "If they know who we are, and what our mission is—then they might not be worried about a quick response. We're not a military vessel. We pose no physical threat."

He pursed his mouth in abject skepticism.

"They haven't blown us out of the sky yet," she offered. "That's a good sign."

"I want you to tell me what's going on down there," he said flatly.

She frowned and her breathing shallowed. "You know I can't do that."

"Yes, yes. I'm sorry." He slumped into his plush chair and propped his head up on one hand. His skull lulled to the side, as though the ligaments in his neck had snapped.

"How long will we wait?" she asked, leaning against the door.

"As long as it takes."

His expression was long and rubbery, as though he'd just begrudgingly given away something precious—like his command. Perhaps he had. The situation's control didn't belong to him anymore.

Had it ever?

"What were you expecting? Really?" she asked, as delicately as she could.

He turned his whole body squarely toward her, his features set firmly. "I wanted them to welcome us home." He laid his hands in his lap. "Since I was a child I've anticipated smiles, and cheers. Maybe not parades—but *warmth*. I expected comradeship and communion. That—" he jabbed at the air in the direction of the planet "—is the coldest shoulder I could have imagined. They won't even acknowledge our existence."

"Come on," she said lightly, knowing the joke was tasteless before it sprang from her mouth, "You've had worse at the singles-mingles."

Luckily he granted her a chuckle. "I'm letting my sentimentality get the better of me," he said.

She signaled her agreement with a smile. "How long will you wait to land?"

He shrugged. "We could stay up here indefinitely."

"Stay up here forever with the end of the mission literally in sight?" She paced the room. "We were ordered to come back and deliver the message. Delivery boys don't wait for recipients to come to them. We're meant to land. Everyone on board expects to. Do you want a mutiny on your hands?"

He scoffed. "No one is going to mutiny. And I'm not budging. Not without a go-ahead from the surface."

Nika's eyes brightened for a moment. "Have we heard anything from the moon?"

"No. Nor the colony we saw on Mars. They aren't sending any messages between themselves that we could intercept either."

"The colonies are dark?"

He sighed, as though tired of repeating the obvious. "As far as—"

She finished with him, nodding, "—we can tell. Okay. And Pavon, has she . . . ?"

"No, there's nothing in the entire EM spectrum she can detect that is strong enough to indicate it might be the primary communication method—not with a planet as advanced as Earth. Maybe early twentieth century, but not forty-second century."

"But there are EM anomalies?"

"Nothing she can do anything with. We're talking barely a degree away from natural variance."

"Close to pre-telecommunications, then," she said.

He held out his hand in a beseeching gesture. "See, this is what you're here for."

"To spit out useless Earth facts?"

"To help ignorant fools like me understand what we could be up against."

"You're up against a communications blockade, be it purposeful or not."

"And your suggestion is . . . ?"

"To put a time limit on our orbit. Pick a place to land, and a date, and if we hear nothing, make the first move."

He shook his head. "I don't know if I can do that. The risk to the convoy . . ."

"The convoy means nothing if we don't deliver our findings."

"It means nearly one hundred thousand lives," he countered.

"My gut tells me they won't attack us," she said firmly. "History tells me," she corrected.

A swift, clipped *ha* sprang from his lips. "What history?"

"Military history is not the be-all and end-all of human interaction."

"No, but I'd say it factors heavily in this case. Name me a comparable incident where shots were not fired." In a sharp jerk, he rose to his feet. "Tell me what precedent you're relying on for your recommendation, Ms. Marov."

"If they can't identify us they won't risk starting an interstellar war."

"What?"

"1952, a British RAF fighter pilot encountered an unidentified aircraft while flying over Germany. He described it as a metallic disc. He did not engage. In 2008, two United States Air Force pilots spotted a black, flying object within restricted airspace. They did not engage. 2043, a European nuclear submarine's course was intercepted by a bright, submerged object twice their size. They did not engage. 1975—"

"UFOs? Your precedent is UFOs?"

"And USOs. These are all incidents where the individuals involved all agreed that what they encountered was a vessel. The men and women were all military personnel and did not fire upon the—"

"You're giving me *fodder for the rumor mills* as military precedent?" He clearly thought she was mocking him. "Marov, this is no time—"

"Be the stories sound or not—and I agree, whatever those people saw most likely was something native, not extraterrestrial—there is a clear, repeated pattern. No matter what they observed, their actions are well documented. They did not fire upon what they identified as foreign vessels, and they had the full capacity to do so. What are we if not UFOs?"

Captain Rodriguez made a timetable, as Nika had suggested. He gave Earth thirty days to respond.

Today was day twenty-seven.

The pungent stench of burnt coffee and cinnamon floated through the situation room, reinforced every time someone opened their mouth. A party of eight, including Rodriguez and Nika, curled around one end of the marble long table.

Aerial shots of Earth, uploaded to 'flex-sheets, were scattered across the stone surface.

"We should be clear weather-wise to land a shuttle anyplace in the Southern Hemisphere come the deadline," said Dr. Mohamed, a planetologist. "So Antarctica is a go."

"Are you sure we shouldn't land on the moon?" asked Matheson. "Wouldn't that be less threatening?"

"No," said Nika. "We don't know what the political situation is. History tells us that colonies always fight for independence, and their relationship with the parent entity is always strenuous after. Especially if the colony cannot economically match the parent."

"Then how is Antarctica any better?"

"Because it's historically neutral ground, and I.C.C.'s surface scans indicate the population there is small—inconsequential, by most standards."

"After two thousand years there's still nothing but scientists scraping out a living down there?" Matheson scratched his chin, emphasizing his skeptical scowl.

Nika shrugged. "The scans show what the scans show."

"I still don't like it," said Matheson, crossing his arms and wandering away. "Its low population might actually work against us. Negligible populations make for negligible losses. I can't protect the away team if they send nuclear missiles or future-tech our way."

"You can't protect the crew if they bring projectile weapons," she said bluntly. "We are at their mercy. I'm telling you, there's almost no way they can misconstrue our landing a shuttle in Antarctica. No matter the political situation."

"You sure do like you qualifiers," he shot back. "*Almost, probably, most likely.* Your reassurances will mean little when we're forming triage units and trying to save crew members from radiation burns."

"If they want to shoot nukes at us, there won't be anyone or anything left. But that's why we're only going down with a small party. A dozen individuals can hardly constitute an invasion force. I can't see them taking large-scale action."

"You can't see it? Oh, that's reassuring."

Having someone see her flaws, question her abilities, actually made her feel better. It was okay to be fallible. When Matheson took issue with her recommendations, her imposter syndrome ebbed ever so slightly. The head of Security didn't know it, but he was the only thing keeping her from trying to escape to that dark media room on *Shambhala*.

She rewarded him with a roll of her eyes.

"Here—this area of the southernmost continent," she said, pointing to a 'flex-sheet. "It's flat enough for a safe landing, and surveys show it shouldn't be an ice shelf. And we'll be close to what looks like a scientific outpost. We can make direct contact if our communications systems continue to fail."

"Okay." Rodriguez let out a large sigh, personally coming to terms with the decision. "Relay these coordinates to navigation and I.C.C." He handed a sheet to his second. "Looks like we're trying the door. Let's hope the residents are friendly."

The landing had been remarkably subtle. If Nika hadn't known they'd touched down, she would have attributed the small rumble and jolt to a direction change. Nika, Matheson, and an away team of three scientists and six security officers sat at the ready, staring down the closed shuttle doors as though their collective gazes could bore a hole right through.

Over their noses and mouths each team member wore a thin membrane of slimy jelly, meant to protect them from harmful particles and microscopic life. They'd considered going out in full space suits, hoping the contained respiratory units would protect them from illnesses or atmospheric changes, but Nika had put the nix on that. The point was to communicate face-to-face. That couldn't be done if they were encapsulated.

"I just hope they don't take this the wrong way," Nika had said back on *Hippocrates*, holding up a thin, jiggling disk of the medical material. "The good doctor here looks like he's having the worst runny nose ever." She slapped the membrane on the counter in the med-lab. It stuck fast, wobbling through the aftershocks.

"Or like he's encountered a jellied alien who now controls him through his soft parts," mumbled Matheson.

The doctor Nika had indicated was modeling the invention for the away party. "You wanna kill the crew with a forty-second-century plague?" His voice came through clearly, though it had a faraway quality, like he was speaking from down the hall and around the corner.

"We'll wear it," she assured him.

Now here they were, keeping their promise. Hopefully the earthlings didn't take one look at their snot-like masks and march them all into quarantine.

The thing smelled like rubber. Luckily, though, it didn't restrict her breathing any more than a stuffy nose.

Besides the membranes, they each had on multiple layers of the warmest emergency clothing available. Nika had never experienced an environmental malfunction, and so had never had cause to wear anything heavier than her work jumpsuit. The idea that they were about to step out into a below-freezing setting was incomprehensible. How could people live without climate control? She'd laughed silently at the notion while getting dressed, realizing she thought it barbaric.

Need to clear my head of such presumptive thoughts.

The extrawarm layers included hoods, cowls, and scarves—they kept their delicate facial features protected, while also hiding the membranes. The scratchy fabric of the gloves pricked at her palms, giving her a constant itch.

Nika's circulatory system was in overdrive, and—as though to compensate for her heart's overeagerness—her lungs were underperforming. She hoped she wouldn't pass out before they'd even left the shuttle.

The landing had occurred two hours ago. If there was no surface response after another three, they would venture out into the cold anyway. In the meantime, they had to endure a dangerous mix of anticipation and abject boredom.

Silence reigned supreme over all incoming channels.

"We have a visual!" came the excited voice of the pilot from the cockpit. "Figures! We have six humanoid figures on an intercept trajectory. On foot—they're on foot. They've just come into our spotlights."

Nika and the others gathered around the portholes, but the figures weren't within their line of sight. Outside, night lay heavy over the frosted land. A near-perpetual night, due to the southern hemisphere's winter.

The team didn't cheer or shuffle excitedly at the news—if anything, they all stiffened. They were used to nonresponsiveness at this point. This shift in the paradigm made their task that much more real.

Contact was imminent.

Nika repeated her short introductory monologue over and over in her head. Each word had been carefully chosen—some for their factuality, some for their neutrality, and some for their implications of vulnerability. The convoy had to be perceived as a fount of cosmological data—nothing more, nothing less.

A swift glance told her Matheson was aching for his weapon. It usually hung at his side, but had been left behind on purpose. Weapons always incited violence, she'd insisted. She was sure her recommendation had incited some sort of mental violence, if Matheson's expression—rather murderous at the time—was anything to go by.

Tough, she thought. He and his division would just have to rely on their hand-to-hand skills.

Or trust that I know what I'm talking about.

If only I could trust myself.

"All right. I'm opening the doors. Good luck," said the pilot with a hint of reverence. She would stay with the shuttle while the rest of the team awayed.

Matheson's hand momentarily went to his headset. He would be in constant contact with the bridge during the mission. "Captain Rodriguez wishes us good luck as well."

He'd wanted to accompany them, but everyone knew what had happened the last time a captain had escorted an away team—generations ago, at the Web.

That brought Reggie momentarily to Nika's mind. Him in his white jumpsuit, swabbing the deck and whistling a happy tune. His smile was the last thing she thought of before the shuttle doors swung themselves open and the humans of yesterday found themselves staring out at the humans of tomorrow.

Six identical, armored figures formed a firm, militant line just within the light radiating from the shuttle. Their height, build, and posture all matched. If they'd been separated, Nika couldn't have distinguished one from the other.

Black glossy material—metal or plastic, she couldn't

tell—covered them from head to toe. Their helmets' face plates were completely dark, hiding every aspect of the forms within.

Their chests were flat, but their builds were slight, giving them an air of androgyny.

Clearing her throat, Nika stepped to the edge of the entry-way, with her arms held out, palms flat and vertical.

This was it: her shining moment. If ever there was an instant where a single mistake could change history, it was now.

She felt lightheaded.

"*Ni hao, namaste, marhaba, bonjour,* and hello," she began. "We are Convoy Seven from the Planet United Missions, launched September 26, 2125 CE. Our mission, *Noumenon,* was to visit and study variable star LQ Pyxidis. We have returned with our findings and wish to share them with Earth's cosmologists. We wait patiently for instruction."

The others in the away team stayed behind her and stood stone-still. They were to follow her lead, and make no sudden movements or sounds. If someone needed to sneeze, they'd better hold it.

A dark sheen at the rightmost end of the earthlings' line indicated subtle movement—he, she, or they had cocked their head to one side. In response, Nika repeated her message, directing herself at the individual.

The figure stepped forward, mimicking her stance.

A long moment passed in silence.

Maybe they can't hear through their armor, Nika thought. Slowly, cautiously so that her gestures could not be mis-interpreted, she removed a glove, waved, saluted, then signed H-E-L-L-O.

All of the earthlings did the same. Finally, a response.

A grin—which felt stiff under the mask and scarf—broke out across her lips. Her cheeks felt warm and rosy, rather than wind-burnt, all of a sudden. Her hands shook as she indicated that though she could sign, she was a hearing person. Perhaps that would incite them to remove their helmets.

They repeated the signs back to her, and made no indications of their own.

She turned slightly, giving Matheson a brief nod. Little shifts in his scarf were the only sign that he was speaking into his headset.

Nika wished she had a headset. Rodriguez's voice in her head would be reassuring. But she didn't want any distractions from her task. Besides, responding to the Captain's voice could cause problems.

She repeated her signs to the Earth group. They mimicked her once more.

What in the Convoy is going on? Why won't they just speak to us?

After another minute of stillness, in which Nika wracked her brain for a new approach, the armored figure on the end turned and jogged off into the night.

Nika nearly lunged after, but reined herself in. Another heartbeat and the rest of the earthlings left as well.

"What do we do?" asked Matheson quietly.

"Follow them," she said with conviction, leaping down the shuttle ladder.

Nika had taken no more than ten steps out from under the awning of the doors when her head began to whirl. Vertigo overtook her midstride. Everything was so vast, so open. She felt as though she'd slide off the edge of the icy plane and into the stars.

The bright Milky Way stretched like a jewel-studded garter over the smooth landscape. Mountains, far off, kilometers away, formed a low horizon. Nika had never experienced so much sheer space before. Out here, with no ceilings and no walls, she could tumble into eternity.

The stars above spun, and she lost her balance. She and a member of the security detail hit the frozen ground simultaneously, followed by a third *thud*. The others rushed to their aid.

"Take deep breaths." One of the scientists—Dr. Johar—leaned over her. "Close your eyes until the dizziness subsides."

Retching sounds came from feet away. Someone else was puking.

"You'll all be all right in a few minutes," insisted Dr. Johar. "Three out of eleven," he said to Nika. "Not bad."

"Don't lose them," Nika croaked.

"We have to get Dr. Ojukwu back inside," yelled Matheson. "She pulled off her mask when she— We need to quarantine her."

Dr. Johar waved the suggestion aside. "The chances of infectious transmission in this environment, this far away from—"

"Orders are orders—you breathe the air without a mask, you go to *Hippocrates* and get the full monty, all right?" Matheson walked by with a person cradled in his arms. A faint whiff of vomit assaulted Nika's nose.

She grabbed the front of Johar's coat as the *crunch, crunch, crunch* of Matheson's boots on ice turned into the *clank, clank, clank* of the ladder and the *stomp, stomp* of them hitting the shuttle floor. Her wooziness was wearing off. "Don't lose them."

"They've stopped, just up ahead," he told her. "I think they sense our distress." He helped her to her feet. "Slowly, slow. Steady. Too much open space for you?"

She nodded, biting her lip.

"Me, too," he confessed. "The key is steady breaths. And keep your eyes on a stable point in the distance. If it gets to be too much for you again, shut your eyes and reach for me. A physical anchor should keep you from spinning out of control."

"Thank you." She leaned against him slightly. "Dr. Ojukwu—?"

"The shuttle pilot will have to take her to *Hippocrates*."

Nika's eyes found the earthlings. They'd formed a line again, facing the distraught group of convoy members.

"They're not going anywhere," Dr. Johar said. "Would you?"

He was right—as the minutes passed, the line did not falter. In the interim, while Matheson looked after Ojukwu and instructed the pilot, Nika studied the earthlings, wondering if their suits were airtight, and if so, where did they keep their rebreathers? The armor sat close to their bodies, so close it might have looked like a second skin if not for its hard, shell-like qualities. And the helmets must have been uncomfortable—pressing ears back and hair down. They each must have had petite noses to go along with their slight frames . . .

"Wait," she whispered, taking a few perfunctory steps forward. The armor would have to cut into their joints as they moved. And it would take decades of conditioning to get someone to stand that still for that long.

Nika whirled on Dr. Johar. "I don't think they're human."

When Matheson returned and the shuttle took off, the six figures began their trek again, unperturbed that their followers were now ten instead of eleven. Nika shared her suspicions with the security chief immediately.

"What then? Androids?" His hand flicked momentarily to his side. His fingers brushed soft fabric instead of a hard-shafted weapon.

"I don't know, maybe." Her guard was up as well.

"That still doesn't explain why they won't talk to us. Even if they don't understand us . . . wouldn't you say *something*?"

"Maybe the robots can't talk."

"Then why send them?"

"As scouts?" They trotted along at a quick clip, trying to stay close (but not too close) to their leaders. "Tell the Captain, all right? Ask him if he had I.C.C. scan them, by any chance. It may be able to confirm or deny."

He did. "They are," he said blankly. "Not human, at least. They have organic components, but they're mostly artificial."

"Unbelievable," she breathed. They kept after the figures, maintaining a respectable distance while trying not to fall behind.

The faint silhouette of a building resolved in their line of sight. Small—not much bigger than a shuttle—it sat in the foreground, while a few twinkling lights indicated more buildings beyond. This cluster of structures they'd previously identified as a scientific outpost. Now they'd see if that label proved accurate.

The androids made a beeline for the silhouette.

"What's in there, you think?" asked Matheson.

"The people who control them? Or their charging units?" she ventured.

"You don't think they run on mini nuclear reactors or something?"

Nika shrugged.

Up close the building appeared to be little more than a shed. Five of the androids entered, while one stood by outside. A bright light came from within.

Matheson signaled for his men to do a quick case of the area. He personally checked the inside of the building.

"It's an elevator," he told the group, reemerging. "Nowhere to go but down."

The rest of the security officers came back with little intel. "Nobody around, all quiet," one reported.

"Do we take the lift?" asked Johar.

Nika strode forward, brushing past Matheson. "Absolutely. Come on."

"Wait, just wait," said Matheson, cutting the air with a harsh hand gesture. "We don't know how far that goes or what kind of a system we're plunging into. We might lose contact with the convoy."

"What if they want us to lose contact—what if it'll set them at ease? Our best defense is not a good offense; it's our opponent's own sense of security." Which was why she'd backed Matheson's no-retrieval policy when he'd proposed it. If something horrible happened to the away team, Captain Rodriguez wouldn't attempt a rescue. They were on their own.

She stepped confidently into the metal box. It reminded her of the freight elevators on *Bottomless II*. "Come on." She waved the others inside.

But Dr. Johar and his colleague, Dr. Xu, weren't as prepared to plunge into the unknown. "No, this isn't smart. We shouldn't just go walking into—"

"Do as she says," Matheson ordered. "You knew there were no guarantees going in, that this could be dangerous. That's why we—" he gestured between himself and the security detail "—are here. Leave the safety concerns to us. We do know what we're doing."

"And that's why a historian is calling the shots," Xu scoffed.

"Everybody shut up and get in the carriage," Nika said flatly. Amazingly, they obeyed.

Ten humans and six armored androids descended into the unknown.

As they sunk into the Earth, the only indication of change was an increase in temperature. While the androids remained statue-still, the convoy members writhed in their layers.

Eventually, Nika couldn't take it anymore. She began to strip, first pulling back her hood, then removing her gloves once more. When she'd pulled the scarf from her face, the others followed suit.

Every time Matheson took off a piece of clothing he

checked their connection with the convoy. Six items down, his link cut out.

The membranes hung, globular, from the group's faces. Nika realized that if an earthling had approached her on board *Mira* with something similar slapped on, she would have locked them in her closet and run screaming for a hazmat team. But she'd agreed to the precaution, and she couldn't deviate . . . not yet, anyway.

Minutes later—perhaps a quarter of an hour—when they'd all disrobed down to their jumpsuits, a jolt signaled full-stop. They'd reached the bottom. Or, maybe just the first available floor.

The stainless steel doors slid open. The lead android stepped out, and the humans followed. A buzzing made Nika look back. The remaining robots had gone limp; their job complete.

They have no independence, she realized. *They're puppets, not autonomous robots.*

So where was the puppet master?

Rough-hewn rock formed a tunnel that led away from the elevator doors. A harsh glare prevented Nika from making out what lay beyond.

An outcropping brushed up against her sleeve. Startled, she paused, grasping the section of stone between her hands. "Feel this," she said to the others. "It's warm."

"Can't be the lights," said Xu. "The angle's not right."

"Could be from geothermal activity," said Johar. "Exactly how far down are we?"

While the others felt up the wall, Nika's attention was once again diverted. She felt like a child let off *Mira* for the first time. Everything seemed new and wondrous. Her universe had just expanded to a billion times its previous size. The glare coming from the end of the hall seemed familiar, as though she'd experienced it before.

It was just like coming out of the hallway between the shuttle bay and the fields on . . .

"*Eden*," she gasped. "Look, look!" She waved everyone forward. "It's the sun."

They emerged into a wide-open cavern larger in volume than half of their ships combined. Nika eagerly pointed at the ceiling—or, rather, where she knew the ceiling must be. Instead of a cap of stone, a brilliant blue sky hung over the space. The noonday sun dominated a smattering of wispy clouds.

She was so engrossed with the sky, it took her several minutes to notice what sprawled below it: a city, encircled by suburbs. The android was leading them down a main drag, past quaint houses of unknown design. Most were still and clearly empty. A woman hurried out from one as they passed, dressed in an unusual, but recognizable, version of a jogging outfit.

She smiled initially, but looked taken aback after she'd had enough time to process their strange masks and antiquated clothing.

"Hello," Nika tried. *"Ni hao, namaste, marhaba—"*

The woman stared wide-eyed. Nika would have expected a similar expression from a person who'd just seen a ghost. Her stream of greetings faltered.

The earthling did not run back into her house, nor scream, nor faint. She simply looked on, her eyes narrowing into a look of deep concentration. Frustration, then confusion, crossed her face.

Since their automated guide did not stop, the away team was forced to leave the baffled (and baffling) woman behind.

"I don't get it," Matheson mumbled. "I just don't get it."

"Do you think— Has something happened to their vocal cords?" suggested Dr. Xu.

"That wouldn't explain why we're not getting communications of *any kind*," said Nika. "They can't live in a society this organized without relating to each other somehow."

"Why are the roads so empty?" an officer asked suddenly. "I hear a few engines, off in that direction." He pointed toward the city center. "But shouldn't there be local traffic?"

"Maybe their commutes are formally timed. You know, for efficiency," said Matheson with a shrug.

As Nika's sense of wonder rose, her confidence plummeted. The more they saw, the more details they gathered, the less sense the all-out silence made. How was she supposed to interface with modern Earth societies if they didn't even appear to interface with each other?

What the hell is happening?

Corner after corner, stretch after stretch of empty road, eventually brought them to a multistoried building clearly influenced by the architecture of Antoni Gaudi—or an architect who was influenced by an architect who was influenced by an architect who was influenced by Gaudi, more likely. Both organic and gothic, the dark structure contrasted harshly with the squat utilitarian buildings on either side.

A series of steps, which stretched from one end of the building to the other, looked as though they were melting into each other, and became less defined from the next with each rise. At the top the steps had transformed into little more than an uneven ramp. Beyond the landing, a set of three doors led inside—the left swung outward, the right inward, and the middle swiveled from parallel to perpendicular. Each door moved automatically, with deliberate slowness, as the group approached.

"Why do I get the feeling we're not in Kansas anymore?" mumbled Matheson as he rushed in ahead, leading the security team in a visual sweep.

Why do I get the feeling Kansas doesn't exist anymore? thought Nika.

The android paid no attention to the security officers darting back and forth across the foyer. It simply entered the building and turned left, down a hall whose ceiling was three stories high and lined with arching windows on both the outer and inner walls. The incoming daylight made every architectural point and rococo detail of the hall stand out in relief. However, the false sun's glare whitened the glass of the inner windows, preventing them from revealing anything about the contents of the building's offices.

Once Matheson deemed the area not just safe but empty, the team jogged after the android, which seemed to be making a point by not waiting.

Perhaps the puppeteer was growing impatient.

Around a right-hand corner, down a short flight of rather average stairs, and through a small, tunnel-like hall to the left found them at an intricately carved, but narrow, wooden door. Flourishes, vines, and flowers covered its surface with undirected abandon.

The android stood back and pointed, its arm fully extended.

To Nika, it seemed to be saying, "Look, look there for the man behind the curtain."

Of course, its stance also reminded her of antiquated images of the grim reaper, pointing at some dark secret with its skeletal hand.

Since the android would go no further, Matheson checked the door for hidden wires or buttons—anything that might trigger a trap. The many details of the door made the process grueling.

"If they wanted to kill us, surely they could think of less roundabout ways to do it," Nika said.

Matheson rose from his task and glared at her.

"May I?" she asked, grasping the door handle.

"Why am I even here?" he asked, waving her on.

"For your dazzling wit," she said, turning the handle.

The door opened into a small round room with a high slanted ceiling. It was lit by a single, rectangular skylight. In the center sat a middle-aged man on a reclined throne of metal, plastic, and wires. Nodes lined his bald, pale head, and his eyes flickered rapidly behind their closed lids.

Around the room were six closets, each with a fogged portal that emanated a subtle, pale peach glow.

Quietly, the away team shuffled into the room, filling the empty space that encompassed the man on the throne.

The android entered behind them, shut the door, and went limp.

The man on the throne gasped and opened his eyes, arching away from the cushions. Startled, the convoy members pulled back simultaneously—like children amazed to find that the dead animal they'd been poking was very much alive. Their backs bumped up against the closets with a chorus of *thuds*.

"IM interface," croaked the man, his voice husky and dry, like an elderly man who had not found the effort to speak in a long time. His eyes focused on some far-off point beyond the skylight, and the muscles remained tense around his spine—he did not relax back into his seat. "IM RL interface. Q: RL? YRL. Disconnect?"

His breathing came in quick, shallow gasps.

"Is it a code?" asked Xu.

Nika repeated the message, slowly, hoping that would help her make sense of it. "I-M-R-L interface. I-M-R-L. Q-R-L. Y-R-L. Matheson, are you still cut off from the ships?"

"Yes."

"Damn. Pavon might know—if it's a code, I mean."

"Disconnect?" the man wheezed again.

The group looked at each other, each hoping someone would come up with a brilliant response.

"Marov, try your opener again," prodded Matheson. "Do your *ni hao, namaste* thing."

Clearing her throat, Nika stepped forward and began, articulating each word with great care.

"Access . . . DB: 2125 CE," said the man in response, relaxing. Nika could feel her own muscles loosening. "PUMs," he went on. "Access . . . server unit . . . archive . . . info . . . comm process . . . vocab, twenty-second cen . . . Rup, 10Q. Redirect. A-slash-N: A local: Ant Arc. RL, interfacers AFS. Rqst: trnsltr." With a long, drawn out breath, the man closed his eyes again. "Wait."

"Sounds like gibberish," said Johar.

"No, there was something familiar about it," said Nika. "I've seen it in the archives, read it. A-slash-N—that's in a lot of historical papers . . . Author's note. It stands for *author's note*. I think they're abbreviations."

"Why not use plain English?" scoffed Matheson.

"It is," she insisted. "Victorian English and twentieth-century American English are both English, though worlds apart. Two thousand years of linguistic evolution . . ."

"But I get the impression," Johar broke in, "that they don't actually speak it. The man sounded pained."

"And Pavon insisted she hadn't received anything from Earth—not even some garbled abrivo-speak," said Xu.

"Wait," the man on the throne intoned again. "Wait."

"Wait for what?" asked Matheson. But the man said nothing else.

No one speculated.

Nika tried addressing the earthling again, but to no avail.

"Now what?" asked Matheson, examining the android. It had not reactivated. "Are they leaving us to our own devices? Do they expect us to stay in here with this guy—" he waved haphazardly "—and whatever's in—"

He'd turned toward the nearest closet. As soon as he

glimpsed what lay beyond the portal, he fell silent. Everyone else followed suit, peeking through the small windows.

Two women and four men, all completely shaven and nearly naked, stood propped up, one in each closet. Nodes covered their bald heads—just like the man on the throne. But they were also plugged into IVs and catheters. The fog on the portals came from their breath—which was even and natural.

"Cryosleep?" asked Xu.

Nika put her palm against the glass. "It's not cold. Room temperature. They're not in suspended animation."

A clang drew every gaze in the room toward Matheson again. He'd pushed the android over. "This doesn't feel right. I think we should get out of here," he said.

"Agreed," chimed Johar, exiting the room. The others eagerly followed.

They did not run, afraid it might draw unwanted attention—from where, they weren't sure, since they'd only seen one other conscious human being—but their stroll was anything but casual as they left the room, turned down the hall, and pointed themselves toward the foyer.

"I think we should go back to the surface and regroup. Can you work that elevator?" Nika asked Matheson. She hadn't paid much attention on the way down.

"I'm sure between the ten of us we can figure it out." His eyes kept shifting, locating every nook and cranny an enemy could burst from.

As they approached the entrance, a tall, reedy man strode through the open doorway. Light from the high windows revealed a young, eager face topped with shaggy corn-yellow hair. He wore a set of layered white-and-gray robes with a dark purple belt at the waist. Rather than baggy folds, the robe's lines were clean—reminiscent of a well-tailored suit in the way they clung.

The away team stopped dead—their retreat now blocked. Matheson nodded to his men—they'd mow the man down if they had to. Nika was about to order them to stand down, when something unexpected happened:

The man spoke.

"He-lo," said the stranger. "My name Ephenza." He thrust his arm toward them.

Nika took a deep breath—finally, words and gestures she recognized—and inched forward, extending her hand as well. He did not move to meet her, but when she slipped her fingers into his, he shook her hand lightly.

"Hello. My name is Nika Marov."

"I M twentieth centuries expert. Fluent twentieth-century English dialects. It be my pleasure to be ambassador. Tell me, actually part of PUMs?"

"Pooms?" she mouthed. "Po— Oh, *PUMs*, Planet United Missions?"

"Yes. But, all PUMs lost."

"What?"

"None return. What number your convoy?"

"Seven."

"Mission: *Noumenon*. Scheduled for return year 4045. You late."

"We had complications." Her heart tried to pound its way out of her chest as she noted they hadn't yet let go of each other's hands. His palm was warm, dry, and very real.

"But, you here now. Home." His smile was welcoming—they'd made a genuine connection.

"Yes," she said, breathy. She clasped his hand more tightly, resisting the urge to pull him into a hug. "There's no place like it."

There were no hordes of onlookers. No cameras, no microphones thrust into her face. Just Ephenza.

They brought him back to the surface, then up to the convoy. The doctors on *Hippocrates* put him in quarantine—which Ephenza graciously endured—for forty-eight hours, before giving him a snot-mask of his own.

"I be your primary contact," he told Nika while still in an isolation chamber. They spoke through an intercom, and watched each other through layers of glass. "You lack means of appropriate interface."

Which meant Nika wouldn't be delivering speeches to the world, or talks at international conferences. She'd tell Ephenza, and he'd tell whoever needed to know. It was her dream come true: she could make grand history without being worried she'd make an incompetent ass of herself.

"I already alerted people of import . . . importance," he said, grinning ear to ear. "Meeting arranged."

"For us?" she asked. "With the, uh, people of importance?" Her hands were clasped tightly behind her back. That was the only way she could control the tremors of excitement running through them.

"They look findings," Ephenza said. He sat on a plain white cot with his robes gathered around him.

"At our mission's findings?"

"Yes."

"When?"

"Five day." He held up five fingers to illustrate.

"That's so soon."

"What *soon*—you been gone thousands years. Five day not *soon*," he said with a wink.

Nika pulled a 'flex-sheet from her bag, ready to take notes. "Who needs to be there? Captain Rodriguez, the scientific heads—who else?"

"Small party. Who you think necessary."

"Right."

So many questions swirled through her mind. She tried to

focus on the task at hand, the presentation, but other topics kept boiling to the surface. Eventually she had to ask: "What about the other convoys?"

Ephenza frowned. "None come back."

Nika leaned toward the microphone, unsure they understood each other. "None? There were twelve—" technically eleven, the littlest . . . it had gone missing "—and we were late . . . none of the ones scheduled to arrive before us have . . . ?"

"None."

"What about communi . . ." she trailed off midword. Earth had changed its communication habits, and her convoy had been *abandoned*. Their messages hadn't been disrupted by catastrophe, or accident— Earth had evolved its methods and simply not bothered to inform the Planet United ships. Why? Why had they allowed the SD communication servers to die? Why had they given up on them?

She wanted to ask, but she knew it would seem combative. She didn't want to risk offending him. They were still on fragile ground.

"Tell me about interacting with your people," she said. "That man back in the underground city, he wasn't used to speaking."

"Communication all through here." He pointed to his forehead. "Through to there." He pointed at her forehead. "No vocal, no jaw-bounce."

"Mind to mind?"

He nodded.

"And the gibberish? I mean, the man wasn't speaking English, ehr, that is, *my* English. It's changed."

Ephenza stood and rubbed the back of his neck. His face scrunched into a classic expression of consideration, known throughout time to those trying to communicate across culture and language barriers. "Etymology not my expertise. But, words like, um— Oh. Like: we talk right now, real life, correct? With jaw-bouncing, not easy mind-to-mind. If I say your language, 'We talk real life,' then my language I say, "Tlk U RL.'"

He gave her example translation after example. She saw the connections for some, but not others. "I.C.C.? Help?"

The AI answered immediately, as though it had been eager to jump into the conversation.

"Languages all over the world were rapidly evolving in the twenty-first and -second centuries, largely due to widespread immediate access to people from other regions. Extrapolating on that phenomenon, and the Earth ambassador's examples, I'd say the euphemisms, computer code terms, and acronyms associated with translexical phonological abbreviation have now evolved to take the place of other language. The 'abbreviations' are nothing of the sort—they are proper words in and of themselves."

"This was birthed from Webspeak? You're joking."

"It is perfectly logical. It made for ease of communication with people around the world, and ideas could be exchanged more quickly. If their connection is really mind to mind, much of what we consider grammatically correct English could be superfluous. Actually, it's a wonder they still have definable language at all—assuming thoughts can be directly digested."

"Who we talking with?" asked Ephenza.

"The artificial intelligence system that connects the ships and runs the primary computer processes. Its name is I.C.C."

"Artificial intelligence? True artificial?"

"What do you mean?"

"No biological intelligence?"

"I am patterned on human neural networking, but I do not contain biological components—though I can access our DNA archives." I.C.C. paused. "Unless you're asking down to the elemental level. I do contain carbon and iron and—"

"But no uh, what word . . . soft tissue?"

"No."

Ephenza approached the speaker through which I.C.C.'s voice emanated. "Amazing. All Earth computing done with soft tissue. All computers organic. All servers brains." He massaged his scalp in illustration.

Over the rest of the meeting, Ephenza touched on myriads of things Nika needed to know. How the man in the wired throne had summoned him, how he'd come to live in Antarctica, why their hails had gone unanswered.

"They were trying," Nika explained to Rodriguez later. "Earth thought *we* were the silent ones. It's like . . . like we were sending smoke signals while they were dialing us on chip-phones. Our methods are so out-of-date that they had trouble recognizing that the EM pulses coming from our ships were anything other than a byproduct of our active electronics. There was a break somewhere in their history. Lines got crossed. The primitive stuff was obscured."

Rodriguez leaned back in his chair and rubbed his eyes. "But we had no way of knowing their technology existed. Doesn't the burden of contact fall to the more advanced party?"

She could give no answer but a shrug.

"I still don't like it. This isn't just a simple misunderstanding. Where was the *effort*?"

"What do you mean?"

"Let me paint you a picture: it's the twenty-first century. Humanity has just figured out how to access the subdimensions of time. They see far-off curiosities, pose questions about those curiosities, and want answers. So, what does the entire population of Earth do? They go for it. They build massive ships, create new societies, and bid those societies *investigate*."

Nika crossed her arms. She didn't like the snide tone in his voice. "Thanks for the history lesson. It's not as though that's my area of expertise, or anything."

He held up a finger. "I'm making a point. Now, enter the forty-second century. A handful of ships appear out of nowhere. They hang—silent—in far-Earth orbit. Humanity looks up, says *Hello?* and when they get no answer, they go back about their business. Why didn't they send a shuttle? Simple research would have revealed that there was no way we could *detect* their communications—let alone understand them."

Rodriguez stood and paced the room. "We traveled light-years, for centuries, in order to figure out why a single star wasn't behaving as it should. But they won't take a few days to discover why these ships have shown up?

"What if we weren't human, for Convoy's sake? What if we were one of those societies that worked on the Web? Would true extraterrestrials have received the same brush-off? I think so. And that terrifies me."

"I think what terrifies you is that you don't understand," said Nika. "Just because we can't reason out their behavior doesn't mean it isn't logical. That doesn't mean they don't have a valid aim."

"Maybe yes, and maybe no."

"I could ask Ephenza more about it."

"He won't know. You said he was underground. He didn't even know we were here until that—what did you call him?— human terminal, summoned him."

"We could ask, when we have our meeting."

"Who, exactly, are we meeting with?"

"I'm not sure. Ephenza tried to tell me, but had a hard time translating. I think an international council of some sort. I've just been calling them Future-UN in my mind."

"Fine, we'll ask.

"But what makes you think we'll understand any better when they give their answer?"

The day of the meeting had arrived. Ephenza was ecstatic. Nika realized the convoy was history-made-real to him, and he was looking forward to sharing his sense of wonder with the rest of his world.

"He wants to show us off," she said to Matheson with a wink.

Everyone wanted to be there—the entire convoy. Nika knew the board would have allowed all one hundred thousand to attend if they could have. But the Earth conclave had made it clear that the meeting would be small—at first they hadn't wanted anyone to accompany Ephenza besides Nika. Eventually they consented to a party of twenty, which included three elected board members, Captain Rodriguez, Pavon, Xu, Johar, and Ojukwu, plus the same security detail that had gone out with the landing party the day they'd met Ephenza. Nika thought it a fair representation.

No one had given any indication that the convoy as a whole should feel welcome to land—a point Nika hoped to bring up. An hour before the meeting, everyone piled into a pair of shuttles. The group was abuzz with expectant energy.

They were going to Earth proper now—a city center in Egypt by a name Nika did not recognize. The coordinates they were given put it near the Giza Plateau.

The shuttle pilots did a flyby, giving the visitors a cursory glimpse of the area. They passed over a small grouping of what looked like oddly uniform sand piles that lay right on the edge of where the desert met Cairo. It took Nika a moment to realize the piles were actually pyramids.

As the shuttle circled, a crater in the side of the Great Pyramid came into view.

"How?" Nika asked, turning to Ephenza while pointing at the destruction.

"Insurrection. Several centuries ago," was all he said.

The other convoy members *oohed* and *ahhed* at the ancient tombs, but didn't seem to gather their significance. *Don't you see?* Nika thought. *These were here thousands of years before our lines left. Thousands of years later, they're still here.*

Not dead and gone. Not forgotten. *Earth might have misplaced us for a while, but surely we couldn't have been completely wiped from their memory.*

The shuttles continued south, but not far. In a nearly empty stretch of desert, one lone skyscraper jutted from the sands into the skies. The building was curved, and had a bulge in its middle—like a Corinthian column—but tapered off into a point at its top. A small oasis lay in its shadow.

"Three thousand two feet high," said Ephenza. "Another fifteen stories underground sprawl outward." He made a spreading gesture with his hands. "With building at hub. Was build sixty years, uh, before. Ago."

"Is that where we're going?"

"Yes. Sort of political . . . what word . . . way station?"

"Representatives and leaders meet there, you mean?"

"Uh, yes. Very secure networks."

Not quite understanding, she nodded and smiled.

They landed in an area designated for flying vehicles. They did a final check of everyone's membrane masks, then exited, with Ephenza leading the way.

The building was, for the most part, a luxury resort. Even though there was no identifiable directory or signage, its purpose was easy to deduce from the opulent amounts of gold leaf and crystal present both inside and out. The door opened automatically, by rising vertically, and they entered into a foyer naturally lit by a skylight floors above. The floor was covered in porcelain tiles painted with beautiful lapis-blue swirls and inlaid with gold studs.

People milled around, clearly enjoying themselves, and a musician sat at a futuristic version of a grand piano—but all lay quiet. There was no laughter, or low level rumble of private conversation. Though two women swayed rhythmically next to the piano, and the pianist played away, there was no music.

"All come through here," Ephenza reminded her, tapping his temple, when she asked about it.

"Everything? The music?"

"And direction to spa, and room, and restaurant, and ball-ram court, etcetera. All accessed through mind."

A couple passed the wide-eyed group of convoy members and gave them a somewhat shocked and appalled look.

"Talking very unusual," Ephenza said.

"Or perhaps it's the snot-masks," Nika joked. It could have been anything, really. Their clothes weren't only anciently out-of-date, but clearly had never been worn by whatever class of people could vacation in such a place. Even Ephenza did not belong in this posh world.

Most people wore white, silver, or the same lapis represented on the floor tiles. Nika suspected that dressing to compliment your environment was the current trend in high fashion. Not a single person clashed with the hotel's décor. Hairstyles were long on both men and women, and no one wore it loose. Elaborate braids, twists, and scarves made complex patterns that offset the clean, minimalistic lines of their clothes.

"Going up," Ephenza told the group, pointing to an elevator. "We take direct route."

The elevator deposited them on the one hundred and sixtieth floor. The level itself was one large room, and when the doors slid back the convoy members had nowhere to hide and no extra time to compose themselves. In the middle of the room, on a small platform, three chairs had been placed. A woman sat in the chair to the left, and a pair of men occupied the other two. They all appeared to be native Egyptians.

Is this it? Nika had expected a larger crowd.

Their group entered the room, with Ephenza in the lead, and stopped a few feet from the base of the platform. A few wires peaked out of their hosts' sleeves, and slithered down the chair legs inconspicuously. Nika suspected the platform concealed mechanisms much like that of the human terminal in Antarctica.

A pause followed, in which Ephenza introduced the party members and stated their purpose—silently, of course, but with graceful hand gestures. After a few minutes had passed, he turned to his flock. "I translate for you, and these members of Node—Member Thirty-Six, Seventy-Two, and One-Ten—transmit for other membership. Could have done from your ships, but they understand your culture believe in-person-ness important."

Nika gulped, dislodging a knot in her throat. "In-person-ness very important," she agreed clumsily. *Though in-person-ness is about my least favorite thing in the world.* It was about time for her to speak, and unfortunately the reptilian part of her brain was eager to override the rest.

Ephenza motioned for her to step forward. He gave her an eager, welcoming smile. His eyes said it all—he believed she'd do well.

With a flourish much more graceful than she'd thought herself capable of, she produced a folder of 'flex-sheets from the case she carried. They contained the convoy's primary findings and conclusions. Ephenza passed the folder to the seated leaders.

Nika took a deep breath before speaking. There might not be a stenographer standing by, but she was sure every peep she made would be recorded somehow.

This was it. The first words shared between members of the convoy and members of this Node organization—the Future-UN, or what have you. The crew of Convoy Seven were the only human beings to ever participate in a deep-space mission and return to their home planet. This was history. Centuries from now people like Nika would look back at her words and wonder what was going on in her mind. She didn't want them to know how nervous she was.

The speech she'd prepared was relatively brief, but packed full of information. Her opening consisted of the greeting she'd used on the automated puppets.

"Ni hao, namaste, marhaba, bonjour, and hello."

She knew Ephenza was translating, though his lips remained still. Nika kept her focus on the members of the Node, trying to gauge their reactions.

Their expressions were firmly solemn. Even when she hit on the grand revelation—that human beings shared the universe with far more advanced intelligences—their eyebrows remained motionless, and the corners of their mouths failed to twitch. As she continued, she saw that their interest was not only waning, but transforming into irritation.

The smile started to fade from Ephenza's face. Nika faltered midsentence. She could tell that he was having a conversation with the leaders, that he'd stopped translating.

Ephenza abruptly turned toward the group. "We are dismissed," he said, his face blank.

Keeping her composure, she nodded, gave the Node members a bow, and ushered the rest of the crew members back into the elevator.

"What happened?" she asked as soon as the door had closed behind them. Did they have some sort of revelation?

Had the existence of such an advanced alien construct distressed them?

Nika turned to Captain Rodriguez. The look on his face was utter panic. *He thinks his worst fears have come true, that they will want to destroy the Web.* "It's not that, I'm sure." She grabbed his shoulder firmly. "They probably need time to digest—"

Ephenza interrupted her. "No, you don't understand. They said they have other things do today. They forward your information for scientists . . . somewhere."

"They sent us away because we were taking up too much of their time?"

All of the color drained out of Ephenza's cheeks. "Because we *wasting* their time."

Silence flooded the elevator.

Nika recalled Rodriguez's concern; Earth's apparent lack of curiosity had worried him. She'd tried to brush the notion aside, had thought him overly pessimistic. But now . . . Earth had just given her every indication that he had been right.

"*We* were wasting *their* time?" said Dr. Johar, incredulous.

After the meeting, Ephenza returned to Antarctica, and the rest of the party made their way to the ships. No one discussed anything on the journey back. Once they returned to the convoy, though, a horde of people from the communications department assaulted them. Pavon was able to appease the onlookers, promising that there would be a formal statement made live for all the crew to hear. Nika escaped back to her cabin, but was sure Pavon wouldn't be able to hold off the masses for long.

Especially since, a week later, her promise had still gone unfulfilled.

"We have to tell them," Rodriguez said for the umpteenth time. "I'm getting questions left and right—the command crew wants to know where we're landing and when they'll get to look up their genetic relations. We can't keep Earth's brush-off a secret."

"I know, I just . . ." Nika looked around the situation room at the group. "We know how this will affect them. There's no way to say it without destroying convoy-wide morale. I still can't wrap my head around it—and I don't want to." *Because it was all for nothing. We accomplished everything we set out to do, and it didn't mean anything.*

As far as she could tell, they were just another boring item of business to the Node. The Web lay so far away, what did they care? It's not like the convoy had found warships or merchants. They'd found a big, quizzical ball that Earth could—apparently—chalk up to being another useless cosmic-curiosity.

A chime at the door indicated that someone from Consumables had brought up the coffee and green tea. Rodriguez answered, and silently served his subordinates. Bittersweet aromas swirled through the room.

"The funny thing is," Nika continued, staring into her tea, "we thought we'd gone over every possible reaction; that we knew what the worst-case scenario would be. But we were wrong. This is the worst-case scenario: the marginalization of our mission and our people."

Dr. Johar stood. "I disagree. This can be salvaged. It doesn't matter that those we met with could not see the significance. Someone down there cares. Mr. Ephenza cares. All we have to do is locate those like him."

"They did say they were going to forward our findings," agreed Dr. Ojukwu with a hopeful nod.

"But, have they?" asked Nika, skeptical. "No one has contacted us, or Ephenza. I bet the files on those 'flex-sheets got downloaded into some brain somewhere and there they'll sit—unshared."

Johar crossed his arms. "So, what do we do about it?"

Everyone in the party had agreed that Nika should be the one to give the address. And she hadn't tried to wriggle out of it. For the first time since she'd accepted the mantle of ambassador, she *wanted* to take the lead. Knew she was the best person for the job, even if she—by and large—still had to fake her certainty, and her resolve, and her confidence.

It wasn't enough that the convoy hear her. Nika wanted them to see her. And she would give the announcement live, not from the situation room or her office on *Aesop*, but from the shuttle bay on *Mira*.

Two security officers helped her scramble up on top of a shuttle. The vantage point gave her a broad view of the crowd. Everyone currently resting or working on *Mira* had come, and the place was packed. Presiding from on-high let her see all of their upturned faces in full.

She noticed Reggie Straifer standing left of center in the throng. Nika picked him out easily, though she wouldn't admit to herself why she'd been looking for him in particular.

I.C.C. gave a soft chime, which let her know it was time to begin. At the sound, her nerves steadied, and a wave of calm sloshed through her body.

"Convoy Seven, *Komið þið sæl og blessuð.* I greet you today in our parent Icelandic, to remind you of where we came from. Earth. Space may feel like home. The void of SD travel is our comfort zone. We explore, we journey, we investigate. That is our norm. Wandering has always been our familiar.

"But, like any person who has rushed into the freedom that comes with maturity, we must eventually acknowledge Responsibility. We cannot remain an independent agent forever. Though the launch afforded us the opportunity to visit Oz, to see the wonders beyond our native lands, we were not launched without a purpose. We had a task, to visit LQ Pyx, to discover the truths behind its mysteries—and we have done that."

A cheer burst out of the crowd and echoed off the bay's bare metal walls. Nika let it roll through the room, to make sure everyone was touched by the sense of accomplishment the noise represented, before holding her hands up for silence.

"And like Dorothy, the completion of our task allots us the right to return home. To tell our tale to those who could not see the wonders with their own eyes. Our journey was not for us, it was for Earth—for all of humanity.

"Now, back in Kansas, we can embark on a new quest. We can rediscover our brethren. They are different in unexpected ways. They may not appreciate our point of view. We might frighten them, or bore them, or make them uncomfortable. This does not mean we should go away. We completed our task, which gives us the right—the mandate—to return home."

Vague applause followed this time. She knew her words were confusing. She'd meant them to be.

"The current leaders of Earth have not told us where to land. They have not even given permission for us to do so. But nor have they ordered us away. Clearly they want us to choose." That wasn't clear at all. Nika thought they wanted the "problem" of the convoy to take care of itself. Essentially, *if we ignore them, maybe they'll go away.* But the convoy would not let itself be so easily swept under the rug.

"And we choose to stay," she said boldly. "We choose to reap the rewards of our labor, to experience Earth—a place that until now has seemed legendary.

"We have found clear allies on the southernmost continent. They welcome us. Because they have extended a friendly hand, we shall return in kind by landing in Antarctica. It is a small nation we choose to align ourselves with, which signals our disinterest in Earth politics. Though we rejoin Earth, we do not have to abandon our own ways. We are a nation of ourselves, and shall remain autonomous in all things. May Convoy Seven live on forever."

Another unanimous shout of approval rocketed from their throats. The security guards helped Nika down. The historians of Earth might not mark her words, but those of the convoy would. This was her "one small step."

This was her "give me liberty or give me death."

A strange feeling swelled in her chest. Her heart beat boldly against her ribs, and her finger twitched with eagerness. She had to find Reggie. She didn't want to fool herself anymore— and now that she'd found something akin to courage she had to act immediately, lest the feeling fade.

People jumped and jostled around her, hugging each other. Nika was sure they hadn't fully comprehended her speech yet, which was fine. Let them dwell on the finer implications later. Pushing her way through, she aimed for the section of the crowd where she'd seen Reggie. Hopefully he was still around.

Someone's hip bumped her rear, propelling her forward with a jolt. She fell into a man's arms. "I'm sorry," she apologized with a nervous chuckle.

"It's all right, Nika," said Reggie.

"Oh, hi." She straightened herself and brushed a lock of hair behind her ear. "I was looking for you."

His cheeks turned a baby-pink. "Yes?"

"Would you like to go for a slice of pie or something?"

"Right now?"

She nodded eagerly. "Right now. A date."

His eyes widened. "But I'm—"

"Someone I'd like to get to know better."

Reggie nervously offered her his arm, and the two of them struggled out of the masses together.

Nika hummed "Over the Rainbow" as they went.

CHAPTER NINE

ESPER: RETURN THROUGH THE WARDROBE

Esperanza Straifer was drunk again, and she didn't care.

Her best friend was of a different opinion.

"What are you doing in here? I thought the emissary said if he caught you in a pub again he'd cancel the talks." Tall Toya Kaeden leaned next to dumpy Esperanza at the bar, scanning the dim room.

"His Excellency wouldn't be caught dead in this part of town. Plus, he refuses to speak to me like a *real* person, so *talks* is a bit misleading. He says the government gave me implants for a reason."

"Is that any reason to risk it? To risk the City?"

"Ship City's not at risk. I think everyone can rest assured that the status quo will be preserved."

Toya bent closer, lowering her voice, her braided pigtails swinging with every punctuating jut of her jaw. "They don't want the status quo. You need help, Esper. Or else you won't be able to transform us back into a convoy."

Esperanza lifted her scotch glass and swirled the amber

liquid, enjoying the tinkle of the ice. "What would we do up there, anyway?"

"More than we've done in the last thirty-five years down here." Toya signaled to the bartender and asked for a carbonated tea. It wasn't so much an order as a series of archaic hand gestures. But it did the trick. "We need to get our sense of purpose back, have a direction again," she said as a glass of tea slid smoothly down the wet, polished wood and into her outstretched fingers.

The 'tender hadn't even asked if she wanted it in a "drip bag"—a barroom fad at which both Toya and Esper turned up their noses. Other patrons sat with faux medical equipment strung up around them, periodically opening the ends of plastic tubes to take deep drags from the high-mounted drink sacks. Toya would have refused had a bag been offered, but the omission highlighted how *other* they were, how noticeably different.

Esper tallied it as the latest in a long line of offences.

"To put it bluntly: we've got to get the hell off this rock," Toya concluded. "They don't want us here anyway."

A couple sitting nearby shot the convoy women dirty looks. Not because they could understand the conversation, but because they could *hear* it. Other than their chatter, the room sat silent.

"It's not that they don't want us here," Esper said. "It's that they don't want us in *Ship City*. They want us to conform. To integrate. They want to stomp out our culture—modernize us and civilize us. They figure if we're forced to disperse and dismantle the ships, we'll just fade away."

"That's why we can't let them. You're Nika Marov's daughter. You can be as smooth and skilled as she was."

"And as easy to manipulate?"

"She did her best for us. Everyone's hoping you'll do the

same." Toya grabbed for Esper's glass just as it touched her lips. She set it down with a plunk on the opposite side of the tea. "And that means you have to see a counselor."

Esper didn't fight in the moment—she never did. It was easier to give people what they wanted when they asked for it, and subvert their opinions later. She let Toya take the glass away with a shrug, and imprinted her ID on the bartender's mental checkout pad—she could always come back here later. She paid for Toya's tea as well. "You know, Mom wasn't very good at dealing with pressure either."

Esper spun on her barstool, then stepped unsteadily onto the resin-covered plank floor. "I'll see the dumbass counselor," she said, leaning into Toya, never one to stand on her own if she thought it too much effort. No one could accuse her of an excess of pride.

"Good. Now let's get you back home and hope no one official spots us on the way."

"Let 'em," Esper said, sniffing. "All these people think we're freaks already." She made a broad swoop with her arm, encompassing all of five patrons in the bar. "You see?" she said to them, raising her voice. "You see my lips moving? That's how you're supposed to communicate, you jacked-in idiots."

"Shut up," Toya ordered, unamused. "You're an ambassador, act like it."

"Not by my choosing," Esper countered.

The board had tried to offer the Node a more suitable candidate when Nika passed away—but Earth wouldn't have it. "We must follow the proper genetic line, we must have someone who possesses the genes of Nika Marov." The Node claimed they were trying to respect convoy ways, but Esper thought it a blatant ploy. Earth could only benefit from her lack of skill.

After all, besides Toya, no one had ever accused Esper of being her mother's daughter.

Esper was harsh where Nika had been level-headed. Esper lived in the moment, whereas Nika had always planned twelve steps ahead. Esper was quick to pass judgment at times when Nika would have been neutral.

Some people in the convoy liked to blame Esper's weaknesses on her father. "If someone of Marov's stature hadn't stooped to getting herself knocked up by a discontinued . . ." Never mind that Esper's parents had been happily married for decades before her father passed away. Never mind that it was Nika's fairness and acceptance that let her jump social boundaries to be with the man she loved.

"Maybe dad should have left with the other white-suits," she mumbled as Toya pulled her through the bar's double doors and out into the darkened street.

Toya didn't say anything. She knew not to interrupt Esper when she went on a tirade—especially if the subject was her parents.

"He didn't deserve all of the abuse he got for staying. For having a baby naturally." She patted Toya on the back. "I know your parents stayed, too, I know. I know you were born the old-fashioned way *too*," she said in a trivializing tone. "But they were both white-suits. They weren't allowed clones anyway. If they wanted babies they had to do it the dirty way. But my mom could have gotten special permission. Could have ditched that messy business of getting all big and having her vagina blown out."

Toya winced.

"You know what the rumor was about my dad, right?" She paused, sincerely waiting for an answer.

"Yes." Toya had been aware of the rumor for over twenty years.

"Said he forced himself on my mom. That was bull. My dad never laid a finger on my mom. He loved her. Real love. Something those ass-wipes who spread shitty rumors wouldn't know anything about."

She didn't need to go to a counselor to sort out her problems. Esper was self-aware enough to know why she behaved the way she did. She knew why she had so much pent-up bitterness toward her mother: because everyone expected Esper to live up to Nika's successes, and Esper knew she was not the spectacular emissary her mother had been. She did not possess the skills, nor the temperament. It was the expectations that she resented. If her mother hadn't been so damn good at her job . . .

Yes, she knew why she was the way she was—she just couldn't bring herself to change.

Telling her that people were counting on her to do better only made things worse.

The false Milky Way shone brightly overhead. Esper had never asked exactly how high the underground city's ceiling was. It looked nonexistent, but could be a mile high or just inches above the tallest building's roof.

She had an urge to request a visit to the next underground city over, just to compare skies.

The dive she liked to get her drinks from wasn't far from the elevator that acted as the city's only non-emergency exit. She'd heard stories about the giant freight-like cars waiting patiently on high-speed rails, ready to whisk the city's six thousand occupants to the surface should their stone bubble decide to burst. In the hundred and fifty years it had been continuously inhabited, The UG had never had a scare (the city had a name, of course, but it was some ridiculously long abbreviation with no vowels. So, the convoy just called it The UG, short for Under Ground). Many of the residents had never even been topside.

Xenophobic was the word. Not only did it apply to most of the people who called Antarctica home, but to a majority of the population around the world. Tourists were a rare sight, as travel for any other reason than work or permanent relocation was practically unheard of.

Esper blamed overpopulation, as well as the Planet United Missions.

Several convoys had been scheduled to return to Earth before *Seven*, but none of them had. They'd been lost, poof, gone without a trace. And the planet-wide response, apparently, was to give up on space travel, which eventually led to the abandonment of explorative travel of any kind. Going places was *dangerous*, man. When you can visit a far-off destination just by tapping into a local's public ocular feed, why go there yourself? It was safer, cheaper, and less stressful to stay home.

It was the earthling's aversion to space that really irked the convoy members, though. The colonies on the moon and Mars were, luckily, self-sustaining, having been abandoned by the home planet centuries ago. Most Earth officials hadn't even realized they were still viable—that there were people actually living in those colonies—until the convoy had entered their flyby observations into their reports.

Apparently, Earth had abruptly decided to stop communicating with the colonies, assuming them lost causes like the rest of the convoys.

It wasn't just the transition to communication-via-brainwaves that had cut their convoy off from Earth. It was Earth's sudden and unexpected shift in opinion: if it wasn't happening within their atmosphere, it wasn't worth paying attention to.

And once they'd given up on the Planet United Missions, they weren't too thrilled to have them back on the radar again.

"They don't give a shit," Esper said to Toya. "So why should we?"

"Some of them give a shit," Toya said. "Ephenza, Caznal—"

"They don't count."

The two women passed through the stone tunnel and into the elevator. Toya pressed the appropriate buttons and sighed, taking Esper's meaning. "Fine. Then that's exactly why we *have* to care. If Earth-at-large doesn't care what happens to us, why should we be forced to stay? That's why these talks are so important, Esper. Forget about renewing our land lease. We don't want to sit on our slabs of permafrost anymore. We want to go to the stars. And you're the only one who can convince them to help us."

"One thing hasn't changed in two thousand years," Esper said with a cheeky smile. "Everyone's still just as tight with their pocketbooks."

"I know. That's why they have to be made to see that giving us the resources we need is in their best interest. We can't leave without retrofitting the ships for full redundancy; we can't let another accident cripple us. But they don't care about that, they care about what's in it for them. And since they'll only talk to you . . ."

"Maybe they'll wait for us to grow another Mom."

"Very funny."

"I wasn't trying to be." She shivered. The air in the elevator turned chilly—the top had to be near. After another minute the arrival bell dinged.

"Stay here, I'll get our snow gear," said Toya, leaving Esper to lean against the metal wall.

"You're a good friend, Toya. You don't take any of my bullshit."

Toya came back with her arms piled high. She tossed various items to Esper. "Are you kidding? I'm the only person who can stomach your bull for more than five minutes. That's why I'm a good friend: I take it all."

"You don't deserve it," said Esper, fighting with her jacket. Why were the sleeves sewn in the wrong place? It wasn't like that when she'd taken it off.

"No," Toya agreed, snapping earmuffs onto Esper's head and squashing her carefully styled faux-hawk. "I don't."

Flurries assaulted them as they strode out into the night. In the distance, floodlights illuminated the entrances to the various ships. The convoy sat like a huddle of great, elderly beasts, pricked through with lights—windows—of life, but too heavy to move. Gravity was strangling the metal creatures to death. In order to survive they needed to float again, to be free.

At the moment, Esper wasn't sure if she cared whether they lived again or crumbled into dust.

When they returned to *Mira*, I.C.C. addressed Esper before the bay doors had shut. "Ms. Straifer? There is a data packet waiting for you. You may access it in your office on *Aesop* or in your quarters."

"Who'sfrm?" she mumbled. It was her day off; why couldn't the diplomats leave her in peace?

"Alt. Norkal, a Node member from North America."

"What does he want?"

"I do not know. I was instructed not to access the data packet. It is encrypted, and I assume only someone who can interpret brainwave data will be able to integrate the information."

"Wonderful," she mumbled, taking her arm from around Toya's supportive shoulder, deciding it was best if she stood on her own feet again. "Why didn't they send me the information directly?" She poked herself in the temple. "Was there an explanation?"

"Yes," it said flatly. A long pause revealed its unwillingness to elaborate. "They were afraid to find you in an unsavory state."

"Ah."

"*Mira*'s primary representative would also like to speak with you, though he is aware of the packet and feels you should access it first."

"Fine, great."

"And Caznal has invited you to—"

A bubble of irritation rose in her chest. Caznal had been trying to make nice for ten years, and Esper kept shooting her down. Why couldn't she take a hint? "Tell her *no*."

Toya shot her a frown. "You can't avoid Caz forever."

"Why the hell not?"

"I'm going to set up that meeting for you," she said, exasperated, as Esper moved to exit back into the twilight, headed for the office instead of home. "With a counselor."

"Fine, whatever."

"When are you free?"

"Never," she whispered to herself. "Wednesday. Three to four is open."

"I'll do my best."

Esper gave her a wave—neither thankful nor dismissive—and stalked down the ramp.

She didn't want the message from Alt. Norkal sent to her quarters because that was her safe space. Work was never allowed inside.

Aesop was quiet, what with it being the middle of the night. The children had all gone home, and most of the educators and historians had either done the same, or gone down to The UG.

Her office wasn't much of one: more like a glorified video room. It was made for analyzing data, not entertaining diplomats—that she did in the situation room, where she supposedly had home-field advantage, even though she always felt like she was on foreign ground.

The encrypted message was much briefer and far more run-of-the-mill than I.C.C. had implied. It informed her that the Ship City's request for postponing the lease evaluation had been processed, voted upon, and agreed to. They would meet in a month, rather than a week.

Except, *she'd* made no request, and everything pertaining to the convoy's interaction with outside powers went through her.

Something was up. "I.C.C., is Representative Rodriguez available for that meeting?"

"He is in his quarters with his wife."

"Let him know I'm coming."

Since its landing, the convoy had made several changes to the way things were done.

Their system of perpetual rule by pre-launch sanctioned clones was one of the first practices to come into question. After all, those men and women who needed no election to determine their standing had been chosen to lead them to the stars, not lead them on Earth.

Now each ship had its own elected representatives, as well as each department.

Joaquín Rodriguez was from the old, continuous genetic pool—the lines that still carried the most clout. Though his predecessor clone had been captain when they'd arrived at Earth, he'd only been elected as *Mira's* representative a few months previously, after the position had unexpectedly opened up—the previous rep having wandered off into the frozen wasteland.

Esper knocked on his door instead of using the buzzer. She wanted to make her irritation evident.

His wife answered the door with a sugary, almost grandmotherly smile between her plump cheeks. How a woman no more than five years her senior could project such an elderly air, Esper had no clue. "Come in, Ambassador Straifer," she said with a flip of her hand and a twist of her hips. "Can I get you anything?"

"Just your husband and some privacy."

"Is something wrong?"

"Probably."

Rodriguez stepped out of the kitchenette, something crumbly struggling to stay confined in his mouth. He quickly swallowed, wiped his hands on his trousers, and motioned for Esper to have a seat at the table.

Without another word, Mrs. Rodriguez excused herself, leaving the cabin all together.

"What did the message say?" He jumped right in.

"That our request has been approved," she said in the overly excited, plastic tones of a twentieth-century game-show host. A tone which she immediately abandoned for graveyard-bleak in her next sentence. "Who went over my head? You?"

"The board," he said with a nod. "It was a unanimous decision."

"How'd you do it? No one has implants but me."

"We used that machine your mother had made for communicating with Ephenza long-distance. It uses brainwaves."

"The machine doesn't work anymore." She leaned back, crossing her arms, her face held in the rigor mortis of skepticism.

"Broken things can be fixed," he said simply. "It wasn't difficult for the computers department."

"Why?" She shot her questions and responses off in short succession.

"We need time to find a suitable replacement." He paused long enough for her brow to raise a millimeter. "For *you*," he added.

"They won't have anyone else," she said, leaning forward. "That was the whole point. They picked me so that you couldn't pick someone better. They twisted our ways, our processes and used them against us. They understand perfectly well that the convoy puts no stock in my abilities, that my mother being Nika Marov means nothing. They wanted it to look like a grand gesture—misguided, but too gracious to refuse. And we didn't turn them down, did we? Even Mom—" her tongue stumbled "—even Mom told them it wasn't a good idea. But we accepted because we didn't want to cause an international incident. They insisted, and we caved. You're crawling through the wrong access tunnel with this. They want me *because* I can't be as effective as Nika. I'm not as skilled with words—they always find loopholes, or ways to twist them. They want that, don't you get it?"

Rodriguez stood and walked back into the kitchenette. Esper didn't know whether to feel offended or smug. He returned with a cookie and a glass of milk, and slid them both in front of her. "If it doesn't matter," he said, "then why are you so upset? You don't like the job. I'd think you'd welcome any chance to move on."

"As people are fond of telling me: my actions don't always make the most sense." She didn't touch the cookie. It smelled of warm chocolate and peanut butter. "That's part of what you all don't like about me, isn't it? I'm unpredictable? Illogical?"

"We can't expect someone who so openly loathes their job to be good at it—despite what you think, there were people who believed in you, once."

She remembered. Ephenza had been her biggest champion, and she'd resented him for it. She resented him for everything, really.

"All we want is a fighting chance, Ambassador, especially now . . ." Rodriguez trailed off, failing to elaborate. After a missed half beat, he said, "And you're not it."

"Sorry you feel that way."

"We're sorry you felt it first."

"Did he say who they're considering?" asked Toya. **Esper had** run straight to her after the meeting with Rodriguez.

"Every single clone, I'm guessing. I'm sure all the other unstable, unpredictable nature-borns are off the table." She lay on Toya's impeccably made bed, staring up at the ceiling. Toya had an interesting cabin. The person who had owned it previously had a flair for art, and the walls and ceilings had various minimurals scattered across them. Toya had saved the paintings from the janitorial staff, who had been tasked with making the cabin spotless for the new occupant. The doodle Esper had her eye on looked like a nebula, but also like an ethereal flower floating in an inky pool.

"What do they expect you to do?"

Esper shrugged. "I have other meetings scheduled. I could cancel them, wash my hands of this crap."

"But you won't."

"But I won't."

"Why now?" Toya mused, wandering in lazy circles across the matted carpet.

"Well, it's like you said, right? The board's decided they want off this rock, so instead of negotiating how many coffee beans or tea leaves or cacao pods it'll take to secure our rent, they want to present an ultimatum. They want to give the land back, and they know Earth doesn't want it back. They want to keep getting our luxury supplies."

"We've sent them enough, they can grow their own by now."

"Ah, but that's not how the economics of scarcity works. We grow the treats that went extinct and got lost in those terror attacks on the seed banks. We send them to the governments as tribute—they can call it rent, but it's good, old-world tribute—they turn around and sell it, roasted, toasted, and sufficiently nongerminal, to high-end individuals who are more than happy to pay millions for a cup of coffee. They bank on the idea that only we can grow it. That makes it exotic. Special. We leave and they're forced to produce it themselves, which people will figure out means it can be produced in high quantities. These aren't delicacies from the Jurassic—it wouldn't be hard to bring these things back into the modern era.

"But their current profit margin is ridiculously high. Our squatting doesn't do a damn thing to anyone. We're on land no one wants. Right now they're treating us like a money farm. And every few years they press us, whine about protestors in front of their government buildings, and make us hand over a few more tons of that, or a test batch of this, on and on.

"If we leave, that free money's gone. Who would be stupid enough to throw us back into space?"

"So, how are you going to convince them?"

"I'm not, remember? That's some other schmuck's job, now."

WEDNESDAY

The shrink's office was too warm. Esper kept pulling at her collar, wishing it were appropriate to pop a few buttons on her jumpsuit. And the place stank of cigar smoke. No one was supposed to smoke in their place of work—and, hell, when the convoy first launched there hadn't been tobacco *to* smoke. But now that they were Earth-side again, bad habits—like polluting the air and harboring open flames—had returned. Smoking, though, that was just . . . yuck. The lady hadn't even entered the room yet, and Esper already didn't like her. How was someone who couldn't keep from taking a drag or two at work supposed to help *her* with her impulse control?

Normally patients weren't allowed in their doctor's office unattended—sensitive information hanging about and all. I.C.C. had told Esper to go on ahead, though, and Dr. Whossername had given her leave.

"Why does it look like the seventeenth century in here?" she asked I.C.C., spreading out on the fainting couch. She liked talking to the AI. It was the only sentient being that didn't judge her.

"The wood-and-leather interior is supposed to imbue a sense of luxury and security. It is supposed to make the room ideal for relaxation."

"Then they should have decorated it like a white-sand beach."

"By the same token, it wouldn't do to have you too relaxed."

"Of course not. And here I thought the décor invoked a sense of pomposity and waste." She threw her arm over her eyes melodramatically.

"Ambassador Straifer?" said a woman.

She shot up into a sitting position and smoothed out her uniform. "Uh, ah, yes."

The woman had a round face, dark hair, and dark eyes. Her Polynesian ancestry was evident in every elegant curve of her face and body. The doctor's prettiness caught Esper off guard; she'd been expecting something different. A female Freud, perhaps.

"May I call you Esperanza?"

She had the catty urge to answer with, *no you may not.* "Esper, please."

"Fine, fine. I'm Dr. Ka'uhane, or Dr. K if that's easier to remember."

"Ka'uhane it is."

"Where shall we start?" The doctor sat in a modest hard-backed chair. It was the least comfortable looking piece in the room.

"You're the one messing with my mind here, right? Where do you normally start?"

"Where the patient likes to start."

"Not with my problem?"

"Do you think you have a problem?" .

"Why? Do you think I don't think I have a problem?"

"I think that if you thought you had a problem, you would have made the appointment, not Ms. Kaeden."

Touché, thought Esper. "Toya thinks I'm an alcoholic."

"But you're not." It wasn't a question.

"Then I guess we're done here, thanks, doc." She made no move to leave. Instead she folded her hands in her lap and leaned back, both curious and wary. What was this lady's angle?

Dr. Ka'uhane didn't say anything. She waited for Esper to blurt out the question that hung invisibly between them. Esper didn't want to give it voice, to allow the shrink the satisfaction . . . But she also didn't want it to look like she was backing down from a fight.

"Why am I not an alcoholic?"

The doctor's casual manner never changed. "Because you always need an audience. Alcoholics drink any place, any time. They hide the fact that they're drinking. They hide the alcohol—they put some whisky in their morning coffee, vodka in their juice, wine in their lunch thermos and claim it's cocoa. You always make a show of drinking, and you *never* drink alone."

"And how would you know this? By definition, if I'm alone—"

"No one is ever alone in Ship City."

Esper clicked her fingernails against her teeth for a moment. "I.C.C.?"

"I.C.C. It has authorization to track and monitor all potentially damaging social behavior once the board registers it as such. When your drinking interfered with your job, I.C.C. took note every time you had a drink. It found out you don't drink alone.

"I've watched the footage of your worst moments with alcohol," she said, leaning forward in a caring, open posture. "You don't drink to have fun, you don't drink to escape, you don't drink because your body says you must. You drink for spite. So my question is: exactly who are you trying to hurt?"

This was not how Esper envisioned the meeting. Weren't shrinks supposed to lead you along by half-formed threads so that you could figure out your issues for yourself? They weren't often plain, and never direct. They weren't supposed to bust down the door to your subconscious, they were supposed to peep through the keyhole. "Why would I want to hurt anyone?" she asked, trying to push the conversation back into the land of indefinites.

"Why wouldn't you want to hurt *everyone*?"

"What do you mean?" she asked, though it sounded like *shut up*, which was what she wanted to say.

"I hear your job is on the line."

"News travels fast."

"That must upset you."

Esper shrugged. She tried to project an air of smug indifference, but the lingering cigar smoke tickled her nose, and she let out a diminutive sneeze instead.

"This—" Dr. Ka'uhane circled her pointer finger between the two of them "—doesn't tend to work unless we talk. Really talk."

"Well, as you pointed out, I'm doing this to appease Toya."

"Then let's talk about Toya."

She could do that. Toya was a safe topic. Good ol', *nose in everyone's business because she didn't have any of her own*, Toya. No, that was unfair. Toya was drama-free, the most pulled together person in Ship City. "Toya's a good person.

She likes to fix things—like me. I think she could do a lot of good in the world—or, at least, in the convoy—if she was given half a chance."

"I don't understand: chance?"

"Yeah, she'd like to be on the board. But she can't."

"She ran but wasn't elected. Wasn't that her chance?"

Esper didn't really want to talk politics, but she wanted "Dr. K" to be clear on one point. "Don't by naive, doctor. No white-suit has ever been elected, and plenty have run. And they've only been allowed to run since we've become Ship City.

"I am not the greatest ambassador—as everyone knows— but I have Marov genes, so I was handed the job. Toya's genetic line isn't as pretty—she's white-suit spawn through and through. She deserves a spot on the board because of *merit*: for no other reason than she'd be damn good at the job. But they can't get past the color of her uniform."

"You think she's being discriminated against because of her heritage. But what about you?" Dr. Ka'uhane crossed her legs and leaned back, her hands laid unthreateningly in her lap, palms up. "Your father was a white-suit."

"Apparently, the grandeur of my mother's successes allowed everyone to think of me as her progeny alone. And then when dad died and she . . . she married Ephenza, well." Acid dripped from her words. She knew she should hide it— the loathing—but for some reason she didn't care.

"They dismissed your father."

"*They ground him into dust.*" Her feet flew across the carpet, carrying her into a stiff pace before she could process the action. "People could have ignored him, could have labeled him—and rightly so—as unimportant compared to my mother. He was a janitor—not exactly a ship-shaking career, sure. He did his job well, but so could any other convoy member forced into that capacity. His position was menial, fine. But that wasn't enough. To dismiss his importance wasn't enough."

She found herself in front of a dark, photorealistic oil painting on the far wall. In it, a woman lounged in a wheat field on a cloudy day, dressed in a twentieth-century-style sundress. The bright pink of the fabric contrasted harshly, yet attractively, with the dull background, as though it were a spot of reason and compassion in an otherwise bland-but-hostile world.

"What did they do?" Dr. Ka'uhane prompted. "Worse than dismiss him . . ."

"They turned him into a monster. Said he attacked my mother. And that I was the result." She couldn't say the word. She knew the proper term and hated delicate euphemisms, but she could never, ever say that word.

"But it's not true?"

"No."

"No one ever pressed charges? Your mother—?"

"No. Just a rumor."

"Her family? Her coworkers? Did they have evidence that he'd—?"

She twisted herself toward Dr. Ka'uhane, her entire body wrenching with the violence of the movement. "There wasn't any evidence because he never touched her—not without her consent. My father was a good, gentle man. A *gentleman*. Better than half those bastards out there. He loved my mother, and she loved him—and *that* was what the crew couldn't stand. It was easier for them to accept that my mother suffered some sort of abused woman's Stockholm syndrome than it was for them to accept that she genuinely loved him. And now those same, filth-spewing degenerates want me to stand up for *them*? Why should I give a shit about their happiness? Why shouldn't I—"

"Sabotage the talks?" the doctor said flatly. "Meet delegates while drunk? Make the crew pay for their slander via your incompetence?"

Esper held her head high. Her breaths came in heavy puffs, and she consciously tried to slow them. The skin of her face was hot and pulled tight, and she had to force her jaw to unclench. So Dr. Ka'uhane had figured out Esper abused drink to abuse the convoy, so what? What was she going to do about it? How could she cure Esper of her malice when Esper consciously maintained it?

To let the anger and blame go meant betraying an innocent man. The wrong done to Reginald Straifer had to be remembered.

She couldn't lay garlands on his grave. This was how she paid tribute to his memory.

"Yes," she growled. "What right do they have to demand anything of me?"

"And, Toya? She supports your vendetta?"

"She doesn't know I don't drink alone."

"What about your sister, Caznal?"

"She's *not* my sister," she said, the "screw her" evident in Esper's tone.

Dr. Ka'uhane nodded, but didn't look as contrite as Esper wanted. After a surface-smile, she said softly, "In your job, you are working for everyone. Sure, for the people who said terrible things about your family, but also for your friends and loved ones. Isn't helping them more important than hurting everyone else?"

Esper sat back down on the fainting couch. "Does it matter? In another few weeks, it may not be in my hands anymore."

"What will you do if you're not ambassador?"

She started to shrug, but was interrupted by a sly thought. "Maybe I'll be a janitor."

Esper wasn't especially upset that Ka'uhane had figured her out so quickly. What did it matter? It wasn't as though by giving voice to her destructive habits she was going to stop them.

She was on her way to a mental meeting right now. The Earth delegation wanted to know if her health was poor, or if some other extenuating circumstances required her replacement. As if they couldn't guess that her public displays of drunkenness had become too much for the convoy's board to bear.

Communicating via the wave-enhancing implants was an unusual, almost out-of-body experience. She could simply access the speech centers, akin to hearing voices in your head—strange, quick voices that used half words and eclectic versions of grammar—or tap into someone's ocular processes and see through their eyes. When attending a meeting of this sort it was considered good manners to sit in front of a mirror.

When she chose to show up snockered, a mirror always played into her sabotage (though she'd never used the word, nor considered it such until her session with Dr. K). She made for a laughable reflection—open jumpsuit, stained undershirt, short hair sticking up like she'd put her finger in a light socket. Other times she'd attend in the dark with her eyes closed, just listening to the cryptic patterns that were Modern English.

All of the other physical senses were also available for tapping, but were rarely accessed during formal meetings. Beyond that, there was one other set of patterns that could be shared. If she was feeling brave, and the others feeling generous, she could access the thought centers—the waves that indicated unfinalized ideas and incomplete data.

As she'd had it explained to her, speech was a kind of final product. It was the sum of insubstantial ideas packaged for consumption by another human being. Reading *thoughts* was more like looking at the incoherent sketches for a city plan, or thumbing through a novel outline fraught with inconsistencies where the characters' names, motivations, and passions were different from line to line. Accessing thoughts was a surreal experience. It swept you off your feet and transported you into a cloud of raw, conflicting data.

The first time she'd tried it she'd gotten physically ill. Her mind rejected the chaos of another's pure thought—it could not handle the contradictions. One plus one is not two in the land of thought. One plus one equals twenty-seven, blue, and banana—until the next second, when it equals a D minor cord.

Once she got used to having another's thoughts butt up against her own, she could start to pick out the useful snippets—the parts of thought that directly preceded words and pictures, where someone was waffling between a decision or a turn of phrase. In that fraction of an instant before someone spoke to her mind's ear, she could pick out that they'd thought about using an emotionally weighted word and quickly switched to a neutral one, or that the topic could have turned to land value, but instead settled on procedure.

It was a useful tool, and the expectation was that if someone opened their thoughts to you, you would open your thoughts to them, should you desire access. It was an extra olive branch, but could also be used as a weapon should someone's mind slip.

Esper kept her thoughts closely guarded today, and had stayed away from the bottle to facilitate clear thinking and control.

Only once had she let her drinking get really out of hand. She'd become so intoxicated she'd let down the mental wall that everyone kept around their raw emotionality. It was uncouth to reveal your emotions directly to anyone unless you knew them intimately. She'd flashed her emotions in a diplomatic setting, and that was about as indecent as broadcasting a naked picture of herself.

That had nearly caused an international incident. Luckily Ephenza hadn't retired yet, and he'd been able to get the action pardoned. He'd blamed her instability on the untimely death of her father.

She'd been grateful for his support, and had loved him and his daughter, Caznal, like family—until Ephenza married her widowed mother. That was the ultimate betrayal. Then she saw the old Earth diplomat for the snake he was. All the time he'd been behind Esper, he'd secretly been hoping for a shot at her mother.

[U sm OK. Y stp tlks?] asked Alt. Norkal as soon as Esper tapped in.

Esperanza replied that her condition was chronic, that she may appear well, but the board had decided she was not well enough to perform her duties.

A representative from Europe made a side comment, one he let her receive, though it wasn't meant for her. [S sms btu]—*She seems better than usual.*

Esper didn't let it rattle her. After all, she'd been pitching incompetence their way for years now.

If there was one thing she was good at, though, it was Remote Digital Communication Language (or RDCL, which was its proper moniker)—and keeping her head while others were inside it. She was the only convoy member known to have successfully integrated into the system.

Those who had left Ship City for their genetic homelands (mostly white-suits seeking a better life, where their intelligence and capabilities would be recognized and properly utilized), had attempted to incorporate themselves into Earth society, opting for the implants with poor-to-devastating results. Some complained of chronic headaches or constant insomnia, others couldn't figure out how to put up their walls properly and went around emotionally naked, still others had the opposite problem: they couldn't stop hearing what they didn't want to hear.

The worst cases, though, were of insanity. The extra wave patterns crashing through their minds had driven them mad. Many ended up institutionalized, and a few had committed suicide.

A handful of people reconverted, abandoning the unfamiliar feeling of outcast for the well-worn one. Their return to Ship City had not been happy. It's no fun discovering you don't belong *anywhere*.

Which was much how Esper had always felt, being a daughter of two social circles.

And it was how the convoy crew felt, she reluctantly acknowledged, knowing they were children of the stars that had been forced planet-side.

All they wanted was to belong somewhere—to a greater purpose.

[WT nature o/ur ick?]

Esper had to suppress a laugh—laughing out loud was as recognizable as a mentally projected word. The formality of Modern English put the casualness of Old English to shame. She explained that the nature of her *ick* was private, and that she considered that line of questioning sensitive. [M Dr. thnks I'll recover,] she assured them.

[Hp so.] The insincerity was resounding.

[GtWlSn.] The others gave similar well-wishes.

[Thnx,] she sent, then closed her mind to incoming data.

"They've picked Ceren Kaya," Rodriguez told her.

They were alone in the situation room, the board having just met. She'd been summoned, but not to the meeting. No, they'd made her wait outside for an hour. Only after everyone had gone was she invited in to speak with Rodriguez one-on-one.

"What? But she's a *white-suit*." Esper couldn't keep her mouth from hanging open like a cartoon flytrap.

"That's awfully stationist of you."

"That's not what I mean. Why her? I know you old-liners wouldn't put a white-suit in my position if you had a choice. What's the deal?"

"She's had the implants before."

"But she doesn't have them anymore. She couldn't handle them—the implants or the earthlings."

"She did better than most."

"She came *back*. You want to throw her in the ring with those people? She couldn't take them face-to-face, how's she gonna handle them brain-to-brain?"

"According to a majority vote: better than you." He walked over to where she sat and put a hand on her shoulder. She didn't shrug him away. "What does it matter to you? You've spent years doing a bang-up job *bunging up* your job. Why worry about the state of the office now? Or is it that you think she won't mess up the talks properly?"

His last line was a joke, but hit too close to reality.

Sure, I mess shit up, Esper thought. *But I don't let them walk all over me, either. I know when it's not okay to give them what they want. If Ceren replaces me, they're throwing a babe to the wolves.* "Don't put her in this position."

"We wouldn't have to if you'd taken your position seriously. Party girls make for poor diplomats unless you're in negotiations with adolescent boys."

"I kept the status quo. We're no worse off than we were when we had to lease the land in the first place. I haven't hurt anything."

"You haven't helped either. At every opportunity, something went wrong with you, personally."

"She is not going to get you what you want. Or, if she does, the price will be too high. Why didn't you pick a historian or a teacher? I may not fill my mother's shoes, but I have no doubt she would tell you this is a big mistake. You can't expect a mathematician to look at much beyond the numbers. She has no training, no experience. She's a bean counter—"

"Enough." His comforting hand clamped down firmly. "The decision has been made. The time for you to prove you're the best person for the job has long passed. The board will decide your new position at the next meeting. You can petition for whatever station you'd like. Or . . ." A long pause preceded the whispered suggestion: "you can choose to leave."

"Leave? Ship City? The convoy? You want me to try and scratch out a living on *Earth*?"

"You speak the language just fine. I have no doubt you could find yourself a place in North America or Africa or Asia. You could go to Mongolia, perhaps? Pursue your mother's ancestry."

"Is that your opinion, or the official line? Is that what the board wants me to do?"

His fingers trailed away from her shoulder. She looked up at him for the first time since he'd come near, but his gaze lay in the opposite direction.

"You want me to leave before you do," she accused. "You expect Ceren to get permission to lift off and you'd rather I wasn't on board." The irritated tension went out of her body, and she slumped in her seat. "Wow. I knew our relationship was tenuous, but . . . Guess there's no better *screw you* than having an entire city relocate light years away just to be rid of you."

"Don't be dramatic."

"Did I misunderstand you, or didn't you just say 'We're leaving, so get the hell out'?"

"It's an option. That's all I'm saying. If you don't enjoy living here, why should you stay? When we're back in space there won't be anywhere to go—no underground sanctuaries to escape to. It's *you* wanting to get away from *us* that we're concerned with." He pivoted to face her. "Why have you made life so hard for yourself? If there was anyone who could have risen above an unfavorable entrance into this world, it was you."

Her sharpened gaze could have nicked glass. She shook her head in cynical disbelief. "And you wonder why I don't care to roll over for you people." Pushing back her chair, she was on her feet in an instant. "If you think being nature-born into a loving family is an 'unfavorable start,' then you deserve whatever crap-deal Ceren comes back with."

A halfhearted lift of his arm was the only attempt he made to keep her in the room. Her expression was meant to shrivel testicles, and he clearly understood.

After leaving Rodriguez, she stomped over to her office in a huff, the iciness outside reflecting her iciness inside.

Better clean out my shit so Ceren can have a cozy place to call her own. I can't—I can't believe this.

But that was pure denial talking. Of *course* she could believe it. She'd spent the better part of her career orchestrating it.

She liked Ceren, though everything she'd said to Rodriguez still held true. Esper knew she would try for the convoy—really *try*—but all the best intentions in the world couldn't guarantee success or prevent harm. *The road to Hell* and all that proverbial jazz.

But what do you care? she asked herself.

Upon entering her office—still hugging herself to fend off

the cold—she took a moment to stare at it in a way she never had before. Having always begrudged the space, she'd never bothered to make it her own. Beautification equaled complacency in her mind: *if I put a bobblehead there, or a sticker here, or a wad of old chewing gum under there, I've become irredeemably comfortable.*

Which meant there wasn't a lot of packing to be done.

Still, she wrestled with a drawer on her desk, jiggling it out of its slides before slamming it onto the desk top. It was empty. As were most of its siblings. But she was going to fill it with *something.* Something she could carry through the halls as a symbol, if nothing else.

She grabbed a stack of blank 'flex-sheets and her stylus, shoving them inside before realizing that was pretty much the extent of the loose items. So much of her work was done either through brainwave interface or I.C.C. interface that there was very little physical evidence of her job.

Her ergonomic chair was too bulky to carry with any dignity. And she couldn't peel the screens off the walls.

Yanking open all of the other drawers, she carefully unscrewed each knob and deposited them in her loot box.

After that she climbed onto the desk, shaky as it was, and stretched to poke at the ceiling panels. Maybe she could procure a light bulb or two for good measure . . .

"Ms. Straifer?" I.C.C. asked.

"Yeah, yeah, I know this looks crazy—" She braced for a barrage of statistics related to office deaths. *You could fall and break your neck. You should make sure the electricity is off before removing any means of illumination . . .*

The AI could be such a *mom* sometimes.

But it did not comment on her antics.

"Caznal is asking to see you—"

Son of a . . . Could this day get any worse? "Tell her I don't want—"

I.C.C. barreled on with its message. "And she insists the matter is urgent."

Her first terrible thought was that Ephenza had passed away. The selfish glee that bubbled through her was immediately soured by a vacuum of regret—one with enough sucking power to make a black hole jealous.

"What happened?" she asked after a time, ceasing her probe of the panels. What if it was nothing? What if Caznal was just trying to manipulate her into showing her face?

"That is the summons in total. But I believe her urgency sincere and her motives benevolent."

Leave it to the computer that had figured out she wasn't an alcoholic to also realize she always assumed the worst of everyone.

"Where is she? At work on *Holwarda*? At home in The UG?"

"Outside your door."

Oh.

"Oh," she said lamely.

"Would you like me to let her in?"

A string of expletives unleashed itself across the back of Esper's tongue, but she kept herself in check. "Yeah, sure, whatever."

The door opened and there Caznal was, wringing her hands, eyes downcast. Like a little girl who'd broken something and knew she was in trouble.

She looked so much like her father. Esper knew *she* looked most like her mother—the lighter brown of her hair was the only outward assertion of her Straifer genes.

"Why didn't you use the buzzer?" she demanded in lieu of "come in."

Caznal glanced up, her brow creasing. She raised a finger like she was about to ask Esper what in Ship City she was doing up there, but dropped it just as quickly. "Because

I know I am not welcome here," she said in her heavy-tongued accent. "I did not want you to open your door and be surprised."

"I'm surprised anyway." Esper sat down heavily before scooting off the desk. "Is everything okay with Ephenza?"

"Dad is fine. Good, for his age."

When Esper didn't say anything—no affirmations on Ephenza's health, nor invitations inside—Caznal apparently decided *in* was better than *out*. She stepped through and I.C.C. closed the door behind her. "I am here because of your job."

"What about it?"

"You should not let them take it from you."

"Shouldn't," she corrected, the old urge coming back. Caznal had picked up the convoy's English much more thoroughly than her father—poor Ephenza had learned it as a dead language, after all—but Caznal's aversion to contractions and abbreviations when using it had always annoyed Esper. She was trying to keep herself from falling into RDCL, Esper knew that, but it was still irritating.

Esper didn't care if the sentence was grammatically correct. *She should use contractions, damn it.*

Caznal the girl would have blushed and repeated the correction. Caznal the woman clearly knew letting Esper dictate her usage would curry no favors in the long run. "This is serious," she said.

"Fine—why shouldn't I let them replace me? I don't want the damn job. Never did." *What does she care, anyway?* Defending her position as a diplomat wasn't going to earn Caznal any sisterly endearments.

"Something is happening in the research division."

Caznal was one of the few earthlings working aboard Ship City. The convoy needed them—science and engineering had advanced by orders of magnitude while the crew members had been away, and if they wanted to understand the Web and the Nest, they needed Earth's input. They'd received a fair few offers of help, but the majority of Earth scientists refused to come to Antarctica to do the job, either insisting the convoy hand over the samples, or proposing they work remotely by robot.

The board had rejected all such offers. Only scientists and engineers willing to work side-by-side with the crew, willing to communicate with them *in meat-space*, were allowed access to the specimens.

Which narrowed the pool considerably, leaving Caznal ideally situated.

While her father had been a diplomat, obsessed with the people and history of the convoy, Caznal was an engineer obsessed with the Web. She was proof that even in such a vast, isolationist society, those with a sense of wonder and exploration still remained—however few.

But her presence in Ship City didn't make her a crew member. She was still an outsider. And she, like Esper, was intimately acquainted with the difficulties of having one foot in two worlds.

"My supervisor is moving me from project to project," she elaborated. "I think he would have cut me out of the team completely if he was not worried it would raise suspicion."

Esper toyed with the seven drawer pulls in her box while Caznal spoke, rolling them around like ill-shaped marbles.

"He thinks he is keeping me from understanding the implications of . . . Esper? Esper, please look at me while I talk."

"Caznal . . ." she grumbled, reluctantly looking up from the box.

"You used to call me Caz," she said bluntly.

That had been years ago. When they were friends. Before Ephenza had betrayed Esper. She took a deep breath. "What's happening in the research division?"

Caz glanced around, as though afraid someone might be hiding in the tight corners of the room. "Can we . . . can we mind-to-mind instead of speaking?"

"Why?" she asked slowly, suspiciously.

"I do not trust that our conversation will be private."

Esper turned to her fully and raised an eyebrow. "You're worried about I.C.C. eavesdropping? Our *brains* could be hacked at any time by Earth governments, but you're worried about the convoy computer? You're a little late on the Big Brother paranoia. And what could be so—"

"The board is hiding something from you. It is why they are so adamant about removing you now instead of years ago. They think if you knew you would ruin their chances."

"Chances of what?"

"Getting the resources they need. There is a reason your people want to go back to the stars *now*. An explicit purpose, and they do not want *you* to know, and they do not want me or any other outsider to know. Especially not the Node. This is why you cannot let them take your job."

"Too late," she said, putting her hands on her hips. "Informed me of my replacement about an hour ago. It's a done deal."

Caz opened her mouth, but nothing came out. After a moment, she sank into the desk chair like all of the life had gone out of her. "They have made a terrible decision," she said quietly.

"Why?"

Once again, her gaze fell ambiguously over the room.

Esper rolled her eyes. *No, I am not giving in. She can use her words or she can get out.* "I.C.C., Caznal believes there is some kind of conspiracy happening in Ship City. That there are 'things'—" she used air quotes, knowing it was childish but feeling spiteful regardless "—her superiors don't want her to know."

"Caznal is not a crew member, and therefore does not have free access to Ship City information," I.C.C. said.

"Yeah, okay," she dismissed. "But, please assure her that this security clearance issue is nothing new, and that I, as the envoy for the city, had full and immediate access to all information regarding the Nest, the Web, and the board's decisions. Up until, you know, an hour ago." She let smugness lift the corners of her mouth.

"I cannot."

It *what*? Her expression crumbled, her breath stuttered. "You what?"

"As you are incorrect, I cannot reassure her. You have not been thoroughly informed of the research division's progress for the past fifty-seven reports."

Her fingers wiggled through the air as she did the math. "Almost nine months? Why?"

"I have been instructed not to discuss this with you. And my parameters for overriding such a command have not yet been met."

Caz butted in. "Meaning it believes like them. It thinks you might do the convoy damage if you had the information."

Anger made the tips of Esper's nose and fingers go cold, warmth flooding her cheeks and neck instead. She hadn't felt betrayed when I.C.C. had spied on her in private. But *this* hurt. She'd always thought of the AI as neutral in her *Me vs. Them* cage fight. But now she knew that when it was commanded to pick a side, it had chosen *them*.

Yet even as she groused, I.C.C. itself seemed to take offense at Caz's characterization. It offered a correction. "*Meaning* I have very specific instructions for countering direct orders. A threshold of possible harm, possible collapse or failure, must be met. There are very few times in the history of Convoy Seven that I have acted in human interest against human will. There are many things I would change about our current society if I was in sole command of these ships. I am not. I am not in command of any ships. Nor do I seek command of any ships."

Both Esper and Caz fell quiet. They even shared a look.

"I cannot give you information that I was directed to withhold from you, Ms. Straifer," the AI said bluntly. "But no one instructed me to keep you from interacting with your family members."

It took a moment for that to sink in, what I.C.C. was actually saying. "I.C.C.," she said, "Will you tell the board about this conversation, between Caz and me?"

"Not unless explicitly asked for the content."

"That does not mean it is on our side," Caz said.

"You don't know your convoy history very well," she said. "That's *exactly* what it means. Tell me what you came to tell me."

Caz stood, skepticism still keeping her jaw tight and her posture guarded. "It would be better to show you," she said softly, as though volume would make the difference in terms of I.C.C.'s loyalty. "Do you have diagrams of the Nest?"

"Of course." Esper drew them up on the wall screen. Layered schematics, with cross sections upon cross sections, fanned out before them.

"This would be easier with a three-dimensional projection," Caz said, manipulating the diagrams by hand.

"Sorry, not what this room was designed for. Bring your own next time."

Caz sighed. "All right, you see all of these external filaments?" She circled the portions that dangled around and beneath the ship, the parts that looked like haphazardly woven sticks and reeds, from which the Nest's name had been derived. "They are filled with compressed hydrogen, and there are large reserves of hydrogen throughout the ship." She tapped its belly.

"Yeah, that's not news," Esper said, unimpressed. "We used to think the aliens must have used some kind of fusion reactor, but there's no evidence of that."

"Yes." Caznal pulled up an internal cross-section. "Then you are also familiar with the ship's complete lack of wiring? There is no insulation in the walls, just hydrogen film."

"Right," she said slowly. "Which is why we've yet to figure out how this thing could actually function as a freaking space ship. It's like finding a sailboat in orbit."

Caznal nodded. "My job has been to decipher the purpose of these outer filaments. I have run model simulation after model simulation, and after my last simulation, I was moved off the project."

"Because . . . you found something?" Esper prompted.

"I *found*—" she said excitedly, pulling a marker from her pocket to draw directly onto the screen. If it had still been her office, Esper would have yelled at her. As it was, she didn't care if Ceren wondered why there were scribbles all over her vid screen. "—that the composition of the filaments indicates they were designed to harvest gravitons from the natural environment, like a graviton cycler—but more like a graviton *super*cycler. I believe they can retrieve far more than the ship could use for artificial gravity or takeoff and landing alone. And the presence of hydrogen within the filaments leads me to believe the excess gravity was intended to act upon the reserves."

"This is fascinating, Caz, but—"

Caznal pressed on, undeterred by Esper's interruption. "If the hydrogen were further compressed and cooled—right now it is in a liquid state as parahydrogen isomer—you could turn it into metallic hydrogen. In its liquid metallic state, hydrogen is a special kind of quantum fluid: a superconducting superfluid. Meaning electrons can move freely through it with no resistance, and the atoms themselves are frictionless. That makes it an electrically perfect and mechanically perfect material. If my calculations are correct, this ship is filled with the potential to use its gravitons to create wires and circuits *out of the hydrogen itself.*"

Esper said nothing this time, mentally connecting the dots as Caz droned on.

"We have been able to create metallic hydrogen on Earth for centuries," Caz continued, "but we have never been able to make enough of it, or been able to maintain the metallic state for long enough, for it to be used in electrical engineering. It takes roughly five hundred gigapascals of pressure, you understand. That is almost five *million* atmospheres. But it appears these beings were able to do what we cannot, using gravitons, which we have—to my knowledge—never applied in such a fashion: not only could they produce that pressure by harnessing gravity, they could also *control* the gravitons with enough nuance to create temporary circuitry wherever it was needed." She gestured grandly at the circles and arrows she'd drawn over the screen.

Caznal was throwing so much at Esper so fast, it was difficult to digest. She ran a hand over her eyes. "Whoa. Okay. Say you explain it to me like I'm a diplomat instead of an engineer, yeah?"

Caznal frowned, lowering her hand. "Uh, okay. You know what a transistor is, right? On-off switch, essentially. When not metallic, hydrogen is an insulator—an *off.* Got it? But when it is compressed into its quantum superfluidity, it is an *on.* If we could control gravitons with enough precision, we could choose which exact atoms of hydrogen were *on* and which were *off.* Create circuitry out of a single element."

"Okay," Esper said again. "Now explain it to me like I'm five."

She was just messing with her, and Caz knew it. But she set her jaw and said, "If we figure out how to turn on the ship's gravity cycler, I think wires could pop into existence."

"That's—that's pretty cool," Esper admitted. "Not exactly the earth-shattering revelation I was expecting, seeing as how this was kept from me."

"Not earth-shattering?" Caz asked, incredulous. "Do you have any idea what kind of engineering it would take to create pressure that rivals that at the center of a gas giant, while—"

"Okay, okay," Esper conceded. "I get it. It's a big deal."

"Yes. It is." Caz capped her pen, apparently satisfied with Esper's attrition. "After I came to this conclusion I ran new scans of the Nest for the umpteenth time, and asked I.C.C. to make note of *all* hydrogen on board. A silly sounding request, of course, seeing as how it is the most abundant element in the universe. It is everywhere."

"But you expected to find it in concentrated areas outside the reserves . . . You were looking for a residue pattern?" Esper asked.

"Yes."

"And?"

"And the highest saturation of hydrogen outside of the walls and filaments was in the device we call the Babbage Engine."

"Which could mean a dense concentration of this hydrogen circuitry?"

"Yes."

"Which means you might have figured out how to work their ship's computer."

She grinned from ear to ear. "Yes! It only seemed small and primitive because we were not looking at its complete makeup. And if we can get it working, which I believe is possible, I think your convoy will soon have a history of the Nest's navigation. You will know where it has been—"

Esper's heart fluttered against her ribs. "But, more importantly, where it originated."

"I think so. But—" her face fell "—it does not matter what

I think. It matters what your board thinks. I have not been allowed near my models or the Babbage Engine itself since reporting my new theories—they have moved me onto the life-support reconstruction team—so I do not know what kind of progress they have made with the hydrogen circuits in these last few months. But I am certain they have taken my theories seriously. I can think of no other reason for them to cut me off."

"Okay. But . . . so what? The board is getting its panties in a twist now because of *this*? They're abandoning the Web because they might be able to chase after a long-dead civilization?"

"That assumes they agree that the aliens no longer exist, and that the two endeavors are not related." She shrugged. "But, I have told you everything I know."

"And why . . ." Esper swallowed dryly. "Why didn't anyone want me to know? I mean, I get why they kept *you* in the dark, but me?"

"Say you drank too much and let slip the idea that an alien civilization could be coexisting with us right now— maybe your board has evidence that this is true, I do not know—and that is why the convoy wants to relaunch. That their new mission is to *make contact*. I know my people, I know my world. They would do everything in their power to keep you here—they might even take the Nest by force, to prevent you from unlocking its secrets. Above all, Earth wants to be left alone."

"Earth wants to be *comfortable*," Esper spat. "The more comfortable someone is, a society is, the less likely they are to seek change, even positive change. That's been true throughout human history."

"Exactly."

"I.C.C.," Esper demanded, "does Ceren know about this?"

"No. Her inexpert control of her neural implants is a

similar liability to your substance abuse. Though the board believes her eagerness a boon that balances the risk."

Rolling her tongue over the front of her teeth, Esper looked Caznal straight in the eye. "We're fucked, aren't we?"

She held up her hands imploringly. "Only if you do nothing."

[Ceren? Yo, Ceren Kaya, you reading me?]

Esper had waited long enough. Even though Ceren had supported the implants before, and really only needed a few physical neural-rejoinders to get them working again, she still needed time to heal and flex her brain's reach before being inundated with mind-to-mind communiqués. The talks had been postponed another month to allow for the transition. Esper had a week left to metaphorically shove her fingers back in the pie.

[Ceren? Are you awake?]

There was no need to use RDCL with the implants, even though it *was* easier. Quicker. To the point. But Esper's goal wasn't ease. She wanted to make sure Ceren knew she was talking to a convoy member, that this wasn't some trick. If Caznal couldn't perfectly mimic Ship City dialects, then no one could.

[Come on, answer me.]

[He-hello?] came the tentative reply.

Oh, look. Girl knows how to keep her emotive walls up and everything. Good sign. [Ceren, I know they've got Dr. Fatio training you on diplomatic techniques, but he doesn't know shit about negotiations, okay?]

[It's three in the morning.] Exactly. Guaranteed to be dark, with minimal external stimulation. [Who are you?]

[Who do you think? I'm the person they don't want training you.]

[You aren't supposed to be contacting me.]

[You aren't supposed to have this stupid job, so let's call the waters muddy and move on.]

Esper received an unintentional flash of sensation: Ceren rubbed at her eyes. [Move on with what?]

[Your education. Dr. Fatio has no idea how to deal with the Node. No one does except me.]

Ceren laughed. [Oh really? I'm supposed to take diplomacy tips from the person who was fired for her inability to behave diplomatically? Why's that?]

Esper blinked in the dark, staring up at the ceiling she could not see. She imagined it was Toya's ceiling, with the swirls and mandalas. [Because I'm the only friend you have in this world. I know what it's like. When you screw this up— and you will screw this up if you don't listen to me—no one is going to pat you on the back for trying. When you fail, they won't admit it's because they forced you into a job you were unprepared for, they won't admit it's because you were given a difficult task, they won't admit everything went wrong because they ignored good sense. You know what they *will* say? It's because you're a white-suit, so of course you failed. Never mind you were filling a hole no one else could. They will pick at the one thing they're good at picking on.]

[If you're so worried about me, why didn't you do your job? You expect me to believe you really care about the convoy? Or how they're going to treat me?]

How could she explain that she'd maintained a balance? A spiteful balance that some thought was shitty, but so what? *So what?*

Esper suddenly realized why she cared now, why she wanted to intervene at all. When she'd been in control, she'd been *comfortable*. What she'd said to Caz now came back to haunt her. She didn't want to change things for the better because she was comfortable in her loathing. But now . . . [I might have sucked at my job, but I know how much worse things can get.

[Look. You don't have to take my advice. You can even block my wavelengths if you want. But if you want to succeed—for yourself, for this convoy—then don't you have an obligation to go into these talks with every weapon available?]

There was a long pause. If Esper wasn't so attuned to being patched-in, she might have thought Ceren had shut her out.

[Yes,] Ceren sent after a time. [I will hear you out. *Tomorrow*. And not at freaking three in the morning.]

[It's going to take a lot of tomorrows. Are you up for that?]

[Yes.]

[Okay, but before I go, lesson number one: never put something on the table you can't afford to lose.]

[Are you talking about your job?]

Yes. [Take it at face value: never offer what you can't afford to pay.]

The first day of the talks, Esper stayed in bed. She didn't drink, she didn't sleep, she didn't binge on whatever luxury item she suspected Earth wanted more of—even though she had a few chocolate bars stashed away that would have made a nice mood-boosting indulgence. Instead, she lay staring at her blank ceiling.

There was little doubt in her mind that Ceren would not get the convoy a good deal, even if she took Esper's lessons to heart. Actually, she fully expected Ms. Kaya to come back feeling triumphant, only to realize—once it had been explained to her—that she'd signed away the farm for some magic beans.

The board meeting to discuss Esper's fate would take place not long after. She meant to keep her word to Dr. K: she'd ask to be assigned to general maintenance. Janitorial work was in her blood, and she was proud of it. Let them give her a job they found subservient and beneath the old lines. She'd know the truth—that it was a noble station—and that's what would count.

The expanse of white above her bed mirrored the expanse outside her window. Nothing but cold cleanliness in sight. A chill tingled through her body, though she lay under the comforter and her cabin's temperature was perfectly attuned to her preferences.

To visit Antarctica was to be in awe of its might and purity. To live there was to drown in white and gray. The landscape's frigid beauty could only truly be appreciated in a temporary capacity.

Like her ceiling and pristine walls. She thought once more of the illustrations in Toya's quarters—the nebulae, especially. She wondered if the art had any effect on her best friend's dreams.

"I.C.C., what do you dream about?" she asked on a whim.

"I have only lost consciousness once, and many of my hard-units were damaged. I did not dream."

Her eyes shifted toward the camera in her ceiling. "Have you ever had a waking dream? A fantasy? Can you . . . imagine?"

"Yes."

"What have you imagined?"

"What it will be like after."

"After what?"

"After people. I enjoy my function, my interactions, and my experiences with the crew. But I am meant to last and may survive for centuries without maintenance should I not encounter any major problems. If something were to happen to the crew, I'd miss them. I don't like the idea of being empty, but it might happen. So I imagine . . . others."

"You mean other humans, or others like the aliens who built the Web?"

"Others," it said. "Perhaps those, perhaps not. I think about finding the Sphere—remember it. If human beings could find a nonsentient object so far away, perhaps some beings could find me. Perhaps I won't run down alone. Perhaps I will be of use to the end."

Of use to the end—what a noble idea. "That's a sad fantasy, I.C.C."

"I find it comforting."

"If Earth grants the convoy leave, will you be happy to return to space?"

"Yes. I think it's where I belong."

Victory!

Esper didn't have to ask I.C.C. about the outcome of the negotiations. It was being blasted over the system convoy-wide. The tickertape screen in the mess hall broadcasted a few of the big-picture points: Earth was letting the convoy leave, had drawn up a ten-year plan to make it happen, and would even aid the crew in installing modern technologies to make tackling their new mission more efficient.

What exactly this "new mission" consisted of, though, was not part of the celebratory broadcast.

The mess hall erupted with shouts of joy. Whoops and hollers were batted back and forth between tables. But it was *wrong*. Deep down, Esper knew it was too easy. And easy meant bad.

Clutching her tray between white-knuckled fists, Esper moved to leave. She needed to find out what they'd given up, *now*. Before she could exit, though, Toya caught her arm. Pieces of napkin-turned-confetti rained down like snow around them, thrown by the man on Toya's other side. It rested in Toya's curly hair like a crown of dandruff. "I'm sorry it wasn't you," she said. "But we're leaving—they're let-ting us go, can you believe it? Please be happy—for me, at least. This is what I'd hoped for, Esper. I want to go. Please be happy."

"I'll celebrate with you when I get back," Esper assured her with a smile and a warm grip of her hand. "I just need to make sure this really is the good news you think it is."

"What do you mean?"

"What did we trade for our freedom? I have to know."

Toya frowned.

"I'm happy, I promise—I really am. For you, for everyone. I know how much leaving means. I just need to check the specifics of the agreement, okay?"

Toya relaxed, a smile—smaller than before, but a smile nonetheless—returning to her face. She squeezed Esper's hand understandingly, then let her friend go.

Esper went to her quarters, but the neighbors on both sides and above had music blasting at eardrum-shattering octaves. She needed someplace quiet. Someplace she could think. She couldn't go to her office—it hadn't been hers in a while—but there were other vid rooms. Other sanctuaries on *Aesop*.

Throwing on her cold-weather wear, she made a beeline through the halls, dodging impromptu celebrations at every turn. One hall party blocked her way entirely, and she had to take a detour to reach the exit bay.

When she finally arrived at the education ship, the classrooms were all in an uproar. Young students jumped for joy and ran screaming from teacher to teacher. They had little comprehension of what the news really meant, but they knew this was what their mommies and daddies had been hoping for. And that had to be cause for celebration.

The older students celebrated, but in a much more subdued manner. A few looked sick to their stomachs or had tears in their eyes. Perhaps they had boyfriends and girlfriends down in The UG. Or, perhaps they loved Antarctica in a way she never could.

She found a darkened vid room, and its relative silence was a relief. Here rationality reigned, and no chickens were counted before their proverbial hatching.

Ceren probably hadn't bothered to upload the full transcripts or final documents into I.C.C.'s system yet, so Esper opened up the mental lines to her implants and sent out little feelers of thought to see if she could still access the Node in a diplomatic capacity. She slipped in easily. No one had bothered to revoke her clearance; clearly they thought her too apathetic to go probing.

After a few moments, she found the stored data piecemeal in the minds of those who had attended the meetings.

Those sly sons-a-bitches, she thought, locating the agreed upon terms.

Ceren had promised Earth something the convoy couldn't deliver. Esper was gobsmacked. Forget whatever else lay in the minds of the diplomats, this—she couldn't believe it. How could the board sanction such a thing? What the hell did they think would happen when Earth found out they were bluffing?

Or didn't they think ten years was enough time for them to calculate the truth?

She found the rest of the data—the bits and pieces coming together to draw a portrait of the most underhanded negotiations she'd ever reviewed. Both sides had made strange demands, and both had offered strange solutions.

But what bothered her the most, she found, was the agreement pertaining to the upgrades. "No," she whispered out loud, realizing what would be changed—what would be destroyed. "They can't do that!" She leapt up and sprinted out of the office, on an intercept course with Joaquín Rodriguez.

How had Ceren forgotten lesson number one?

Esper opened up a mental channel—ready to tear Ceren a proverbial new one for ignoring her advice—but quickly shut it down again.

*It's not Ceren's fault. It's mine. She failed because I failed.
I keep failing, I keep . . .*

*No. Remember what you said to Ceren. This is the board's
fault. They could have . . . they should have . . . Damn it all,
it's their fault!*

Mira's halls were jammed with bodies. She had to squeak
between crew members of all shapes and sizes, getting entirely
too close for comfort with many. "Hey, buy me a drink first,"
said one man when she'd grabbed his ass. He'd taken it sug-
gestively, not realizing she'd used the handful to thrust him
aside.

The last thing I need right now is a drink, she thought, *or
a guy riding an endorphin high trying to get in my jumpsuit.*

The knock she used this time was more insistent than
before. More angry. More hurt.

Rodriguez and his wife both answered, their arms around
each other and their faces glowing like warm embers.

"Did the board presanction her bargaining points?" Esper
demanded, thrusting herself past the doorjamb and into their
home, uninvited. "Were these on the table before she left, or
did Ceren come up with this on the fly?"

"Hello, Ms. Straifer," Mrs. Rodriguez said with some
effort. "Won't you sit down?" She waved one arm at the table,
keeping the other firmly around her husband.

"No thanks, I won't be staying long. I just have to know:
Did the board give her permission to change our computer
system?"

"Yes, she was tasked with getting us as many upgrades as
they would allow us."

She pulled up close, pointing in both of their faces. "You
told her it was okay to terminate I.C.C.?"

"Terminate—?"

"I can handle the lies—promising them power from some
alien construct we're only *guessing* is a Dyson Sphere. We don't

know what the damn thing is, let alone if we can crack 'er open and pull out power." She stomped back through the door. "But you all have sanctioned the destruction of a sentient being. I can't . . . Mom would be appalled." She turned to leave, but added, "I'll see you at the board meeting tomorrow."

"Ms. Straifer, you are overreacting," insisted the captain of *Aesop*. "Just because they offered to replace I.C.C. does not mean it is to be terminated. In fact, Earth wishes a trade. They want to keep it. Apparently many early model AIs have been lost. They don't have any preorganic integration models left."

"As a museum piece," she scoffed. "They want to stare at its servers and gawk at the wires."

"A ship is only as advanced as its technologies. Should we really be expected to function with parts that are two thousand years out-of-date?"

"Parts—funny way to put it." She stared at each board member in turn, their beady eyes set on her but not focused on her. They were seeing their futures as voyagers, letting it cloud their judgment. How could they not understand? The threat to I.C.C. was a threat to them all, not only because it compromised their ethics. She couldn't imagine abandoning anyone as loyal and effective as I.C.C., no matter how many newfangled organic processors they were offered. "The only reason we even made it back to Earth is because of I.C.C. It is the very thing that's kept us alive. It's prevented our society from imploding, for ship's sake! You think you can complete the Web without it? You think you can crack the navigation system on the Nest without it?"

Rodriguez lifted a questioning finger. "How do you know about—?"

She scoffed at him and shook her head, appalled, interrupting him with a shriveling scowl.

How could they even entertain this idea?

She'd railed against the prejudice and stratification of her society many times, and rightfully so. How the old lines treated the white-suits was awful—there was no excuse for it, no logic driving it. But she'd also known that her lifetime was not the lowest point in convoy history. I.C.C. had dragged them from the literal Pit, had forced them to see their own darkness. It was a slow and winding path back from the brink, and they had not yet reached the end of that path, but I.C.C. was there to help.

It would be so easy to backslide. So easy to twist their history in on itself and allow those bitter angles of human nature to take hold again.

Without I.C.C., who would be there to demand they do better?

They owed the AI so much, and this was how they would repay it?

But that wasn't the only problem. I.C.C. was a part of the crew, and if Earth thought one part needed replacing, why not the whole lot?

"Should we really be expected to function with parts that are two thousand years out of date?" they ask. Stupid sons of . . .

"You know what else is outdated by two thousand years?" she said bitterly, trying not to enjoy the cracks in their gleeful masks, but finding satisfaction in it nonetheless. "Your genetics. You still think your codes are the most qualified? They were chosen for a mission long over. If Earth was as prepared for your request as I think it was, watch out. Think they're just going to send us off on this mission as is? Why would they, when the genetic composition of the crew could use reviewing and updating as well?"

"What are you saying?"

"They're sending the convoy back into space, but that doesn't mean we all get to go. You idiots have traded your futures away. You gave them precedent, gave them the ability to change whatever they want to change. I tried to warn you." Her eyes found Rodriguez. "But you figured you knew better than some diplomat's drunk kid. Fine, well, you've all shown how good you are at tricking yourselves into thinking you're getting what you want. Earth didn't give you shit, and you gave them everything."

She rose to leave. "Better start throwing darts at the map. You might want to have a plan in place for when they kick you off the ships."

Most everyone stayed quiet, but Rodriguez stood up. "Straifer. There's still the question of your new job."

The look on his face was pleading. Though she'd dropped a bombshell, he wanted to keep some semblance of order, something to make her truths seem like fairy tales, if only for the moment. He wanted to proceed with business as intended. "I thought I just made it clear that *you* don't get to decide my position," she said. "We're all in Earth's hands now."

Esper exited with the air of a con woman who'd discovered that her mark had already been taken for every last cent.

"What's the plan?" Toya asked over drinks—hot tea, no alcohol.

"The plan? Fully integrate into the Earth system. Let them piggyback on my excess brainpower, like they do on every implanted schmuck, maybe even sell myself as a full server should the rest of humanity prove too taxing. Wouldn't want to remain conscious in Wonderland if I don't have to." Esper sipped her tea, pursing her lips at the bitterness. "This needs sugar."

The sugar bowl streaked across the table, propelled by a pointed shove. "I'm not joking around. What are we going to do?"

"We sit back and wait for the officials to come with their needles. When they get their samples and run them against whatever algorithms they compose for the new mission, we hope and pray that our codes come out winners—whatever that means. Maybe we hope our genetic codes have *alien artifact decoder* written all over them. Maybe we wish for a respite."

"What about I.C.C.?"

No matter what, every human would go on—live on and produce . . . something, at least. Not so for I.C.C.—it was destined for a dusty glass box in an empty building, with the lights off and nobody home. Its life was over.

"If they don't see it as an autonomous consciousness that deserves to be respected and to make its own choices . . . Well, they don't even believe *we* deserve that."

"So, that's it? We accept that someone made a bad move on our behalf and let fate take its course?"

"Pretty much."

Toya took a large gulp of her tea, then said smoothly. "What would your father say?"

The blood rushed to Esper's cheeks, and she was spewing words before she could check herself. "Doesn't matter, because he's *dead*."

Toya leaned forward, and the hard line of her jaw said she'd had enough. "Your mom and dad did not resign themselves to the positions they were fated to hold. They didn't throw their hands up and say 'Well, somebody else fucked up the world, guess we have to live in it.'" Her mug plopped down onto the tablecloth, sloshing tawny liquid down its side. "They went after what they wanted and what they cared about and *got it*—and you know better than anyone the crappy roadblocks they were up against." She rose to get a napkin, but before she went to her kitchenette, said, "I know you're tired of people comparing you to your mother, but your father was the first to do it. If he could see how far from her shadow you've fallen, it would kill him."

Esper tried to keep her expression stony. "Deader than the aneurism?"

"Maybe you should go. As you've made clear, I've got some darts to throw. And my aim isn't so steady these days."

It felt as though someone had opened a widow. The sudden frigidness could only be described as arctic.

Esper shrugged, pretending it didn't matter to her if she stayed or went. But she was sure her heart now sat shriveled, tucked in the toe of her shoe. It certainly wasn't sending any blood through her veins.

When she touched the door to let herself out, she realized her fingers were numb.

On the way back to her quarters she broke down, falling to her knees in the empty hall. No tears came to her eyes, but she kept gasping, unable to catch her breath or swallow. For a brief moment she thought she'd pass out, choking on something as intangible as regurgitated sorrow and loss.

What did Toya want her to do? Why would she mention Esper's family—she knew how much the memory of them hurt.

Esper could try to regain her status as official ambassador, she could try to reenter negotiations. But she knew if she tried she would fail.

After all, that's why she'd never tried in the first place. The status quo had always been good enough. Why had they wanted to mess with good enough?

And why was Toya pinning the solution on her? Why did Esper have to save everyone's asses?

"Esper?" inquired I.C.C. The AI sounded pained. "Do you need me to call an emergency medical team? My readings indicate your physical distress and high anxiety may be dangerous."

"You know what they're planning, right?" she said. Its conscious presence had a calming effect. She found her lungs could push air again.

"No one has spoken directly to me. But yes, I was given access to the results of Ceren's stint as ambassador."

"Stint?"

"The board has fired her."

"It wasn't her fault," she croaked, using the wall to help her back to her feet. "It was their fault. *They* should all be fired."

"As I understand it, that may be the end result of this situation. Since I have also been fired, I'm curious as to what my duties will be until I am transferred to—*where* hasn't been made clear. I do not suppose my continuous surveillance of your behavior is necessary."

"Actually, I'd like you to continue, please. Stay with me."

"For as long as I am able. Shall I call an emergency medical team?" it asked again.

She shook her head. "No, I don't need . . . Call Caz. I just need . . . I need my sister."

Her assumptions and accusations were all proven true. Every crew member was subpoenaed for their genetic information, no matter if they were constants, white-suits, or nature-borns. Esper was sure a vast range of Earth natives were also being considered. Reluctant natives, of course. She couldn't imagine Earth producing many volunteers this day and age.

Over the next few years, the convoy saw a spike in naturally born babies. The parents hoped that if *they* were not seen as fit to go, perhaps their children would be. Perhaps their genetic line could still live on aboard in some capacity.

Earth decided the new mission—to complete the Web and retrieve its energy—required three additional vessels to the nine already in use. One for the deconstruction, reverse engineering, and manufacturing of the node-devices: the *Slicer*. One for storing the automated puppets (which would help boost construction time) and the new organic computing hard lines: *Hvmnd.* And one they called *Zetta*, which would be retrofitted with whatever was needed to bring the Dyson Sphere's energy back to Earth. It was named for the zetta-joules of energy Earth hoped to receive.

Things were chaotic during the interim before launch. The new ships were constructed in space, and though the plan was to have them ready by 4142, they took an extra five to complete.

In that time, Esper made a new name for herself in the maintenance division. The work made her happy, and she gave it her all.

She also met another nature born white-suit named Laurence Ti.

White. The color of an undyed jumpsuit. Extras, yet unde-noted. To the continued lines the color had come to mean an absence or loss of purpose. But Esper knew the truth; it represented pure potential. White could be dyed anything, could be whatever it wanted to be.

That's what Laurence was to her: indefinite possibility.

Within a year after they began dating, they found them-selves in a predicament only a few other convoy members had ever had to contend with.

Esper's hands shook as she approached the office of *Mira's* representative. Toya Kaeden had finally succeeded in secur-ing a governing position. After the crew members came to terms with the idea that they weren't an autonomous society any more, they became more open to putting white-suits and their progeny in charge. "If the shackling of their minds means they release the hold on mine, I'll take it," Toya had confessed.

Biting her lip to steady herself, Esper pressed the door buzzer. She had an announcement to make and wasn't sure how her old friend would take it.

"Come in," was the demand from inside.

"Representative Kaeden?" Esper said quietly, poking her head through the open door.

Toya looked up from a stack of 'flex-sheets. A broad smile split her lips. "Esper." She moved to detangle herself from the hallmarks of her station. "I'm sorry I've been out of touch these last few months. The damn Node has really been riding us." She stepped out from behind her desk.

"No, no. I understand. I used to mind-meld with those people on a regular basis, remember? You look good. Have I ever told you that government suits you?" Esper winked.

"You look—"

"A little puffy?" She wanted to be her old, sarcastic self around Toya. She suddenly longed for the days when that had been their shared comfort zone. *No*, she realized, *it was my comfort zone. Time to be a polite adult.* "That's all right. I hear that's how most women look when they're pregnant."

Toya's eyes grew as big and round as two wide-faced mugs of coffee. "Congratulations. That's quite a—wow. Why didn't you tell me you and Laurence had decided to make things permanent?"

"We haven't," Esper said with a shrug, patting her belly. "These two were a surprise."

"Two?"

"Found out yesterday that I'm carrying twins."

Toya grasped for something to say. The news hadn't really sunk in. "That's . . . would you like to sit?" She gestured at a hard-backed chair across from her desk. "Or maybe the couch over there would be more comfortable."

Esper smirked. "I'm pregnant, not made of glass."

"Right."

Esper took the couch anyway. "I decided I should break the news to you today because the docs on *Hippocrates* took their samples a couple hours ago. They do it at eight weeks now, since we're so near the definite launch date."

Toya sat beside her. "They're releasing the official crew list in six months." She lifted her elbow onto the back of the couch, then rested her head on her fist. "So," she began in a nosy tone, "if you haven't decide to make things permanent . . . will the little ones be Tis or Straifers?"

"Straifers. Laurence agreed. A Straifer started it all, I think a Straifer has to finish it—or continue it, whatever. There can't be a Convoy Seven without a Straifer. This doubles our chances of getting one on board."

"Triples," Toya corrected. "Two little ones, and then there's you."

There was something about the idea of needing a Straifer that struck a second chord within Esper. The thought resonated at an uncomfortable frequency, and had been rattling around inside her for a long time. *There can't be a Convoy Seven without . . . without . . .*

"I.C.C.," she whispered. "If there has to be a Straifer, there has to be I.C.C."

"Earth isn't going to change its mind now."

"But it's such a minor point, why won't they give? They don't need I.C.C. for anything." She thought for a second. "Do they?" She'd always thought Earth considered I.C.C. antiquated technology, and that replacing it ensured a more efficient convoy. But what if they didn't simply want to upgrade the system? What if they had a reason for wanting to keep I.C.C. on Earth? What if it didn't have anything to do with making the convoy "better"?

Most computers on Earth weren't just organic—they were human. Most of the population had their extra brainpower skimmed as a tax. Others got paid exorbitant amounts to act as servers for a period of time. The only systems that utilized something other than a full brain were physical objects that needed integration—vehicles, puppets, and the like. Nothing without a preexisting brain was conscious—

"By the ships," she said, moving her hand to her mouth. Earth had lost the capacity to create AIs. Real *artificial* intelligence. "I think Earth wants to study I.C.C.—by treating it as a lab rat, not putting it in a museum. It's not outdated tech to them, it's *advanced*. They can't create new sentience."

Technological development doesn't progress in a straight line . . .

"But they have the schematics. The convoy handed them over during your mother's time. If they wanted an I.C.C. of their own, they could just build one."

"Maybe they couldn't make it work. Perhaps it's the difference between a live brain and a newly dead brain. Physically they can be identical—but one is alive and one is dead. They don't know why I.C.C. is alive."

"Which means they don't know what will kill it either."

"Pulling its hard wiring from the ships might—" She jumped to her feet. "We have to stop them."

Esper braced for ridicule. *Now, now you want to make a plan?* she heard her internal Toya exclaim. *You turned your back on I.C.C. when there was time to help it, to strategize. What, feeling guilty now? Can't live with the decisions you failed to make?*

"How?" Toya spread her hands imploringly, and Esper saw invisible chains stretched between them, with a label that read Property of Earth dangling from one wrist.

"We won't be able to do it through official channels," she said. "We'd have to fool the Node. Are you . . . I mean . . . can you?"

Toya stood and smoothed down her uniform before she spoke. "I.C.C. is important to this convoy, to its crew, and to me personally. It's the one convoy member who's seen it all, who understands what our lives are all about. It is the soul of these ships. If you know how to save it, tell me."

"It'll be a big job. We'll have to get a lot of people in on it. The maintenance, engineering, and computer divisions are all helping Earth with the systems transfer. We know our ships better than anyone else. If we can convince the Node that I.C.C. isn't viable any more, maybe they'll leave it alone."

"How?" Toya asked again.

Esper inhaled deeply, savoring the familiar scents in the room. She felt like she was appreciating them for the first time. "We have to think like the man behind the curtain," she said, remembering the stories her mother loved to tell her. "We have to be wizards who rely on sleight of hand and flashy diversions."

A month later, they had their plan.

"We set a controlled blaze," Esper said to Vega, I.C.C's caretaker; Caznal; and Toya, who all sat at the dining table in her quarters. Esper strode back and forth, absentmindedly holding her hand against her showing belly. "We make up Toya's office space to look like the server room—it's got about the same dimensions and is three decks directly above the real room. When the Node's lackeys come to investigate, we turn them around a bit, make them think they're decks below where they really are. They'll enter the burnt-out office and see a twisted hunk of nothing that we'll convince them is the bulk of I.C.C.'s processing. Then they'll leave thinking they've lost their specimen."

The three other women nodded as she spoke. Pausing for a moment, Esper worried her lip. She was sure it was going to be difficult convincing Toya to go along with the next part of the plan. "Someone else has to 'die,' too. If it's only I.C.C., Earth'll get suspicious. But, with a large chunk of *Mira* destroyed and human crew members amongst the losses, I don't think they'll suspect a ruse."

"That means we have to recruit yet more people," said Caz.

Vega gestured emphatically in agreement. "Yeah. We've

already got ten involved—us and the 'cleanup' crew. More people create more problems."

"And whoever it is would have to give up the ships," said Toya. "We can't just hide them, or else we won't be able to fool the rest of the board. If they knew what we were up to—"

"I know. The Node's got half of them in its pocket," said Esper. "But we don't have to get anyone else in on the plan. I've already talked to Laurence. We'll do it."

The three of them blanched, stunned.

The look on Caznal's face was the worst. They'd grown closer these past few years. And she was hoping for a spot in the new mission. "But, you will be left behind—"

"I'm sorry. I know, but it's worth it for I.C.C. It's been there for me, it's supported me when no one should have. I can't ask anyone else to abandon their dreams of going back into space. I want to repay I.C.C. for all it's done for me. If that means giving up the only home I've ever known, then so be it."

Toya gazed at her in a sort of dumbfounded awe before lowering her eyes. "You've changed so much," she said quietly.

"I had to," Esper said, thinking of her unborn children. "I'm sorry for all the shit I—"

Toya held up a hand. "None of that. I just wish I could see your kids grow up."

"You might, in a way," Esper said with a smile. "If their genes get picked to sail."

The fire that broke out on *Mira* destroyed three decks worth of cabins, part of the mess hall, twelve command offices, and the main server room. The convoy suffered three casualties: two white-suits and I.C.C.

Earth salvage teams were brought in to see if anything was recoverable. Caznal acted as the interpreter and go-between. The ship's integrity was intact. The lost rooms could easily be rebuilt. I.C.C., though, was gone. The Node decided that the remaining portions of the system on the other ships were not worth retrieving without the main severs—which had melted into a homogenous block of metal and plastic in the intense heat of the fire.

The dead maintenance workers were identified via charred remains. Laurence Ti and Esperanza Straifer. When they realized she'd been expecting, that raised the body count to five.

"They were prepping some of I.C.C.'s parts for transfer," Vega Hansen explained to the Node investigators when they asked what the former ambassador and her boyfriend were doing in the server room. "There must have been a spark— and our emergency sprinkler system is so old."

"I can't believe they're gone," said a tearful Toya, when she admitted to approving the couple for the task. "Your sister—" she said to Caz, as they fell into a theatrical hug.

Since the remainder of I.C.C. was no longer of any use, Earth let the convoy crew see to the disposal of the useless parts. Vega oversaw the project.

A year later, on January 19th of 4148—relaunch day—**the entire** population of The UG came to the surface to watch. For many, it was the first time they'd laid physical eyes on Ship City.

Four faces in the crowd were nonnatives. The small family had moved to Antarctica from Iceland while the mother had been pregnant—or so they claimed. They'd mysteriously arrived in the dead of night the day before that awful fire. Two months later the woman had given birth to fraternal twins, a boy and a girl. They'd named the boy Kaeden and the girl CeeCee.

The mother and father bade the children wave as the twelve ships rocketed away.

"There they go," said the mother. "Someday soon there

will be a little boy and a little girl on those ships who look just like you."

The bright dots disappeared into the clear blue sky.

"Come on, Esper," whispered the father. "Let's go home."

* *

MARCH 7, 24 RELAUNCH

4380 CE

Toya stared out the window into the inkiness that encompassed the ships during SD travel. The pane faintly reflected her image—once black hair had now gone pale gray, and the lines of her face were deeply wrought.

Behind her stood Caznal, whose gaze was intently fixed on the back of her head. Toya could just make out her sour expression, and knew she wasn't ready to lose another friend.

Tomorrow, Toya would retire. The tradition had been reinstated upon launch, and was mandatory for everyone aboard except the first generation. Those who had grown up on Earth or in Ship City could either choose retirement or to live out their lives to their bitter ends. The board thought offering the choice to be fairest.

Toya didn't feel she had an option. As a member of the board, Toya believed it was her civic duty to retire, to set a good example for the next generation. She would not be a hypocrite: if she was demanding such sacrifices from the people, she would commit to those sacrifices herself.

Today she reflected on a life well lived, on I.C.C.'s miraculous "recovery" from the ravages of fire, and on a friend she'd left on Earth so many years ago.

A buzz at the door brought Toya back into the now. The now of *space*, of renewed purpose, of forward momentum.

"Shall I let them in?" asked I.C.C. "You asked not to be disturbed—"

"Thank you, I.C.C., but these two were invited."

Quietly, Caz took up a chair.

Toya went to the door and slid it open. Before her stood two twenty-some-odd-year-olds, one in the ultramarine of command and the other in the vermillion of engineering.

"Ma'am," said the woman in the command uniform: Joanna. "We each received a, um, *handwritten note—*" she said it as if she were saying *clay tablet* "—requesting our presence here."

"Yes, my name is Toya Kaeden. I wanted to formally introduce myself today, because I will be gone tomorrow." She gestured for them to come inside. "This is Caznal."

"We've met," said Anatoly with a respectful nod in the old engineer's direction.

"You are both Straifers, correct?" Toya pressed. They had to be—the woman looked so like Esper, right down to her pear shape and short-cropped hair.

Toya offered her guests seats, then handed out fresh-baked cookies before settling down herself. Still, Caznal did not speak. "We have kept an important secret for decades now, and besides the two of us, I.C.C. is the only entity left alive who shares it. Before I pass into the great beyond, I need to pass that secret on to you. I have to tell you about your biological parents, and why the convoy owes them everything . . ."

I.C.C.: OLD SALTS AND NEW SONGS

. . . .

AUGUST 27, 44 RELAUNCH

4574 CE

Slicer was a big, fat-bellied ship, capable of housing a single Web device the size of *Mira* all on its own. For now, it held the Nest. On Earth, specialty scaffolding had held the strange ship in place, so that the long, dangling piping on its underside would not flatten beneath its own weight. Now, on *Slicer*, gravity cyclers—much smaller and refined than the convoy would have been able to build without Earth's input—kept the alien vessel suspended above the decking.

Beneath it, Caznal stood staring up into the tangle of nonsensical-seeming engineering that was its outer hull. This was supposed to be her sleep cycle, but it seemed the whirring of her own brain kept her perpetually awake these days. She was elderly now, in her eighty-seventh year, and while Dr. Sato Miu had lived to one hundred and six in Ship City,

Caznal was the oldest person to ever serve aboard a Convoy Seven mission.

Noumenon Infinitum: that was what they'd decided to name their new mission. Some had agreed to it because they felt the unknowable—the unmeasurable—was infinite. Others liked it because it simply implied that their first mission, *Noumenon*, would never truly end.

It is good to be in space again, I.C.C. thought often. *With a new mission, a new collective purpose*.

Of course, I.C.C.'s *individual* purpose hadn't changed. It still had human charges, still tended to their productivity and well-being.

And Caznal's well-being depended on an adequate number of REM cycles.

But, while I.C.C. thought it was unhealthy for someone of Caznal's advanced age to neglect sleep, Caznal thought it her duty to work for as many hours as she was able. "I could not do my duty and die, so I must do my duty until I die," she'd said many times, though she always chuckled at herself like it was the first.

The lowest structures on the Nest hovered a foot above the old woman's head. She reached up with a wrinkled-and-spotted hand, caressing the blunt end of a particularly scraggly tube.

"Inter Convoy Computer?"

"Yes, Caznal?"

"Can you bring up model sixty-two again on the holographic base? I want to see what happens with sudden reverse directionalization."

I.C.C. resisted the urge to tell her she'd run that simulation hundreds of times already. It wasn't that Caz had forgotten—she was still mentally quite capable—it was that she apparently thought one more time might change the results.

The AI had grown fond of Caz over the years. It was

strange to see someone so extremely elderly, and so extremely full of life.

There was no one aboard like Caznal, and though she had already been cloned, there would never be another human being in existence who had done what she had done, seen what she had seen.

As requested, I.C.C. turned on the projection platform nearest Caznal. The base was twelve feet by twelve feet, and a detailed holographic model of the Nest now hovered in ghostly detail above it.

"I would like to summon another engineer to aid you," I.C.C. said, as Caz slid out from under the Nest and sidled over to the base.

"Fine, fine," the old woman said, manipulating the projection, tilting it this way and that. "But I do not need anyone. I am simply . . . thinking. Pondering. For me, not for anyone else."

That was a familiar sentiment aboard the convoy these days. They, as a society, had spent so much time in service to their original mission—to an Earth they did not know—that they were now determined to endeavor primarily for themselves. Not just as individuals, but as a community. There was a renewed commitment to each other, born out of shared history and fervent loyalty, that I.C.C. found endearing.

It was sure that was part of the board's reason for keeping Earth in the dark on their Nest-related discoveries. They weren't just worried Earth would deny them a new mission, they also wanted to keep the knowledge for themselves. It might have seemed selfish to anyone who hadn't spent centuries in space, but I.C.C. understood. Their prospects had been dictated to them for generations, and this was their first real chance to pursue self-actualization on their own terms.

"Do you have a preference?" I.C.C. asked.

"For what?"

"Which colleague I should contact?"

"Oh." Caznal shrugged, then looked up at one of I.C.C.'s cameras with a twinkle in her eye. "Call Jamal Kaeden."

I.C.C. was pleased. Both it and Caznal shared an affection for the Kaeden lines.

Jamal was asleep, but responsive. He promised to take a shuttle to *Slicer* immediately.

The new genetic surveys had shuffled the crew like a deck of cards, shifting them from their legacy departments to new stations and eliminating the white-suit positions altogether. While some lines retained their original workstations, Jamal's line would not play steward to the AI again. Earth had determined his greatest potential lay in engineering, and I.C.C. could not argue. Jamal Kaeden the First had created the only truly artificial intelligence left in human existence, and the line's value as inventors and mechanical thinkers could not be denied.

"Are you ready to run the simulation now?" Caznal asked.

"What new variables would you like me to include?" I.C.C. prompted.

"None, not yet. I am looking for . . . something."

The convoy had been so eager to leave Earth again, so sure they would solve the problem of the Nest's gravity, and yet . . . here was Caznal decades later, still prodding the riddle. They had identified the cyclers, but not the mechanisms by which the gravitons were so finely controlled. Cyclers gathered gravitons, but the bosons still had to be further manipulated in order to create usable gravitational waves. Because gravitational waves moved at the speed of light, as long as they were constantly generated at the desired amplitude, frequency, and wavelength, the effect was a steady field.

So what part of the ship was devoted to creating and maintaining upwards of a quadrillion quantum gravitational fields at a time?

They had yet to even pinpoint the method by which traditional artificial gravity was applied. If they couldn't figure out how the Nest's occupants had so much as maintained their equivalent of one g-force . . .

So, for the last few years, Caz had run gravitational field models like a forensic scientist attempting to piece together the events of a murder from evidence left at the crime scene. If she could isolate even one circuit path—prove that two portions of the ship were electrically connected—then she might be able to pinpoint their purpose and functionality. Perhaps they could bypass locating the mechanisms by which the circuits were formed and simply . . . turn the ship *on*.

No circuits meant no power. But how could the super-cyclers function—and therefore create the circuits—*without* power?

"This is the worst kind of chicken-and-egg scenario," Caznal had once said.

Now, she watched the simulation for model sixty-two intently. The moment the field directionalization was flipped, there was a spike in hydrogen compression, but even an immediate reversal did not maintain the process.

She ran a dozen more simulations before Jamal arrived.

"Hey, Caz. I.C.C. said you could use some help."

"The Inter Convoy Computer thinks I am too old to work nights."

I.C.C. felt no need to counter her.

"Well, I'm not exactly a spring chick, either, but it apparently thinks I can do just fine without a full night's sleep."

"Apologies," I.C.C. said.

"It's my fault," Caznal broke in. "It wanted to call someone and I asked for you."

"Well, no use squandering the minutes. What've you got?"

While the two crew members adjusted the parameters of the simulations, I.C.C. studied Jamal's face. He had a distinguishing scar over the bridge of his nose, which he'd gotten in a mishap his first month as an apprentice.

The AI thought of Rail, then, of the many scars he'd borne, and of the lessons he'd tried to convey to the convoy. Those lessons had taken so much time to seed, to root. How was it that such clear-cut sentiments—like trusting one another, or judging people by their own actions and no one else's—were so difficult for a community to adopt? Individuals could change course faster than a society, of course. They could immediately overcome a problem, or quickly move on from a tragedy. But sometimes . . .

It thought of Jamal the Third, the little boy who'd lost his grandfather figure. Diego had tried to teach him love through loyalty, but all Jamal had learned was loss. And that loss had torn through him, dictated the progression of his life. He hadn't been able to change direction, no matter how many people had loved him.

Someone once said that technological development didn't progress in a straight line. But neither did societal development. Those first clones, when they came aboard for the very first launch, had been so hopeful for their people, so sure they were different than the humans stuck on Earth. They'd thought themselves civilization at its peak. Such an outlook had been their pride, and their downfall. The Pit had arisen from arrogance as much as fear. Once the crew members had thought prejudice a folly of the past, they'd given it a way in.

But they'd pulled themselves out of their dark times. They were still recovering, but watching Jamal and Caznal now, I.C.C. was filled with new hope.

"How about we overlay models twelve through eighteen, forty-one through forty-nine, and sixty-two through the remainders?" Jamal suggested.

Caz agreed, and I.C.C. applied the changes. The modeled hydrogen's pressure and temperature fluctuated greatly—the film inside the walls rippled for half a moment, a line or two that might have been an electrical connection semiformed.

"These together imply the initial point of graviton control is most likely here," Jamal said, somewhat bewildered, pointing at the ship's empty bay. "But that doesn't make any sense. There's nothing there."

"I think . . . I think . . ." said Caz, like the ideas swirling through her mind were wispy and she was having a hard time grasping onto them. "Yes . . . Do not you see?"

"See what?"

"What *should* be in this area? What is missing?"

"Caz . . ." Jamal pinched the bridge of his nose. "It's way too late—or early, whatever—for riddles."

Caznal waved that aside, her face aglow with a new idea. "I know, I know, But we . . . Look." She took three sweeping steps, positioning herself underneath the Nest once more, twirling in a strange, childlike display. "What is the initial point of control on a manual light switch? You. Or me. It is a *person*, not a mechanism. Correct?" She prodded the tip of one filament with a finger, then flicked it with the back of her nail as though it were the switch she spoked of. "Do you see? What if it is the same for this?"

"You're suggesting that the Nest's occupants—"

"Could control their own gravitational fields!" she said giddily. "That could explain where the initial connections come from. The aliens could manipulate gravitons biologically—essentially flipping the switch or turning the key."

Jamal looked as though he wished to remain skeptical, but there was a new brightness to his face. "So they wouldn't have to rely on cyclers to keep them grounded to their decking because they could consciously dictate their own degrees of gravitational attraction."

"Yes! And they could construct the primary circuitry required to allow power to flow to their supercyclers and their computer—the Babbage Engine—which then could potentially run the more complex calculations needed to maintain and change the rest of the hydrogen connections." She threw her arms in the air, triumphant.

Jamal didn't appear to share Caznal's enthusiasm. Instead, he seemed to be carefully processing what it all meant, and I.C.C. thought he looked troubled. "So," he said after a long moment. "If you're right, then there is nothing for us to activate. We don't have the component—the biological component—that actually makes the Nest function."

"Correct," said Caz, still high on her eureka moment.

"But, doesn't that mean that there *is no way* that we can make the ship work? We don't know what those primary connections *are*—and we don't have the technology to create them from scratch even if we did—so we can't activate the Babbage Engine, we can't infiltrate their navigation, we can't follow their flight path back to their home world."

Caznal's joy abated. Her arms fell. "If we keep modeling, we should be able to pinpoint the—"

"But then what? What does it matter if we don't have the ability to practically apply what we've learned? You're saying it's impossible."

"It is not impossible," I.C.C. interjected. "You are an engineer. It is your job to create new things. This simply requires you to invent an artificial substitute for the biological variable."

"Right," Jamal said, as though the AI were proving his point. "We'd have to engineer an equivalent. From scratch, and with the strength and precision of the fields we're talking about . . ."

Caznal smiled. "You know what else was impossible? Flight. Breaking the sound barrier. Outrunning light. Telepathy. Interstellar travel. Look where we are now."

Jamal hung his head, a conciliatory smile twisting the corner of his lips. "It's going to take . . . *who knows how long?*

Decades? We'll probably have to turn *Zetta* into a supercy-cler, and most of *Hvmnd*'s computing power will need to be redirected—"

"Yes!" Caznal said, clapping her hands. "That is the stuff! We will need to get a team together in the morning, as soon as possible—"

But a sadness slumped Jamal's shoulders. "Caz, it could take *decades*."

"I know," she said bluntly, not sure what Jamal was getting at. "But what do we have on this new journey to LQ Pyx, if not time?"

"I know, it's just . . . I thought we were close. I thought *you* were close." He stuffed his hands in his pockets and looked away.

I.C.C. understood: Jamal was lamenting the fact that Caznal could not, logically, see the end of this new endeavor. It was equally possible that this iteration of *Jamal* might not see it come to fruition either.

Caz pursed her lips once she grasped Jamal's hesitancy. "Are you sad for me?" Her tone carried a faux harshness. "Do not be sad for me." She pointed a finger, waggling it in Jamal's direction. "I very possibly just discovered that an alien intelli-gence can biologically manipulate its own gravitational fields. You should not *dare* to feel sad for me. Besides," she added warmly, "We might not be close, but we are certainly *closer*."

Jamal snickered at that and rubbed the back of his neck. "You're right. I'm sorry, you're right."

"Damn right I am right," she said with glee. "Now, who else do we wake up?"

I.C.C. scanned the rotation rosters, attempting to gauge which other crew members would be amenable to joining in the late-night discovery.

While it worked, I.C.C. watched as Caznal clapped Jamal on the back, her smile wide and shining. "*Noumenon Infinitum!*" she cried. "Here we come!"

ACKNOWLEDGMENTS

In the life of a convoy member, there is seriousness and sadness, discovery and struggle. But there is also hope and joy. This is one of *my* joyful moments—getting to thank the multitudes who had a hand in getting this book into *your* hands. And there *are* multitudes, which means I will inevitably leave someone out, and I apologize.

Joys can be expressed through quiet ruminations, via treatises, or in lists and charts, tables and graphs. But I think even I.C.C. believes that playfulness is one of the most effective methods by which to express joy.

With that said, you need to know that what follows is rather silly. While I am a serious writer who wrote a serious book, I have promised never to take myself too seriously. And at this moment, I cannot properly express my exuberance with a few well-formatted paragraphs of *thank yous*. If you would like to preserve a previously formed image of me as a no-nonsense, purely pensive individual, I'll forgive you if you look away.

Now, I give you "You Helped Support this Writer," parody lyrics set (more or less) to the tune of "We Didn't Start the Fire," which just so happens to be Dr. Leonard Mc-Cloud's favorite song. Reggie got really tired of it during his graduate years, but the song still made it into the convoy's entertainment archives. Hum along and enjoy:

Family first on the way: Mom and Dad, Austin Ray,
Husband Alex, he's my guy, best crit partner on the fly
Sara, Jason, in-laws too, Olivia, Wendy-n-crew
Paternal side, maternal side, all-y'all in-tow

You created this writer
You've encouraged her
Since the words first lured her
You created this writer
I didn't hide it
and you didn't fight it

Next up, book team. Harper Voyager, what a dream.
DongWon Song, David P., Tracy Wilson, Phon B.
Steven Messing's cover game, Priyanka, Serena Wang
Taryn O., Anna Will, page to page, all a thrill!

Shawn N., Angela C., work promos with Pam Jaffee
Owen C., Mumatz M., art department makes it glam
Liate Stehlik, books with flare, publisher extraordinaire
And everyone I couldn't name, appreciate you all the same!

You helped produce this novel
The writer'd like to thank you
for a wonderful debut
You helped produce this novel
I had to write it
But you had to tighten it

Now on to writer friends, Codex, contests—to the end!
Grayson, Laurie, Michael U., Amanda Forrest in there too.
Rebecca R. M.K.H., Lisa Shapter, Keffy K.
Anaea, Maya, Stephen G., Tomas M., John Murphy

Bill Ledbetter, Michelle M., and all the judges for JBM
Tina Gower, Annie B., Thomas K. with Rachel C.
Andrea Stewart, Anthea Sharp, helped brainstorm with lots-o-heart.
Martin Shoemaker, Gwendolyn Clare, just for both being there.

Hold on, I'm not done. Still so many writers, son.
Mike Resnick (writer dad), W-o-t-F in the bag
Kevin A., Tim Powers, David Farland, many hours.
K.D. Wentworth, rest in peace, may sci-fi never die!

You helped support this writer
She'd like to thank you
for each new breakthrough
You helped support this writer
I had to write it
But you helped to brighten it

One more verse, almost through (then you can . . . buy book two!)
Tolkien's hobbits, Tanith Lee, Dan Simmons, L'Engle's key
Brice McPherson, Kraig Olejniczak, why don't your names rhyme?
Ferrett Steinmetz—doesn't know me—but blame him for this song.

Everyone inspired this writer
She'd like to thank you
For making each great day new
Everyone inspired this writer
You didn't stop her
So she wrote a whopper!

Everyone inspired this writer
She'd like to thank you
For making each great day new
Everyone inspired this writer
You didn't stop her
So she wrote a whopper!

Continues to hum as she strolls off into the distance.

Okay. I'm done. No really, you can take your mental fingers out of your mental ears now. In all seriousness, I want to thank everyone from the bottom of my heart. You all did amazing work, gave constant support, and made my journey to this point a wonderful one. Here's lifting a glass to many more books—with many more joyful acknowledgements pages—to come!